e **Jay**'s short stories and poetry have won prizes and appeared in
logies. Her PhD explored the link between creative writing and
dreaming, and she has led 'Dreaming into Writing' workshops at
national conferences. Clare has lived in five European countries and
lled extensively in South-east Asia. Her critically acclaimed debut
l, *Breathing in Colour*, is set in India.

t Clare at: www.clarejay.com

Praise for Clare Jay's debut *Breathing in Colour*:

'A poignant and at times heart-breaking debut'
Kate Furnivall, author of *The Russian Concubine*

'Clare Jay's prose is compelling and her debut is impressive.
he is a remarkable new talent. Expect big things in the future'
Aesthetica

'Jay's poetic sensibilities are stretched to the maximum
and results in some of the most innovative imagery I've
read in prose. Buy the book'
Cinnamonpress.com

'A beautifully told story that may have you grabbing
for a box of tissues'
Lovereading

'Imaginative and beautifully written'
Sun

n addictive debut novel that went everywhere with us as we
ourselves silly, even sneakily at work (sorry boss!). The story is
a urney, and has all the best bits you could hope for: an intriguing
ath, unfulfilled dreams and a painful discovery. It rips along in
nthesised psychedelic India – book the ticket, buy the book'
Grazia (Australia)

60000

D1650132

Also by the author:

Breathing in Colour

Dreamrunner

Clare Jay

piatkus

PIATKUS

First published in Great Britain as a paperback original in 2010 by Piatkus

A CIP catalogue record for this book
is available from the British Library.

ISBN 978-0-7499-2979-4

Typeset in Times by M Rules
Printed and bound in Great Britain by
Clays Ltd, St Ives plc

Papers used by Piatkus are natural, renewable and
recyclable products sourced from well-managed forests and certified
in accordance with the rules of the Forest Stewardship Council.

 Mixed Sources
Product group from well-managed
forests and other controlled sources
www.fsc.org Cert no. SGS-COC-004081
FSC © 1996 Forest Stewardship Council

Piatkus
An imprint of
Little, Brown Book Group
100 Victoria Embankment
London EC4Y 0DY

An Hachette UK Company
www.hachette.co.uk

www.piatkus.co.uk

For Yasmin, who dreamed herself into existence
while this book was being written

Chapter One

Blood changes everything.

It's cool in the house after the heat of the street, but nothing is the same as before. Father's linen jacket falls away from me when he sets me down on the green-edged tiles I learned to crawl on, birds and vines at their centre. Flying from one of the rooms with her happy step, Aunt Marina sees the red all over me, soaking through my white shirt, sticky on my skin. Her eyes turn huge and shocked.

'Carlos!' she cries, rushing towards me. 'You are hurt . . .'

Father's bellow stops her. 'Get back, Marina. Get back and forget what you see.'

She stands for a moment more and the pink of her blouse is too bright, like a flower in the wrong place.

'Get away!' shouts Father, and she backs away, her eyes flashing wet.

It isn't my blood.

He pushes me into his study. It's all brown leather and old cigar smoke, and everything here is serious: the books, the hard wooden ruler on the desk, even the picture of Mãe when she was a girl. All I can see in my head is the gap in the black plastic wall around the building site down the road from our house, feel the squeeze of it against my body as I climb through.

When Father kneels, he's as tall as me. He's stripping off my wet clothes, warm with blood and sweat, and dropping them onto the lining of his jacket, which he has laid out on the floor. His fingers are hurting my arm but the pain is far away and everything looks whiter than usual. When I'm naked, he shakes me so I have to look at him. The black points in his eyes are tiny and hard, his beard and eyebrows spiking out towards me.

'You have done a terrible, terrible thing,' he says, and his big hand crashes into my ear. I think I might fall and smash into the floor, but he's still holding me so I only stagger, noise ringing through my head.

Father takes something from his trouser pocket – the amulet. The gold chain is broken and he loops it around his fingers. Mãe never wears it, she's too sick to dress up all shiny the way she used to. The shaking of Father's fingers makes the amulet shiver and I see its blue sparkle, the colour of the Tejo, Lisbon's wide river that I can see from my bedroom window.

'You will never speak of what happened,' says Father. His breath is hot in my face. The amulet slides out of his fingers and onto his desk. 'This will all have to be burned,' he says through his teeth, tying the arms of the jacket together so it looks as if all the blood is being hugged in the centre of it like a horrible secret.

The light from the building site, that strange sunlight, the brightness, it's all over the study now. I'm squeezing through the gap in the wall . . .

'Stop that!' Father has turned back to me, and his voice makes my skin hurt. 'You must never think of it. I'll know if you do, Carlos. *I'll know.*'

His face is very close to mine now, bigger and darker and smellier than my own, and I know he's telling the truth – he can see into my

2

thoughts. '*Tens que esquecer isso.* You must forget,' he says, 'or even worse things will happen. You're going to get in the bath now and scrub that blood off you, boy. No one must know what you have done today. Not your aunt, not your sister, and especially not your poor mother. You understand?' He waits for my nod. His hands are still shaking as he straightens up.

'If the police come,' he says, and his voice is low now, as if he thinks someone could be listening at the door, 'you must not speak of it.'

I nod again.

'You must forget,' he says.

Chapter Two

Leo is happy. His parents promised him weeks ago that on his seventh birthday they would all go to the park to play his favourite art game, which is like a happiness spell, full of colour and messy beauty. This morning, his mother gave him an acrylic painting she'd done herself in the workshop she's set up in the garden of their yellow-and-blue-tiled house in the old Alfama district of Lisbon, a stone's throw from the castle. The painting is abstract; an energetic swirl of purples and blues, Leo's favourite colours. A scattering of small marbles are pressed into the paint, staring out like cat's eyes, because Olivia knows Leo likes texture, likes things to be different. Carlos gave his son a sturdy, sky-blue mountain bike that Leo has wobbled joyfully all the way through the park on, his father loping beside him gripping the saddle tightly, his expression oscillating between pride in his son and alarm that he might fall and hurt himself – he is a fearful father, although he tries not to be.

Above them, the sky stretches high and still, reaching in slivers through the knotted branches of the dragon tree. Olivia unfolds the bulky rectangle of plastic sheeting. Shaking it out so that it crackles and leaps in the sunshine, she allows it to settle onto the rough spikes of grass as if she were spreading a picnic sheet. Leo's eyes – blackest brown, impish – follow the rise and fall of her arms and, as soon as the sheeting touches the ground, he rushes onto it to stamp the creases flat with his bare feet. Jardim da Estrela is Lisbon's prettiest park, a fifteen-minute car ride from the house where they have lived since Leo's birth. Rolled up tightly under one muscular arm, Carlos has three sheets of 60 cm by 45 cm paper. These are almost as thick as cardboard, with a matt white surface. He tosses them onto the sheeting and Leo, on all fours now, flattens these out too, laughing at their tendency to spring up at the edges.

'They're alive,' he exclaims, slapping at them with his hands.

'They'll lie still if you flip them over,' advises Carlos, watching him with a smile.

As they stand for a moment waiting for Leo to sort out the paper, Olivia sees Carlos glance at a blond hair, sparkling like a gold filament, caught on the front of his black vest top. She watches as he picks it off and lays it across his hand, a lone wave following the curve of his lifeline and floating off, beyond his supple fingers, to touch the air. He coils it around and around his two fingers and pushes it carefully into his pocket. His green eyes meet hers. This gesture – keeping her hair as if it were too precious to lose, rather than tossing it away – goes back to their first kiss under the giant fig tree on Príncipe Real Square in Lisbon. It's one of Carlos' many ways of telling his wife he loves her. Olivia thinks of last night: the way that Carlos, home in the early hours after photographing a wedding, had hugged her sleeping form until she awoke, and when she wriggled around to face him they were both suddenly so aroused that he didn't have time to pull off his evening clothes. He flicked his silk tie back over one shoulder, and this for some reason made her laugh. Then they made love and she succumbed to a firestorm of orgasms so wild that she had to bite down on a pillow for fear of waking Leo.

She knows by the look in his eyes that Carlos is remembering, too.

He steps forwards and folds her into his arms and the smell of the sea mixed with his summer sweat reaches her. As they pull apart, Olivia laughs out loud, shaking her head, and after a moment he laughs too, lowering his head so that his nose touches hers.

'Come *on*,' calls Leo impatiently.

The two of them turn, smiling. 'Have you got the containers?' Olivia asks Carlos.

Carlos pulls the bulging hemp bag off his shoulder and empties its contents onto the grass. Half a dozen plastic food containers slide out, along with a selection of vegetable-based paints which always remind Olivia of the squeezy bottles of tomato sauce and mayonnaise found in fast-food cafés. There's a bag of white flour, a random scattering of encrusted paintbrushes, and a two-litre bottle of water. Olivia sits down cross-legged in the middle of it all in her cornflower-blue sundress and begins to sort out the containers. Leo scoots over to help her with the paint-mixing; she knows that this is his favourite part, like cooking an inedible cake, heaping spoonfuls of flour onto squirts of red paint, green paint, yellow. Tipping in water and pounding it all together with a gummy brush until each container is glistening with colour.

Leo mixes purple in super-fast circles. 'Dad?'

'Hmm?' Carlos splashes more water into a doughy yellow mix.

'Why is seven a dangerous age?'

Under his year-round tan, Carlos blanches. He glances rapidly at Olivia. Leo must have heard his comment this morning.

'It isn't really,' he says, screwing the cap back onto the water. 'So don't worry, Leo. But it's true that seven-year-olds sometimes have adventures with tree-climbing anacondas or speckle-backed crocodiles,' he adds beguilingly.

Leo sits very still, his paintbrush dangling from his left hand, eyes raised to his father's face. Olivia looks at her son's bony knees which already have smudges of dirt on them. She looks at Leo's spiky black hair and his bold, friendly eyebrows. He's a replica of Carlos, except for his eyes, which have skipped both her English blue and the unusual green of his father's, and are the liquid black of generations of Portuguese.

Watching them both, Olivia can read the foreboding in Carlos' face, although he's trying to hide it. She knows he's struggling with the familiar feeling of love mingled with terror and the desire to protect Leo – he's spoken to her of this paternal emotion many times, and it's always seemed normal, even inevitable, to her. But in recent weeks his protective instinct has been growing stronger and is now verging on the paranoid, in her opinion: Carlos has started insisting on walking Leo to and from school whenever he can, even though it's only a five-minute walk through friendly neighbourhood streets that Leo has been doing alone since he turned six. He's also started checking on him at night to make sure he's safe and breathing, as though he were a newborn. That morning in the kitchen, when they'd thought themselves to be out of earshot, Carlos had paused in the act of slicing pineapple and melon for Leo's birthday breakfast and turned to her with a disturbed look.

'I know it's irrational,' he'd said, 'but I can't stop thinking that seven is a dangerous age, the sort of age when death is close.'

Olivia had stared at him, her fingers tightening on the pile of plates she was holding. 'Don't say things like that,' she said. 'Why say something like that on his seventh birthday? If you voice that sort of superstitious fear, it'll only give it more power. Just stop worrying about him, Carlos, OK?'

Leo is looking up at the trees, his eyes filled with possibilities: Carlos has effectively distracted him with the thought of a magnificent anaconda coiled slitty-eyed on a branch somewhere close by.

'In fact,' says Carlos, 'I wonder if it's worth checking whether there's a full-sized adult anaconda up the dragon tree.'

Leo looks at him in amazement. Olivia suppresses a smile. Leo's face is so expressive he can be read like a book: his father has guessed his thoughts, and this can only mean one thing – that there is indeed an anaconda draped in deadly spirals along one of the branches above his head. He swivels his head up and scans the tree.

'Oh, Carlos, you've got him all wishful now,' Olivia laughs. 'Leo, there is no snake, but there's plenty of treasure right here.' She pats the bag beside her. 'Come on – I need you to open up the booty bag.'

'But my back's prickling,' protests Leo. 'That means there's an anaconda with a hundred sharp teeth, watching me!'

'No, it just means the booty bag's waiting for you to see what's inside it,' says Olivia, and she squeezes the bag so that it crackles like an extra birthday present. The bag is full of things Leo collected a week ago with his aunt Rosa. From the booty bag, Leo pulls seashells from the beach by Rosa's place in Cascais, along with strips of eucalyptus bark, fallen rose petals, sand, moss ripped from one of the boulders at the duck pond, peat from the garden and handfuls of dried flowers. Leo heaps these treasures onto the middle of the plastic sheeting. Then Carlos holds his finger poised over the play button on the portable stereo, which he has placed by the trunk of the dragon tree, and says, 'Ready to start?'

They all know Carlos won't press the button until Leo shouts, 'Ready!' Leo savours the moment. Olivia meets his eye as she hunches over her sheet of paper, holding her paintbrush as if she can't wait to begin, her eyes fixed on his. When he looks at her, she widens her eyes and jiggles her slim body, conveying enormous impatience. Leo is grinning, trying to keep his mouth closed so that he won't shout just yet. He looks at his father, strong and graceful in his vest top and cut-off jeans, his broad feet tanned and bare. Carlos is watching Leo's face with a look of love and waiting, waiting. A burst of joy races through Olivia, from her stomach up to her heart.

'Ready!' yells Leo, and Carlos presses the switch.

Today's music is 'The Can-Can'. They have the length of the

song – maybe three minutes – to create their artwork. Carlos leaps into position by his blank sheet and they start flinging loops of liquid paint onto their canvases, mixing the colours indiscriminately, using both hands at once to grab handfuls of anything they fancy – peat, petals, bark – and add these to the collage. There is no glue to hold it all together, no wind to blow it all away. Leo's paper rapidly turns purple and yellow. When he sees that Carlos is building a pyramid of peat in the centre of a mass of scarlet paint, he sends a stream of yellow streaking over the top of it all. Carlos retaliates by throwing dried flowers onto Leo's paper, then flour all over Olivia's, which is already a heap of bark, moss and green paint. By the time the music stops, they are all frantically adding to each other's collages, their faces covered in splashes of paint, their fingernails clogged.

Olivia throws her paintbrush onto Carlos' pyramid as a final touch and sits back, laughing breathlessly. 'We haven't done that for months, and it does me so much good,' she says.

Carlos nods to Leo. 'You have a fan club, birthday boy.'

Twisting around, Leo sees a scattering of children standing on the path, staring along with their parents. One little girl of about three is open-mouthed with wonder, her hair tied back in a scarlet bow. Leo grins at them all, full of pride and mischief. Olivia reaches across to brush flour from Carlos' jaw and, as she does so, she murmurs: 'I don't want to hear any more talk about danger, please, Carlos. He's got his own destiny, like all of us. Just relax and let him enjoy being a kid.'

When Carlos nods, Olivia moves in closer and kisses him on the mouth.

Chapter Three

It's as if an electric shock runs through Carlos' body in an intense spasm.

Olivia judders awake, and in the half-light she sees him leap from the bed with astonishing speed and height, as if he has the power of flight. He's yelling something incoherent at full volume, and the desperation in his voice cuts straight to her heart. She sits up, groping for the lamp switch with one hand, the other stretched out towards Carlos as if this will calm him. He's standing at the foot of the bed in his boxer shorts and, as the light clicks on, Olivia sees his eyes, wide and fearful, unseeing. Sweat shines off his bare torso and he is hyperventilating, his breath hoarse and panicky.

'Oh, God, what's wrong?' she cries, struggling from the bed half blinded by her hair, her nightie tangling in the sheets. There must be some disaster. Is it Leo, a snake in the bed, an earthquake?

Carlos doesn't register Olivia's voice or even seem to notice the sudden light. His muscles are bunched as if he's about to fight and, before she can say another word, he runs from the room with a prolonged groan, crashing heavily into the corner of the wardrobe as he goes but not reacting to the pain, his staring green eyes focusing on nothing. He's asleep, she realises, and the eeriness of it makes a shiver run through her because he seems like a stranger. She rushes after him, calling for him to stop.

Out on the landing, Leo has woken up and stumbled out of his bedroom. He's standing uncertainly against the wall in his pyjama bottoms, streetlight from the window gleaming on his silken chest. He is open-mouthed at this impossible scene: his gentle father beside himself, hurling broken words into the strangeness of three in the morning. When Carlos sees him, something seems to break inside him. He howls and rushes towards his son, sliding onto his knees as he does so, and grabs him roughly by the shoulders, effectively barricading him against the wall. Leo and Olivia both yell in protest – Carlos is never rough with him, but clearly he has no idea what he's doing.

'Stop, please – it's a *dream*, Carlos, not real!' Olivia shouts, pulling on his arm. They say you should never wake a sleepwalker, she thinks frantically, but what if they're being violent like this? 'Wake up, please stop, you're *hurting* him . . .' He's a wall of muscle that she cannot move, even to protect her son. Leo's eyes are round with fright. 'It's all right, Leo my sweet,' she tells him rapidly as she tightens her grip on Carlos, 'Dad's just having a bad dream.' Leo's face compresses as he tries not to cry, attempting to twist away in his pain, but unable to move. Carlos, absolutely heedless of Leo's distress, is shouting something that Olivia can just make out through the slur of his dream-speech.

'My *luck*!' he yells, clutching Leo's shoulders even harder.

Abruptly, Olivia's fear turns into anger. 'Don't you hurt him!' she shouts, wrenching Carlos' shoulder back with both hands.

He barely notices; the strength of him is like nothing she's ever known. She can see his powerful fingers biting into Leo's shoulders, hurting him. Kneeling, she shifts her grip to his forearm. Without warning, Carlos' arm jerks out to the side to shake her off and she is a rag doll, flung aside, her head hitting the wall or the floor, she doesn't even know which because she's up in a flash, the red in her head throbbing as she pulls at him again.

11

'Wake up, Carlos!' Olivia's shriek doesn't seem to enter Carlos' consciousness. It's like dealing with a madman; he doesn't see them for who they really are. Olivia wonders what crazed scenario he's acting out, what nightmare? Whatever it is, it's making him cry, and she's never seen Carlos cry before. Tears of compassion fill his eyes as easily as the warmth that radiates from his heart, but not tears like this: she has never seen such anguish.

As Leo and Olivia both struggle to no effect, Leo crying now under the brutal strength of his father's fingers, for the first time it hits Olivia how powerful Carlos is. She'd never realised those beautiful muscles could swing like steel ropes; the two of them have no chance against him. Pulling and pulling on his arm, she realises she's never thought how helpless they'd be if he turned on them, only he never would, she thinks, he's normally a lamb of a man, full of tender love. Where has her husband vanished to?

Faintly, beyond the blood booming in her head, Olivia hears the doorbell ringing urgently: they must have woken the neighbours. She can't do anything but ignore it and hope they'll give up and go away.

'You're dreaming, my love!' she shouts, right in Carlos' ear. He turns to look at her, and in his tear-soaked eyes she sees deep confusion and terror, and below this, the faintest glimmer of recognition. 'Yes,' she tells him more gently. 'It's me, Olivia. This is a dream, and you need to wake up now.'

Just as suddenly as it started, the nightmare ends.

Carlos' tears stop, his hands slip from Leo and he gets to his feet looking dazed, while Leo cowers on the floor. As soon as Carlos is up, Olivia positions herself in front of Leo, facing Carlos full on. His knees are bleeding from where he skinned them sliding full tilt across the rough wooden floorboards, but he is calm at last. She studies his face. He seems almost awake, almost compos mentis again, apart from the slight filminess in his eyes. Still shielding Leo with her body, she tells him, 'Go back to bed.'

With unquestioning obedience, he goes. Her heart pounding, Olivia watches him disappear across the hall. This may turn out to be a one-off bout of sleepwalking, but part of her suspects it's something altogether nastier: it's like witnessing a slice of madness. I've just seen my gentle husband transform into a desperate version of himself, she thinks in shock; a man who doesn't even recognise his wife of eight years and his son, the jewel of his life. If this happens again . . .

She turns to help Leo, who is crouched white-faced and silent on the floorboards, his face streaked with tears. If Carlos gets violent again, she thinks, if he has another nightmare and mistakes Leo for a threat that he needs to destroy, then what might happen?

She doesn't want to think the words, but, as she gathers her trembling son into her arms and leads him back to his bed, they come anyway.

Accidental murder.

Chapter Four

Leo wakes up with dried tears on his cheeks and purplish finger bruises on his shoulders, but at first all he thinks of is his blue bike, waiting for him in the garden. He can't wait to show it to his best friend, Concha, who has a Spanish father she hasn't seen since she was five, and a love of thrills that makes her the most exciting person Leo knows. She will ride his bike far better than he ever could, no-handed and with a daredevil swish, her long dark hair streaming in the wind.

His mother's voice drifts over from his parents' bedroom, sounding indignant and panicky. 'How can you *not* remember?' There's the sound of their door opening. 'It happened right here, Carlos. Look at your knees. Look at my eyebrow!'

Leo stiffens, remembering.

'. . . can't believe it . . . what does it all mean, Olivia . . . am I losing my mind?'

'All that ridiculous talk about danger!' Olivia cries, and Leo can tell she's trying not to speak too loudly but it isn't working; he can hear every word. 'See what it triggered? You have to *stop* worrying about Leo. He's a normal, healthy little boy and he's going to live a long and wonderful life. Just believe it, for all our sakes!'

'I know, I know . . .' Carlos groans, and Leo hears him say, 'Aunt Marina . . . what if madness is hereditary?'

'Last night was just a one-off,' says Olivia urgently. 'A freak incident. It won't happen again. Our bruises will fade, the neighbours will have the decency not to complain, it will be forgotten, Carlos.' Their voices recede back into the bedroom. For a long time, there is nothing but muffled talk.

Then Carlos puts his head around Leo's door. His short black hair is as spiky as his son's and, although his eyes are troubled, he wears his habitual expression of deep and patient kindness, the sort of expression that makes everything all right, always.

'Leo,' he says, coming into the room where Leo is now crouched on the bare floorboards, arranging beach stones in complex patterns that only he understands.

Leo looks up at him with a grin. '*Olá*, Pai.' Hi, Dad. The two of them tend to speak Portuguese when they're alone, and English when they're all together as a family.

'Mum just told me what happened last night,' says Carlos, sitting cross-legged next to him and flinching when he sees the livid bruising on his son's bare shoulders. 'I'm so very sorry that I scared you and hurt you.'

'It's OK, I know it wasn't you, Pai.'

Carlos looks startled. 'Then who was it?'

'It was the sleep monster.' Somewhere between struggling to escape his father's grip and playing with his stones this morning, Leo's imagination, never idle, has set to work to make sense of what happened. He knows his father is neither steel-fingered nor a cry baby. He knows his father was asleep and dreaming, because his mother had told him so. He knows that monsters exist, that they can slip into different disguises, shed wings, enter people's dreams, become men. And now here's his father, fully himself again, looking at him beseechingly. Leo feels sorry for him. Leaning forwards, he touches his arm. 'Come on, Pai, I'll let you have a go on my bike,' he whispers enticingly. There's a moment's hesitation, and then Leo

15

is rewarded by his father's warm smile and the familiar weight of his hand caressing his head.

Out in the small garden, which is thick with oleander plants, budding olive trees and pink blossoms, Carlos has crouched to check again the saddle height, the stretch of the pedals, the efficacy of the brakes. Leo is sitting astride the bike clutching the handlebars, hoping to persuade his father to let him go out on the street, but all set to go shooting off in tight circles around the garden, when his mother comes out carrying a metal tin. He sees immediately that her right eyebrow is swollen into a thick, bluish bruise.

Leo thinks of the sleep monster, his mother's screams.

Olivia looks at Leo in amusement. 'What are you looking so dark and dangerous about on that bike of yours?' she teases. 'Are you practising being Evil Knievel?'

Leo has no idea who Evil Knievel is. He looks at his father. He can see the sleep monster lurking somewhere at the back of his eyes. 'Don't hurt my mum,' he says, his fists tightening around the handlebars.

'He's fixing your bike, sweet. How could that hurt me?' Olivia walks briskly across the garden and puts the tin down on the mosaic-tiled table. Leo can see that it hurts her to blink; she keeps wincing. 'We're having almond and honey cake for breakfast today,' she announces. 'And then I'll put some arnica on your bruises, Leo my love, and Dad's going to make us all Sunday pancakes.'

But when he looks back at his father's face, there's such unhappiness there that Leo can't look away.

'I will never hurt your mum,' says Carlos helplessly. He thrusts his hands through his hair, holding his son's gaze. 'I will never hurt her,' he repeats, 'and I'll never hurt you again either, Leo.'

Bent over the almond and honey cake, Olivia looks up. 'How can you make such promises?' she asks quietly, and Leo sees tears in her eyes.

Carlos spreads both hands out. 'Like you said, *querida*, it was a one-off.'

'Well, if it does happen again, we'll have to take steps,' says Olivia despairingly. Leo hopes her tears will stay in her eyes and dry away to nothing. His mother almost never cries, but, when she does, her eyes look less blue and such sad red threads run through them that Leo wants to cry, too. Olivia extends one slim arm and sweeps it across the green grass and the limpid sky, encompassing Leo astride his bike with his father crouching protectively beside him. 'I just don't want all this to go wrong,' she says passionately, and Leo sees that she has mastered her tears. She is strong, his mother.

She smiles at them both. 'I want everything to stay the *same*.'

Chapter Five

There are square, earth-coloured floor tiles in Aunt Rosa's living room, and Leo is sitting on one of them, trying to squeeze himself so small that no part of him goes over the lines. It's Tuesday, three days since Carlos' violent dream. Whenever Olivia is painting a commission, which is often, Carlos' sister picks him up from school in her battered white Peugeot and he spends the afternoons here in Cascais, a thirty-minute drive from Lisbon. Rosa is in the kitchen, which has a sea view.

Through the gap in the door Leo can just see her slim wrist moving rhythmically as she stirs a pot of codfish stew on her gas stove. The smell of the food is mixed, as always, with the fragrant scent of herbs. Rosa gives aromatherapy massage courses at the local Centro Cultural, helps out at shelters for women, and fills her kitchen with the pungent aromas of raspberry leaf, ginger, aloe, fennel, lavender and essential oils. Condensed and shrunken on his tile, Leo hugs his knees to his chest and peers down at his elbows, his toes, pulls them inside the line and starts to count to seven. His aunt has told him that seven is a magic number, one you can make wishes on, or cast spells with. Leo is seven; an age where he knows that anything can happen.

He knows that both wishes and spells need loud thoughts;

thoughts which are shouted bold and solid inside the head, with the mouth closed and quiet. He's holding his breath as he counts . . . five, six, seven. Now he tilts his head back and lets out his breath through O-shaped lips, like a plume of smoke from a dragon's mouth. He closes his mouth and eyes, and shouts inside his head, so loudly that the veins in his temples pulse with red energy:

Save Daddy from the sleep monster!

Save Daddy from the sleep monster!

Some moments later, Leo is startled from his mantra by Rosa's touch on the crown of his head.

She sighs, and he can smell the scent of peppermint on her breath; she has been chewing mint leaves. 'What are you doing, *menino*? Eh, lad? You look like a giant hazelnut, all compressed down there on the floor.'

He gazes at her, recovering himself after all that shouting. Rosa always speaks to him in Portuguese, and if he forgets and addresses her in English, she doesn't like it. Leo thinks of Rosa as a second mother. Sometimes she has boyfriends but he knows she can't have any children of her own, and this, she has told him before, makes him even more precious to her. Her cotton dress is swinging towards his face as she leans over him. It's midnight blue, and his hand sneaks out to touch the wide yellow hem. 'Tia Rosa, what does the sleep monster look like?'

She moves away from him and sits on the sofa, her cheeks flushed from the steamy cooking pot, her hair a witchy black streaked with grey. She has drawn it up into a bun which is tumbling down, as it always does, making it look as if she has been dancing a jig and is still whirling, breathless. Five years older than Carlos, Rosa has inherited the same fine Portuguese features as him; her nose is straight, her jaw is defined and her chin juts slightly, giving her a determined, regal air in spite of the state of her hair. The only still part of her is her steady gaze; at thirty-eight, she has boundless energy.

'Which sleep monster might that be?' she asks.

'The one that's got Dad.' He watches his aunt absorb this for a moment. Her face doesn't change, but her dark eyes turn very black.

When she speaks, her voice is velvety around the edges. 'What do *you* think the sleep monster looks like?'

Leo feels ashamed. He doesn't want to say; he twists on his tile and his foot slips over the line. He stands up, but he can't take his eyes from hers and eventually he blurts it out. 'It looks like Dad.'

She throws her head back and releases a peal of laughter which offends him. Certain that he's being ridiculed, Leo stands his ground and stares at her, waiting for her to stop. Then he finds himself saying, 'It looks like him only the eyes gleam like underwater stones, and when the throat opens the sound comes out boiling angry.'

His aunt isn't laughing any more. 'Leo,' she says, leaning forwards with her hands on her knees. 'Have you seen . . . the sleep monster?'

He nods. 'It held me against the wall and Mum couldn't make it get off me.'

She makes a sound between shock and dismay; an expletive so fast and low that Leo can't grasp it as it flashes off her lips. 'This happened in the night, Leo? He didn't know who he was, and he hurt you, is that it?'

Leo shifts from one foot to the other. 'Well . . . the monster had metal fingers that dug into my shoulders, and it shouted.'

Rosa clutches both hands to her face. 'It cannot be,' she mutters. 'Surely not.'

Leo frowns. His aunt's sudden change of mood is unsettling, and her face looks strange, all bent out of shape by the pressure of her fingers. He tries to diffuse the situation. 'I did a spell to make the sleep monster stay away,' he says with studied nonchalance, walking over to the table and fiddling with the pile of felt-tip pens scattered across it.

But Rosa isn't listening. 'Carlos should have *told* me this,' she says emphatically. 'I must speak to him.' Her eyes are blacker than night now, Leo sees. She seems to have forgotten her fish stew, but he doesn't like to remind her about it. He hopes he hasn't got his father into trouble. He squeezes his fist around a clump of felt-tip pens so that they click together, red against yellow against white, and wonders miserably what he's done now.

Rosa has summoned both Carlos and Olivia to Cascais to collect Leo that day, and, as soon as Leo runs upstairs to get his beach things, she reveals like a war flag her chip of information about Carlos' violent behaviour.

As Carlos has no memory of his episode, Rosa extracts the full story from Olivia as they all walk through the cobbled town centre and out to the string of sandy beaches which ebb and flow along the coastline. When they reach the first beach, the three adults head down to the point where the waves meet the shore. Leo spots a couple of boys about his age with a beach ball and runs over unselfconsciously to join in. Olivia steps into the light foam, lifting the hem of her sundress and feeling the suck of sand around her flip-flops as the waves pull away.

Rosa looks curiously at Carlos. 'I assume you do remember what happened all those years ago?'

Carlos tenses. 'No.'

The three of them form a close triangle, their feet sinking into the wet sand. Beyond them, the tight black bodies of surfers tumble through the waves.

'When you were a little boy,' says Rosa, 'you went through an intense period of violent dreaming. Like a sort of sleepwalking, it was, only nothing peaceful about it. You actually screamed and did things. I'm pretty sure it started when I was doing my year at boarding school, the year Mãe died, and it must have gone on for a good few months. Do you really not remember?'

'All that stands out for me about the time around Mãe's death is that Father seemed to be upset with me for what seemed like months before she died, but I have no idea why. We were never close,' he adds for Olivia's sake, although she already knows this, knows that it's an understatement. From what little she has gleaned from Carlos, his father, the last in a line of wealthy maritime merchants, completely withdrew from both his children after his wife, Isabella, died from breast cancer. He committed suicide five years later, when Carlos was twelve. In that five-year span, he stopped working and became a recluse, losing a lot of money, so that when he died, Rosa had to sell the grandiose family house to pay off his debts. She used half of the remaining money to buy her own house in Cascais, and later Carlos used his half to buy the Alfama house they live in now, just a five-minute walk from the former family home.

Rosa nods thoughtfully. 'Father *was* upset,' she agrees. 'He used to give you troubled looks whenever you came into the room. But why?'

'No idea.' Carlos spreads his hands wide. 'I'm sure he never gave me a reason. You know what he was like. But did you ever see me sleepwalking? What did I do?'

'It was so long ago,' says Rosa, 'and I was away most of the time, so I barely know any more exactly what happened. I do remember hearing you shouting out in the night, when I was home for the holidays.' She frowns, her gaze moving out to sea. 'It was this absolutely fearsome yelling, as if the worst thing in the world was happening. Hard to sleep to. You used to do that a lot, but I never actually saw you running around the house banging into things, which is what Inês said you did.'

'Inês?' asks Olivia.

'Our housekeeper,' says Carlos, without taking his eyes off his sister's face. Olivia tries to imagine her husband as a small, disturbed boy, screaming in his dreams.

22

'You think this is only sleepwalking then, what I did the other night?' Carlos asks Rosa. 'When Olivia told me about it and I saw the bruises I'd inflicted on them both without even being aware of it, I thought . . . well, I thought I must be going insane.' He takes a deep breath. 'And there's this feeling of doom. I don't know why or where it's come from but it's been creeping up on me for weeks, and we've got madness in our family, as you know – didn't we have a mad Aunt Marina . . .?' He trails off.

Rosa's expression grows sombre. '*Sim*, I thought of her too, as soon as Leo started talking about sleep monsters,' she admits. 'Carlos, there's something I need to tell you, but don't take it as gospel because I was only a little girl myself.'

'What is it?'

'Before she was taken away to the psychiatric unit, Marina used to do odd things. At night.' Rosa hesitates. 'The family thought she was possessed by demons. It came on suddenly, when she was in her early twenties. Inês told me a story about finding Marina in the kitchen stark naked late one night, trying to smash her way into a frozen pie with a cheese grater. When Inês challenged her, she got aggressive, but she had no memory of it afterwards, couldn't explain why or what she'd been doing. Apparently on another occasion she even threatened Father with a knife. I think that's when they carted her off.'

'So this *could* be the start of madness?' Carlos looks stricken. Olivia moves close and snakes her arm around his waist.

Rosa waves her hands at them both. 'No, no, no, I'm sure there's no connection really. I just needed to tell you this, so that you can be vigilant, you understand? We have to make sure Leo stays safe. You said you thought of Marina, I instantly thought of her too . . . Maybe Inês was wrong, or I haven't remembered it right . . . Tell you what, I'll do some digging,' she promises. 'I can ask some of the neighbours who still live close by our old house. Better if I do it – I can say

I'm researching family history or something. Someone's mother or grandmother is bound to remember something about Marina. You know what it's like in the Alfama, it's just a village really, same old faces, same old families. But don't worry too much about madness, Carlos. After all, you've only done this strange thing once in your adult life, and it might never happen again. And besides,' she adds, her eyes narrowing slightly, 'Father managed to put a stop to your sleepwalking, so it can't be *impossible* to control.'

Her eyes skip past him to Leo, who is sauntering down the beach towards them with a sunny smile on his face. Rosa waves at him.

'Just quickly,' urges Carlos, 'tell me how Father stopped my sleep-walking.'

Rosa looks at him oddly. 'Do you really not remember?' she asks. 'He used to tie you to the bed.'

Chapter Six

January 1984, Alfama

My father's name is Aníbal Alfredo Casanova de Albuquerque Moniz. When Father speaks, you have to listen. Father smokes three Havana cigars a day, always. They come in a box he calls a coffin and they look a bit like peeling brown crayons, but once he told me they taste of burned gold. Since Mãe got so ill, Father is most cheerful when he's been filling his study with blue Havana smoke. Sometimes I still think about last summer when we went for a family picnic and Father held me close as we walked into the woods and called me his *príncipe*, his prince, and later he whirled me through the air, gripping my ankles so that I flew, the wind bringing me to tears, with Mãe there, standing among the trees and clapping her hands to see me fly. My sister Rosa says they aren't the same parents any more.

Mãe's name is Isabella, the most lovely name in the world. Before, she was more beautiful than stars. I remember her spinning in a red dress, her dark hair swinging to her waist, sparkling dots around her throat. Now she lies in bed, yellowish, and closes her eyes. Her hair is gone. When she's awake, she puts on a colourful headscarf and tells me about the waterfalls and butterflies and big piles of rocks up in Gerês, where she grew up. Sometimes she forgets what she's told me, and tells me again, but I don't mind. Gerês is hours and hours in a car from Lisbon, and Mãe doesn't think we'll be going there again any time soon. She lets me play with the hill of jewellery on her dresser. I pull out diamond bracelets and swing them like lassoes so they come alive in the light and make Mãe less yellow, or I turn them into snakes that slide across her bed. My favourite is the amulet that she says is made from one big sapphire. It used to belong to Father's great-grandmother, and I could look at the blue of it for ever. It glows even if there's not much light in the room. The blue bit of the amulet is a circle about as big as a marble, only flatter, and it hangs off a gold chain.

It's night time, but not very late. I'm in my room, which has wooden floors and wooden walls so it creaks a lot and it's like sleeping in a ship because from my bed I can see through the window and out on to the river where all the boats flash their lights and move slowly up and down. From my other window, which I have to get out of bed to see out of, I can see Castelo de São Jorge, the castle which is lit up gold at night above all the old houses of the Alfama, which is our district, and Mãe always says we sleep at the heart of Lisboa because Alfama is the heart.

When Father and Marina and I ate together tonight, they argued because sometimes, in the middle of the night, Marina gets very hungry, so she gets out of bed and goes into the kitchen and does funny things with food, things she can't remember in the morning. Last night Father found her making pancakes at half past two in the morning, only she wasn't neat about it the way she normally is – there was a raw egg broken on the table and sugar spilled all across the floor. Father nearly slipped on the sugar and he doesn't see why he should put up with it, or why Marina gets so hungry when she eats a good meal every evening. Marina kept saying she was sorry but she really couldn't remember cooking any pancakes, and Father kept saying that she must remember because she was rude to him when he told her to go back to bed, and I wished Rosa was at home, but she lives at her school now so I never see her. I wasn't allowed to finish my roast duck because when I leaned over to get some bread, I knocked a candlestick onto Father's polished floor so he sent me to my room. I should have just asked him to pass me the bread but, since Mãe got ill, he's much sterner and sometimes I'm scared to talk to him.

Now my belly is making music, talking to me as the boat lights wink. I can hear Father in Mãe's room now, and there's something wrong with his voice, it's like cracked mud. I sit up in bed to hear better, and now I can hear a sort of groan that seems to go on and on, and I think, Father never cries. I run to the door and hold it open. I can see the light from Mãe's room spilling onto the corridor, which means the door is open. *Is* he crying?

Then Father cries something so loudly that I nearly race back to my bed.

'It's a terrible death!'

I grip the door tight, ready to run as soon as I see him.

My mother's voice is angry for the first time in months. 'How dare you? I'm not dead yet. Look at me, Aníbal. *Look* at me.'

Father's sobs grow less clear. She's holding his head in her warm arms, I'm sure of it. I stand very still, my hand curled around the edge of the door. What do they mean? Is Mãe going to die? I think of Tak-Tak, my red-bellied parrot, who hopped and whistled and flew around dropping feathers and made me and Rosa laugh until we ached. One day I found him cold and stiff at the bottom of his cage and Rosa said he'd run out of morning whistles and not to be sad, even though she was crying herself. And the dead cat behind the bins on Portas do Sol. When I think of the cat, I wish I hadn't because it looked just like any other sleeping cat until I poked it gently with a lollipop stick and it was as hard as anything under its fur. And sometimes when Mãe sleeps she's so still.

I wish it was me being held by Mãe's soft hands, not Father. He is sobbing quietly now, saying her name, Isabella, Isabella. I open my door very carefully and slip down the curving marble staircase. The day help have gone home now – Rita, who is big and stern and cooks, and Paula, who has sweets in her pockets and talks to herself as she cleans. Inês, our live-in housekeeper, who wears black and is everywhere and sees everything, won't be up any more, but my heart has jumped into my throat so that I can hardly swallow as I twist the big handle on the front door. I've never left the house on my own before at night and the door seems heavier than it does in the day, but the black sky and its stars pull me outside. I pull the door very, very slowly behind me so it looks closed but is really a tiny bit open, the gap no bigger than my little finger. Our house is just up from Miradouro de Santa Luzia, the viewpoint where tourists come to take photos of the river and all the pretty houses. I don't know where I'm going, but I don't want to think about Mãe's yellow face, her thin bald head.

The cobblestones are chilly und uneven under my bare feet. I'm wearing my blue Thai-silk pyjamas and a cold breeze comes up the Tejo from the sea and moves the silk like the wash of a boat. There are people on the street, only these are night-time people, dressed up to go out together, and there are less cars because it isn't a weekend. I think I must be invisible tonight because the people don't look at me, they just take their shouting voices on. I walk towards the river, shivering a little, keeping close to the wall. There's a cruise ship out there tonight, bigger than ten houses, and it has so many round and square lights and big funnels.

Then I see him, standing alone under the gold of a street lamp; a boy of about seven, my age, but thinner, his dark hair so long and kind of gritty that it curls under his ears which stick out a bit. He's wearing a black pullover too big for him so that you almost can't see his shorts which Inês would call 'tatty' because bits of thread run off the ends of them. In his hand he has a wooden hoop as round as the moon. Like me, he has no shoes on even though it's winter. I walk up to him, my heart still banging high in my throat.

'Who are you?' I ask him.

'Pedro.'

'Where do you live?'

'Here.' He swings out his arms, towards the river lights, the tram stops, the castle. '*Em todos os lados*.' Everywhere.

He speaks differently from me; his voice sings up and down. Something in my face makes him laugh. His laugh is like a blackbird opening its wide throat to the sky. I look and look at Pedro, at his violet eyes and burnt-brown face. He is where I want to be. 'I'm Carlos,' I say.

'Why are you wearing a suit?'

I look down at my pyjamas. 'It's not a suit.' I fiddle with the cuffs, and suddenly I can hear Father's ugly sobbing again, see Mãe in her yellowing bed.

'Whatsa matter?' He twiddles his hoop but his face is kind.

I shake my head, too proud to say.

Pedro looks at me for a moment and I clench my fists so the tears won't reach my eyes, but I think he sees anyway, and maybe he sees the fresh bruises on my wrist where Father gripped me after I dropped the silver candlestick and made a scar on his floor.

'Tears are no use,' says Pedro, swinging his hoop. 'Just go to the sun,' he adds, as if this is easy, something he does all the time. 'It's better than trying not to cry. No one can hurt you when you go to the sun – no matter how wicked people are, it's too bright and too far for them to follow you there.'

'But it's night-time.' My fists are still tight and hard by my sides.

'*Não faz diferença*.' Doesn't make any difference. He laughs again. 'The sun's always there.'

'How do you get there?' I think of aeroplanes, hot air balloons, tall trees.

29

He smiles a big smile. 'Like this,' he says, and closes his eyes and goes still. I watch him for a moment and his face softens, as if he's looking at something inside his head. If I squint, I can nearly see the sun as I look at his long eyelashes, the streak of dirt on his chin. The street lamp is sending gold all over him and I'm standing in the gold too. When Pedro speaks, his voice is different – slow and wonderful.

'When I close my eyes,' he says, smiling, 'I am at the centre of the sun.'

My mouth is open, my hands relaxed. Mãe and Father are far away and as small as toy soldiers. I look at Pedro's sleeping smile, see the sun all around him. My legs twitch and I can't stop watching him. Then his eyes fly open and they are bright with light, as if he really has just come back from the sun, and he raises the hoop with his dirty hands and puts it over me so fast that I don't have time to hold out my arms to stop it. It falls right down to my feet and Pedro laughs as I pick it up and then he's turning his belly in a circle, showing me how to spin the hoop like a waist bracelet but of course I already know how, we do this all the time at school, so I show him and his eyes shine in the night like a tiger's and I think: He is my brother.

Chapter Seven

Zebra is old. Exactly how old is impossible to judge. His dark face hangs between the tree branches, perspiring in the sun, surrounded by a shock of white Afro hair and an equally white beard which dangles forty or fifty centimetres to finish in a twisted point. People always feel the jolt of contact when they look into Zebra's eyes, which are black and mesmerising; the kind of eyes that see into and through a person, strip him down to the essentials.

The view from Lisbon's castle, Castelo de São Jorge, is so clear this afternoon that on their way to Zebra's tree, which is tucked out of the way of the main tourist thoroughfare, Carlos and Leo pause and stare.

'You and me have lived in Lisboa all our lives, haven't we, Leo?' says Carlos, squeezing his son's hand. 'And we love it like part of our own soul, don't we?'

Leo nods emphatically. The castle sprawls on one of Lisbon's seven hills, overlooking the wide, shining strip of the river estuary as it broadens into the sea. From the spacious courtyard they can see the imposing Cristo Rei crucifix on the opposite bank and Lisbon's bridge swooping in red highs and lows across the water like an escaping bird. Cruise ships are lined up in gleaming rows in the port. When Carlos collects Leo from school they often wander up here together as it's just a few minutes' walk from their house. Leo notices what his father pointed out to him last time – the contrast between the gridlike structure of the Baixa district which was rebuilt after Lisbon's earthquake, and the higgledy-piggledy red rooftops that cluster at the base of the castle.

'The Alfama didn't fall down in the earthquake, did it, Pai?' he asks, knowing the answer, knowing his father will be pleased to see how much he has remembered. 'Not like Baixa.'

But Carlos only nods vaguely, and Leo can see tears brimming in his eyes. Carlos' free hand clutches his digital camera which rests on his chest in its leather case. He told Leo he could come with him today while he collects new shots for his commissioned photography book, which is on the street people of Lisbon. Leo is always happy to play up at the castle; he knows it inside out. He breaks free from Carlos' loose grip on his hand and runs ahead to find a hiding place near Zebra's tree. 'Spying' on one or both of his parents has recently become one of his favourite games.

When Carlos arrives at the foot of his tree, Zebra looks into and through him, and Leo hears him croon, as if to a small child.

'Why so sad?' he asks, holding a whippy branch back with one hand. 'Can't take good pictures if your own lenses are blurred, can you, man? *Não é, pá?*' Gathering himself up, he rises in a steady wave of sheets so small they might be cast-off tablecloths. He tiptoes daintily down the tree branch, which thrusts outwards from the mammoth trunk at twenty-five degrees; the perfect angle for sleep. Within half a minute, Zebra is on the ground and is stowing his folded sheets in a Jumbo shopping bag riddled with punctures.

When he's finished, he stretches his sinewy body, linking his hands above his head. 'Nothing like an afternoon nap.' He yawns. He's wearing an ancient black T-shirt with a yellow circle on the front and writing too faded to read, and worn jeans. His feet are bare, but he presses them into a pair of bent plimsolls. Then he straightens up and looks at Carlos.

32

'*Então?*' he asks. 'Well?' Zebra's Portuguese moves in slow, beautiful lilts, his rich voice coating the words. His real name is probably José, shortened to Zé and then lengthened to Zebra, but nobody remembers or cares. He is Zebra. Originally he is from Boa Vista, the easternmost island of Cape Verde, but the past forty years of his life have been spent in Lisbon, so that he knows every pavement crack, every face on the street. Carlos often jokes that Zebra has become Lisbon itself, the beating red heart of the city.

'Leo,' says Carlos, turning calmly in Leo's direction. 'You're a master-hider. Not even a hawk would be able to spot you behind that olive tree!'

Leo explodes into laughter, his head bobbing out from behind the stick-thin trunk. 'I know!'

'So come on out and say hi to Zebra.'

Leo steps out of his hiding place and runs across the courtyard to Zebra, who he knows well. He finds his hand enveloped in a huge, callused one, and Zebra brings his gigantic head with its white, Zenlike twist of beard close to his face. He smells of wood smoke and stale beer. As always, Leo wants to touch Zebra's dangling string of a beard – wants to tug it, in fact, but he's never plucked up the courage to do so. Instead he asks, 'Why are you called Zebra?'

Zebra looks at him, very serious. 'Why do you think?' he asks. Leo stares straight into his liquid eyes and gasps at the flickering image he sees there: stripy zebras grazing under an orange African sun, then kicking up their hooves and running into a yellow dust cloud which hangs in the air like an explosion. Through Zebra's grip on his hand, Leo senses the sinewy muscle of Zebra's body. He's old, he thinks, but he's stronger than twenty men.

'It's because you run and disappear into dust, just like zebras do.'

Zebra's smile is wide with delight over bad teeth and red gums. 'Exactly, *menino*. You said it.'

'Now, why don't you go and find out how many peacocks there

are up here today?' suggests Carlos. Leo looks at him, not fooled by this blatant ploy to get him out of the way of something interesting. He turns without a word and scampers off towards the castle ramparts, then doubles back as soon as he's certain his father's attention is elsewhere. There's a far better hiding place than the olive tree: if he can sneak up unobserved to Zebra's wide tree, he can stand behind it and listen to what they're saying.

Leo sees Carlos sit down sideways-on to him on the thick stone edge of a potted plant. Zebra is leaning against the stone wall just down from the tree, glancing towards the river and taking in the colours and shapes of the afternoon. They are talking. As long as Carlos doesn't turn his head, Leo has a clear run to the tree. He darts across the courtyard and leans breathlessly against the trunk. He's just three metres from his father, maybe four or five from Zebra. He tries to blend in with the thick grey bark – not easy in a red shirt. Then he leans out very slightly, so that he can see around the trunk.

Zebra has turned back from the river and his attention is on Carlos. 'You telling me you hurt your boy and your woman *in your sleep*?'

'I did, yes.'

'First time?'

Carlos nods, and Leo sees him blinking back tears. 'Leo has bruises on his shoulder blades where I grabbed him viciously. Olivia has a bruised eyebrow, the skin around her eye is purple, the neighbours must all think I beat her or something, I don't know . . .' He trails off in despair. 'How can I accept that I, Carlos, a peaceful man . . .'

'Known for your gift for listening to the hearts of people,' prompts Zebra generously.

Carlos shrugs off the compliment. 'I'm responsible for incomprehensible violence.' Leo sees him press the palm of his hand into his forehead. 'That I had no control over myself, no memory of it afterwards, is the worst part of it. It means madness, surely? The onset of schizophrenia, perhaps, the first tremble of a mental earthquake.' He stares at Zebra. 'I had a mad Aunt Marina,' he says, his voice sinking low. 'She was taken away and she never came back.'

Zebra looks at him solemnly. 'In Cape Verde, some would say it is a spirit. You are possessed by a spirit. Perhaps the spirit of this mad Auntie Marina.'

Leo's eyes are wide. He has heard Rosa speak of her Aunt Marina, and he knows she's dead, but not that she was mad, which makes her much more interesting.

'Thanks, Zebra,' says Carlos. 'That's really helpful; I'll be sure to tell my wife that's what it is. It'll reassure her no end.'

Zebra gives him one of his patient looks. 'Where has it come from, this night-madness, this thing?'

'It could have come from anywhere, anything,' Carlos replies, looking down at the cobblestones. 'Olivia thinks it could be from a traumatic memory, although I have no idea of what, or from when. Rosa tells me I used to sleepwalk during the year my mother died of cancer. But this is worse than sleepwalking – it's violent and it's mixed with this terrible feeling of doom, and I'm frightened that *Leo* will die.' (Leo's hands clutch the tree trunk involuntarily.) Carlos hunches forwards, his hands on his knees. 'I'm just praying it was a one-off thing because if it happens again, that makes me a madman, you know?'

Zebra shrugs. 'Maybe, maybe not.'

'It happened on Saturday, the night of Leo's seventh birthday.'

'So it was a birthday present from the ghost of mad Marina, perhaps. A night of madness, for old times' sake. A one-off thing, Carlos.'

'You think so?' Leo sees his father's face rise and brighten.

Laughter growls deep in Zebra's throat. 'I have no fucking idea, son. No idea! All I'm saying is, when the shadow comes looking for you, you're the one who needs to be looking for reasons.'

'Shadow?'

Zebra rubs his belly roughly. 'Yeh, the shadow, the dark side of yourself, man. What d'you think happens to a leper whose face dissolves? You think they're not there any more? When things shift, when they go dark on you, you got to find the place where you're nothing and no one but yourself. Find it, claim it, and there'll be no need for more mental eruptions.'

'That might be easier said than done.'

Zebra shakes his head. 'No. What shifts once can shift back again, like sand, you see? Easy! It's you that has to stay steady.' He flips a cigarette out of a crumpled pack in his trouser pocket and positions it between his lips. Leo thinks of dragons as Zebra pulls out a green plastic lighter and lights up, sucking in smoke and blowing it out from flared nostrils. He strokes his fingers down the length of his beard and Leo stares harder, wondering what it feels like to touch. 'It was a *dream*. And dreams are like thoughts – you can change them. Stay light, man, don't give this nightmare so much weight or it'll drag you under.' Abruptly Zebra seems to lose all interest in the subject. 'Now it's time for a Super Bock beer, what you say, man? *É pá*? Set the world to rights again, *sim*?'

Heaving himself away from the wall, he picks up his carrier bag and shuffles off towards the back exit of the castle without another word. Leo ducks back behind the tree, uncertain as to what to do. He has the uneasy feeling his father might not find it so funny if he discovers that Leo was right there, listening to all that. He hears a rustle as Carlos stands up, and presses himself to the tree trunk, willing himself invisible. After a moment or two, he realises he can't hear his father any more. He risks a peep and, to his relief, he sees him wandering down to the main viewpoint, his camera freed from its case, his hands fiddling around attaching lenses, making adjustments.

Leo extends his arms and hugs the tree to him, glad of its huge strength. He hasn't understood all he heard, but when he closes his eyes he sees himself lying on his back looking as if he's asleep except that nobody and nothing – not even his mother's screams – can wake him up, because he's a seven-year-old dead boy.

Chapter Eight

'You don't seem to believe us,' observes Olivia in frustration.

Silver-haired and thick-set, the doctor gazes at her myopically from behind round, gold-rimmed glasses which catch the light from the one high window in the room. He has a Father Christmas-style beard that on first sight makes him look soft, almost comical, but the longer they sit opposite him, the less approachable he seems. They've never seen this doctor before; he's a GP who works in the same large, Cascais-based medical practice as their family doctor, who is on holiday for two weeks.

'As I say, I have no doubt that your husband was responsible for your bruised face, if that's what you both claim,' he remarks, his hand tightening around his pen. It's been five days since Carlos' episode but Olivia's bruise is still large, deforming the shape of her eyebrow. Her eyes narrow slightly as she thinks of the looks she's been getting from shop cashiers and passers-by when they spot the bruise she has tried to cover with make-up and her largest pair of sunglasses. They are looks of sympathy mixed with something less charitable – perhaps she's only imagining the thin strand of contempt? Olivia has resolutely cancelled arrangements to see friends over the next week; she doesn't feel she can face explaining her bruises away. Her friends are used to her 'disappearing' from time to time anyway, during phases when she's working intensely on a painting. She has a sense of hunkering down, closing off from other people until the situation is under control.

'I simply haven't come across such an elaborate story before,' the doctor continues bluntly. Olivia has spent the first minutes of their consultation explaining in a nervous, convoluted way the electrical-type charge that propelled Carlos from their bed out of the blue, and describing the events of his episode.

'It's more than a story,' says Carlos patiently, his hand moving to Olivia's knee to calm the tension he feels radiating from her. 'You need to imagine it.' Dr Freitas looks at him as if he has never needed to imagine anything in his life and resents being told to do so. 'That's what I've been doing, imagining it,' says Carlos, 'since I can't actually remember it.' He shifts forwards on his seat. 'Try to imagine removing everything from a theatre play and leaving in just one actor, who hasn't noticed that all the rest have gone. This one actor continues his act, perhaps arguing with people who aren't there, or lashing out at nothing at all.' Carlos throws out his arms to show the doctor what he means. 'It's ridiculous, laughable, even. But according to my wife, who is *not* prone to exaggeration, that's kind of what I did on Saturday night. I must have been dreaming a very vivid dream, and just acted it out. Sleepwalking,' he adds, since the doctor looks unmoved.

'You claim to have no memory of the event, but you assume you were sleepwalking?' asks Dr Freitas.

'When I shouted at him to wake up, he did,' explains Olivia, her hand scrunching her cream skirt and then smoothing it again.

He switches his gaze to her. 'The first time you shouted, he woke up?'

'No. No, at first he didn't seem to hear me. He stared right through me.'

The doctor leans forwards. 'He appeared unaware of your voice?'

'Yes.'

'And he continued with these violent movements and shouting, like a man possessed?'

'I wouldn't use the word "possessed",' protests Olivia loyally, although in fact the label fits and she subsides into silence. At least the doctor seems to be taking this more seriously now, she thinks. He's taking notes in a scrawling hand, and for a moment there is only the sound of his pen scratching across the page. He looks up.

'This could have been a one-off fit of sleepwalking, brought on by stress,' he says. 'But if it really happened the way you say, it seems too extreme for that. I'm inclined to think there's more to it.'

'Like what?' asks Carlos.

At first the doctor sits and says nothing in response to this. He places both palms on his desk and purses his lips. Then he begins to wield the names of big illnesses as if they weigh no more than balloons. 'There are many possibilities. This could be the onset of epileptic seizures,' he says, his lips moving thickly. 'It could indicate depression.' Olivia notices the clod of silver bristles blocking each of his nostrils. 'Or an anxiety disorder. We could even be looking at schizophrenia.'

Carlos jumps, his knee jolting the underside of the doctor's desk. 'Schizophrenia?' he asks, his voice faltering.

'Is there a family history of any of these illnesses?' asks the doctor, his fountain pen poised.

As Carlos stammers out the few details he knows about his Aunt Marina – her strange night-time behaviour and removal to a psychiatric hospital – Olivia watches the doctor's podgy hands, noticing that their backs are also covered in sprouting grey hairs. He is taking illegible notes in his squeaky leather chair, nodding his head all the while as if this explains everything. For a moment, Olivia detests him for this bandying around of awful illnesses as if one or more of them might be the name of Carlos' fate. How dare he shift from disbelief to this punishing list of diseases in the space of seconds? She feels in some way abused by him, and listens woodenly as he questions Carlos about feelings of depression, frustration, violent urges, alcohol and drug consumption. Carlos, perhaps feeling the same way as she does, responds for the most part in monosyllabic negatives.

Dr Freitas checks Carlos' blood pressure and refers him to a neurologist for further tests. He is in a frenzy of paperwork now, his unseasonally festive beard touching his desk as his hand flies across the thin paper, signing it all with a flourish. Olivia realises neither of them have spoken of Carlos' fear about Leo dying. She thinks she mentioned it when she described Carlos' episode but the doctor had listened to her account with such a condescending air that she might have skipped it in her nervousness.

As they step out on to the street, Olivia is fuming. 'If you don't fit into the narrow schema of what doctors like him know about, they dismiss you out of hand,' she says, flipping her plait behind her neck with unnecessary force. 'How *dare* he mention all those grim diseases? Bloody ignorant Father Christmas lookalike. He doesn't know what he's talking about.'

Carlos shrugs. His face is drawn and Olivia's heart contracts as she looks at him. Further down the street, a musician in a tall blue hat is playing the didgeridoo. The pavement is so narrow that passers-by have to step over the end of the instrument to get past. As they approach him, the music wraps around them and Olivia feels her jaw unclench for the first time in half an hour.

'We can't tell anyone about what I did on Saturday night, you know that, don't you?' asks Carlos in a low voice. 'If even a doctor has trouble swallowing the truth, what will other people think? We can't tell Senhor António and Senhora Madalena. They'll think we're liars.'

Olivia nods, squeezes his arm. They haven't seen the neighbours since that night, but she knows it's only a matter of time. 'We'll just say you had a fit and that we're getting it checked out,' she agrees. 'That's pretty much the truth.'

'All those awful possibilities he came up with, but nothing concrete,' says Carlos. 'I wish he could have just told me what's wrong, why I went crazy like that. *Bolas*,' he sighs. They reach the street musician and step over his didge, Carlos turning back afterwards to toss a coin into the velvet bag beside him. 'I can't believe he tried to make out at first that we were bluffing to cover up a case of wife-battering.'

When he says that, Olivia is assailed by an image of her own pale face staring back at her from the bathroom mirror on Saturday night, when she'd shepherded Carlos back to their own room and tucked Leo up in bed. The bruise on her eyebrow was vicious in the instant, prominent way that bruises sometimes are, and blood was seeping from a tiny abrasion at its centre. Her eyes looked huge and fearful, and there was blood at the corner of her mouth where she had bitten her lip. In a way, I *am* a battered wife, she thinks in alarm as she follows Carlos past a pile of debris from a building site that is spilling onto the pavement. He didn't mean to do it, but he hurt me, hurt us both.

Carlos turns back for her and, when she sees his worried face, Olivia pushes these thoughts from her mind. 'I'm not sure the charming Dr Freitas was too impressed with your actor analogy,' she remarks, and finds herself giggling unexpectedly as she remembers. 'It was just *so* absurd,' she continues, and laughs harder.

'What?' Carlos is half frowning, half smiling, confused by her sudden change of mood.

Olivia stops walking outside a *padaria*, the warm smell of bread and croissants drifting out. Her face is contorted with laughter and she struggles to control herself. 'He was so . . .'

Carlos stops too, his smile growing as silly as hers as he catches her mood.

'He looked as if he'd bitten into a lemon!' Olivia is gasping for breath now, her giggles relieving the knot of tension in her belly, making tears roll helplessly down her face.

They laugh together, Carlos dabbing at her tears with his fingers, and optimism surges in Olivia like a joyous paint stroke spanning a canvas, filling it with light.

Chapter Nine

If Leo's father wasn't a man, he would be a dolphin.

This is what has made Leo choose to do his primary school animal project on dolphins. His friend Concha often arrives at school with a dirty face and has wild dark hair and can do backward flips as well as any television gymnast in a sequinned leotard. She has chosen Pegasus for her animal, a choice their teacher, the kind-faced Professora Celeste, was initially unsure about as she claimed that Pegasus isn't real in the same way that sloth bears or green parrots are. But at this sign of dissent, Concha had stood staring at the teacher with an expression so desolate that she had got her own way (she flashed Leo the grin he thinks of as her monkey grin as soon as Professora Celeste had turned away from her).

Today, Concha is making a pair of wings from wire and white tissue paper for her Pegasus. The airy classroom with its bright cut-out flowers on the walls is buzzing with excited voices, and Leo is pressed against a sink in the far corner, making a glutinous soup of a spell with paint mixed into warm water, a fat sponge with honeycomb-like holes in it to suck up and spit out liquid, and a blue plastic dolphin. Leo looks especially smart this week – his mother has made him wear high-collared shirts since Monday, rather than the oversized T-shirts he likes to wear, to ensure that his bruised shoulders remain well hidden.

Leo loves dolphins for their gentleness, their smiles and playfulness, the effortless strength of their bodies. But in doing his project, he has discovered they have a vicious side. In a documentary that his mother let him watch last week to help him with his project, Leo saw that dolphins can tear up prey just like lions, can hunt and destroy, drag flesh through clear water, staining it a sorrowful red. Since learning this, and since seeing what he saw when the sleep monster turned on him and his mother, he has been feeling anxious. He doesn't know why he has gravitated to the sink. He knows that dolphins can't survive without water.

As he stands grasping the sponge, Leo wishes fiercely that he was as big and strong as his father. He has made this complaint to his mother many times and she always soothes him by saying, 'All in good time. The important thing is to be happy with the Leo of the now.' Finding his hands suddenly empty, he looks down and discovers to his surprise that he has shredded Professora Celeste's fat yellow sponge to pieces, so that the sink is now decorated with random pieces of floating honeycomb. Leo swirls his mud-coloured water and, grasping the dolphin in his fist, he plunges it through the pieces of soaked sponge, then zooms it up and out of the water, making it fly in an arc, in and out, sending water splashing over the edges of the sink and soaking his pale-blue shirt so that it clings to his chest in dark panels.

Professora Celeste is there in a moment, her black hair brushed into its usual chignon which begins each school day impeccable and gradually frees itself into strands which cling to her vivid cheeks.

'Leo, *querido*, no mess-making, please. When water falls on the floor, it makes it slippery, doesn't it? Someone might fall and hurt themselves.' She is bending down, armed with paper towels which turn dark as she swipes at the spilt water. When she stands, her face flushed, she looks down into the sink and sees the filthy water, the destroyed sponge. 'Ai, Leo,' she protests. 'Did you do that to my sponge?'

Leo looks down at the sponge pieces and nods, ashamed. '*Peço desculpa,*' he murmurs. I'm sorry.

'You must ask me before tearing things up for your project.' She pauses. 'Are those pieces of sponge going to be part of your project?'

Leo looks at his teacher with big, anxious eyes, the dolphin gripped tightly in his fist. 'I'm making the dolphin swim through them,' he explains.

'Well, no dolphin would be happy swimming in dirty brown water full of sponge fragments,' says Professora Celeste briskly, scratching at a fleck of yellow paint that has found its way onto the sleeve of her cream blouse. 'And just look at the state of your shirt, Leo – where are your overalls? You'll have to get changed, but first I'd like you to fill the basin with a *small* amount of fresh water. If you don't need the pieces of sponge, throw them in the bin, and please don't do any-thing like that again.'

The teacher ruffles his hair with a smile before walking over to help another child who is calling for her above the noise.

When he has dealt with all the limp, soaked pieces of sponge and refilled the sink, Leo places the dolphin carefully in the clean water. 'Swim away,' he whispers. But it seems unable to swim. It rolls on to its side and stares up at Leo from its plastic eye. Leo thinks back to all he's learned from Rosa about spells and magic-making.

Saying or thinking the same thing again and again is a spell.

Making a wish your first thought when you wake up and your last thought before you go to sleep is a spell.

Something that happens three times is a spell – Rosa calls this the rule of magic three.

Leo ponders this one. He thinks that perhaps something is only a spell if you *make* it happen three times, thinking magical thoughts as you do so. Rosa has taught him that what happens in your mind is the most important magic, the pictures you make, the thoughts you think.

Mixing different things together in a magical way is a spell.

The artwork they did in the park was a spell – Leo sees again his father's volcanic red mound. Do some spells show you the future? Now he needs a powerful dolphin spell to scare away the sleep monster. He looks at the plastic dolphin bobbing weakly on its side in the water. This is no good. He needs to find real dolphins, ride on their backs, ask them for help.

Concha appears triumphantly at his side, the fingers of both hands spread. She pushes them close to his face and Leo sees they are sticky with glue. Slivers of coloured paper and white blobs of tissue paper are stuck to them like tiny, budding feathers. The glue peels off her palms in shreds, a silvery second skin. Leo laughs. If Concha wasn't a girl, she'd be a monkey, although he isn't sure which kind. One with a very pretty face, he decides. 'Concha,' he says in what he hopes is a mysterious whisper. 'Will you help me find a real dolphin?'

Concha drops her hands and agrees immediately. 'How?' she asks.

Leo frowns, deep in thought.

'Oh, I know,' says Concha quickly. She leans in and her hair swings against Leo's arm. They are exactly the same height. 'But it'll only work if you come and stay the night at my house,' she says pleadingly. 'My mum has a dolphin film and sometimes when she's watching it, the dolphins come right out of the television, she says.'

Leo looks at her doubtfully. He can feel that Concha wants him to stay at her house, possibly more than she wants to find a real dolphin, but he doesn't know why this should be. He has never stayed with her before, or met her mother: the school bus takes Concha home. 'But if they come out of the television, are they really real?' he asks. It sounds very strange, but not impossible, he thinks.

'Yes, she says they are.' Concha nods exaggeratedly, her eyes wide. 'We could try it.'

'I'll ask my mum,' says Leo. Already he is imagining huge, smiling dolphins emerging in a stream into Concha's mum's living room, ready to make the spell that will banish the sleep monster for good.

'Leo.' Professora Celeste is at his side again, her indulgent smile gone. 'What did I say about changing into your overalls? Come with me. Concha, dear, perhaps it's time to wash your hands?'

Leo finds himself ushered away from Concha's colourful hands and towards the back of the room, where the clothes pegs are. His teacher lifts down his overalls. 'Off with that wet shirt – no, please use the *buttons*, Leo, or it'll rip, it's so wet.' She helps him struggle out of his shirt, and that's when she sees the bruises. It's been six days since Carlos' violent nightmare, and Leo's bruises have been changing colour spectacularly. They barely hurt any more to the touch but are currently a greenish yellow, and some still have tiny purple centres where the blood vessels have broken. There are two deep ones on the fronts of his shoulders, caused by Carlos' thumbs, and when Professora Celeste turns him gently around, she sees seven or eight more spread across his shoulder blades.

Uncertain of why he has been turned to face the peg rack, Leo turns back to face his teacher and is shocked to see tears in her eyes. He thought teachers never cried. He looks up at her questioningly, waiting for her to pass him his green classroom overalls.

'Leo,' she says very seriously. 'How did you get those bruises on your shoulders?'

Leo is startled. He had forgotten about the bruises. He squints down to look at the only ones he can see: the thumb marks. He knows he isn't allowed to talk about this. He reddens and answers, 'I don't know.'

'It's all right, *meu querido*, I know it wasn't your fault,' she tells him, her voice soothing. 'I'm just wondering how they got all over your shoulders, that's all. Was it your *pai*?'

He hesitates for a long time, then drops his eyes from hers and shakes his head.

Professora Celeste sits on the low bench that runs underneath the clothes pegs. She leans towards Leo solicitously. 'Then who was it, my little man?'

Leo looks into her eyes and knows he can't lie to her. 'It was a monster,' he says. 'It came to our house in the night.'

To his surprise, she nods. 'I see. I see, Leo. Well, if it ever happens again, do you promise you'll come and tell me?'

He nods, trying to keep his promises in his head. He knows he has already broken a promise to his mother, the one about not talking about the sleep monster, but he also knows it's wrong to lie to your teacher – hasn't his mother said so before? Professora Celeste eases him into his overalls, getting another good look at the bruising as she does so. Her lips are pinched together as if she's in pain. Leo swallows apprehensively, but then her face seems to shake out of itself so that within a moment she's her usual self. 'You're allowed to play at the basin for five more minutes,' she says kindly, 'and then you need to sit back down and do some drawing or cutting out. OK? *Tudo bem*?'

Leo nods again. '*Sim*, Professora.' He smiles at her, one of his big, beautiful smiles, relieved that she's dropping the subject of his bruises, and he darts away, back to Concha, who has been busy weaving strips of discarded sponge around her sticky fingers. She raises them as Leo approaches, wiggling them so that they look like sea beasts, her monkey grin flashing wide.

Chapter Ten

'Marina's story was sadder and more terrible than I knew,' says Rosa as they stand within touching distance of the lit water of the central aquarium in Lisbon's Oceanarium. Leo is pressed up against the glass as if he'd like to swim through it into the water. 'Although she was always very sweet with you and I, Carlos, stories about her peculiar behaviour filtered from our household out to the neighbours, probably via Inês.'

Olivia's eyes are lost in the velvety undulations of stingrays and the sight of a shoal of electric-blue fish which scurry past, as sharp and metallic as jeans zippers, but she's listening intently to Rosa.

'The Rodrigues family lived opposite Father's house – d'you remember, Carlos, the son had a funny arm, no left hand and wrist? Anyway, I spoke to the grandmother, Senhora Dona Conceição,' Rosa continues. 'She remembers hearing that Aunt Marina used to smear herself in food in the dead of night, and fling everything out of the kitchen cupboards onto the floor. She also remembers that shortly after her madness started, Marina was removed to a mental institution in Almada and died there soon afterwards.'

'*Soon* afterwards?' Carlos asks. 'But she couldn't have been more than twenty-five!'

'She was just twenty-three. There was talk of some family scandal, over and above the madness, but whatever it was, it was kept dead secret – maybe Inês knew she'd lose her job if she told anyone the details. In any case, the Rodrigues didn't know. All the grandmother could tell me was that shortly after Marina was taken to the asylum, she died, and rumour has it that it was suicide.'

Shocked, Olivia turns to look at Rosa. 'How dreadful.' And frightening, she thinks, her gaze sliding over to Carlos who is standing with one hand stretching over Leo's head to rest on the cold glass, the fingers splayed.

'Mum, *look*!' Leo spins around and grabs her hand, pulling her towards the glass. Olivia looks at a passing shoal of circular yellow fish, their patient, silver eyes. 'No, up there – a monster fish!' Leo is beside himself. The fish he's pointing at *is* monstrous, no more than a huge, armoured head with glaring eyeballs. It's slower than a falling balloon, its ugliness as loud as the cry of the little girl packed into the crowd of children around Leo.

'*Feio!*' she exclaims. 'Ugly!' and the other children laugh and crane upwards to see, and now the word is among them like an upset bee, '*Feio, feio, que feio!*'

'His mouth's big enough to bite my head off,' marvels Leo.

'I don't think he's ugly,' says Olivia, feeling sorry for the fish as it slides past the taunting children. 'He's just out of place next to the tropical fish.'

'He's out of his depth. He should be in the deepest, darkest waters where sunlight never penetrates. That's probably why he's called *peixe lua*. Moonfish,' says Carlos, and his free hand makes its usual brief exploration of Leo's head, the large fingers spread, sending warmth through his son's scalp.

They all watch as the fish turns slowly, like a submarine, and floats upwards, out of sight.

Leo tugs at Carlos' shirt. 'I need to see it again.'

'There are penguins just outside, Leo,' says Olivia enticingly.

'And otters!' adds Carlos, his eyes flashing.

'And things that look like plants,' says Rosa, 'but are really sea horses in disguise.'

Leo nods at them all calmly, as if he is the adult. 'I know, but first I need to see the moonfish again.'

They climb up to a higher viewing platform and watch the slow circles of the *peixe lua* through all the other fish. Carlos stands behind Leo, hugging him against his belly. Rosa and Olivia are on either side of him, pressed against the railing.

'Do you remember anything of that family trouble, Carlos?' Rosa asks.

'No – what trouble?'

'I don't really know what, but some sort of trouble happened around the same time Marina was carted off. I bet it had to do with that valuable family amulet.' Olivia leans in to hear better as other families crowd against the railing. 'When I'd spoken to Senhora Dona Conceição Rodrigues, I remembered Inês whispering something about an amulet to me, and now I'm wondering whether the two things were linked – this other scandal involving Marina, and her being shut away and made so miserable that she . . . well, you know . . . finished things.'

'I can't remember anything about any amulet,' says Carlos. 'Although –' He stops.

'Although what?' prods Olivia.

'Although I do remember playing with Mãe's diamond bracelets, them flashing in my hand . . .' Carlos falters. 'She used to wear a headscarf in bed, didn't she?'

'She wore a headscarf for a whole *year*, Carlos,' says Rosa in surprise. 'Are your memories of that time really so vague? The chemotherapy made her lose her hair. *Querido*, try to think back. You may have heard or seen something – you were living there when all that happened with Marina.'

'Since Inês has been dead for years and Senhora Dona Conceição doesn't know the full story, I think we should visit Marina's asylum and find out what actually happened,' says Carlos. 'If nothing else, they'll be able to give us an exact diagnosis. It looks as if I might have whatever she had, so . . .' He tails off, but not before Olivia catches the misery threading through his voice. She presses closer to him.

'Look, a hand!' cries Leo. A slim, female hand stretches down into the water and starts thrashing food around – seaweed? The food swirls on the surface in long, green tendrils, and the moonfish rises slowly towards it. When it reaches the surface, it eats, careful not to put its jaws too close to the fragile fingers. It trails seaweed, chomping.

'That's settled, then,' says Rosa as they watch. 'We'll go to the asylum.'

Two hours later, they've seen it all, the penguins and the starfish and clownfish and seahorses and the oily fur of the otters and glimpse after glimpse of the *peixe lua* from behind, from the side, face on, its sad, gaping mouth. But instead of seeming satisfied, Leo is agitated as they leave the complex. His head swivels and he walks on tiptoe, eyeing the river.

'*Tudo bem, filho*? All right, son?' asks Carlos, laying a hand on his head as they walk.

Leo stops dead. 'Where are the dolphins?'

The adults stop, looking at him in faint amusement. 'There aren't any at the Oceanarium,' says Olivia. Seeing his face fall, she adds, 'Is this about your dolphin project?'

Leo nods miserably. 'That's why I asked to come here,' he said. 'For the dolphins.'

Olivia sees that he's on the verge of tears. 'Carlos, could you get him something to eat – a sandwich, a cake? Come here, you.' She draws Leo close to her and closes her eyes. 'We'll find you some dolphins,' she murmurs.

Her thoughts drift to the dream workshop she and Carlos are

53

going to attend tonight in the Baixa district's Centro Cultural. When she discovered that the neurologist Dr Freitas had referred Carlos to was booked solid for the next seven weeks, Olivia spent some time Googling phrases such as 'bad dreams,' 'sleepwalking', 'violent nightmares', and even 'dream madness' in the hope of shedding some light on their situation. Her search did nothing to reassure her; the amount of information on the internet about dreams and nightmares was overwhelming and, as she skipped from dream dictionary websites to sites on mental health, she felt increasingly confused and anxious. The one thing she found which she's hoping will help Carlos and her to get to the bottom of his behaviour is this workshop on dream enactment. Olivia visualises a small group of men who have had similar violent nightmares, and a workshop leader who will calmly explain to them what it is, why it happened and how to ensure it never happens again. As she breathes in Leo's little-boy smell, she smiles slightly, knowing it probably won't be that simple, but happy to believe it for now.

While Leo is wolfing down the cheese sandwich his father brings him, Carlos, Rosa and Olivia lean against a low wall, looking out to the sweep of the river, and talk about how to find dolphins.

'The zoo,' suggests Rosa and, when Olivia sighs at this, she says, 'it's the only place he can get up close.'

'We've never taken him to the zoo before,' observes Carlos.

'That's because zoos are nasty places really,' says Olivia, gazing out towards the Vasco da Gama bridge which stretches seventeen seemingly endless kilometres across the river. 'All those animals imprisoned behind bars.'

'The fish are stuck in the aquarium,' points out Carlos, but gently, because he knows Olivia feels strongly about animals being poorly treated.

'I know,' she says. 'I know. But Leo wanted to go . . . and it's educational,' she adds feebly.

'I could take him to see the dolphins on my own,' suggests Carlos, watching her face.

'Or I could take him,' suggests Rosa.

Olivia half turns to them, the breeze blowing a strand of hair across the bridge of her nose. 'I like dolphins, too.'

Carlos chuckles. 'We'll all go.'

'Yeah!' shouts Leo, having swallowed the last bite of his sandwich. He jumps up and down as if he's on a pogo stick, the energy from the food coursing through him already.

Olivia's mobile rings and she searches for it in surprise. 'Didn't know I'd brought it,' she mutters as she answers. '*Boa tarde*, Professora Celeste,' she says, startled. Leo stops jumping when he hears his teacher's name. Olivia listens, looking fixedly at Carlos. '*Sim*,' she says, two or three times. 'Monday, as soon as school finishes. We'll be there.' When she slides the phone back into her bag, Olivia looks at Leo sadly. 'Did Professora Celeste see your bruises, my sweet?'

Leo nods tensely. 'My shirt got wet.'

'Never mind. These things happen.' She smiles at him as reassuringly as she can before turning to Carlos. 'She said she'd been debating whether to ring or not, and that she's decided she must speak to us both urgently.'

'Busybody,' mutters Rosa, but she sounds half-hearted. They all look at each other for a long moment.

'Why does Professora Celeste want to speak to you?' asks Leo.

Olivia hesitates, and is thankful when Carlos turns to him and demands playfully, 'Where did all that excited jumping about the zoo vanish to? Come on, Leo!' Carlos crouches in front of him. 'Imagine it,' he says warmly. 'There's going to be a pool that glimmers and glistens in the sunshine, as blue as any swimming pool, with lovely dolphins jumping and twisting in the air and making big splashes of cold water that'll land all over *your* head!' Carlos drops his fingers

55

onto Leo's head like a splash so that Leo shrieks and leaps away, laughing. With a burst of energy, he zooms off across the paving stones, the movement firing his young blood with oxygen, then he doubles back and races, full pelt, towards his father, who crouches in readiness, his arms outstretched.

'Flying dolphin!' cries Leo as he is lifted high above his father's head. He holds his body as straight and tight as a dolphin's and, as Carlos spins him in rapid circles, he yells in a most un-dolphin-like way so that despite the apprehension that Professora Celeste's call has caused, Olivia can't help but laugh.

Chapter Eleven

Through the door of the dilapidated Centro Cultural in the heart of Lisbon's Baixa district strides a tall, wiry man, as blond as Olivia, his hair curling past his ears.

He smiles at everyone and no one, remarks on the heat in accented Portuguese, flings open windows and switches the fan up a few notches. Everyone is active all of a sudden, pulling chairs and desks back against the earth-red walls, following his directives. Olivia realises how big the room is, how strange this workshop could turn out to be, and she calms the nervous flutter of her stomach, glad that Carlos is with her, his shirtsleeves rolled up to his elbows, his face open and friendly as he clears furniture with the rest of them. Rosa and Leo are at home with a Shrek DVD, tired after their visit to the Oceanarium.

From the leaflet Olivia picked up at the door, she knows that the Centro Cultural has a steady stream of workshops offering everything from making finger puppets to painting with your eyes closed. For May alone, there are several on dreams, all offered by Miles Courtney: 'Draw a Dream'; 'Sandplay: a Jungian approach to therapeutic dreamwork'; and tonight's 'Dream Enactment'. Surely that's the perfect way of describing what Carlos did, thinks Olivia – he physically enacted a nightmare while asleep.

When all fifteen or so of them are standing in a loose circle, the blond man steps into the centre, and silence falls.

'I'm Miles Courtney,' he says, 'and I promise I'm not going to talk for very long.' His British accent resonates through every word he speaks, but his Portuguese is reasonably fluent, so Olivia assumes he lives here. 'This workshop is about acting out your dream, or part of your dream, to gain a better understanding of it,' Miles announces.

Carlos nudges her arm and whispers, 'I thought you said it was about the kind of thing I did last week?'

'I don't know, do I? It just said "Dream enactment", that's all.' Olivia barely listens to the rest of Miles' introduction, hoping she hasn't wasted their time. In her summer dress, green cotton with a gathered skirt, she is sweating. She wishes she'd thought to put her hair up, but at home a cool evening breeze had been blowing through the house so she had left it down. Now it clings to the back of her neck like an animal. Sighing, she gathers it up briefly in her two hands, and lets it flop back down, creating a brief coolness. Above her head, an elaborate silver ceiling fan in the form of a rose rotates at a snail's pace, barely touching the warm air.

'The dreams of all workshop participants are to be respected and treated as confidential,' Miles says. Then he invites them to think of a dream they'd like to work on. Carlos shifts impatiently and Olivia knows what he's thinking – how can I work on a dream I don't remember? 'The first exercise,' continues Miles, 'is to think of your chosen dream and extract from it one sentence, one snippet of dialogue, or just a thought that sums up the dream. Keep it short.' Olivia looks at Carlos, raising her eyebrows meaningfully. He nods.

'Let's get rid of the circle, everyone come together, that's right, stand around randomly. Now – here, could you go first?' he says to a stout, soft-eyed black woman beside him, who baulks but then smiles her agreement. 'I want you to say your sentence loud and clear in the tone of voice that best goes with it – you might say it angrily, sadly, you might sing it, and I'd like you to combine it with an action that goes with it, like running, collapsing, spinning, whatever seems best. And we, the rest of the group, are going to copy you for one minute, repeating over and over again the words and the action. That clear? Now go!'

Everyone looks at the woman. The room is very quiet. Poor thing, thinks Olivia. This is really hard. We're not actors.

But the woman seems composed. She looks down at the floor and when she lifts her face she looks stricken. Raising her arms slowly to her face in a gesture of distress, she says in a high, quavering voice: 'A baby rabbit, covered in tar!'

The second time she begins her sentence and gesture, the group joins in, tentatively at first, but rapidly gaining confidence so that Olivia finds herself in a roomful of distressed, quavering people who have just found a baby rabbit covered in tar. And she is one of them. This is beyond weird, but she has to admit that the effect is strange, electric. They have to keep raising their hands to their faces, mirroring the woman's distress, feeling it. The room sings with the woman's dream image.

Abruptly, Miles signals the next person with a pat on the shoulder, and on it goes, the peculiarly arresting pattern of dream phrases combined with actions. This is what acting class must be like, thinks Olivia, as she crosses both hands over her heart and says blissfully, yearningly, along with all the others: 'Such beautiful mountains!' It's incredible how quickly her own emotions change with the dream images.

Then Miles pats Carlos on the shoulder.

Carlos is tense. He doesn't look at Olivia. With the eyes of the group on him, he sinks to his knees, his arms shoot straight out, gripping imaginary shoulders, and he shouts with great force and emotion: 'My *luck*!' It hurts Olivia's ears, that shout, it penetrates to the red muscle of her heart.

The second time he repeats this, the group takes up the refrain and it feels like madness, all this anguish in the room, these people whipping their arms out just as Carlos had that night, kneeling and shouting in dread . . . Olivia feels tears at the back of her throat as she shouts. Her eyes rest on Carlos and she is shocked by the intensity in his face, which reflects her own, reflects that of everyone else present. The sound in the room is unbearable and the strangeness of what Carlos did in his sleep hits her with renewed force. Then she realises that Carlos has stopped shouting and is kneeling in the centre of the room in his lemon shirt and black jean-shorts, staring around him in dawning horror as strangers enact his words and actions. He claps his hands to his ears, and on his face she sees the same look of inevitability that she saw on Leo's birthday night, the same deeply etched despair.

He scrambles to his feet and runs from the room.

Olivia freezes in shock, sees Miles tap the next person on the shoulder to indicate that they should carry on with the next dream phrase and, as Miles' eyes fly questioningly to her face – he must have noticed that she and Carlos are here together – she is prompted back into mobility. Signing that there's no need for him to follow them, Olivia too slips from the room.

Carlos is at the far end of the dim corridor, leaning his head against the glass of an ornate, shabby window. When he hears Olivia approaching him, he starts to speak. 'Anyone walking unprepared into that room would write those people off as raving lunatics,' he says heavily, 'but they *know* they're just acting out a dream, they *know* what state of consciousness they're in, they're more in touch with reality than I am.'

Olivia stops walking as he turns to face her. Behind him, night is darkening the window; all the colours have gone from the sky.

'This workshop was a bad idea, it's like being thrown into the middle of a public therapy session,' Carlos goes on. 'Can't you see how nightmarish it is to see the darkest part of your psyche reflected in the faces of strangers?'

'I'm sorry.' Olivia's voice cracks a little on the words.

He shakes his head uncomprehendingly. 'When I saw them all mimic me . . .' He sighs, and Olivia realises that, until now, the instant amnesia he suffered after his episode has protected him from a direct encounter with his actions. 'When you saw me like that, you must have thought I was completely mental.' Something in his face reminds her of Leo when he's exhausted and needs a hug. Instinctively, she steps towards him, but Carlos raises both hands as if to fend her off.

'No – I need to be alone,' he says, and she falters. 'Go back inside and carry on, tell me later how it went. Olivia, *por favor*,' he adds when she tries to protest. He cups his hands to his face, breathing through his fingers. 'It's madness,' he groans. 'Olivia, don't you see? I'm losing my fucking mind.'

Carlos so rarely swears that Olivia's eyes widen, and he misreads her expression. 'That's right,' he says grimly, 'this is the curtain rise on to insanity, schizophrenia or something, I don't know . . .' Before she can do or say anything to reassure him, he turns and disappears down the stairwell without saying goodbye. Olivia stands alone and listens to his footsteps clattering down three floors. After a time, she composes herself and goes reluctantly back into the workshop, meeting Miles' eye briefly to indicate that all is well, even though it isn't. She has decided she must speak to him at the end of the session.

They divide into small groups and act out their dreams wordlessly – no narration is allowed. Unable to face the idea of working with Carlos' nightmare, Olivia chooses one of her own dreams, a recent one in which she saw the approach of a tsunami. Again, during the dream-enacting, they all look as if they're slightly crazy, but to her surprise, it's absorbing, taking her mind off the weight of her situation with Carlos, and Olivia is impressed by how much of a dream can be expressed using the body. The artist in her is already working as she watches the bending, long-armed shape of a woman representing a dream tree or plant blowing in the wind. She imagines a painting with human shapes telling a story. She imagines bold greens and reds, perhaps some silver in there, too.

Working in this simple, physical way with complete strangers is gratifying. Each group puts on a production of one of the dreams, and Olivia plays the part of a temple on a hill. It feels good to be serene, imposing, solid. At the end, they give feedback and the group spontaneously claps Miles, who laughs and bows his head. Then people say their goodbyes and begin to disperse. Olivia waits. She's aware that Miles is watching her; she can feel his grey-blue gaze on her. He must sense that she needs to talk to him about Carlos fleeing the class like that. When the room has almost emptied, Miles comes across to her. He's as tall as Carlos, his frame skinnier. He's smiling at her.

'Your friend didn't seem too comfortable with the workshop,' he says kindly in Portuguese.

'I'm sorry about him leaving like that,' she replies in English.

'No problem,' he says, switching languages. His accent is southern, like her own. 'Dreams tend to split people wide open if they aren't ready to work on them, and the timing isn't always right. I hope he's feeling OK now.' He gives her a lopsided smile. 'So you're English? I thought you could be Dutch, or even Swedish.' His eyes skim her hair appreciatively.

'Definitely not Portuguese, anyway.' She smiles.

'Definitely not, although you speak it brilliantly. You must live here?'

'Yes. And you?' Olivia feels slightly frustrated; she didn't want to exchange pleasantries. She should have stayed with speaking Portuguese and kept on the subject of Carlos.

'I've lived here for two years,' he tells her smoothly. 'In Lapa. It's a lovely area of town – know it?'

Olivia nods, and decides to take the plunge. 'My husband – the one who ran out of here – is interested in learning more about dream enactment,' she says hurriedly. 'But not like in this workshop. We had a bad situation a week ago – he enacted a nightmare involuntarily, while he was asleep.'

'Ah.' Miles looks taken aback, but he recovers quickly. 'How intriguing,' he says. 'Go on.'

It's such a relief to talk about it. As she speaks, the words tumbling over each other as she describes what Carlos did that night, Olivia realises how much angst she has been hiding from her family in Cornwall, from their friends and neighbours, from Leo. Living so far from her parents and oldest friends makes it easier to gloss over the difficult parts of her life when they speak on the phone. Even when Leo is feverish or otherwise ill, Olivia rarely tells her parents until he's recovered, wanting to spare them from worry. With Miles standing in front of her, his arms folded loosely across his chest, his expression grave, Olivia feels some of the dreadful weight she has been carrying inside her fall away.

'His eyes were open, but glazed over, seeing only the action of the dream,' she says, her hands fluttering in the air as she attempts to explain. 'It seemed as if he was hallucinating the dream on to the real world, which to him only had the substance of a shadow. He couldn't differentiate between me, his wife of eight years, and a random dream figure.' Although unburdening herself like this is a relief, some instinct makes her avoid mentioning Leo's involvement in the violence. 'I'm exhausted by the state of tension I find myself in now at night, when Carlos is sleeping beside me,' she admits. 'I keep thinking it might happen again any second. It's all getting too much and we need to know if this is the beginning of some kind of dreadful madness, or whether it was just a freak incident.' She gives a short, embarrassed laugh. 'I'm sorry. You're the first person aside from Carlos that I've really talked to about it,

63

and he can't remember anything, so I've been feeling sort of on my own with it.'

Miles unlocks his arms and for a moment she fears he's going to take hold of her hands, but he doesn't. 'I deal with psychological and therapeutic aspects of dreaming, and I'm not an expert when it comes to this kind of thing,' he says. 'But I have colleagues in the field of dream studies who will almost certainly be able to tell me more. If you like, I could try to find out more for you.'

Olivia's heart leaps. 'Oh, yes, please. That would be fantastic.'

Miles smiles, and she sees the shine of something like tenderness in his eyes, which haven't once left her face. 'I'm more than happy to help,' he says. 'I'll be out of town all next week though, so how about meeting the week after that?' They arrange to meet on Wednesday 26 May, in the artistic Café Amarelo by the cathedral. As she leaves, Olivia turns one last time to smile her thanks, and Miles is standing in the centre of the room, the breeze from the giant rose-fan stirring his blond hair.

As she rides the wasp-yellow *eléctrico* back up towards the castle, again and again Olivia's thoughts return to the moment when the whole room rang with Carlos' cry. The dream anguish reverberating around the room felt too raw to be repeated, too frightening. From her intense questioning, all she's managed to get out of Carlos is that when he woke up from that nightmare, he felt exhausted, as if he'd just experienced the most brutal bolt of fear, the most intense adrenaline charge possible. His heart, he told her, was beating as fast as a hummingbird's wings, sweat was flowing from every pore, a residue of dread thrummed through him as she had ushered him back to his bed. But apart from that, there were no anchoring images, not even the sliver of a memory of what had taken place.

Olivia jumps down from the tram and walks home through yellow-lit streets with the smell of grilled sardines on the air and the strains of a fado singer reaching her ears. If only I could see right into the depths of Carlos, she thinks. If I could have watched that night-mare spool past, I'd understand why he went so crazy, I know I would.

She pauses at the top of the hill to turn, as she often does, and look down at the beloved sweep of cobblestones, the twinkle of restaurant lights, the calm old walls of the Alfama. She inhales deeply, can smell the sea on the breeze. What the hell is Carlos so afraid of?

Chapter Twelve

March 1984, Alfama

The red-haired man tips his head back, puffs his cheeks and blows out a column of orange flame which shoots into the air like lava before disappearing in a shimmer of light. I want to grab Pedro's hand for safety but don't dare, and anyway he's holding his hoop and smiling with the sun on his brown face as we watch. We're standing right up close and the flame is so hot that if the fire-breather turned his head and breathed on us we'd be burned as black as paper in the hearth, along with all the other people who are watching him, tourists and old men in baggy shirts and children younger than us, held high in their mothers' arms. The fire-breather has thick wrists like Father's, only with orange and yellow rubber bands wrapped around and around them, and he stinks of fire and sweat and whatever it is that he drinks and swills around his cheeks to make fire.

'If he breathes in,' says Pedro, nudging me with his bony elbow, 'he'll die.' The fire-breather hears him and his eyes catch Pedro in their grip as he breathes out another wing of fire so hot I wonder why his mouth doesn't melt to nothing.

'Why will he?' I whisper.

'Because the fire will be sucked back into his lungs and burn them to nothing, and he won't be able to breathe at all after that.'

'How d'you know that?'

Pedro squares his shoulders, flexing his wooden hoop so that it flips outwards towards the fire-breather. 'My brother told me,' he says. 'He's tried fire-breathing but he didn't like the taste of paraffin.'

Paraffin. Pedro knows words as exciting as adventures. Paraffin sounds like pirates with eyepatches and whirling swords.

'I wish *I* had a brother.'

Pedro grins at me. I see him nearly every day now, after school. He waits for me on the low wall at the corner of Rua da Galé, swinging his legs. Every day, he has something new to show me – a white kitten, its pink nose peeking from the cork satchel his brother got for free, the dried body of a newt stuck by sunshine to the wall of the church, Igreja de São Miguel, the houses where the baker hangs plastic bags full of fresh bread rolls off the doorknobs every morning so that one roll is never missed, the tiled window where the ginger dog barks at us when we go by, no matter how fast we run. Pedro has no shoes to pinch his feet, no Father to roar at him, no tie to choke him on Sundays. He doesn't go to school, but he loves the coloured pencils I give him and when I showed him my exercise book, he said he wants to learn to write his name, only I don't know how to spell it so I'll ask Marina first and then teach him.

The fire-breather is crouching on the ground, sorting things out for his next trick. His face is as red as his hair, and he is half-naked, with green trousers and silver rings on his toes. 'When you can write your name,' I say to Pedro, 'I'll show you how to write mine, and then we'll be brothers.'

Pedro nods. '*Sim*,' he says. 'That's what we'll be.' And my chest hurts with happiness so I don't care that when I get home today Inês will be standing at the front door with scolding words. She says I get home later every day and she's going to speak to Father about it, but I think Father's too busy being angry with Marina to care, and it's not even about the leftover casserole he found her eating with her bare hands a few nights ago. No one will tell me what she's done. Mãe shook her head when I asked her and said, 'You're too young, Carlitos. Leave it for us adults to wear out our heads with worrying.' Her lips were white and I touched them to make them red like before but she just frowned and said I should run along and practise my piano scales. When I asked Marina, her eyes looked everywhere except at me, and I saw tears there ready to fall, as heavy as Mãe's diamonds. 'I'll tell you another day,' she whispered. 'It's too soon, too much, too hard.' And then she hugged me and I smelled the rose-petal-Marina smell only this time it was like petals that had fallen off the flower and were dying on the ground and I knew how sad she was.

A blast of flame rushes into the air and everyone gasps and some of the smaller children cry out. The fire-breather is dancing now, dancing with his legs bent as he breathes fire through the world. Beside me, Pedro is scratching the new tattoo on his left arm that his brother took him to get done in a shop with skulls in the window – it's a winged thing, in green and red, and Pedro says it's a phoenix that can never die, but comes back to life always, and even if he washed it every day the phoenix will never leave him, it's part of his skin now. As the fire-breather coughs between one flame and the next, and the sun rings my head and Pedro stands close by, twiddling his hoop and whistling low between his teeth, I promise myself that one day I'll have a phoenix tattoo.

When the show is over, we walk up towards my house. Squatting in the dust further up the street is a dirty man with black hair and a sharp beak of a nose. He's wearing an anorak even though it's boiling hot. 'He looks like a crow,' I whisper to Pedro as we get closer.

'He's *maluco*. Crazy. My brother says he's killed many men.'

'Killed? How?' I stare at the crow-man and he lifts his head and stares back as if he knows we're talking about him.

We pass him in silence, and I keep my shoulder close to Pedro's. 'He kills with a razor,' whispers Pedro. 'He chops cats' heads off for kicks. He lost half his brain to white powder, Fernando says.'

White powder? I imagine an aspirin, fizzing his brain to nothing. I have a bad feeling – I'm sure the crow-man must be looking at me, I can feel his dark stare on my back. I twist my head around and he *is* staring – right at me. 'Pedro!' I say in panic.

'Keep walking. Fernando says he sits in one place for a while, then he disappears and sits in another patch in a different part of the city. And he leaves at least one dead man behind him each time.' Pedro is breathing fast; we're walking as quickly as we can up the hill. When the crow-man is out of sight, we slow down and clutch each other, laughing until we're dizzy.

It's night time and I'm lying in my boat-bed. I've been asleep, I think, but I wake up with Marina's sobs in my ears and Father's shouts but it's far away and I don't understand. Then Father comes upstairs and I hear him talking with Mãe. I kneel up on my bed. My window is easy to open quietly. The night air comes in, dark but full of the sparkle of boat lights and the smell of the river. I choose the boat I'd like to take tonight – a small one with a bright blue light at its bow, blue enough to light our way across the water, Mãe, Marina and I. We'll take turns to row, with Marina singing fado songs to us and Mãe laughing in a headscarf and me touching the cold water with my hands, and we'll fetch Rosa from her school and we won't come back.

I hear Father's voice, suddenly loud again so that I go very still. '*Nobody* must know about Marina,' he says, and I hear Mãe coughing into her tissues. 'We are the Casanovas de Albuquerque Moniz . . .' Father's voice is stern, and I hear their door closing.

Down on the street, outside the shoe-man's shop with its dark windows and piles of brown shoes for mending, I see bright orange circles dancing like three suns. I push myself forwards and the circles are moving around and around and I see the boy who's making them move and it's Pedro, his arms spinning until suddenly they all fall, rolling in different places so he has to chase them, laughing his blackbird laugh. How are they so bright? He catches one, two, and runs after the third, which he kicks to the wall to stop it rolling down the hill.

'Pedro!' I call very quietly – too quietly? But he hears, and I see his head lift and search the faces of the houses. I wave, and when he sees me his smile opens up.

Another boy comes up then, bigger than Pedro, with a cap pulled down over his ears, and he has a yellow dog with floppy ears and a bouncy walk. The big boy puts his hand on Pedro's shoulder and they walk away towards the river with the sun-balls filling Pedro's arms, and I think, that's his brother. When they turn the corner onto the tram lines, I can't see them any more.

Chapter Thirteen

Despite the ache of unease in her chest, Olivia smiles as she watches the children run to their parents, trailing the paper lanterns they have made that afternoon at school, the wind rippling across blue, red, and yellow tissue paper. Leo, she knows, will be the only child left inside today, settled with some colouring pens in a classroom near to the room where she and Carlos will have their interview with Professora Celeste. Carlos is silent as he walks at her side, his shoulders tense, but when she glances at him she sees tender amusement in his eyes as he watches the children's faces.

Inside the building, Professora Celeste, looking flushed and slightly dishevelled, beckons them into Leo's classroom with a restrained smile. The classroom is peppered with tiny pots with name stickers on them and feathery green ferns shooting from their centres; the kids must be growing their own plants, the way Olivia remembers growing mustard and cress at her own primary school. She looks around for signs of Leo's dolphin project, but the classroom is neat, everything has been tidied away into the big cupboards which line the walls.

'Do sit, please,' says the *professora*. 'Leo is next door playing a spelling game – he likes spelling. Will you be all right sitting on these chairs? I know they're rather small. Or you can sit on a desk, if you'd rather.' Carlos settles himself gingerly on a desk, and Olivia sits on a chair beside him. She has tidied her mass of hair into a chignon and is wearing a large pair of sunglasses. Her gaze doesn't leave Professora Celeste as she moves briskly to her desk, which is stacked with little piles of Sellotape, board pens and what look like pompoms scattered with glitter. Leo's teacher is wearing a tight red shirt with wide lapels which gives way to a flowing skirt of the same red. Since she started teaching Leo a year ago, Olivia has always liked and trusted her, but she realises she has absolutely no idea of how this meeting will go.

'Leo is a lovely child,' Professora Celeste remarks gravely as she sits down. 'He's very well mannered and, most importantly, his heart is in the right place.' She pauses. 'Although sometimes I worry that he's too sensitive, his imagination too powerful: he regularly seems entranced, lost in a complex imaginary world.'

Olivia is nodding. 'He's the same at home.' She smiles. 'Leo has a vast imagination and it takes up almost all the space in his mind.'

The teacher tilts her head in acknowledgement of this. 'Perhaps at times his dreaminess becomes frustrating for the two of you?'

Carlos and Olivia exchange a brief, baffled look.

'No,' says Carlos. 'His dreaminess is part of being Leo.'

'Well,' says the *professora*. 'I've asked you here today because on Friday, Leo soaked his shirt and had to get changed into his overalls. I saw bruising all across his shoulder blades. He told me a monster did it in the night. At home,' she adds significantly, then sits back in her seat and looks at them both.

Olivia's hands, still pressed together, are sweating. When she glances rapidly at Carlos, he is studying Professora Celeste's desk with an expression of deep unhappiness. 'It isn't what you think,' she says. 'We've never hit Leo, even when he's been naughty. We don't believe in striking children.'

Professora Celeste's eyes darken, but her voice remains even.

72

'Well, Senhora Olivia, there are more ways of being violent to a child than simply hitting him. The bruises I saw on Leo's skin are clearly finger marks. It seems that Leo has been gripped most brutally and possibly shaken hard.'

'Well,' says Olivia faintly. 'We had a –' she glances at Carlos. '– an unusual situation at home last Saturday night and things got out of hand.'

'Would you like to tell me about it?'

'It was a sort of . . . conflict. There was a lot of shouting.' An uneasy pause fills the room and Olivia looks at Carlos again. He is studying his hands now and she experiences a flash of anger. Why does she have to be the one to bluster their way out of a situation which is not her fault? Following the doctor's sceptical reaction, they've agreed not to attempt to explain that Carlos hurt Leo during a violent nightmare. 'Either she'll think we're lying, or she'll think I'm going crazy,' Carlos had reiterated urgently, clasping her elbow in a panicky way as they approached the school gates. 'And if she leans towards the crazy conclusion, she might contact the authorities and have me carted off like Aunt Marina.'

Professora Celeste shifts her gaze from Olivia to Carlos, and back to Olivia. 'So you're saying that Leo's bruises were caused by yourself or Senhor Carlos?'

Olivia nods. 'He . . . We were arguing and Leo got in the way.' This is the best excuse they could come up with, having the merit of being as close to the truth as they can allow, but as she speaks she sees how reedy it sounds, how weak. Professora Celeste allows the awkward silence to stretch, and Olivia sees that she doesn't believe them. Without thinking, she removes her sunglasses and leans forwards, her wide, sincere eyes fixed on the teacher's. 'Professora Celeste, we would never mistreat our child.'

When the teacher's eyes jump in shock, Olivia remembers too late the fading bruise on her right eyebrow which is now in plain view.

Professora Celeste's expression deepens in sympathy as she takes in the sheen of pale-green discolouration which spreads from Olivia's eyebrow down onto her eyelid like inexpertly applied eye shadow. Panicked, Olivia rams her sunglasses back onto her face, flinching as the movement disturbs her bruise. She wants to shout, it's not what you think, my husband is no bully, this was an accident, he was asleep for Christ's sake.

'My husband is not a violent man,' she says definitely.

Professora Celeste looks over at Carlos, who is huddled on the desk like a white eagle in a storm, his shoulders hunched high, his head jutting low in misery. He returns her gaze unflinchingly. But he looks repentant, thinks Olivia, guilty.

'I realise I have a small bruise on my eyebrow,' she adds quickly, 'but it wasn't Carlos' fault, he had no idea what he was doing . . .'

The teacher's attention has shifted to Carlos. 'Senhor Carlos,' she asks politely, 'had you been drinking?'

Carlos shakes his head, regarding her sorrowfully. 'No. But I didn't remember anything afterwards.'

'So you simply forgot what you'd done?' Professora Celeste looks flustered, and Olivia turns to Carlos tensely. This doesn't sound at all convincing: he'll have to come up with something better.

Realising the same thing, Carlos straightens in his seat and backtracks hastily. 'Maybe I did have a few drinks that night.'

Olivia nods encouragingly. 'He's not used to drinking.'

'Let's hope for his family's sake that he doesn't start getting used to it,' says Professora Celeste. A steely note has crept into her voice; for the first time, her understanding front is slipping, and Olivia wonders how she could have assumed that this woman who spends her days interacting with children has little more to her than an easygoing nature and her characteristic bursts of quick laughter. 'Leo has already shown mild signs of dissociation,' continues the teacher, smoothing her skirt and sitting very straight at her desk. 'He's not normally a wilfully destructive little boy, but he shredded one of my sponges without seeming to know why, or even that he'd done it. And he had his head in the clouds all last week. I'll be observing his behaviour for further signs of disturbance, and I think I'll know if anything like this happens again.'

'It won't happen again,' says Carlos, opening his palms. 'It was a one-off, a terrible mistake.'

'Well, if in future I find further marks of violence on Leo, it will be my duty as his teacher to notify the social services.' Professora Celeste pauses to let this sink in.

Olivia's heart hurts as if she's been stabbed. Involuntarily, she raises a hand to her chest. 'I can assure you,' she begins tearfully, but Carlos cuts in, his gaze fixed on the teacher's mistrustful face.

'I *promise* it will never happen again. I love my wife and son more than my own life.' His voice vibrates with conviction. 'You can't imagine how it breaks my heart to see what I did to the two of them when I wasn't myself. I would never purposefully hurt them. Never.' Carlos' regret is visible in every line of his face, and Olivia thinks she sees Professora Celeste's tight mouth soften. She is briefly thankful for her husband's unconscious magnetism. But it isn't enough.

'Then might I suggest, with all due respect, that you lay off the alcohol completely, Senhor Carlos, and put your energies into protecting your family.' The *professora*'s voice is gentle. She switches her gaze to Olivia. 'Senhora Olivia. I'm sure we're both in agreement that a mother's duty first and foremost is to protect her child from harm. I'm sure you're doing your best, and I hope you'll come to me if you need help.'

Olivia manages to force a nod, but she almost chokes on the unfairness of having to accept this misplaced sympathy. They get up to shake hands, and all Olivia can think of is the stabbing in her heart when Professora Celeste threatened to go to the social services. As she follows the other two numbly from the classroom to fetch Leo and take him home, Olivia imagines her son being carried away from her, kicking and protesting, his arms outstretched for her, his small face imprisoned behind the glass of a car window as he is driven away. Outside the room where Leo is, Professora Celeste motions them to wait in the corridor for a moment while she goes in, her red skirt flowing through the door behind her. Olivia turns to Carlos.

'If it happens again . . .' she breathes, her eyes blank with fright.

'It won't,' he says firmly. 'It hasn't happened since, has it?'

'I haven't told you this because it scares me so much,' she whispers frantically, 'but Carlos, over the past few nights, you've been kicking out in your sleep. You get these huge, violent twitches which run over your whole body, just like the night it happened. And I lie there, frozen, waiting to see if you'll cross some invisible barrier and burst out of the bed again. It's *still there*, Carlos. It hasn't gone away.'

'Listen,' says Carlos, his voice low and urgent. 'All that shows is that I've got it under control now. My body has understood that it has to stay in bed, no matter how strong the dream.'

Olivia shakes her head, knowing he's only trying to quell her fears. From within the classroom, they can hear the scrape of a chair as Leo leaves his spelling game and makes to accompany Professora Celeste out of the room.

Carlos pulls Olivia into his arms and she feels her cheek settle into its familiar position on his chest. He squeezes her close and says into her hair, 'Everything's going to be OK, you'll see.'

Chapter Fourteen

'My luck!' Carlos roars, and the pain in his voice is terrible to hear.

In a split second, Olivia is wide awake. In the semi-darkness, she can see his naked form tearing at the thick bedroom curtains with both hands.

'*A minha sorte!*' he shrieks so loudly that she can feel the vibration of his voice in her chest. 'My luck!'

Olivia cringes against the headboard, wishing herself invisible. Only the thought of Leo, waking to hear this, forces her to risk leaving the bed, which will mean crossing the line of Carlos' vision should he turn even slightly from his curtain scene. Who is it he can see?

As she pulls the duvet back, her legs are shaking: this is going to be a bad episode. Carlos wrenches the curtains with such force that the metal rail is ripped from the wall and the whole lot – curtains and slim metal poles and nails and plaster – comes crashing down on his head. Olivia bolts for the door so fast that her nightshirt flattens against her body, but Carlos whips around, the metal curtain poles clanging against the windowpane, and she sees him lunge towards her in the semi-darkness, an unruly shape covered in material and dragging poles. Olivia's fleeting thought as her legs pump into action is that Leo must not see him like this.

'It's *me*, Olivia!' she screams as she races through the door. Her heart is hammering, memories of the last time rearing ugly in her head. Across the landing, Leo's door is ajar and his small white face is visible, peeping around it. 'Get back,' she gasps to him and his head shoots back just a millisecond before she slams his door shut as she passes, running downstairs in the hope of distracting Carlos from Leo's bedroom. She can hear a racket behind her at the top of the stairs but Carlos doesn't seem to be after her or near Leo. He's shrieking incoherently now, and banging against something. Olivia halts just inside the living room door, switches the light on – so sharp it makes her eyes water – and listens intently over the ragged sound of her breathing. What's he doing?

'My luck!' he's yelling still, the panic in his voice tinged with despair, as if something irreversible is about to happen.

Clutching her bare arms, she goes to the foot of the stairs and shouts so that her throat and chest throb with the urgency of it: 'Carlos. You're dreaming, my love. Wake up!'

There's a silence which allows her to hope that the dazed, glazed fog is lifting from Carlos' eyes and that the dreaming part of him, the lost man who is stuck in this nightmare, is rising like a helium balloon to wakefulness.

Then Carlos appears on the wooden landing that links the two short flights of stairs. He has lost the curtain and poles and is completely naked, his chest glistening with sweat, his fists clenched. He stares down at Olivia for a long moment while both of them adjust to the light, and she sees the wordless terror on his face. Oh, Carlos, she thinks desperately. Wake up, be yourself again. She is afraid to speak in case she interrupts what she believes is his awakening. Then he makes a sound of anguish. He's still deep in the dream.

'*Wake up!*' screams Olivia, terrified that he will do himself damage. Looking up the stairs, she cries, 'And you, Leo, stay in your room!' She thinks she hears Leo's protest that he *is* in his room, but to her dismay he appears at his father's side on the stair landing. Leo's face is drawn, his eyes enormous.

'Leave my mum alone!' he screams, heartbreakingly puny beside Carlos' bulk. Olivia has already started running up the stairs when Carlos looks at Leo, and then everything happens too fast. Leo is wearing his pyjama bottoms but is bare-chested, and he's wearing a cheap necklace in the form of a metal disc with a bicycle engraved into it, suspended on a thin metal chain. It was a gift from one of the friends at his birthday party. As he stares up at his father, Carlos explodes again.

'You cannot steal my luck!' he yells. Reaching out in a blur of movement, he rips the necklace off Leo. Before it snaps in two, the metal chain bites into the tender skin on the side of Leo's neck, and he screams. Olivia is there in a flash, wanting to save Leo, all three of them cramped onto the small stair-landing now, with Olivia at the very edge of the top step so that when Carlos whirls away from Leo with the necklace clutched in his fist, his heavy elbow catches Olivia on the chin, sending her off balance. She tumbles backwards, her arms flailing, her head cracking into the banister, her hips bouncing as she slides head first down the stairs, unable to find anything to cling on to.

'Mum!' Leo's frantic screams reach Olivia's ears as she lies dazed and crumpled at the bottom. There were only nine steps to fall down, but they are uncarpeted, so that her spine feels battered and the side of her head is wide and numb where she hit it on the way down. She struggles to get up and, as she raises her head and shoulders, she sees Carlos' eyes narrow, focusing on some threat that isn't really there, and he half runs, half slips down the stairs, almost tripping on Olivia's right elbow as she tries to squeeze out of his way. He runs blindly into the living room and moments later there's a crash, the sound of wood splintering against a wall. Leo is by his mother's side in a moment, and together they manage to right her. She straightens her nightshirt in a daze and sits on the second step, her arm around Leo, who is trembling.

From the living room, Carlos is gasping, and there's a flat, slapping sound that Olivia can't identify. Her head throbs horrendously and her vision is blurred. She tugs Leo closer, knowing she'll have to try to stand up very soon to make sure Carlos isn't hurt.

The doorbell sings out again and again; someone is leaning on the bell. 'Oh, no,' mumbles Olivia. 'Help me up, baby.'

With Leo's help she stands up, wincing.

Carlos is slumped on the living-room floor with his back against the wall, gasping, tears in his eyes. His body is soaked with sweat.

'So much blood . . .' he says, staring straight ahead with a look of horror. He seems entirely unaware of the doorbell. In his closed fist, he's still holding Leo's necklace. Their African giraffe statue, made from dark wood with straw wound around its elongated legs, is lying broken on the floor. Olivia leads Leo carefully around Carlos' outstretched legs, not daring to speak. He could leap up and go mental again at any second, she reminds herself. The doorbell is still chiming; the sound goes right through Olivia's blazing head.

'Keep quiet, my sweet,' she whispers to Leo, who nods, staying very close to her side. At the front door, she switches on the outside light and looks through the grille. Blinking in the sudden illumination are their next-door neighbours, Senhora Madalena and Senhor António. She's in her bathrobe, and he's in dark-blue pyjamas. Both look dishevelled and worried, and Olivia's heart sinks to think of what they must have heard. They only moved into the house next door six months ago and they rarely see each other, but she knows they are decent people. Senhora Madalena, who is as petite as Rosa, teaches music at a private school, and Senhor António, in his early fifties with striking silver hair, is a tax lawyer.

'Senhora Olivia,' says Senhor António urgently. 'Are you all right? Open the door!'

'I'm so sorry we woke you up,' she says, speaking through the grille. Her voice sounds surprisingly calm, if a little rough after all that shouting.

'Open the door. It sounds as if bloody murder is happening in there. I want to make sure you're really all right.' Senhor António's usual composure has vanished; he is red in the face and won't take no for an answer, she can see that. Reluctantly, Olivia opens the door a few inches, keeping it on the chain, and puts her face to the gap.

'Carlos had a funny turn, but it's all fine again now,' she explains quickly before she registers the shock on their faces. Senhora Madalena actually claps her hand to her mouth.

'You don't *look* fine,' says Senhor António. His forehead is wracked with lines.

Olivia raises her hand to her face, feels the stickiness of blood on her left temple, and, beneath it, an alarmingly large lump. 'I fell down the stairs.'

'You were pushed, more like it,' says Senhor António fiercely. 'We heard all the shouting and screaming.' He steps forwards as if to force his way in, and Olivia is suddenly absurdly glad she put the chain on – who knows how Carlos might react if a man confronts him while he's still dreaming? She prays he'll stay quietly where he is in the living room, that he won't roar into life again.

'It was an accident,' she tells Senhor António earnestly, and is aware that she must sound like the classic battered wife, inventing weak and unconvincing lies to keep people at bay.

'Where's your boy?' asks Senhor António. 'I heard him shouting, too. He shouldn't be involved in domestic violence.'

'It's really not what you think . . .' Olivia sighs. 'He's here,' she adds, and pulls Leo partially into view, careful that the side of his neck isn't visible. Leo gazes at the neighbours with haunted eyes.

'Senhora Olivia,' says Senhora Madalena, tugging the sleeve of her husband's pyjamas so that he'll take a step back and let her talk.

She pushes her round, serious face closer. 'Please come back to our house. You can stay with us, both of you. Don't stay here.'

'That's very kind, but we are honestly fine.' Olivia pushes Leo gently out of view again, but keeps her arm around his shoulders. 'I . . . It was just an . . . incident.' She struggles to find the words that will make them return to their beds reassured. 'Carlos, he made a mistake . . . that is to say, he mistook . . . he thought we were . . .' She trails off, faced with the impossibility of a plausible explanation that won't make Carlos sound like a madman.

'Let me speak to your husband,' demands Senhor António. 'Where the hell is he?'

'No, please just leave it.'

'Why should I leave it?' His face is puffed and ugly with a bullishness that Olivia has never noticed in their brief and friendly exchanges about gardening or holidays. It occurs to her that he won't be an easy man to argue with.

Senhora Madalena is shaking her head sorrowfully. 'We can't just let this go. Clearly something awful is happening in your home; this is the second time in two weeks! And you're hurt – you could well be concussed, with that frightful bruise. Please, let me at least call a doctor.'

'Thank you, but I really don't need any help from either of you,' says Olivia, desperate to get rid of them. 'I'm very sorry we woke you but please don't worry – we're all fine.' She shrinks back from them and moves to close the door, but Senhor António has blocked it with his slippered foot. Olivia stares at him. 'Please remove your foot from my door,' she says. The blood is pounding through her head and her voice shakes with the strain of the situation.

'I just want to be clear,' he says. 'This is a decent neighbourhood. We don't want any trouble. We want to help you, but if you refuse to be helped . . .' He looks at her grimly. 'We like Senhor Carlos, but this can't happen again.'

'It won't,' whispers Olivia. 'I promise you, it won't.' She is close to tears.

Senhor António nods. 'You get that cut seen to,' he says gruffly, and removes his foot.

'*Boa noite*,' says Olivia. Goodnight. With no more than the softest of clicks, she closes the door in their faces.

Chapter Fifteen

'Leo, please understand.'

Leo stands unhappily in the narrow road that snakes up from the school gates. He stares at his father, who was waiting to walk him home after school and is now trying to go back on the promise he made last week.

'*Why* can't I go to Concha's tomorrow? You *said* I could!'

'I need you where I can keep an eye on you, make sure you're safe.'

'I *will* be safe at Concha's!'

'I know, I know.' Carlos crouches on the cobblestones to bring his face level with Leo's. 'I just have all these crazy fears, you know – the school bus overturning, or Concha's mum not watching the two of you well enough, or just *something* bad happening to you, Leo. I don't know why I feel this way, and I'm sorry I can't explain it better. I just feel very strongly – more strongly with every passing day – that I have to keep you safe.'

'The only time I'm not safe is when the sleep monster comes, and it looks like you so it must be all your fault,' Leo cries, and when his father flinches, he is filled with remorse. 'Sorry, Pai.'

Carlos shakes his head. 'It doesn't matter.' He looks at Leo for what feels like a long time. Leo waits with all the unfairness boiling up in him, ready to pour out if his father doesn't back down, but eventually Carlos says, 'All right, you can stay the night at Concha's. But I'm going to write our phone numbers on your arm and you must promise to call if you need me, *sim*?'

Leo beams. '*Sim*, Pai. OK.'

Carlos folds him into his arms and Leo has to stop himself from struggling to free himself from his father's smothering grip. On Sunday night, the sleep monster had stolen his necklace and last night, Leo had woken in the dark to find his father crouched by his bed, watching him sleep. Leo had shot up into a sitting position, convinced it was the sleep monster about to attack him, but Carlos had whispered that he was just checking Leo was all right. His father is different; Leo knows he thinks something bad is coming, and surely it must be the sleep monster, coming to kill Leo. He'll need the dolphin spell, and for that he must go to Concha's and watch her mother's magic DVD. When Carlos finally releases him, Leo says, '*Não te preocupes*'. Don't worry. His father smiles his new, thin smile, but the worry in his eyes stays put.

On the way home, they detour to the church square to listen to the music made by a group of street musicians from Uruguay, Germany, Chile and Italy who are passing through Lisbon on a lazy summer tour of European capitals, jamming, smoking high-quality skunk and seeing life. Carlos came across them earlier that day and has returned to immortalise them with his camera. Leo grips Carlos' shirt-end because his father's hands – and all his attention – are on the colours and movements he sees through the rectangle of his camera lens. For years, Carlos has drilled it into Leo's head that when the two of them are alone in a crowd, and Carlos is photographing, Leo must hold him in exactly this way, to stay safe. The musicians are sitting cross-legged at the shady base of São Miguel church on a large woven rug the colour of a sunset. There is a sitar, a clarinet, a South American flute and a string of bells hanging off a string.

Leo sees Zebra crossing the square with his lean and watchful stride, one of his hands grasping a plastic shopping bag filled with his most precious belongings, which he has shown to Leo before – a Thermos flask, tin cup, Swiss army knife, and a miniature glass paperweight in the shape of his home island, Boa Vista. Zebra usually stashes his bedcovers and other gear in a hole in the stone wall outside the castle entrance by day, when the place is swarming with tourists and he is less than welcome. He sees Leo waving, recognises Carlos' white shirt, the slight hunch of his shoulders over the camera, and laughs. A moment later, Carlos receives a hefty slap between the shoulder blades that sends his nose into his camera and ruins his shot. Leo looks up, wide-eyed, to see what his father will do – he knows he is at his strictest when interrupted in his photography – but when he sees Zebra standing there in his holey tracksuit with a big grin splitting his face, Carlos makes a sound of pleasure in the back of his throat.

'Zebra.'

'You always looking through that camera like it's some starry bridge to life,' chuckles Zebra. 'Keeping yourself on the outside, never crossing to the centre, *pá!*'

Carlos looks down at his camera. 'It helps me *enter* life,' he protests, but Zebra shakes his head, grinning.

'*Então, rapaz,*' he says. So, boy. He lowers his giant head so that Leo can see straight into the deep black of his irises. 'You like this music, eh?'

Leo nods. 'It's like a spell,' he says emphatically.

Zebra studies him for a moment, then laughs. 'Right. Right. And I guess if you know about magic, then you know, don't you, that the spell is always – always – stronger than the spell-maker. *Sim?*'

'*Sim,*' agrees Leo, unsure whether he really knew that or not, but impressed by the way Zebra's nostrils flare when he repeats the word 'always'.

Zebra nods and straightens up again. Carlos passes an affection-ate hand over his son's head before moving slightly away, and Leo understands that he is dismissed for now. Still, he retains his grip on his father's shirt, the sweat from his hand creating a damp and slightly grimy stain. Zebra moves to stand on the other side of Carlos, who leans in towards him, telling him something in serious tones. A musician wearing a battered trilby and baggy pants begins to make music with his mouth, tapping his cheeks, while a man with a shaved head and delicate tattoos traced on his neck picks up a didgeridoo. Leo can hear snatches of words passing from Carlos to Zebra, their hiss of urgency sharp above the swinging vibrations of the music: '. . . far worse . . . hurt my son's neck . . . sent Olivia crashing down the stairs . . .'

For a split second, Leo is aware of the rift that exists between lis-tening to their words and letting the music carry him away – if he chooses to do one, he will lose the other. Tension sweeps through him before he makes his choice and tunes into the conversation taking place above his head.

'This jumping, running in your sleep – aren't you tired of it, *pá*?' Zebra demands.

'Tired? Of course I'm tired of it.'

'Then why let it happen a second time?'

Carlos makes an exasperated sound. 'It's not something I choose to do. I have no control over it, you know that.'

Zebra scoffs. 'We *always* have control over ourselves,' he insists. 'Even when I'm dead drunk, I *know* I'm dead drunk.'

'This is different. It's like . . . hallucinations.'

'You been taking LSD? That *invites* the shadow in, my friend. I remember one trip I took years back, I saw a goat with human eyes. I swear that goat followed me around three days after the acid wore off.'

'No, no . . . Olivia thinks the dream imagery I see when it happens must seem utterly real to me, you know how dreams do until you wake up and think, what the hell was *that*? Something major happens when I go into these dreams. It's like a jolt, a fall.' Carlos pushes his hands through his hair. 'I mean, there's a total lack of recognition, for one – I can't recognise Olivia or Leo for who they are. How can I lose the core of myself so easily? It must be madness, right?'

'Maybe.' Zebra stirs the dust with the toe of his plimsoll. 'Makes me think of those stories you hear about kids getting too into computer war games so they can't work out the difference between the game and reality. One kid gave his friend a magic sword from one of these games, a sword stored with power, and his friend sold it, so the kid went and killed him, and not just on the computer, Carlos – he killed him in real life! The difference between that kid and you is he lost his grip on reality, whereas you're losing your grip on a dream.'

'But –' Carlos shoots him a look '– can a dream that bursts violently into the world of solid objects and people still be called a dream?'

'*Sim, claro*. It's a dream that's got too powerful and is overstepping boundaries. It's the shadow in action, *pá*, and only you can stop it.'

'How? It's so real that when it happens, I don't question it.'

'So start to question it,' says Zebra, and Leo sees his hand tightening and relaxing around the handles of his plastic bag. 'Question your eyes, your nose, your ears. Ask yourself: Is this for real, what I'm feeling? Or is it all in my head, am I dreaming?' He chuckles suddenly. 'And those also happen to be the lyrics of a beautiful Café del Mar song, my friend, so you know you're not the first to ask these questions. You are not alone!' He laughs again.

Leo shifts closer to Carlos, wanting his father to notice him. The next second, he feels himself being swept up into the sky, held aloft for one dizzying moment in his father's muscular arms, and settled onto his shoulders so his heels swing against Carlos' chest. Leo is jubilant. Carlos grabs his knees to steady him, and Leo is enthroned, the tallest pair of eyes in the crowd.

A girl with straw-coloured hair in a ponytail, carrying with her a silver hoop, joins the musicians. She bends and flexes her slim body to the beat, spinning the hoop around her hips, her neck, her knees, stepping through it neat as an angel.

'You know, I think I might have had a hoop when I was a boy,' Carlos tells Leo. 'We'll get you one, if you want.'

Leo smiles at the thought. He knows Concha would be even better with the hoop than this pale girl; the hoop would become as much a part of her body as an extra arm or leg. He likes the idea. As the girl picks up her little cloth bag and collects cash from the spectators, Carlos turns again to Zebra, who is watching proceedings with his head held regally.

'What is it that makes this scene so clearly real, so sane and alive?' Carlos wonders aloud. 'Is it Leo's weight on my shoulders, the tap of his heels against my chest? Or is it the music, the girl with the hoop?'

Zebra shrugs. 'Those things could seem just as real in a dream.'

'So how do I *know*?' When Carlos asks this, Leo senses the sorrow in his father's chest, which seems denser against his dangling feet, the breaths heavier. 'How do I know I'm not dreaming this?'

'That,' says Zebra, 'is the billion euro question, *pá*.'

Chapter Sixteen

Olivia leaves the brilliance of the mid-afternoon sunshine by the cathedral to enter Café Amarelo – Café Yellow – which is full of clattering sounds and convivial voices. She has a splitting headache; the fresh bruise on the left side of her forehead from falling down the stairs has teamed up with pain receptors the length of her bruised spine, so that every movement triggers a throbbing from her waist to her head. This meeting, though, is too important to miss: Olivia needs answers. She wishes Carlos could have come too, but he's been hired to photograph a fortieth wedding anniversary party in Parede, one of the beach towns on the road to Cascais, and will be working until the early hours. Leo went to Concha's after school today and is staying overnight with her, which Olivia hopes will be a relaxing break for him.

Dressed in a white vest top and aquamarine cotton trousers, her hair pulled into a simple ponytail, Olivia looks outwardly fresh and relaxed. The scent of ground coffee and croissants rises in a warm fug towards her nostrils. She dips her sunglasses and blinks as her pupils adjust to the relative dimness of the interior.

'Olivia.' Miles' voice is warm and, as he stands up to kiss her on both cheeks, she gets a whiff of his summery aftershave. 'Have a seat.' He looks tanned and youthful in jeans and a black T-shirt, his blond hair swept back from his face. There's a studied casualness about him, but Olivia has the feeling that with just one look, he has noticed everything about her, from the conical bump on her forehead with its ring of purple discolouration to the silver studs in her earlobes. He has already ordered himself a coffee. To avoid Miles' attentive gaze, Olivia glances around the crowded café and its high, domed ceiling as she settles herself into her seat. Her belly is fluttering; she's dreading hearing the results of Miles' investigations into Carlos' night violence, especially now it's happened again and can't be dismissed as a one-off event. This dream expert friend of his, what are his qualifications? If Miles tells her Carlos is definitely going insane, what will she do? She makes a swift, reassuring mental note not to believe all she hears. The waiter takes her order of a sparkling water with ice and a slice of lemon, and Olivia smiles uncertainly across the table at Miles.

'So,' she begins, hoping he won't want to make small talk but not wanting to seem rude. 'What sort of a week have you had so far?'

Miles sips his coffee. 'Well, I've found out a lot about the strange things people get up to while they're asleep and dreaming,' he says with a smile which Olivia returns, relieved he's getting directly to the point.

'Tell me,' she invites him simply.

Miles strokes his jaw as if there's a beard there that he's smoothing down, his long fingers meeting at the tip of his chin. 'Some of the stories I've heard from Jessica – Dr Loverock – are pretty bizarre,' he warns her. 'Most of these aren't her own patients; she's just heard about individual cases.'

'Is Dr Loverock a medical doctor?' asks Olivia quickly.

'She's a PhD psychologist and a board-certified US sleep specialist who's worked with patients with sleepwalking complaints and other night-time disorders – she refers to them as "parasomnias".' Miles looks at Olivia searchingly. 'Shall I tell you everything I know?'

91

'Yes, please.' Olivia's voice is firm, although she is unsettled by what she senses is his reluctance to present her with unpalatable truths. Her water arrives and she allows herself a mouthful of cold, fizzing bubbles.

'There are sleepwalkers who take things far beyond wandering around the house in a daze with their arms sticking out in front of them,' begins Miles, settling back in his chair so that the wicker creaks audibly. 'These special types of sleepwalkers act out scenarios presented in their dreams. Although in most people – and animals – the only muscles that are active during sleep are the diaphragm and the ocular muscles, so that we can breathe and carry out the rapid eye movements that accompany dreaming sleep, in some people, the natural paralysis lifts from their other muscles too, so they leap out of bed and run around the house, or punch, or kick out.'

Olivia is nodding. 'Exactly,' she says. 'That's exactly what happens. He does that – Carlos does that.'

'Yes. I don't know how bad your husband has it –' his eyes skim her bruised forehead '– but there have been some very serious incidents linked to a condition called REM Sleep Behaviour Disorder, or "RBD". People have jumped from high windows while dreaming, or even hurled themselves right *through* windows. The sufferers seem possessed of unusual physical strength while they're having an episode, and since their nightmares are often violent, it can be a lethal combination.' He hesitates before continuing, his eyes resting on her face, still with that watchful look. 'There have been accounts of sleepwalking husbands stabbing their wives to death . . .' He stops at Olivia's gasp.

'People have actually been killed by sleeping members of their family?' she whispers in horror.

Miles becomes very serious. 'It doesn't mean your husband will do anything like that,' he tells her, leaning in across the table, his eyes grave. 'These are isolated incidents. I'm certain the vast majority of people with this kind of disorder never go beyond giving their bed partner the occasional kick, or . . . or maybe accidentally pushing them into walls, or something,' he adds sympathetically, his eyes skimming Olivia's skull so that she remembers giving him a carefully edited version of Carlos flinging her away from him in his first episode. 'Didn't you hear about the tragic case that went to court in the UK last year? The loving husband who strangled his wife of forty years while he was dreaming about being attacked?'

The case rings a very faint bell for Olivia. 'Maybe,' she says. 'I don't read many British newspapers these days, though. I might have heard about it and sort of dismissed it as another bizarre crime, you know?' She shudders. 'Things like that seem beyond belief.'

'Well, there are quite a few cases, just as bizarre as that. Sometimes people even drive in their sleep,' Miles continues. 'Jessica told me this one story about a guy from Toronto who got up one night and drove for miles – while asleep – to his in-laws' house, where he stabbed and bludgeoned his mother-in-law to death and choked his father-in-law into unconsciousness. He was acquitted because he had a history of sleepwalking, and the judge accepted that he didn't intend to murder anyone.'

'But why did he do it?' Olivia is shocked.

Miles shrugs. 'He just got too caught up in the dream imagery, I expect. I'm sure he probably didn't recognise them at all, but mistook them for enemies or something. It's the strangest thing.'

Olivia's hand is cold, wrapped around her glass. She stares at the lemon floating in the water, at the bubbles which cling to it like transparent fish eggs. 'It *is* the strangest thing,' she agrees numbly, without looking at Miles. There's a pressure on her heart, which is beating whoosh, whoosh, in her ears. She can feel her unvoiced fears of accidental murder rising inside her and thickening, sending her deaf, dizzy.

'There are other weird sleep disorders,' continues Miles, unaware that Olivia is hardly listening now. 'Some people eat uncontrollably while asleep. Others have sex with anything that moves. They get out of bed in the night, dreaming, and go and do these things. One person will wake up covered in chocolate cake, another wakes up with venereal disease.'

Olivia is thinking: What if it happens to us? What of Leo? How can I protect my son? The questions are enclosed, unreachable. In her mind, she stretches out her arms for the answers but there's nothing and it's like sitting on a fragile tree branch over a drop of miles and miles. I can't cope with this, she realises.

Miles has noticed her absence from the conversation. He stretches out a hand and touches her lightly on the wrist. 'Olivia,' he says.

She jerks her head up in surprise, and his understanding expression makes her feel as though she can trust him.

'What about Leo?' she blurts. 'My seven-year-old son.'

Miles looks startled. His hand falls away from hers. 'Your son,' he says, as though this is a new concept for him, her having a child, and Olivia remembers being careful not to mention Leo when she spoke to him after the dream workshop. 'Has he . . . witnessed these nightmares?'

'Yes. Yes, he has.' Olivia hesitates, uncertain of how much to say. Her reluctance to tell Miles about Leo's involvement in the violence wins out, so in the end she says, 'Carlos seems very worried that something bad will happen to Leo. It's as if he has a premonition, and it's got much, much worse since he started having the nightmares.'

'Well,' says Miles, 'It may not be about Leo. Carlos may have suffered some kind of abuse or trauma when he was around the same age that Leo is, something that's only now rising into consciousness to be dealt with. Dreams of long-forgotten abuse can appear at any stage in a person's life, and they're inevitably charged with difficult emotions. When I think of the way he sprinted out of my work-shop . . .'

Olivia is nodding. 'We thought it might be some traumatic memory resurfacing.'

'The thing to remember is that although we can speculate to our heart's content about the meaning and source of other people's dreams, the only person who can really know what they're about is the dreamer himself.' Miles sips his coffee, his eyes on her face. 'And if he has no recollection of the dream, obviously that complicates matters. Some people with sleep disorders are able to recall and recount the action of their dream just as they're waking up from it, so it might be worth asking Carlos at that stage, if it happens again.'

'I'll give it a try.' Olivia feels a wave of despondency. The situation seems impossible.

'Sometimes,' says Miles, 'children are caught up in sleep violence. I remember one story about a father who did crazy things in his sleep, hit and punched his wife, but apparently the only thing he ever did with his kids was carry them from their beds to a place he thought was safer. He never attacked them.' He swallows uneasily. 'There was another case Jessica mentioned though, from way back, I think it was in the nineteenth century, of a sleepwalker who threw his eighteen-month-old son against a wall while he was dreaming, and killed him. He was acquitted,' he adds pointlessly.

Olivia looks at him, not bothering to hide the weight of tears in her eyes.

'It's a dreadful thing for any wife or mother to go through,' Miles says gently. His grey-blue eyes are fixed on hers, and she experiences a rush of self-pity.

'It *is* dreadful,' she admits, and the admission feels like a betrayal of Carlos.

'Is he willing to see a doctor? I ask because often adults don't want to tell a doctor that they enact violent nightmares as they're worried they'll be told it's linked to serious psychiatric disease or psychological disorders.'

'That's definitely Carlos' fear, too,' says Olivia. She takes another sip of water and it clears her head a little. 'I knew from the start this isn't simply something that can be ignored, so we saw a GP here as soon as we could, but it really didn't help us – the doctor just produced the names of devastating illnesses that the night violence could be linked to. But what if it *is* a form of mental illness that just isn't talked about? What then? I mean, what happens to these killer sleepwalkers – are they locked up in a psychiatric unit?'

Miles looks uncomfortable. He taps his coffee cup with his fingertip. 'I don't know,' he says. 'But Jessica did ask me to tell you that she'd be interested in meeting your husband to discuss his problem.' He takes a business card out of his wallet and passes it to Olivia. 'Here are her details. She's based here in Lisbon and she's had a lot of experience. She's got a very busy consultancy, so if you're interested, you'd be better off booking an appointment as soon as possible.'

'I think at this stage we're willing to consider anything,' says Olivia with a sigh, sliding the card into her bag. 'He's had two of these attacks now, and the most recent one, on Sunday night, was as bad as the first.'

'I noticed you have quite a shiner there.' Miles' tone is so nonjudgemental that Olivia responds to his unvoiced question.

'He spun around and his elbow knocked me off balance. I went flying down the stairs.'

Miles winces. 'Ouch. You could have broken your neck.' He leans forwards, his eyebrows knotted in concern. 'And your son? Was he involved?'

After a slight hesitation, Olivia sighs. 'He saw everything.'

'So he was close by? He could have been hurt.'

Olivia closes her eyes briefly, seeing again Leo's frightened face, the pain in his eyes as Carlos ripped the necklace from his throat. The metal chain had bitten deep and blood had beaded the skin. Olivia worries that Leo could be scarred for life. Just thinking about it makes her feel ill.

'Olivia.' Miles' voice interrupts her. 'It's not my place to get involved with your domestic decisions, but I'd like to advise you, if I might, to take measures at night to protect yourself and your son.'

'But what measures can I take? I never know when he's going to erupt in his sleep – it's happened twice completely out of the blue.'

'Is there a spare room either you or Carlos could sleep in, preferably with the door locked?'

'No. We don't have much space.' Inwardly, she baulks at the thought of separate rooms. Her parents' marriage had begun its painful disintegration from the moment her mother decided, when Olivia was ten, that her father's snoring was too loud, and moved into the spare room. 'I couldn't not sleep next to him; we're married, for goodness sake. It's . . .' She struggles for words. 'It'd be like never taking an aeroplane because sometimes the odd one crashes. You'd miss so much of the world, all because of a fear-fuelled precaution.'

Miles' gaze travels thoughtfully over her face. 'Then at least lock your son's door at night, to keep him out of harm's way.'

'Oh, but that would be like punishing Leo for something that's not his fault. He'd hate to be locked in.' Olivia looks at him penitently. 'I'm sorry, I don't mean to knock your suggestions, Miles. I just want a swift cure for this, then everything can be the way it was before.'

'Of course that's all you want. And maybe Dr Loverock can help Carlos. But until then, the measures you take to ensure the safety of yourself and Leo need to be as extreme as the situation you're protecting yourselves from.'

Olivia blinks at him. She knows he's right.

'What I'm saying, Olivia,' he continues with that same gentleness in his voice, but a fierce light in his eyes, 'is that the way things are going, it sounds to me as if you'll have to decide which is more important – your relationship with your husband, or your son's safety.'

Olivia bites down on her lower lip until she can feel the short line of pain where her incisors press into her flesh. Miles is voicing something she's been trying not to think about. She turns her eyes away from him and sits mutely, seeing her choice laid out for her as if on weighing scales; Carlos on one side and Leo on the other. I can't choose between them, she thinks. And I won't need to. Everything will work out somehow. Amid the noise and bustle of the café, the silence between her and Miles stretches.

'Thank you so much for helping me out like this, Miles.' She dredges up a smile for him. 'You've been brilliant.'

He looks at her, his expression somewhere between frustration and amusement. 'Is this your way of closing the subject?'

'Maybe,' she concedes. 'It's just so much to take on and it's all very raw, you know?'

'Fine by me.' He sits back in his chair. 'Let's talk about something else. You, for example. You said you paint?'

Olivia visibly relaxes. Yes, she thinks, let's talk about painting; let's get onto solid ground again. She needs to rid herself of the precipitous feeling of being forced to make a decision which will shatter the life she, Carlos and Leo have lived until now.

Chapter Seventeen

April 1984

Mãe is in a strange mood. She said she wants me with her, but now that I'm here, playing with her jewellery which I've tipped all over her white satin eiderdown that puffs up like clouds when you sit on it, she's restless. Her yellow headscarf makes her look too yellow and when I tell her that, she looks sad.

'I thought it might make me look like a butterfly,' she says, and touches her hand to it.

'Mãe, are you going to die soon?' I don't look at her, I look at the ruby bracelet, which I'm pretending is a sea creature, one which looks like it's flying when it swims along.

'Carlitos,' she says, and when she says nothing else, I look at her and she's staring at me as if she's hungry and I'm a cake she'll never get to eat. 'My baby,' she says, and stretches out her hand to stroke my hair. 'Just because I lie here all day turning yellow, it doesn't mean I'm going to die soon.' She laughs. 'I'm tougher than that. You'll see.' Her laugh turns into the cough that makes her sound as if she's being split in half, and I rush for her water. It takes a long time for her to stop coughing.

'Pass me the sapphire amulet, the one that belonged to your

father's great-grandmother,' she says when she can breathe again, and at first I think we're playing the game she likes to play, testing me to see if I can remember the names of all the stones and gems – the diamond tiara from her wedding day, the emerald signet ring that her own grandmother used to wear, the moonstone earrings Father gave her for a long ago birthday.

'My favourite,' I say and I find the amulet as quickly as I can and untangle its gold chain from the mess of other jewellery.

When Mãe's thin hand closes over it, she smiles at me. 'Carlos, this amulet has belonged to generations of Casanova de Albuquerque Monizs. We keep it safe because it brings good luck to our family. And now I want you to look after it. Would you like to put it on?'

'But what if it falls off and gets lost?'

'It won't. It'll stay with you always, and bring you luck.' She seems very certain. 'Sit here with your back to me so I can attach it.'

I do as she says.

'The clasp is good and strong, but I'll have to hook it into *this* part of the chain so it's not too long for you.' She fiddles at my neck.

'What will Father say?' I ask.

'Father won't say anything.' She sounds almost angry, but I can't see her face to check. 'All this jewellery became mine when we married and I can do whatever I like with it. And I want to see you wearing it, my Carlos. Now stand up, *meu amor*, and have a look in the mirror.'

The mirror on her dressing table is three mirrors which open out so that if you pull the outside ones in a bit, you can see your face in three different ways. I sit on the plump seat and look at the amulet, which lies exactly in the dip where my bones meet. It is as blue as the Tejo, and it shines against my skin as if it's alive.

'You're smiling,' Mãe says. 'You like it, don't you?'

'Yes.' I have the luck of the Casanova de Albuquerque Moniz family hanging golden and blue around my neck. I straighten my spine, feeling important, then turn to Mãe and we laugh together.

A little later, I clear the jewellery away and listen to one of Mãe's stories of the green place she grew up, the horses she rode over hedges and fences, and the scent of wildflowers in the fields. Telling stories makes her look peaceful.

'Mãe,' I say on my way out of the door, 'I think you look like a butterfly.'

'Do you really?' She smiles a little.

'A pretty one, with yellow wings.'

Mãe nods weakly. She looks tired and I think she'll sleep now. Maybe she'll dream of being a butterfly. I close her door as quietly as I can.

Downstairs in the dining room, Father is half shouting, but trying not to make too much noise, so that his voice sounds like grit. It's a frightening sound, and I pause at the door. He's in there with his back to me, and Marina is standing a little way from him, on the other side of the long, polished table, with her hands all screwed up in her dress.

'But where would I go, Aníbal? I have nothing, no one.'

'Why couldn't you think of that before behaving like some hussy, stamping our family name into the mud?'

'Nobody knows about this.'

'But everyone will find out, Marina. How could they not when you bloat up like a cow?'

'He'll be back,' she says stubbornly.

'No. He'll never be back now,' says Father, and storms from the room through the opposite door, his back as stiff as a poker.

I run to Marina. Her cheeks are wet, her eyes stony. She takes me by the hand. 'Come and look at the river with me,' she says, and out we go into the fresh air. She doesn't say a word as we walk down the sloping streets under a high blue sky, the sweet custard smell of *pastéis de nata* on the breeze. We don't go right down to the river because our part of the Alfama is up high, the river down below, but we stand at the railings of the Santa Luzia viewpoint, where there's a tiny church and the walls are tiled with pretty *azulejos* that show pictures of curly-winged birds. We look at the sparkling blue, the boats, the white foam the ferries pull out from beneath them.

'Marina,' I ask. 'Will you leave our house?'

She pulls me close to her cotton dress which is flowery and warm. 'I met a sailor with hair the colour of sand who sailed in to Lisbon on the river,' she tells me in her story-telling voice. 'He came all the way from England, a country that looks like a witch-woman when you see it on a map along with Scotland and Wales. He made me laugh and he liked to kiss me on the tip of my nose. When he set sail again, he left something of his with me – a very tiny baby which I've got right here, inside my belly.'

'How tiny is it?'

With her finger and thumb, Marina makes a circle the size of a one hundred escudo coin. 'Maybe like this, maybe a little bigger. And Father is very angry about it, so you mustn't tell anyone, Carlitos, *estás a perceber*?'

I nod. I understand.

'And now I'm not sure if he's coming back at all.' She blows air from her mouth.

'If he comes back, you can give him back his tiny baby, can't you? Then Father won't be cross any more.'

Marina doesn't answer me. She's staring down the river, towards its wide mouth where it turns into the sea.

'Maybe if you don't do your night-eating any more, Father will be less cross?'

She sighs. 'Of course I'd stop if I could, but Carlitos, I don't know I'm doing it. Since it started half a year ago, I've woken with a badly burned tongue from eating scalding porridge I don't remember making. I've woken with crazy mixtures of food all over my face. I've woken with a cut on my finger from opening a can with that horrid old can-opener Inês likes so much.'

'A can of what?'

'Oh . . . I think Inês said they were brown lentils.'

'But why –'

'*Não sei porquê, meu querido.*' I don't know why, my darling.

'Marina,' I say. 'Marina.' I tug on her arm but her eyes stay on the river. 'You won't go away, will you?'

She turns to me then and I see the wet in her eyes. 'I'll never leave you, my Carlitos,' she promises. 'How could I leave such a treasure, hmm?' And she puts her rose-smelling arms around me.

I look out on to the water with her but I'm thinking of Mãe, who might die soon, even if she says she won't, and Rosa, who almost never comes home from her school, and Father, who wants Marina to leave because she eats funny things at night and because the sailor left his baby inside her. I reach for the hard shape of the amulet inside my shirt and close it tightly in my hand. I need this luck.

Marina's arms are hot and heavy around me, and I wriggle away. I grip the railings and lean back to see if there are any clouds in the sky, and someone raps me on the shoulder. I nearly fall back in surprise and it's Pedro, with a silver ring in his ear that I've never seen before. His blue T-shirt is ripped around the neck but he doesn't care, he stands smiling his happy smile and looking from me to Marina's flowered dress.

'*A minha tia,*' I tell him. My aunt. Marina looks round. 'It's Pedro,' I tell her, and she smiles then because I told her about the fire-breather.

'Pedro,' she says. 'The boy who wants to learn to write his name. You're kind to Carlos.'

'I want to do more than write my name,' laughs Pedro.

'What else?' I ask.

Pedro thinks for a moment. 'I want to be an astronaut, get as far as the moon. And I want to learn to ride a camel. And I might try fire-breathing one day!' He grins all over his face.

I look at him, feeling strangely proud. 'He can already go to the sun whenever he likes,' I explain to Marina. 'I'm hoping my necklace will help me get to the sun,' I tell him, and show him the amulet.

'It looks like it's got the sun in it when it flashes like that,' he says, reaching out to touch it with the tip of his finger.

'Oh, Carlitos, did you take that without asking your mother?' asks Marina in a hushed voice.

'No. She said it was all mine. To bring me luck.'

Marina says, 'Oh' without a sound coming from her mouth. I nod my head at her to show her it's the truth, and in a moment she's smiling again. 'Where do your parents live?' she asks Pedro.

'I don't have parents. My *mãe* died when I was three, and my *pai* ran away to sea,' he says, as if none of this matters.

'But . . . who looks after you, poor mite?'

Pedro straightens his shoulders proudly. 'My brother, Fernando. He's seventeen.'

'What does he do for a living?'

He cocks his head. 'Hmm?'

'How does he get money to buy you food and clothes?'

Pedro's fingers clutch the railings and he leans back and looks at the sky the way I did. 'Oh, he does shops.'

'He's a shopkeeper?'

'No . . . he *does* shops, and if he gets anything, he sells it on the market.' Pedro jams a bony knee against the railing and then lifts the other to do the same. He tips his head right back. 'And sometimes he finds wallets that tourists leave behind over there, at Largo das Portas do Sol.'

Marina looks alarmed. 'And do *you* find wallets too?'

'No.' He releases his knees and pulls away from the railing. 'But soon Fernando's going to show me where to look.'

Marina looks at him, then at me, and back to Pedro again. She looks unhappy but I don't know why. For a moment I think she's going to tell Pedro off, but she just says, 'I'll teach you to write your name.' We follow her up the steps and gather close as she licks her finger and writes 'P-E-D-R-O' in the dust on the blue and white *azulejos*.

Chapter Eighteen

Concha's mother sways through the cramped living room for the third time, depositing her empty glass on the table with a flourish next to an ornate green bottle. Leo thinks she looks like an old princess with her shiny brown skin folded into tight creases either side of her eyes, leather trousers, and high, red shoes which tap-tap on the tiled floor when she walks. She has Concha's glorious gypsy hair and Leo is dazzled by her lipstick-red, minty smile and the necklaces like discs of light which have got all tangled up with her sequinned top. But there's something strange about her. From time to time she sends out a crackling laugh for no reason, and her hips and legs keep knocking into door frames or table edges.

'Your shoes are a bit like stilts,' Leo tells her politely. 'It might be easier to walk on bare feet.' Concha's mum eyes him in surprise, then lets loose her laugh again. 'I'm off for a little nap,' she says, smiling, and leaves the room blowing extravagant air-kisses.

From her frayed purple cushion on the floor, Concha watches her mother leave. It's almost 8 pm and the dolphin DVD is running. 'This is the bit where they swim out of the telly,' she says for the tenth time. But the dolphins stay where they are, swimming through layers of light, encased in water which holds them as easily as the sky holds birds. Leo leans forwards, clutching his knees in consternation. Rosa is always telling him that children have many more magical experiences than adults do. So why had the dolphins swum out for Concha's mother, yet appeared reluctant to do the same for them?

'Maybe they only swim out if you drink that drink your mum was drinking,' he suggests, indicating the bottle on the table.

Concha twists around and eyes him curiously.

'Like a potion,' Leo reasons. 'A magic one.'

Concha waits for more, but Leo senses that she is ready to swing away from him and dismiss what he has to say unless it's something really good. He thinks quickly. 'Potions,' he continues, 'can make you change into things. Like a Pegasus,' he adds, beguilingly.

Concha sits up straight. 'Or a dolphin, Leo!'

They stare at each other, wonder-struck. 'I could turn myself into a dolphin,' says Leo with a surge of excitement, 'and save my family from the sleep monster.' He's told Concha about the monster, and she seems to understand, although she was troubled to learn that it looks like Leo's father, whom she likes.

'I'll get some cups from the kitchen,' says Concha, and runs out.

The feel of the air has changed: it has become charged with the shimmering quality of adventure. Leo is thrilled by the knowledge that Concha's mother is curled up close by like an ageing Sleeping Beauty, unaware of what they're up to. He's enchanted by the glimmer of light through the tantalising green bottle, and the knowledge that it very likely contains the potion that will take them to a direct dolphin experience. He imagines streams of dolphins fanning out around them, their fins brushing against Concha and himself. And he imagines the moment of transformation, his body streamlining, his nose lengthening, a ridge appearing on his spine and becoming a fin. And then? Anything could happen. All that he can be certain of is that such powerful magic would drive the sleep monster away within minutes, never to return.

Concha returns with two large plastic beakers, and closes the door behind her as quietly as she can. As soon as the lid is off, a strong aroma of mint rises out. It smells like polos, or peppermint sorbet, or a particularly sweet menthol chewing gum. The two of them are delighted. 'Sometimes potions taste disgusting,' says Leo knowledgeably, 'but this one's going to taste better than ice cream.' They fill the beakers to the brim.

It's like drinking fire. At the first taste, they splutter and their eyes burn. When Concha has recovered from the initial shock, she croaks, with tears rolling from the corners of her eyes, 'Last one to finish is a *baby*.'

Leo thinks of the sleep monster, waiting in the dark to come alive again. He thinks of the dolphins, his graceful saviours, the starry side of his father. He takes a deep breath and drinks to the last drop.

Their beakers are empty. After draining his manfully – beating Concha by a full two seconds – Leo feels queasiness pulling side by side with the fire, and his racked coughing makes this worse.

Twenty minutes later, the nausea has receded but his eyes are burning. So are his tongue, his throat, even his stomach.

'Concha!' he cries, his head zooming, his heart roaring. She is laughing, shaking her wild head, her wild hair, falling back on her hands in weak-limbed slow motion. Then she turns over and seems to be attempting a squat thrust, or possibly a more complicated gymnastic manoeuvre. Her knees are bent up like a cricket's and her hair is tumbling over her hands where they are spread, firm and brown, on the tiled floor.

'Can't balance,' she announces, and sits up, red in the face. Her eyes are unfocused, but very bright. 'Hey, maybe I'm turning into a Pegasus already,' she says excitedly. 'I feel like I've got four legs.'

'You always feel as if you've got four legs. That's why you walk on your hands.' The living room looks strange, blurry around the edges. Leo staggers upright and gapes at the sleek bodies of the dolphins on the TV screen. They could swim right through a sleep monster, could stop him in his tracks for ever. Under his high-collared shirt, Leo can feel the soreness of his neck. He lifts a finger and lightly traces the thin red line of pain.

'Let's shake them out of the telly,' he says, and is astounded by the simple beauty of this idea. Why hadn't they thought of this before?

Concha lurches to her feet, her eyes bloodshot and fiery now. She takes one side of the high-definition flat-screen television which her mother is paying for in the lowest possible monthly instalments, and Leo takes the other. They stare in at the dolphins, who flick their tails expectantly, and then they begin to shake and rock the slim screen, building up a rhythm which becomes unstoppable, out of control, so that somehow the television breaks from their grip and crashes face down onto the hard tiles with an alarming cracking noise and at the same time a blue flash leaps from the wires protruding from its spine and Leo's hand jolts into the air and he screams and flies backwards, tripping over his own feet so that he lands on his back on the hard floor.

They stop. Everything stops; there is no sound from the dolphins. The room is spinning slowly and, through the shock and the shooting pain in his hand, Leo sees the door blast open and Concha's mother runs in, crying out in alarm when she sees Leo on the floor, Concha standing like a drunken sentry beside the fallen television. What she shouts is a blur to Leo; he registers her arms waving, her red mouth. She hauls him up into a sitting position, demanding to know if he is hurt. He clutches his limp right hand and she examines it, turning it over in her own.

'Make a fist,' she orders. Leo does so, his fingers trembling uncontrollably. The pain is as bad as if his hand had been stamped on. 'Now spread your fingers out,' says Concha's mum. He manages it, and the pain begins to lessen. She nods, satisfied. 'Rub it,' she tells him dismissively, and releases him so suddenly that he sways. She turns on Concha, but before she can begin to ask what happened, she sees the open bottle of turquoise potion and the two beakers in plain view on the table in the middle of the room. She becomes very still.

'It was my idea,' Leo says into the booming silence, ashamed of the tremor in his voice.

'*What* was your idea?' she snaps.

'Mãe,' Concha says weakly. 'It was a magic potion, to make the dolphins come out. We didn't mean –'

'Quiet,' snaps her mother. She snatches up the bottle and holds it up to the light, observing how much they have drunk. 'This,' she says, bending to put her face close to Concha's, 'is not magic. This is like gin. Do you remember what gin did to your daddy?'

Concha nods. Her eyes meet Leo's briefly, then slide away, as if she's ashamed.

Jinn? Leo doesn't know the word. Might it be like the genie that comes out of bottles? he wonders, feeling dizzy and sick. Concha's mother's sudden entry has made the fun effects of the potion vanish, and now all that's left is a hand that aches with pain and the start of a cruel hangover. He can tell Concha is feeling unwell, too. Concha's mother notices their pallor. She begins to laugh her crackling laugh, as if all is forgiven.

'Well, well,' she says. 'Both of you, come here and take a deep sniff of this.' She waves the bottle. They approach warily. She makes Concha take several deep breaths through her nostrils. Concha's face turns green. When Concha tries to turn her head away, her mother grasps her by the back of the neck. 'Keep going.' Concha dry-retches, and her mother releases her, satisfied. It's Leo's turn. When he sniffs the minty, alcoholic smell of the potion, his stomach instantly rebels. He clutches a hand to it. Why would the potion suddenly smell unbearable, when it had smelled sparkly and exciting before? He knows he never wants to smell this smell or taste this taste again. Concha's mother seems to know how close he is to vomiting, because she whips the bottle away and screws the top back on. Then she reaches over and struggles to right the television, swearing. The screen is black and silent, but it looks intact.

'No more stealing drink,' she says as she turns back to them both. 'And no more of this dolphin nonsense.' She shoots Leo a meaningful look. 'I won't tell your parents about what you've done to my lovely television if you don't tell them about drinking my special drink and getting that little electric shock, OK?'

Leo nods, relieved. He's about to say that he wouldn't mind going home – all he wants now is his mother's hug, her warm arms sending the sickness away, her kiss on his forehead propelling him safely into sleep – but Concha's mother again seems to know how he's feeling. It will be harder for him and Concha to get through their hangovers and their shame together, so in a wearied tone, as if she's not used to giving instructions, she tells them to get themselves ready for bed, and then she sweeps from the room with the mint liqueur in her hand.

The next day, Leo is at his desk, a shiny, plastic-topped brown table into which compass scratches have been scored. The remnants of paint and Biro decorate the wooden edges and legs. Professora Celeste is talking but he can't hear the words because they are rolling above him like thick clouds. His hand doesn't hurt any more but it won't curl tightly enough around his pencil. Concha's mother made them go to school today although both of them feel terrible, their tongues furry and swollen in the aftermath of the potion, and a dry, sharp ache in what Leo thinks of as the lining of their heads. Concha has been wild and irritable, upturning a jug of water over another girl's head at break time. Now the headmistress will be asking her why she did it. Leo's head feels like a giant, sad balloon. He thinks of the moonfish, the one all the others had called ugly.

'Leo.' His teacher's voice shocks him. 'Whatever's the matter?'

Leo realises he's sitting with his head slumped in his two hands. He raises his head and it's heavier than firewood. Professora Celeste is by his side in a moment, her cool palm on his forehead.

'You're very hot,' he hears her say.

He tries to look at her, to tell her he's waiting for Concha to come back from her telling-off, and her expression grows more concerned.

'Your eyes look odd. I think you might have to go home, *querido*.'

Soon, Leo is ensconced in the passenger seat of Rosa's old car. She has come to collect him because the school can't reach his parents. Rosa fields Professora Celeste's keen questions deftly, assuring her this is no more than a slight fever, he stayed at a friend's last night, it's just the excitement, lack of sleep too, perhaps, and no, of course it's not significant that neither of his parents can be reached; Olivia is probably doing an exhibition, Carlos is doing a photography session in Palmela, everything's normal, no need for drama, the child will be as right as rain in the morning.

Leo leans back and smells the familiar scent of Rosa. 'You have shadows under your eyes,' she tells him as she drives, 'and you're pale, but you aren't ill. Something's happened, hasn't it?' Without waiting for a reply, she continues. 'Well, *meu amor*, I can't take you home; if Olivia's not reachable, then she may well be painting in her workshop without her mobile, but she could also simply be out somewhere for the day. I know what we'll do,' she says, expertly guiding the car through lanes of traffic onto the Marginal road that leads to the beaches, 'we'll go to the beach to blow some freshness into you.' That decided, she passes Leo a small flask of spring water to drink, and when he's drained it, he falls asleep until they draw up in a stony car park.

Praia Grande is a stretch of sandy beach towards Sintra. Today, although there is no wind, the waves are high and fierce, dotted with surfers. Sunbathers are scattered about and there are people paddling or swimming in the foamy shallows. As Leo slips his good hand into

112

Rosa's, which is rough from gardening and, he thinks, all the spell-making in her kitchen, his thoughts turn to Concha. 'The dolphins bit you,' she'd told Leo the night before, 'because they don't want you to try to turn into them.' But how can he save his family if he doesn't turn into a dolphin? His eyes skim the breakers and he knows there are dolphins out there somewhere.

Rosa interrupts his reverie. 'What happened at Concha's to make you so tired and pale?'

He stoops to pick up a purplish shell, delicately ribbed. 'We tried to turn into dolphins. To magic the sleep monster away for ever.'

'And I'm guessing it didn't work?'

Leo shakes his head sadly. There's something he wants to tell Rosa, something to do with that new word he has learned, 'jinn', and the way Concha's mother had walked as if on stilts, but he can't put all this into words.

She squeezes his hand. 'You mustn't exhaust yourself with worry, *meu amor.*'

Leo's eyes are roaming across the sand in front of him. With a startled cry, he tugs his hand from Rosa's and crouches quickly to retrieve something half-hidden in the sand. In its former life it was a tile, perhaps one of the traditional Portuguese ones, varnished a deep and arresting blue. The sea has eroded it for so many years that it has been worn down to an almost perfect circle just three centimetres in diameter and perhaps half-a-centimetre thick. Sitting on the palm of Leo's hand as he brushes the wet sand from it, it looks like a shining, sea-blue eye.

'It's a dolphin-eye!' exclaims Leo, as utterly amazed as if he had in fact discovered a real dolphin's eye.

'So it is,' Rosa agrees, admiring it closely. 'You know, Leo, even if we can't change bad things, like the sleep monster running wild, we can still hope for the best.'

His eyes flick to her face but return quickly to the marvel in his hand. The dolphins *do* want me, he thinks fiercely.

'And not only hope for it,' Rosa adds with a hint of sternness so that Leo lifts his gaze to hers. 'We must *believe* that things are changing for the better, and imagine them working themselves out with wondrous ease. And we must put effort into this working out.' The eye is sparkling in Leo's hand but now he is fully focused on his aunt's voice and on the magic she is teaching him.

Rosa counts off points on her fingers. 'We take a dolphin-eye stone and trust that it will help us. We whisper good spells into the wind, or at night, in the special moment when images appear in our mind before we fall asleep. And –' she grasps her third finger '– we never give up, do we, Leo?'

Chapter Nineteen

As Olivia paces, ignoring her throbbing spine, she isn't seeing Carlos' African masks, carved from ebony and staring from the walls. She doesn't register the spray of yellow roses on the bookcase which holds Carlos' photography manuals, her art books and Leo's stash of fairy tales and English language early readers, most of these given to him by Olivia's mother. She sees only her husband, roaring in the bedroom with curtains and poles fuelling his confusion and distorting his form. She sees him running naked through the house with a look of abject terror on his face. Why should any of them have to live with this fear, sleep with it, wake up to it? There's something impossibly ominous at the root of these nightmares, she thinks. But what is it?

Paintings come to Olivia in flashes, astonishing in their completeness, the colours so startling that she can feel them buzzing in her hands. The painting-to-be will rise before her and then vanish so that she has to rush to reproduce its essence as fast as possible, using anything to hand – one of Leo's crayons and a scrap of telephone paper; shells and debris lying on a beach; or even, once, the contents of their packed lunch when they were on the motorway returning from holiday in Spain and all her pencils were in the boot. That had made Carlos groan – crisp packets laid out to represent the pattern of abstract orbs she had seen, cheese sandwiches precisely arranged around them in the passenger footwell until they made a service stop and she could get it all down on paper.

As she turns smoothly at the door to stride back across the room for the umpteenth time, Olivia has the sick feeling that Carlos is on the brink of the unmentionable, about to make some irreversible mistake. It is out of this darkness that she sees the image she has been waiting for, the one she will paint.

She sees a man running towards her wildly, in desperation, his arms flung out like the victim of a crucifixion, his face contorted in horror, his eyes flat and unconscious. The colours are dreadful – bloody, vicious reds, the browns of sludge and drudgery, the unrelenting black of the unknown, a pallid death white.

For a moment, Olivia stands stock still, reeling from the impact. Then, dazed, she looks around her for something with which to record the image. Part of her is reluctant to give the image more power by painting it, but the artist in her cannot let such potency be lost, so she hurries into the kitchen where there is a shopping pad on the wooden table and begins to sketch. She finds herself grabbing metal scissors, knives, a stone that Leo has brought in from the garden. The stone becomes the man's open mouth. The knives and scissors are his limbs.

Fifteen minutes later in her studio, a converted garden shed with big windows, Olivia grasps a paintbrush, the tip of which is glutinous with scarlet and black acrylic paint, not quite mixed, so that the scarlet is threaded with black, the black veined with scarlet. If Carlos' desperate nightmares had a colour, she thinks, they would be red – the scarlet of freshly spilled blood. And black, the blackening that signifies irreversible decay. Olivia's gaze is fixed on the square canvas before her, which she has swiftly painted a thick, ridged yellowish-grey. She is hunched, intent.

In an instant, she uncoils, whips her slim body forwards and flings the paint so that it flies momentarily, a blur of colour, before it hits the canvas. It judders like a teardrop, becoming a scarlet and black slug surrounded by tiny repetitions of itself. Olivia admires the fatness, the wet lines of her paint-slug. If she could, she would touch it now, let it crawl across her fingertips. Instead she dips her brush into the water pot and watches the colour swirl from it. Raising a hand, she touches her forehead, feels the weight and shape of her newest bruise. She's no stranger to violence.

At the core of Carlos is gentleness, so that over time, Olivia had grown certain he would never hurt her – that nobody would ever hurt her again. But now she's wondering, doubting. Has something inside her triggered this unconscious night-time violence to surface? As she begins to build her painting, adding splinter-thin slashes of midnight blue and black, she wonders whether the pattern of her previous life, the life she lived while she waited to meet Carlos, has been stamped so strongly on her psyche that it will beat through into the peace and trust she and Carlos have built together.

Her ex-boyfriend, Gary, had been prone to violent rages (without the excuse of being asleep, thinks Olivia drily). She'd met him when she was just twenty and had fallen for his tightly coiled energy and his belief in his music – he was lead guitarist of a Bristol-based band called Clarity. Their love affair had been so intense that his anger and abuse became inseparable from his charmingly wild side, and for three years, although he bullied and hurt her, Olivia had found it impossible to leave him until during one bitter row, his hands closed around her neck and began to squeeze. After that, Olivia left the relationship without looking back. Despite Gary's despairing efforts, the songs he sent her, his heartbroken and repentant emails, she never set eyes on him again. She jacked in the undemanding job she had taken working in a small art gallery in Bristol on completing her art degree, and accepted a work placement helping a sculptor, Samuel Briant, in his atelier in Lisbon. After just four months in Portugal, she met and fell in love with Carlos.

The background of Olivia's painting is a savage mess, an angry explosion. She can feel it all coming out of her, the fear, the frustration. It occurs to her that she's never gone into much detail with Carlos about her relationship with Gary; in the early days part of her had felt, ridiculously, that this Portuguese photographer with his way of making her feel as though he needed nothing more than her, would lose interest if he knew how badly she had let herself be treated. Intent on becoming a new person, one to whom violence could never happen, Olivia had glossed over the darkest scenes of her time with Gary, and rarely allowed herself to think of them. With this new violence, though, it's all returning to her in flashes of scarlet and black.

Miles' words ring in her head as she works. She hasn't found a moment yet to relay his findings to Carlos; he was home too late for them to talk that same night, and the next day Rosa had returned Leo with some tale of having to take him out of school because he was poorly, so Olivia had spent the evening fussing over him. Still, she knows that soon she must take her courage in both hands and say what she has to say. Today is Friday, and Carlos is working all morning. He mentioned something about going to his sports club afterwards, but he should be back an hour or more before Leo returns from school. That, she decides, will be her opportunity to speak to him. She presses more colour into the painting, her movements deliberate now, the initial frenzy spent. Her resolve is strengthening.

'They have killed, Carlos. These people have killed! No, don't walk away from me. I need you to hear this. You – Carlos!'

Olivia snatches at his arm as he backs away from her, but he avoids her grip, shaking his head. This is going badly. She has no choice but to follow him into the house. Carlos is panther-like in a black muscle-top and jogging pants, his thick eyebrows furrowed. He had come into the studio after his workout to find her sitting despondently in front of an unfinished portrait she'd been commissioned to paint, the jaunty orange headscarf she wore to protect her hair at odds with her glum mood. The nightmare painting she'd begun hours before was hidden from view, put in a corner of the studio to be continued another day. Concerned, Carlos had asked what the matter was, and all Olivia's worries, which had been building as she painted and agonised over their situation, came flying out of her with brutal honesty.

Part of Olivia knows this is not the way to tell these tales – they require tact, delicacy; they should be told with reassurances that this will never happen to Carlos. They should be held up as Miles had held them up: as extremes of behaviour, cautionary tales; a catalyst to act early, take precautionary steps. But, loosened by fear, her mouth is unstoppable. When she has shouted out the bloody story of the baby, smashed against a wall, she hears an unfamiliar and disturbing sound, like a bursting, or a rent in the air, and realises that Carlos is crying.

She runs to him. He won't look at her, but he doesn't push her away either, so Olivia stands on tiptoe and holds him in her arms, breathing in his sea-salt smell, crushing her face against his deep chest. For a long while, neither of them speak.

'I'm sorry,' says Olivia after a while. 'That was brutal. I should have . . .' She tails off. 'Miles says he has a colleague who knows a lot about this kind of thing. We should talk to her.'

He smears the tears off his face, focusing on her as if he's only just noticed she's there. 'What colleague? A psychotherapist? A psychiatrist? Who?'

'A psychologist and sleep specialist. She's done lots of work with patients who have sleep disorders.' Olivia walks into the living room to get a little space, knowing that he'll follow her now. She lowers herself onto the sofa and waits.

Carlos walks in looking lost and leans against the wall. 'So Miles thinks I have a sleep disorder? This – what was it – RBD?' He sounds uncertain. 'I've never heard of anyone doing this sort of thing in their sleep. Those stories . . . it all sounds so grim.'

'I know, but if we try and look on the bright side, at least if it's a sleep disorder, we can rule out your fear that it's the start of some weird hereditary insanity.'

'Oh yeah, sure, because those sleep murderers sound like really rational people.' Carlos narrows his eyes, which are still wet, so that his long eyelashes stick together. 'Not a mad bone in their bodies.'

Olivia shrugs off his sarcasm. 'I shouldn't have blurted it all out like that. Miles told it far better, he kept saying these were extreme cases.'

'And you don't think I'm an extreme case? *Meu Deus*, look at that huge bruise on your face. Look at the marks on our son's *neck*, for God's sake . . .' Agitation moves through his body in a wave and he shifts position, hugging his arms to his chest.

'Carlos.' Olivia raises her hands in a calming gesture. 'Miles raised the possibility that when you were a child you may have suffered some kind of abuse, maybe sexual abuse, and that's what's resurfacing to cause these terrible dreams.'

'No way,' says Carlos immediately. 'That's ridiculous. I'd remember.'

'Many people don't remember childhood traumas, they block them out. But whatever happened, you need to remember it, because only then can you exorcise these nightmares.'

Carlos clicks his tongue impatiently. 'Stop simplifying everything, Olivia. Life isn't always so black or white. Not everything can be traced to a childhood trauma, and I *know* I wasn't abused.'

'Then what happened? You have to remember, Carlos!'

He stares at her. 'Do you think I'm not trying?'

'Well, try harder,' she pleads. 'We can't carry on like this indefinitely, you do see that, don't you?'

He tenses. 'What do you mean?'

'I mean that you're endangering all three of us. Leo's teacher is watching us like a hawk, we're hiding Leo's neck with shirts this week – what will it be next week? A balaclava because he's so bruised up? We've been avoiding all our friends . . . And Leo isn't coping well – Rosa is worried about him. *I'm* worried about him, I'm worried about you . . . Carlos, this thing is upturning our lives. We *have* to make sure it never happens again.' She shakes her head in disbelief. 'To think that just a few weeks ago we were seriously discussing trying for another baby. Lunacy!'

At this, Carlos comes to her where she's sitting on the sofa. He crouches in front of her and she looks into his sad, handsome face. 'What are you saying?' he whispers. 'No baby after all?'

Tears well in Olivia's eyes. 'It's not the right time, is it?'

'Us having a second child, after all your excuses over the years for putting it off so you can make a name for yourself as an artist, is now off the cards because of two isolated incidents?' Carlos is staggered. 'Admit it, Olivia,' he says softly, 'you don't really believe this sleep disorder theory, do you? You think I'm going insane.'

'No, *querido*,' says Olivia. 'You're the one who thinks that.' She turns her face from him but he gently eases it back, with a finger on her chin.

'Please, Olivia,' he says, his eyes bright with desperation. 'We'll talk to this psychologist friend of Miles'. I'll do all I can to stop this thing. I'll tie myself to the bed. I'll dredge up all the memories you like. Just don't start closing doors on our future.'

Chapter Twenty

After her evening shower, Olivia wraps one fluffy white towel around her suntanned body and twists her hair up into another. She'll sleep with damp hair tonight; the air is so hot that it'll help keep her cool. As she pads down the corridor, she looks in on Leo. His small body is sprawled across the bed, his arms flung out. He fell asleep happy, having got his parents to agree to take him to the zoo with Concha tomorrow. When she returns to their low-ceilinged, yellow-painted bedroom, the top bed sheet is in a heap on the floorboards and Carlos, bare-chested and in loose pyjama bottoms, is sitting on the bed. They have an old-fashioned, comfortable double bed with wrought iron-bedrails which rise in intricate twists from the head and foot. Carlos is spooling metres and metres of black leather straps across the blue fitted sheet.

'What's going on?' Olivia laughs. 'Please tell me you're not turning into a sadomasochist?'

He grins. 'Well . . . if tying yourself to the bed all night is sadomasochistic, then I guess I am.'

Her smile disappears. 'I didn't think you were serious about doing that.'

'Well, I am.' Carlos' mouth tightens. 'After all those terrible stories you told me yesterday, you shouldn't be surprised. We can't risk it happening again, you know that. And from what Rosa said, it worked when I was a boy. It's either this or sleeping on the sofa.'

Olivia shakes her head stubbornly. 'No separate beds,' she says. 'I want to know if it happens again so I can make sure you don't injure yourself or Leo, you know that.' She sits down on the edge of the bed and watches him grapple with the straps, which she now sees are dog leashes. He's knotting them together to form one long leather strap.

'First I thought of rope,' Carlos says, 'but it's too abrasive. Then, when I was in town earlier, I passed a pet shop and had this idea – it's really soft leather, but of course the knots are a big hassle.'

'Am I going to have to sleep all tied up, too?' Olivia is imagining the straps wrapped around and around the mattress, immobilising them both like flies in a spider's web.

'No, no, of course not.' Carlos pulls the length of leather through his hands, measuring it mentally. 'I hope it's enough. No, I'll be strapped down on my side of the bed. I'm going to attach my ankles to the bedrail and then work out a way of strapping my chest down too so that I can't jump out of bed in the night. It's not ideal, but it'll have to do until I can think of something better.' He begins to fasten the straps around the bedrail, and Olivia stands up to get out of his way.

'It's ugly,' she says sadly, tugging her towel further up her chest. 'We're defacing our bed, Carlos. If this was a painting, it wouldn't be a happy one.' She nods at the snakelike tangle of straps.

Carlos is engrossed in what he's doing. 'We'll get used to it. It's only until we see the sleep specialist, anyway. Shame we have to wait nearly two more weeks until we can.' Their appointment is on 10 June, and Dr Loverock's secretary had only managed to squeeze them in so soon because of a cancellation. When he has run the straps all the way up the length of the bed and knotted them in a compli-cated system to the other bedrail, Carlos comes over to where Olivia is standing at the door, her hands still clutching the top of her towel. He peels them gently away and holds them in his own. He smiles, not so much with his lips as with his eyes. This is the expression that undoes Olivia every time. She presses herself to him, letting the towel fall away as they kiss, and immediately he's hard.

They move to the bed, still kissing, and Carlos eases her down, swiping the loose ends of the dog leashes away with his spare arm, which makes Olivia giggle. She pulls the towel off her head and tosses it aside, then winds her arms around his neck. Carlos lowers himself onto her, his body locked over hers as he kisses her throat leisurely. Olivia closes her eyes and sees her nightmare painting before her, the central figure savage, staring straight at her. She twists slightly to rid herself of the image and when Carlos' arms tighten around her in response, a memory of the impossible strength of his limbs, their violent thrashing, causes panic to rip through her body. She gasps and rams him away from her with her elbows against his shoulders.

'What?' he asks, rolling off her in astonishment. 'Your spine – am I hurting you?'

For a moment, Olivia hesitates. It would be easy to agree that her bruises are hurting. 'I'm . . . I'm frightened of you,' she says, shocked by the admission.

'Of me?'

'Of your body . . . so powerful.' Olivia hugs herself, staring at him. 'Now that you've hurt me, hurt Leo, everything is different.'

'In my sleep, Olivia. I hurt you in my *sleep*!' He gazes at her help-lessly. 'Look at me – I am awake!'

Olivia bites her lip. 'Things have changed. I'm bound to feel . . .'

Carlos reaches out a hand and very gently strokes her damp hair. 'Come on top of me?' he suggests.

Olivia moves on top of him and they get through the rest of it somehow, but the mood is flat, depressing, with Carlos asking her anxiously two or three times if she's OK. They have never had such mechanical sex. As soon as it's over, Carlos pulls his pyjama bottoms back on, and Olivia rewraps her hair in the towel and finds a T-shirt and knickers to sleep in.

'You won't be frightened next time,' Carlos says, more to convince himself than her, she thinks. 'When we make love, I'm awake. I will never hurt you when I'm awake.' When Olivia is silent, he sighs and indicates the dog leashes. 'Will you help me test it?'

She nods, and watches as he manoeuvres himself into the straps and secures them around his ankles. It's awkward. When Carlos has wound the strap around his chest just under his armpits, he takes the end and pulls it tight. Then he hands it to Olivia. 'Knot it to the bedpost, please.'

She stands looking at the strap in her hand. 'This is ridiculous.'

'You'd rather see me slink off to sleep on the sofa?' Carlos' face is neutral but she sees the flash of fear in his eyes.

'Oh, of course not, you *know* that!'

He shrugs as best he can under the straps. 'So tie me up, baby.'

Olivia ties the best knot she can, hating every minute of this. 'I feel like I'm putting you in a straitjacket,' she mutters.

Carlos doesn't reply. When she's secured him, he tests his system with a series of bucks and kicks, which go nowhere: the straps hold him in place. 'Good,' he says, satisfied. 'Come to bed.'

Olivia sheds the towel on her head and combs her hair through with her fingers so that droplets fly outwards. She drapes the pale yellow, summery bed sheet they use in the hottest months over Carlos, feeling better when the unsightly straps are no longer visible. 'The bed smells of leather,' she complains as she switches off the light and climbs in next to him. 'And I can't cuddle you properly.'

'I know, I know,' he murmurs sleepily. 'It's weird, but please let's give it a try, *querida*. Sweet dreams.'

125

'You're the one who needs sweet dreams,' she says, and kisses his ear.

In the morning, Olivia is surprised to find how well she has slept – for the first time in the three weeks since Carlos' explosive night-mares began, she has been able to rest in the knowledge that even if he does have an attack, Leo and herself will be safe from harm. She looks across at Carlos, who is pale, stubble shadowing his chin. He has hollows under his eyes and she knows even before he wakes and tells her so that he has barely slept a wink.

'You should have woken me and told me to untie you,' she laments.

'I'll get used to it, but it's odd not being able to move.' He turns his head and looks at her. 'And Olivia . . . I remember now, what it used to be like.'

'What what used to be like?'

'When Father tied me to the bed as a boy.'

She sits up and leans over him tensely. 'Tell me.'

'In the night, as I lay half awake, I saw him again: he came into my old bedroom all tall and stern with a length of rope coiled in his arms. He wound it right under the bed frame itself – probably a faster method than mine, come to think of it – and I was pinned down, flat on my back. This awful feeling went with the image of him tying me down. As if the child-me had done something too terrible to think about. And I knew Father was trying to protect me. He said, "It's for your own good."'

Carlos' face is screwed up as he thinks back. 'That's all I can remember,' he says. 'Just that one image.' He opens his eyes. '*Meu Deus*, Olivia, what did I do?'

Chapter Twenty-one

Leo and Concha are in the sky. Below them there are lions stretched out on the concrete like dead rats, their bodies bald, tails twitching in the heat, and further along the elephants wave their trunks. Olivia says they make her think of Indian dancers moving their arms and wrists. Even from up here in the air the giraffes look tall, and when Concha hears the apes hooting in the trees she shouts because they aren't in cages.

'I guess the ring of water keeps them there; they probably don't like water,' says Carlos. He's standing at the front of their open-topped metal cable car like a ship's captain, surveying the lush vegetation of Lisbon zoo – banana trees, bamboo hedges, bougainvillea flourishing everywhere, its purple flowers bright against the green.

Concha tosses her head. 'Why would monkeys be scared of water?'

'We're all scared of something,' reasons Carlos.

'I think it's those mean little electric fences they're scared of,' says Olivia, shifting positions slightly. Rosa is booked up giving aromatherapy massages all morning, so couldn't join them. Even so, there's not a lot of space in the cable car; the four of them are standing as it glides around in a big circuit, sometimes almost brushing the tips of the trees.

127

'What are you scared of, Pai?' asks Leo.

'Siberian tigers,' says Carlos, so that Leo remembers standing millimetres from the huge beast, which was prowling on the other side of a glass wall. Leo had looked right into its cat-face and its huge green eyes.

'Not the sleep monster?'

'Yes, I'm scared of the sleep monster, too,' agrees Carlos.

'Me, too,' says Leo.

'So am I,' admits Olivia, closing her eyes momentarily to enjoy the breeze on her face.

'And me,' chimes Concha, not wanting to be left out. And then for some reason, all four of them are looking at each other and laughing, and the sleep monster seems very far away and unimportant as they soar over the rhinos and pink clouds of flamingos.

Later, when they've eaten creamy caramel Cornettos and walked under the burning sun past zebras and llamas, it's time for the dolphin show. They sit in a giant outdoor theatre-tiered space in front of the huge pool along with hundreds of singing five-year-old children. Pop music rocks from the speakers and it's like a party; everyone jives their shoulders to the beat. When the show starts, the dolphins shoot like arrows, make torpedo-like dives, leap clear out of the water so that they glisten and smile. The sides of the pool are see-through, so that when the dolphins close their eyes in bliss at the bottom of a perfectly-timed dive, Leo can see this.

He hunches forwards, his hands on his knees, Concha and his parents forgotten as he learns their graceful movements, sees the way they synchronise themselves with the other dolphins. He watches as the trainer is propelled along by two dolphins who clasp his specially-designed underwater shoes in their beaks. First they swim with him down deep, then they turn and jet up and up until he explodes from the water like a circus acrobat in exactly the right place to punch a red ball, which is suspended high above the pool. The trainer becomes a superhuman, a dolphin-powered man who can bend the rules of gravity and is powerful enough to work magic. Leo can see the magic working on the crowd, which whoops and cheers in amazement. This is the magic he needs.

After the show, the dolphins are allowed to swim around in the deep, see-through pool. The crowd begins to make a mass exodus, but Leo wants to press his nose against the glass and watch the dolphins some more, so they make their way down the steps. Concha's dress ribbons have come loose and are straggling down her back, and she has ice cream stains on the collar. Olivia takes her aside and does her best to tidy her up, with Carlos handing her water from his knapsack. Leo puts his palms flat against the glass and stares into the dolphin world. There are six of them, and they circle the space, almost brushing against the glass. He feels a touch on his shoulder.

'Hello, young man!' He looks round to see Professora Celeste's bright face. She is holding two small boys by the hand. 'My nephews,' she says. She looks very pretty in a white sundress with embroidered yellow straps.

Leo smiles, happy to see her. '*Boa tarde.*'

'Are you here with your parents?' she begins, but then she spots them. Her smile grows fixed and Leo follows her gaze to see Olivia crouching before Concha, dabbing at her collar with a damp tissue. Carlos is bent over, fiddling with the many pockets of his knapsack. None of them are looking Leo's way. Olivia's hair was loose when they left the house, but before the dolphin show began she pulled it into a tight bun on top of her head because of the heat. In the glare of the sun, the bruise on her forehead is very visible, both the conical shape of it and the swirls of yellow-green colouration. Professora Celeste looks grave. She turns back to Leo and notices the thin purple welt scored on the side of his neck, exposed by the low neckline of his T-shirt. Over the course of a week, it has grown less livid but its nastiness still makes her wince.

'Leo, *meu querido*,' she says softly, 'How did you get that mark on your neck?'

Leo's hand flies to his neck and he is startled into blurting out the truth. 'The sleep monster took my necklace.'

His teacher looks into his eyes for a long moment, and Leo looks back. She isn't cross, he thinks, but she isn't happy any more. He hopes he hasn't said the wrong thing. 'I'm going to have a talk with your parents, Leo. Will you stay here with João and Paulo?'

He nods, slightly resentful that he has to share the dolphins with these two younger boys. The three of them gaze into the turquoise pool. The crowd has dispersed and they are almost the only ones left, so he can hear Professora Celeste greeting his parents and asking Concha to run along and watch the dolphins with them. Leo's forehead feels tight, so he presses it against the glass. He wants to disappear through the glass, swim right into the pool and glide away with the dolphins.

'It's not what you think,' Carlos is saying. 'If you'll just let me explain . . .'

'You explained last week. Clearly you've been drinking again, Senhor Carlos.'

'That was just an excuse. I'd like to tell you the truth, but it's rather more complex . . .'

'Oh, I see.' Professora Celeste's voice is colder than Leo has ever heard it. '*Now* you're ready to tell me the truth? Might I ask why I wasn't allowed the truth when we had our interview the other week?'

'Professora Celeste, please understand. This situation is entirely new for us, we're at a loss . . .' his mother's voice is higher than usual, stretched out thin. Leo wants to block his ears but his hands seem to be stuck to the glass. Beside him, Concha has begun a tickling game with João and Paulo, who are twins but don't look the same. Their little bodies twist and yelp with laughter as they squirm away from Concha's quick fingers. For a moment or two Leo is distracted from the adults' conversation. Then Professora Celeste's voice cuts through the air, sounding impossibly stern.

'Nightmares? Last time you told me he'd been drinking. What am I supposed to believe when people lie like this? I'm sorry for you, Senhora Olivia, but I'm not swallowing this story. You and your family clearly need help and it's my job to protect Leo from harm. And *your* job, too, incidentally.'

'I would protect my son with my life!'

All four children stop and stare when Olivia cries this. The adults look over at them anxiously and edge further away. Leo turns back to the pool to see a dolphin swimming straight towards him, slow and deliberate. It reaches the glass and hangs in the water exactly level with his face. The other children gather close, wowing and gasping, but Leo blocks off the sound, blocks out the whole of the rest of the world. It's just him and the dolphin, who looks deep into his heart.

'Come on, boys!'

Leo turns with a start to see Professora Celeste hurrying off with a nephew in each hand. Her white dress is sticking to her spine with sweat. Leo's gaze lifts to his parents and he sees that their faces are black with despair, they hold hands like children and he understands that there are some things even adults can't control. When he turns back to the pool with Concha's arm pressed warm alongside his own, the dolphin has gone.

Chapter Twenty-two

7 May 1984

Pedro is teaching me to juggle. It's so hard! I am chasing the fallen balls, which are orange in the daylight but don't glow, and Pedro laughs to see me grow hot in the sun. We move back to the shade of an orange tree at the side of the road. It's the only tree with no old men on chairs under it. Today the Alfama is very hot; when I ran out of school and saw Pedro he was sitting on the wall waiting for me with a wet T-shirt tied around his head. He'd dipped it in the fountain and it was so wet it looked black rather than blue, and cool water was dripping all over Pedro's face and his thin brown chest. I wanted to do the same with my shirt but what would Inês and Father say? Marina has told me I shouldn't play with Pedro any more, because he's poor and might lead me into bad habits, and his brother could be dangerous, but I can't help it. In the café with all the old men near it, a woman is singing fado. Her voice is as deep as a man's and her neck wobbles like a turkey's and the sound is beautiful.

'Can't do it,' I say when I've picked up all the balls for the tenth time. I lean against the tree and watch as Pedro shows me again, his hands blurring and the balls floating up and down, up and down and around. Then he drops one and we both laugh. I reach out and pat the T-shirt on his head to cool my hands.

The crow-man is coming up the street towards us and this is the first time I've seen him walk anywhere. He's wrapped in a black coat that must make him sweat like crazy, and he walks hunched up, but he's a big man.

'I dare you to roll this so it lands at his feet,' whispers Pedro, handing me a ball. 'And then you have to go and get it.'

My throat is dry but a dare is a dare and I let the ball fall, almost hoping it will roll away from the crow-man and into the gutter. But it goes towards his feet and I have to chase it. I grab it just before it hits his bare, grimy toes, and I leap away as if he's going to hit me. He makes a growling sound in his throat and as we stare, he spins twice in a circle, his arms bunched angrily to his chest. Then he strides on, shouting something in a language we can't understand.

Pedro and I look at each other in alarm. I hold the ball close to my chest. '*Maluco*,' I whisper, and Pedro nods.

'Your necklace is flashing.' His eyes are round.

'It's not just a necklace, it's a family amulet made from sapphire and it's luckier than anything.'

'It's shiny like the sun. I told Fernando about it and he wants to see it too.'

I remember watching Pedro and his brother walking into the dark together, and I'm happy to have something so important that even a big boy like Fernando is interested in it. 'Why does he?'

'He reckons it might be worth a lot. He wants to hold it in his hand and see if it's as sparkly as I told him it is.'

'If you rub it,' I tell Pedro, 'it sparkles even more and probably even makes your wishes come true.' I don't know if this is really true but the more we talk about the amulet and the heavier it feels around my neck, the more I believe in its power.

'Can I try it on?'

133

I shake my head. 'No.' I close the amulet in my fist. 'I can't take it off, even for a minute, in case the luck runs away.' I'd give him anything else of mine – even my wooden train set or the metal plane Father gave me for Christmas. 'I'm not allowed to take it off,' I say.

'Who would know?' His violet eyes gleam with mischief.

'I can't.' The amulet is still hidden in my fist.

'But I'm teaching you to juggle.' Pedro smiles a sad smile. He wants this to be a swap, but what else can I give him? I have nothing in my shorts pockets except for a bit of old chocolate with fluff on it and a paper clip that I found at school and bent into a spiral that looks more like a square. Then I remember. 'My Aunt Marina taught you to write your name!'

Pedro laughs. '*Sim, sim,*' he says excitedly. 'Watch this.' Reaching up to the orange tree, which is short and sturdy, he snaps off a twig. Then he squats down in the dust and uses it like a pen.

'P-E-D-R-O', he writes. Then, grinning all over his face, 'C-A-R-L-O-S'.

'You know how to write mine too!' Marina had written my name on the dusty *azulejos* beside Pedro's that day, but I didn't know Pedro had learned it so well.

He nods. 'That means we're brothers.'

'Brothers,' I say, and my heart shines so hard it feels like it's made of solid gold.

Tonight, I've only been asleep a few hours when I hear Father saying Marina's name angrily, over and over. I pull the sheets away and creep to the door. I've learned how to open it with no noise at all. Through the gap, I can see the staircase bending down and around, right to the ground. It's onyx marble from Pakistan and it glows. Father is standing at the top in his navy and silver pyjamas with his back to me. I can see the round bald bit on the back of his head.

'Marina,' he says again, and I jump. That's when I see my auntie.

She's walking very slowly up the stairs in her long white nightdress and her eyes are as empty as the moon. Her hands and mouth and the top of her nightdress are dark with something and as her hand rests on the banister she leaves ugly smudges.

'Is that some kind of melted chocolate?' demands Father. 'I've had it with the constant mess you make at night! *Stop* this preposterous behaviour and explain yourself this minute.'

Marina says nothing, just continues to climb the stairs at her own pace, and I catch my breath to see someone ignoring Father like that. Father's hands grip the banister and I see the side of his face as he stares down at her. 'What do you think you're doing? Are you play-acting, or are you losing your mind? Do you want to ridicule our family even more than you already have by carrying a sailor's bastard?' Spit flies from his mouth. 'I've had enough of this pathetic bid for attention, do you hear?'

'I'll do what I want.' Marina's voice is thick and careless.

'That's where you're wrong!'

Mãe's voice spans the semi-darkness. 'Please, Aníbal . . . let her be. If she's eaten, she'll go back to bed, she always does . . .'

'But she's getting worse, *minha querida*,' calls Father, making his voice much softer. 'She's plastered in chocolate mousse, and the other night I found her eating a salt sandwich, *pelo amor de Deus*. Salt!'

'It might be her condition . . .'

'Pah! This night-madness started well before she met that damned irresponsible sailor.'

'Ah, what does it matter? Marina has enough grief without you shouting –' Mãe's cough starts and it's so deep, it won't let her speak any more.

Father leans towards Marina as she reaches the top step. 'Look what you've done.' He's trying to whisper now. 'Why are you trying to destroy our family name? Your sister-in-law is getting weaker by the day . . .' His voice stops in the middle as if it's broken, and he turns away from Marina who walks silently past him towards her bedroom, chocolate mousse glistening around her mouth.

I duck back inside the door and into my bed.

In a moment my door is pushed open and I know Father is looking at me to make sure I'm sleeping and my heart smashes so I can feel it in my throat and he waits and looks and I lie very still until he goes away like a shadow, the door closing so it's all dark again.

When he's gone, I put my hands over my face and press hard. 'Please, Mother Maria,' I say inside my hands, 'let Marina stay with us forever. Don't let Father make her go away.'

Chapter Twenty-three

'I *do* remember Marina Casanova de Albuquerque Moniz. Everybody here does. She was here for less than four weeks, but she brought tragedy to our hospital.'

An overweight woman in her mid-fifties, Enfermeira Teresa Pires was one of the duty nurses while Marina was in the women's ward of the Clínica Psiquiátrica de Almada twenty-six years ago. The psychiatric hospital is a dilapidated building just across the River Tejo, set in its own small but secure grounds, with high concrete walls separating it from the town of Almada. The nurse gives the three of them an appraising look, as if deciding how much to say. Her white uniform is crisp and neat, with green bands around the sleeves and hems, but something about the way her eyes peer unfeelingly out of her flaccid face reminds Olivia of the expression her local butcher has as he carves slippery red meat on his counter: focused, but coldly detached from the business in hand. 'Follow me,' says Enfermeira Teresa, and sets off with a light, almost sprightly step through a series of narrow corridors with corroding pipes running along their length. Carlos, Olivia and Rosa follow at a respectful distance. None of them feel like talking. Olivia thinks briefly of Leo, safely at school. It's only eleven so they have hours before they need to return home.

As they pass through the women's ward, Olivia glances uneasily through the scratched windows into a dormitory with steel beds and walls where the plaster has expanded with damp to cause mottled bulges near the ceiling. Only one of the beds is occupied, and she wonders how anyone could be healed in such joyless conditions, alone in dingy rooms where even in summer – and today is the first day of June, she remembers – the smell of damp and rot lies heavy in the nostrils.

'The residents spend most of their days in the recreation room,' says Enfermeira Teresa, as if she has picked up on Olivia's thoughts. 'We don't have the conditions we'd like,' she adds with no hint of apology, 'but improvements are being planned.'

They stop outside a locked door at the end of the ward. A tea-tray with chipped mugs and packets of sugar and coffee is parked outside. Inside, the large room is filled from floor to ceiling with metal filing cabinets. More cabinets have been dragged into a line in the centre of the room to form a partition, behind which is a wooden desk which makes Olivia think of the teachers' desks of her school days. Enfermeira Teresa gestures to them to sit but there are only two chairs so Carlos is left standing, staring around the room with a bleak look on his face. Even Rosa is subdued. As Enfermeira Teresa hunts for Marina's file, which is legally available to them as her surviving family members, Carlos heaves a sigh that echoes around the metal-filled room.

'I'd forgotten many things about Marina,' he says suddenly. 'But since we've arrived here, I've been trying to think back. Rosa, she was lovely – wasn't she?' He asks this as though he's no longer sure.

Rosa nods. Dressed from head to toe in turquoise, with a chiffon headscarf that floats on her head, she brings light and colour into the room. 'Marina had a good heart.'

'I'd been remembering her as little more than a family story – the "mad Aunt Marina" story,' admits Carlos. 'I haven't thought about her personality for years. I wonder why.' After a pause punctuated by the slamming of drawers as the nurse continues her search, he adds, 'I think once or twice she took me right down to the water to watch the river traffic. I remember her joking with the fishermen. She had gypsy-black hair and kind eyes. I don't like to think of her ending up here.'

'*Eu também não*,' says Rosa, shaking her bright head. 'Neither do I. And so quickly dead, too.' She glances at Enfermeira Teresa, who has turned back to them with a slim file in one hand.

'I'd only recently started working here myself,' says the nurse. She has the gravely voice of a long-time smoker, but Olivia hasn't noticed a tobacco smell about her. Enfermeira Teresa settles her heavy frame behind the desk, her hands folded on the closed file. 'I remember the night they brought your relative in,' she says, looking at Carlos. 'As I say, I was new on the job – it was one of my first night shifts, and she arrived in the early hours, wailing and protesting, begging her brother not to leave her here. That sort of scene is shocking when you aren't used to it.' Olivia sees something flicker in the nurse's eyes and glimpses the impressionable young woman she must have once been. 'I felt almost sorry for her – she seemed so convinced she'd done nothing to deserve being brought here. But there stood her brother, tall and sober, along with a physician who testified that she'd thrown some sort of violent fit, unaware of her own actions, and that her behaviour had been degenerating for some time. And of course, now I've worked here so long, I'm well aware of how convincing these people can be.'

'What people?' There's a slight edge to Carlos' voice and Olivia is conscious of his tense posture as he stands facing the nurse, his eyes on the file that she still hasn't opened.

'Those who are admitted to places like this.' Enfermeira Teresa gestures around her with a limp hand. 'Unstable people in the throes of mental illness. Often they truly believe their own stories, you see, just like pathological liars.'

'What was Marina's story?' asks Rosa.

'Let's see,' says the nurse, opening the file. She checks Marina's details with Rosa before beginning to read aloud.

'Admitted 16 July 1984, 4.15 am. Patient hysterical, requiring restraint. Has exhibited aggressive behaviour to family members on numerous occasions. Admitting doctor confirms a state of violent delusion to the point where the patient has become a menace to her family. Patient affects amnesia and denial of her condition. Twenty-three years old. Six months pregnant.'

'Pregnant?' interjects Rosa.

Enfermeira Teresa reads on as though she hasn't spoken. 'Admitted on signature of closest relative, Aníbal Alfredo Casanova de Albuquerque Moniz, and Dr Gabriel Costa Ribeiro. So you see,' she says, glancing up at Rosa, 'her story was that she'd done nothing wrong. The classic conspiracy plot. We get plenty of those.' She allows herself a small smile which none of the others return.

'Maybe she really *did* forget what she'd done,' says Carlos. Olivia sees his hands gripping the back of Rosa's chair. 'Did you take that into account when you locked her up?'

'All cases are thoroughly investigated by professionals in the mental health field,' says the nurse dismissively. She looks at the file. 'It says here that your aunt suffered from irregular nocturnal fits during which she would leave her bed and eat indiscriminately, becoming combative if anyone tried to stop her. So you see, we witnessed her behaviour first-hand.'

Olivia leans forwards keenly. 'Is there any chance that Marina's condition was in fact not mental illness, but a sleep disorder? You see, there's this disorder, where people leap from their beds during a nightmare and rampage through their homes. Sometimes they threaten anyone who gets in their way. People have even killed others while asleep.'

The nurse is shaking her head. 'I've never come across such a disorder,' she says, as if this closes the matter.

'But it exists. My friend told me about all these different cases –'

'Is your friend a qualified medical doctor?'

'Well, no,' Olivia says with a sigh, 'he isn't, but he . . .'

'So I think we could more profitably concentrate on the official reports of doctors who actually met and examined your relative, don't you?' The nurse pats the open file.

'But my husband does it too,' blurts Olivia. 'He runs around in his sleep and can't remember a thing about it in the morning.'

'Are you trying to get me locked away?' asks Carlos incredulously. 'Because that's how they handle people like me in this place, Olivia!'

Rosa laughs unexpectedly. 'Don't worry, we're not going to commit you just yet, Carlos.'

Enfermeira Teresa compresses her lips. 'Might I suggest, Senhor, that you take yourself to a doctor if you are suffering from nightly fits. I'm here to explain your aunt's file to you, not question her diagnosis. Now, would you like me to tell you the rest of her story, or not?'

'We want to hear it,' Rosa assures her. Carlos is still looking in disbelief at Olivia, who pretends she hasn't noticed.

'She was docile during the daytime,' says the nurse, scanning the pages of notes before her. 'But, as I just said, she was prone to strange fits which came unpredictably, although always at night. The night nurses would have to carry her back to her bed and secure her.'

'How did they secure her?' interrupts Carlos.

'We use ankle straps, which are attached to the foot of the bed. Further straps are secured around the thighs, chest and wrists.'

Olivia glances sharply at Carlos. Surely he's not looking for ideas on how to improve his own restraint system? The thought of him lying on their bed shackled like a psychiatric patient makes her shiver.

'Our mistake was in not securing her to the bed every night,'

141

admits Enfermeira Teresa. 'But she was pregnant, the fits were irregular, and we'd isolated her in her own locked bedroom so that she wouldn't endanger other patients should one occur.' She lays her hands flat over the file and eyes them all closely.

Something about the nurse's gaze unnerves Olivia, and she shifts uncomfortably.

'One night there was a security lapse; the door was left unlocked, and your aunt, presumably during one of her fits, made her way to the kitchen. Nobody knows exactly what happened there, but she somehow set the place on fire. The fire spread as far as the start of the women's ward before it was brought under control. Two patients died of smoke inhalation, and Marina herself was found on the upper landing, where she must have run when the fire caught her nightdress. Her body was burned beyond recognition.'

'*Ó meu Deus!*' murmurs Rosa. 'My God. And with an unborn baby inside her.' She crosses herself, something Olivia has never seen her do before. Silence stretches through the room, and Olivia gets the strong urge to get up and run from the building. She has heard enough about Marina's tragic life, has spent enough minutes in this airless, metal room. She can't bear the thought that Carlos might have whatever it was that possessed Marina at night.

Pale with worry, Carlos leans forwards. 'What was Marina's final diagnosis?'

The nurse looks down at the file again. 'There wasn't a final diagnosis, because the doctors were still trying out different medicines and she was having various therapies. But it seems one theory was that your aunt was suffering from a split personality disorder which resulted in brief psychotic episodes.'

Carlos nods, looking defeated. 'Thank you for your time.'

Outside, their relief at leaving the building is palpable. They walk in silence down the asphalt drive to the car park. Olivia is filled with the sick knowledge that Carlos seems to have whatever it was that

Marina had. She realises that so far, Miles is the only person who has suggested Carlos could have a sleep disorder; everyone else is convinced it's something else. The neighbours and Leo's teacher think it's a straightforward case of domestic violence. Dr Freitas sat behind his white beard and told them it could be epilepsy, the onset of schizophrenia, anything. Enfermeira Teresa would say it's a personality disorder.

The hospital looms behind them, its walls containing Marina's final, unhappy weeks of life. Olivia walks briskly despite the heat, eager to get away from the images the nurse has put into her head: a young Marina being forced into the asylum, her eyes big with fear, Carlos' father standing grimly by and letting it happen. *Making* it happen. Why would he do such a thing to his younger sister? Olivia closes her eyes briefly and imagines Marina running from the kitchen with her baby tucked in her belly, her nightshirt on fire, her skin melting as she screams.

They are walking under the trees now, tall Douglas pines whose freshness spills out across the air like a drug.

'I wish we could have done something,' murmurs Rosa.

'We were children,' says Carlos helplessly. 'What can children ever do?'

Chapter Twenty-four

As Olivia layers on paint, she reflects that the nightmare painting is filling with its own power. Her worst feelings pour into it; the fear of the violence that is now between her and Carlos, her memories of his flailing arms, the horror in his face. When Olivia isn't working on the painting, she has to turn it to face the wall and, when she does work on it, it pulls her into its dark centre. Today she is working on the man's lost, screaming mouth, and after a time she decides she has to stop.

When the doorbell goes, Olivia is removing her painting smock. Carlos collected Leo from school on his way back home after a day-long photo shoot, and has peeled off his sweaty shirt and started dismantling camera parts on the kitchen table because his best tele-photo lens has been playing up. Leo is playing with his stones in the garden, setting them into wavelike patterns and balancing them on top of one another like perfectly synchronised dolphins flying through the water. He looks up and sees a bony-faced stranger watching him over the top of the gate. Olivia hurries out of her studio, her hands still dripping wet after her post-painting clean-up, her hair tugged back into a messy ponytail so that blonde tendrils stick to her damp cheeks and neck.

'*Sim*?' she asks, thinking this must be yet another person trying to sell something – in this neighbourhood, people are always ringing on doors to sell insurance or telephone systems, and Olivia gives them short shrift because she dislikes being interrupted when she paints.

'Senhora Dona Olivia Casanova de Albuquerque Moniz?' enquires the woman. She has a low, cultured voice. 'My name is Doutora Lurdes Reis Monteiro and I'm from the Segurança Social de Lisboa.'

Olivia stops dead. 'You're a social worker?'

'I am. We were contacted by your son's teacher, a Professora Celeste Lopes Silva. I'd like to come in and ask you a few questions, if you wouldn't mind?'

Olivia hesitates, wondering whether she should ask this unwanted visitor to return at a more convenient time, but it occurs to her that she needs the woman's goodwill. She nods dumbly and reaches to open the gate. Doutora Lurdes is immaculate in a fitted black blouse and skirt ensemble, her only jewellery silver stud earrings in the form of rosebuds. When she steps daintily into the garden, Olivia is instantly conscious of the way she looks – braless, her nipples protruding through her ivory vest top, her legs on view in a pair of Carlos' Christmas boxer shorts which she'd pulled on for coolness – she always wears as little as she can under her painting smock. 'I've been painting, I'll need to get changed,' she mumbles, but Doutora Lurdes is already bending to greet Leo, asking him what he's doing, telling him she likes his garden. Leo is polite but distant, perhaps sensing his mother's agitation.

Olivia leads her into the house, where Carlos, hearing voices, comes out of the kitchen. He's as underdressed as Olivia feels, and when she's introduced Doutora Lurdes, she excuses herself to pick up her skirt and bra which are hanging over the kitchen chair, and slip into them while Carlos settles their visitor on the sofa.

As Olivia heads back into the living room with a jug of iced water and some glasses, Carlos comes through to grab his shirt and they

145

exchange frantic looks. 'Just be nice,' whispers Olivia as she passes him.

Doutora Lurdes is well organised. She has an A4 pad and a lengthy questionnaire, and she sits on the edge of an armchair with her knees pressed together as her over-sweet perfume gradually clots the room, making Olivia feel dizzy.

'Due to Leo's teacher's concern,' she tells them, not unkindly, 'we're opening a file on your family, and this is just a preliminary visit to help me understand more about you both and the way you work as a family. Are you willing to answer a few questions?'

She goes through every single question, making notes, while Leo plays happily in the garden. The questions begin simply, but quickly become extremely personal. Olivia and Carlos have to explain how and when they met, what sort of people they think they are, the kind of relationship they feel they have. They have to talk about Leo: his character, how he does at school, their dynamics as a family. Throughout, Olivia is aware of the social worker's sharp eyes on them, noticing every detail – the way Carlos keeps fiddling with his shirt cuffs, the baby photos of Leo on the opposite wall, the fading bruise on Olivia's forehead. Olivia feels as if she's being filmed. She is acutely aware of her body language, which she tries to keep relaxed. The questions take almost forty minutes, during which time Leo comes through once for a cold drink and a snack before return-ing to the garden. Throughout this time Doutora Lurdes makes no direct reference to the effects of Carlos' sleep violence, but eventu-ally she puts down her pen and looks at them both in her composed way.

'I assume you're both aware that Leo slipped out of school yes-terday?'

'We are, yes,' says Olivia, her heart sinking. Professora Celeste had contacted her the previous afternoon to say that Leo had left the school grounds during break time and that she'd found him talking to Zebra, whom he must have seen passing by. Olivia attempts a smile. 'He's never done anything like that before, and I think it was only for a few short minutes.'

'A few short minutes can make all the difference between safety and danger, Senhora Dona Olivia. He was found consorting with a tramp, an African man. How did you react when you were told that?'

'Zebra's not unknown to us,' she begins haltingly.

'I'm doing a photography book on the street dwellers of Lisbon,' explains Carlos. 'Zebra's one of them. He's a good person.'

'Good enough to form a friendship with your son?'

'Zebra wouldn't hurt a fly.' Carlos' voice is firm.

'Be that as it may, from Professora Celeste's account, he's a homeless drunk. He had a beer can in his hand when she found them talking together outside Leo's school. I hardly think that's suitable company for a young boy, do you?' Her gaze is steely.

'We talked to Leo,' says Olivia. 'He knows he mustn't leave school again without permission. He likes Zebra, he just wanted to say hello.'

There's a pause, during which Doutora Lurdes looks at each of them for an uncomfortably long moment. 'Would you like to say anything on the subject of the bruising that Professora Celeste discovered on two occasions, the first –' she checks her notes '– on your son's shoulder blades, and the second on his neck?'

Carlos swallows. 'We think I have a sleep disorder,' he begins, and launches into a convoluted explanation of his behaviour, with Olivia jumping in with anxious amendments.

When they've finished, the social worker looks down at her pad, where she has scribbled a few further lines. Then she looks at them both gravely. 'Professora Celeste wasn't entirely convinced by this story, as she said you'd told her previously that you, Senhor Carlos, were drunk on the first occasion.'

'But we're telling the truth now,' says Olivia. 'Carlos never drinks more than a beer or two.'

'So he lied to Leo's teacher about being drunk?'

Olivia sighs, and Doutora Lurdes leans forwards so that her bobbed hair swings around her face. 'You see, my job is to ensure that Leo is in safe hands. When parents change their stories, it's a warning sign that they're trying to hide something. Part of our job at the social services is to make sure that physical abuse isn't symptomatic of other, more hidden forms of abuse.'

'Such as?' asks Carlos. He seems bewildered, and keeps blinking.

'Such as sexual abuse. I've seen this sort of thing before – and worse,' she tells them. 'Purple stripes across children's legs and spines where they have been whipped with a belt or a stick. Raised welts on arms. Bruises half hidden under hair or behind ears. In about thirty per cent of these cases, the child was also suffering sexual abuse, from a grandparent, an uncle . . . or a parent.' She looks at them significantly.

'It's not what you think,' says Carlos, sounding overwhelmed. 'I swear we are not abusing our son, sexually or otherwise.'

'*Claro que não*, Senhor Carlos,' she says pleasantly. 'Of course not. Still, I hope you understand that I'm going to need more than just your word on this sleep disorder story?'

'We're seeing a specialist psychologist a week today,' says Carlos. 'She's sure to be able to help us, and I'm happy to give you her written diagnosis afterwards.'

'Good. Good.' Doutora Lurdes' forehead clears a little, and Carlos smiles reassuringly.

'Anyway,' he says, 'it won't happen again because I've been tying myself to the bed.'

'I beg your pardon?'

Behind the social worker's turned head, Olivia is shaking her head at Carlos, and he sees her but it's too late to backtrack. His gaze flickers for a moment as he thinks.

'Er . . . I've been tying myself down at night so that if it does happen again, I'll be restrained in bed.'

Doutora Lurdes seems mystified and more than a little suspicious, so Carlos jumps up and says, 'I'll show you, if you want.'

Olivia winces, but the social worker is already on her feet. In the bedroom, the bed is unmade and sloppy – they had both left the house in a rush that morning, Carlos to a photo shoot for a little-known Portuguese singer in a smart hotel on Largo do Chiado, and Olivia to deliver a painting of the bay of Cascais to an elderly client on the other side of town. Olivia and the social worker hover at the door, Olivia biting her lower lip so hard that she almost expects it to burst open. Carlos lifts the top sheet completely off the bed so that the black, knotted leather strips are visible. They look ugly and strange.

'Dog leashes,' he says, looking less sure of himself by the minute, faced with Doutora Lurdes' condemnatory gaze and Olivia's reproachful stare.

'How long have you been tying yourself to the bed for, Senhor Carlos?'

Carlos spreads the sheet hurriedly back over the bed, hiding the straps from view. 'Just a few nights, since the last episode. I thought it would help keep things under control until our appointment with the specialist next Thursday.'

'Are you fearful that you might lose control again?'

He straightens his back and looks her in the eye. 'It's only happened twice,' he says carefully, 'but I don't know when or if it might happen again. It may well *never* happen again.'

'But you seem to think it will,' she observes.

'I'm simply taking the necessary steps to protect my family until the specialist has told me what else we can do,' says Carlos tightly. 'I think that's only sensible, don't you?'

She doesn't answer, but fixes him with a level stare that suggests

149

she's uncovered some important evidence here, some looked-for indication of unstable behaviour. Standing beside her, Olivia is in a state of nervous tension but can't think of anything to say to ease the situation. Doutora Lurdes turns her body slightly away, so Olivia understands that they're to head back downstairs. Once there, the social worker asks them a few more perfunctory questions before taking her leave, saving her smiles for Leo as they pass him in the garden on the way out. She pauses to ask him about his stone game, why he's rearranging these stones, what they mean – 'Are they people?' Leo looks at her as if she's mad and tells her they're stones he found on the beach. Eventually she's gone, the gate swinging behind her neat, black-clad figure, her over-sweet perfume lingering in the air along with her promise to return.

Olivia ushers Carlos back inside the house, closing the door most of the way so that Leo will be less likely to hear what she has to say. When they're out of earshot in the living room, she turns to him in amazement. '*Why* did you go and do that, just as we were doing so well?'

He runs both hands through his hair so that the spikes are exaggerated. Olivia sees the panic in his face. 'I thought it might help her to know I'm making an effort to control this thing.'

'OK, Carlos, for future reference, when people like that come snooping around, you answer their questions and look *responsible*. You don't offer information. You don't take them upstairs and show them your damn dog leashes as if you're some weirdo!' She's so incredulous that she's almost laughing.

'You're right. She looked at me as if I was some kind of pervert when I pulled that sheet back.' He clutches his head in frustration. '*Porra*, what a mess! But, Olivia, I needed her to understand . . .'

'Understand what? These people don't want to understand, Carlos, they want to interfere! They come into our home with their long noses and flapping ears and they hunt for an excuse to declare us unfit parents so that they can *take Leo away*, don't you see?' All traces of laughter disappear as she speaks the dreadful words, and Olivia realises her hands are trembling.

'No way can they take him away,' says Carlos firmly.

'Oh, but they can,' she cries. 'That's what they do, Carlos. You heard what she said – we've got a file now, an official file with the social services, where they'll write that our child has had bruises inflicted on him by his father on two occasions. It's the start of a process; they'll say Leo lives in an abusive environment, that he'd be better off in care . . . It'll build like a snowball until they come and take him from us.' She stops and leans back against the living-room wall with her palms spread against its coolness. Her breathing is shallow and she can hear her heart pounding in her skull.

Carlos sits down hard on the sofa and his head drops into his hands. 'We'll be fine,' he mutters. 'We just need to stay calm.'

'Stay calm? This isn't something to stay calm about.' Olivia struggles for words. 'Look what's happened to us in just a few short weeks – we're black and blue with bruises, threatened on all sides . . . Carlos, I love you, but the situation is spiralling out of control. I am *not* losing my son.'

Carlos jumps up. 'We won't lose him! Olivia, look at me, *minha querida*.' Olivia lifts her eyes to his face. 'Come here,' he says, and pulls her into his arms. Olivia is stiff, resistant. Her thoughts are zigzagging between the social worker's words and Miles' concerned expression when he told her she would have to decide what was most important – her relationship with Carlos, or Leo's safety.

She stops resisting Carlos and relaxes into his embrace, inhaling his scent.

'I need you both,' she murmurs, so softly that Carlos doesn't hear.

Chapter Twenty-five

30 May 1984

'Mãe! Where are you going?'

I run down the stairs in my pyjamas and see two strangers, a man and a woman dressed in the same green and white clothes. Mãe is lying on an ironing board with wheels, and the strangers are taking her down the hall towards the front door, one pushing, one pulling. Mãe looks like a baby bird without her headscarf on. Father's big hand rests on her head as if he's trying to keep her warm.

'Go back upstairs, Carlos,' he says in a tired voice, but Mãe holds out her arms to me and I run to her just as the ironing board reaches the door. I clutch her arm and I know she wants to speak but the plastic tube in her mouth won't let her. Her lovely dark eyes smile at me and I kiss her above the plastic, on her cheek.

'Marina,' says Father. 'Keep Carlos out of the way.'

'No!' I hold Mãe's arm even tighter and she starts to cough, deeper than the river. Her plastic tube mists over and Marina is behind me now, I can smell roses and she pulls me gently away, saying, '*Pronto, pronto, pronto*, Carlitos.' The front door swings open and they take Mãe out, her head bobbing as they lift her down the steps and there's an ambulance, blocking the whole road, waiting to swallow her. Marina has her arms around me in a hug so tight I can't run forwards, even though I want to. Mãe disappears head first into the ambulance and Father climbs in too and then the doors close and it slips away down the hill.

'It's not the end of the world,' Marina is saying into my ear, half singing it, in the voice she uses for bedtime stories, a voice that wants you to breathe more slowly and get sleepy and feel safe. But I don't feel sleepy or safe. I make my whole body stiff against hers but she keeps talking. 'Your *mãe* will come home again soon. That cough, it just got too big and hollow for her poor lungs. The doctors will make it go away.'

I twist around to look at her. Marina is always white under her eyes now and she carries a lavender handkerchief because she says she can smell things more than before. Father made her eat a scallop the other night when she only wanted bread, and Marina pressed the handkerchief to her mouth and ran from the room.

There's something wrong with my chest; it's going up and down fast, in and out, and I can't stop it. It's like crying with no tears. I touch Marina's soft cheek and through all the breath in my chest I say, 'Mãe is going to die.'

Her eyes turn round and black. '*Sim*, Carlitos,' she nods. 'One day, she will leave us. But not yet, I hope.'

We press our foreheads together and I close my eyes tight.

11 June 1984

'I have a new trick, a magician's trick, a circus man's trick!' Pedro leaps off the orange-tree wall when I come up the street after school. He's laughing so hard that I start to laugh as well, even though Mãe has been in the hospital for twelve nights and Father is sad and angry all the time and Marina presses herself into corners and hides from him.

'Show me.' I swing my school bag onto the ground. I don't care what Inês says about keeping it clean.

Pedro grins. His hair looks very dirty today, covered with dust. 'Can't yet. I need props, and my brother won't give me them until tomorrow 'cause that's when my birthday is.'

'Props?'

'Things that help you with a trick. My brother's teaching me the best one he knows and it's better than juggling, better even than fire-eating!'

'But what trick is it?' My knees jiggle in excitement. 'Tell me.'

'It's a hiding sort of trick and I can't do it in this,' he explains, tugging at his T-shirt which has holes you can see his brown skin through. 'It needs long sleeves. My brother might come along and watch when I show it to you, to make sure I get it right.'

He starts to walk up the hill and I pick up my bag and walk beside him, thrilled by the thought that I might meet Pedro's brother. The crow-man is sitting at the side of the road with his hands inside a plastic bag. Maybe there's food in there. I think of the way Pedro dared me to drop the ball.

'I dare you,' I say before I even know what I'm going to say. Pedro stops dead and looks at me and I know he'll do anything I dare him to do. But what should I say? I look around for ideas and see an orange tree. 'I dare you to pick an orange off that tree and offer it to the crow-man.'

Pedro nods and runs to the tree where he jumps for an orange. The first two he tries are too well attached to their twigs, but he manages to twist a third one off. It's not a good one – the skin is loose and dry. Pedro walks straight over to the crow-man and holds out the orange.

The crow-man ignores him for the longest moment, so Pedro shakes the orange in front of his face. Then the crow-man looks up with his fearsome eyes and the growling sound comes from his throat again and he leaps to his feet, knocking the orange from Pedro's hand and roaring in fury. Pedro cries out in fear and sprints up the hill and

I run down it because I'm too scared to pass the crow-man. When I'm around the corner, I peep back to see what he does next. He's pacing up and down in his coat, muttering and shaking his head from side to side so violently I think it could fall off. There's a bad feeling in my chest, as if Pedro and I have done something cruel, like teasing a gorilla in the zoo. The crow-man is strange and nasty, and probably it's better to leave him alone. I imagine him coming after us with a razor in one fist and a dead cat's head in the other, and I shrink back, out of his sight, before jogging to the place where another street starts that will take me home. Halfway up it, Pedro appears, and I think he'll say something about the crow-man and the orange but he just whistles a tune as if nothing happened.

'I'll show you a bird's nest,' he offers, kicking a loose cobblestone ahead of us.

The nest is a stack of twigs and dark feathers high in the crack of a wall just down from my house, near to where I saw Pedro walk off with his brother and the juggling balls. We have to climb a bit of the wall to see it properly, and my feet are slipping on the stone when I hear Marina's voice.

'Carlitos!' She's poking her head out of the front door – Father won't let her go out any more in case the neighbours talk – and her voice is loud on the quiet street. 'Come into the house now, please.' She's agitated, her gaze flying from me to Pedro and back again. She keeps telling me I shouldn't play with him.

My hands let go without thinking and I fall away from the wall, banging my shin. When I look up, Father has joined Marina at the door and they are speaking together. Father looks down the road furiously and I know Marina must have told him something bad about Pedro.

Pedro has gone still, like an animal.

I stoop to get my bag and whisper, 'When will you show me the trick?'

155

'Tomorrow, *sim*?'

'*Está bem*. OK.' I run up the road and duck under Father's arm, which is holding the front door open. He slams it behind me.

'What is happening to this household?' His voice makes me stop dead. I turn to face him, but not before I see Marina's blue dress flash into a doorway. Her expression says: I'm sorry. Be careful. Then she goes away.

Father smells of his coffin cigars and the drink he has in a fat glass every afternoon since Mãe went away. 'The son of the house, playing with street filth!' he shouts. 'You are a Casanova de Albuquerque Moniz, not a homeless vagabond. That boy is beneath you, Carlos. His type will drag you into the dust. You will not go near him again, is that understood?'

I stare at him. In his eyes, I see the wetness of tears.

'Father, he's Pedro. He . . .'

'Marina tells me his brother is a pickpocket, a common thief! Do you want to be sent away to school like your sister?'

'No, no.' I would never see Mãe, never see Marina.

'So you will not speak to him again. Have you heard me?'

He takes a step towards me and I back away, nodding. '*Sim*, Pai.'

'Go to your room,' he says, and sighs.

My feet on the staircase are as heavy as stones. I think of Mãe, thin and hairless, her cough stronger than she is, and Marina's sorry face, and Rosa stuck inside her school, and Pedro whose trick I won't be able to watch. I walk up and up to my bedroom with Father watching me from the hall and my hand goes to the amulet around my neck and I wish for luck.

156

Chapter Twenty-six

It's the strangest sound: a cross between a moan and a suppressed howl. Beside Olivia, Carlos is bucking against his straps. Her heart slams against her ribcage as she sits up in the darkness. He's scrabbling now, pulling and twisting at the dog leashes. The incoherent noise continues, painful to hear.

'It's a *dream*,' she cries. 'You can wake up from it, Carlos, just look around – you're in your bedroom with me, Olivia!'

She puts her hand on his arm but withdraws it quickly; his biceps and triceps are strained to bursting as he grapples with the knots in the leashes and this reminder of his powerfulness scares her. For the past few nights, to spare Olivia the struggle, Carlos has been securing the knots himself and untying them in the mornings. What if he can undo them in his sleep?

'Carlos!'

There's a scything sound as one of the straps is wrenched free, and Carlos sits bolt upright, still moaning. His legs are trapped, but it won't be long before he's free. Olivia rolls out of her side of the bed, her breath hot and dry in her throat. She rushes across the landing into Leo's room, thinking only to protect him. Why the hell was I so insistent about not putting a lock on Leo's door? she berates herself. Inside Leo's room, the air is sweet with the smell of his sleep, but

Leo is awake; in the yellowish street light which shines through his thin curtains, Olivia can see the shape of him huddled on his pillows, his knees drawn to his chest.

'It's OK,' she whispers, closing the door behind her. From the bedroom, there's a crash.

'Sleep monster.' In the dark, Leo's voice is small.

'Yes. We need to stay calm and quiet, Leo.' Olivia is anything but calm as she pushes Leo's chest of drawers across the wooden floorboards to barricade the door, swearing under her breath at the scraping noise it makes. It's heavier than she thought and, when she's only managed to shift it half a metre, it gets stuck on an uneven floorboard so that she has to rush around to the front to lift it free.

As if their desire to hide makes them light up through the fabric of his nightmare, Carlos comes crashing into the room, the sound still raging in his throat. When the door flies open, Olivia is dashed against the wall, her spine bearing the brunt of the impact, and there's a dark sensation of spinning, a grainy view of Leo leaping towards his father's silhouette, screaming.

'My luck!' yells Carlos, and there's a bang which sings through Olivia's head as with a sweep of his arm, Carlos flings Leo's little body against the bedroom wall.

'Get *away* from him!' Olivia sees Leo fall, crumpled, onto his bed.

Carlos is oblivious, his eyes glassy. '*Não, não, não!*' he shrieks in horror. No, no, no! He turns and thuds from the room, his breath hoarse and animal-like. Olivia registers his charge down the stairs as she staggers across to Leo. She pulls herself onto the bed and cradles his thin limbs, his fragile spine.

'Leo, Leo. Tell Mummy where it hurts.'

He is sobbing. 'My arm . . . my head.'

'I'm going to turn on the light so I can see. I'm right here, little boy.' She pulls away from him and, as she stands, she hears the garden gate slam violently. Tweaking the curtain aside, she's just in time to see Carlos running barefoot down the street in his T-shirt and boxers in the direction of the city centre. There's something dark and bulky in his arms but Olivia can't see what it is.

'Christ.' She pulls back from the window, finds the light switch. Leo is half sitting on his blue duvet, his face blotchy and bewildered. There's no sign of any blood. What if Carlos had taken it into his head to grab *Leo* and run off with him into the night? As Olivia inspects her son's arm and head, she realises sickly that if he had, she couldn't have stopped him. Stroking her son's temple, feeling for bruises, she thinks of the violence deep inside her dreaming husband and wonders why his dream attacks are focused on Leo. I'm just someone who gets in his way, she realises, whereas Leo is his target.

When Olivia has finished her inspection and satisfied herself that Leo is not maimed, only bruised and shaken, she folds him into the giant safety of her arms and imagines she is warm enough to heat the world, warm enough to make the sleep monster disappear into the cracks between the floorboards.

'My brave boy,' she whispers.

'Are you OK, Mum?' he asks fearfully, his voice muffled against her neck.

'I'm fine, my sweet.'

'Really, really fine?' He pulls back to see her face, to be certain.

'Yes.' Her jarred spine is throbbing painfully but her voice is resolute.

'Where is . . . he?'

'Running around Lisbon like the silly sleep monster he is,' she says, hoping to raise a smile.

'I don't want him to hurt you again.' Leo is close to tears.

'And I don't want him to hurt *you*.' She tugs him closer, her arms fiercely protective. 'I wish you didn't have to experience these things.'

She would do anything to feel the anxiety lifting from Leo's limbs and see his smile. He smells intoxicating; a mixture of the baby he once was and the fresh little boy he is now. She can smell the remnants of kiwi bubble bath mingled with the summer-air smell of his pyjamas, pulled that morning from the washing line where they'd absorbed such intensive sunlight that they were bone dry within an hour. The slightly bitter smell of fearful sweat and dreams lingers around his neck. She rocks him, rocks him.

When she's sure that Leo is sound asleep, Olivia hurries into the dark and silent garden. The force of Carlos slamming the slatted wooden gate made it ricochet back, and it has come to rest slightly open. Yellow street light pools uneasily on the cobbled pavement stones. It's the early hours of Tuesday morning, and a swift glance up and down the street reveals nothing, nobody, only trees and rubbish bins and a great canopy of stars. Olivia closes the gate and sits down at the mosaic-tiled metal table on the lawn to wait, her dressing gown glowing palely in the night. For company, she lights the stained-glass lantern they keep on the table. The air is ominously quiet, and her worry transfers to Carlos, lost out there somewhere, alone and not in his right senses. Should she call the police? And tell them what?

'My husband is roaming the streets. He may be in danger. Would you mind helping me find him? No, he's definitely not drunk. Just asleep. No, he doesn't do drugs ... no, he isn't a pervert ...' Convincing the Lisbon police to do something about a sleepwalking husband could be complicated, unless she convinces them that Carlos is a potential danger to others – which, at the moment, unconscious and crazed, he is. But if the police got involved, if they saw how insane Carlos is when he's dreaming, would they try to take Leo away? Olivia puts her head in her hands, deliberating. After a time, she discards the idea. Carlos wouldn't thank her for involving the authorities in his illness – that's how she thinks of it now, as a destructive disease moving from phase to hideous phase. It's been a month since it started – a month today, in fact. It's like a temporary madness, she thinks; the liberation of some deeply unconscious drive. Sort of like a Jekyll and Hyde thing, a monstrous transformation . . . but now she's only frightening herself.

'Shut up,' she whispers, clenching her fists on the tabletop.

Twenty long minutes tick by, and then Carlos appears at the gate. His face is pale, coursing with sweat. He has ditched whatever it was that he'd carried off in his arms.

'Carlos!' Olivia jumps to her feet and approaches him warily. Is he awake or asleep? She searches his eyes in the gloom.

'Olivia,' he murmurs, sounding lost.

'Come here, my darling,' she says, opening the gate and tugging him inside the garden by his arm. Carlos allows himself to be guided into a seat at the garden table. Olivia remains standing and watches him closely, noticing in the steady light of the lantern that his eyes are filmy but his blink rate is normal. He's awake, but dazed, she decides. Her gaze slips down his blue surf T-shirt and boxers to his bare feet. She winces. The edges look torn up – and is that blood, making them glisten? 'Oh Carlos, your poor feet. Have you been running barefoot across the whole of Lisbon?' She thinks of tetanus shots, embedded glass fragments. She'll have to disinfect his wounds. But first, very quickly, she must ask him before he forgets. 'What was the dream about?'

Carlos shrugs, an uncertain, almost non-existent gesture. 'I think I was just running away from something terrible,' he says eventually, his voice old and cracked as if his throat is raw, which it must be after all that running, thinks Olivia. 'I woke up sprinting through the streets past the Sé Catedral,' he adds. 'When I realised I'd been dreaming, I turned and jogged home again.'

'And what was the terrible thing you were running from?' she prods.

'I don't know.' This time the answer comes too fast.

161

'Tell me,' urges Olivia, and she moves forwards to stroke his head, holding it lightly against her chest. 'Please, just tell me what it was.'

'I think –' He stops, biting his lip.

'What?' She leans in close.

'*É capaz de ter sido um morto.*' It might have been a dead person. Olivia shivers. 'Why do you think he or she was chasing you?'

Carlos sighs. 'Not chasing,' he mumbles. 'He was behind me.'

'Behind you? Who was it?'

'I don't know. Just a dead person behind me.'

Olivia can feel emotions rolling off him in dark, sinuous waves. He's exhausted, she realises. 'Let's get you inside and have a look at that foot.'

They walk together into the house, Carlos hobbling now that the anaesthesia of sleep is wearing off. Olivia settles him in the kitchen and ducks into the bathroom to get what she needs. As she starts rooting about in the cupboard under the basin for an antiseptic, she is overwhelmed by a feeling of isolation. This, she thinks, is a bit like how it must feel to lose a husband to a degenerative disease like Alzheimer's. With every new phase of the illness, they slip further from you, further from the person they used to be, and all you can do is sit close to them giving what comfort you can, while they gradually disappear before your eyes, losing piece after piece of themselves.

She hurries back into the kitchen with a bottle of Dettol antibacterial solution, a wad of cotton, a box of plasters and some tweezers. Carlos is sitting quietly at the table, his head bowed and his eyes far away, lost in nightmares. Where is the man I married? thinks Olivia, and part of her instantly scoffs at her own melodrama.

'Give me your foot,' she says, sitting beside him and pulling her white dressing gown briskly aside, out of reach of any blood. Obediently, Carlos raises his left leg and lays it across her bare knees. The sole of his foot is filthy, bloodied and rent with tiny lacerations, as though he'd run over a beer bottle smashed to smithereens. Frowning, Olivia begins the work of cleaning and disinfecting his foot and extracting slivers of amber-coloured glass from the flesh. Carlos doesn't make a sound, but she feels him jerk involuntarily from time to time when she digs the tweezers into a particularly vulnerable spot. When she glances up at him, his gaze is not on his foot, but on her face.

'Olivia, I am so very sorry for putting you through this,' he tells her. Whenever he's tired, his accent is stronger; the words run together with a distinctive Portuguese lilt. For a long moment, Olivia pauses in her work to look at him.

'I know you're sorry, Carlos,' she says eventually, and her voice sounds strangled. 'But it's not OK. None of this –' she gestures helplessly towards his foot with her tweezers '– none of this is OK. You hurt Leo, do you remember?'

Carlos jerks forwards so that his foot slips out of her hand. 'Hurt him?'

'You shoved him against the wall. He'll have bruises on his head and all down his arm.'

'I'll go to him.' With an anguished twist of his body, he starts to get up but Olivia raises her hand like a stop signal. 'He's sleeping,' she says firmly. 'Let him sleep.'

Carlos lowers himself heavily into his seat and submits to Olivia's tweezers again.

'I just want Leo, you – all of us – to be safe,' Olivia tells him.

'I know,' he says in the feeble old man's voice he has brought back with him tonight. 'I do, too.'

Olivia experiences a pang of desolation. Whatever he says, I'm all alone, she thinks. He has no control over this thing; getting my family through this is down to me. What will happen to our marriage, our family life, if I make Carlos leave? I'll be even more alone, but at least my son won't have to suffer like this any more. She thinks of

Leo, huddled under his sheet, bruises no doubt rising under his skin as he sleeps. Her gaze drops to Carlos' foot and she bends low over her work so that he can't see the flare of tears in her eyes.

'There was this . . . this voice,' says Carlos suddenly.

Olivia's grip tightens on his foot. 'What voice?'

'When I was coming out of the dream. It was a very powerful male voice and it kept repeating, *"Tens que esquecer isso."* You must forget.'

She stares at him, the tweezers hard and surgical between her fingers. 'Forget what?'

'I have no idea.' Carlos frowns, massaging his forehead with his forefinger and thumb. 'It was a very strong voice, it went right through my mind. You don't think it's a sign of schizophrenia, do you? Hearing voices like that?'

Before Olivia has a chance to form a reply, the doorbell chimes, making them both jump.

'Oh, for God's sake.' Olivia throws the tweezers down on the table. 'Why can't those two just leave us alone?'

'Senhor António and Senhora Madalena?'

She nods grimly. 'Bloody neighbours.' She can't face another confrontation.

'I'll go,' says Carlos, and before she can protest he is limping from the kitchen.

'Put your slippers on,' she says urgently.

'They'll get bloody.'

'Then we'll wash them. Carlos, no one must see your feet.' Nothing, she thinks, could be a clearer sign that Carlos was completely out of his mind while he ran through the streets. To not even notice such lacerations! Carlos slides his slippers on and she hears him go through the living room and open the front door. Olivia stoops to wipe at a smear of blood on the tiled kitchen floor, hiding the evidence. Not that Carlos will let them into the house; hopefully

164

he'll send them packing within minutes. Voices in his head, she thinks. Christ.

Male voices float to her ears, but it isn't Senhor António at the door. Alarmed, Olivia gets up and moves cautiously into the living room. Through the window, she sees something that makes her stop dead: flashing blue lights.

Someone has called the police on them.

Chapter Twenty-seven

Olivia freezes in the living room, not trusting herself to join Carlos at the door. From here, she can hear everything; there are two policemen, one older, the other much younger by the sound of his voice.

'. . . disorderly behaviour. Was that you, Senhor?'

'I was out running,' replies Carlos, 'but I wouldn't say I was being disorderly.'

'We were informed that you were heard howling, and that you were running barefoot,' says the younger officer tightly.

'I just decided to go for a late-night jog.' Carlos tries to laugh. 'I'd had a few drinks and I needed to clear my head.'

'You were drunk, you say? So drunk that you didn't put on appropriate footwear before leaving the house for a jog?' The older policeman sounds sceptical.

'Uh, that's right, I was . . . drunk.'

Olivia winces; Carlos really isn't the best liar. Oh, Carlos, if they breathalyse you now . . .! she thinks.

'Is that blood on the floor?'

'Ah . . . *sim.*'

They'll come in now, Olivia thinks despairingly. They'll discover Leo's bruises.

'Now I know why people usually wear running shoes when they go jogging in the city,' Carlos jokes weakly.

'Would you mind removing your slipper?'

Olivia can hear Carlos fumbling about. She is wired with tension, ready to rush through and defend him.

'Your foot is lacerated.' There's a disbelieving pause. 'Yet you've been standing on it showing no sign of pain. Does it not hurt?'

'It's beginning to.'

'Senhor, have you been taking illegal substances?'

'*Não, nada.* No, nothing.'

'We'll see about that.' There's the snap of a pad opening, and the older officer's voice is anything but friendly. 'Your full name, please.'

'Carlos Aníbal Alfredo Casanova de Albuquerque Moniz.'

'You're Aníbal Alfredo's son?' The older officer's tone changes.

'*Sim.*'

'A fine man.'

'He was,' agrees Carlos hopefully.

'And a tragic end.' The officer clears his throat and Olivia thinks of Carlos' father, who died of love; took his own life to end his grief for his wife.

'It was a terrible shock,' says Carlos. 'My sister found him.'

There's a pause. Olivia senses the policeman weighing Carlos' bad behaviour against loyalty to a dead friend. *Let it go*, she pleads silently.

'It's a sorry day when a child finds her father dead. I trust your sister is well?'

'She is, she is, *graças a Deus*. Did you know my father well?'

'*Claro*. Aníbal was a fantastic Sueca player. We used to play in the Eduardo VII club house.'

'He did love playing cards,' Carlos says with a false heartiness that makes Olivia's lips twitch.

'Does Aníbal have any grandchildren?'

'Only one. My little son, Leo. Of course, Father didn't live long enough to meet him.'

'*Pois*. True. The lad's in the house now, with you in this state?'

'Yes, but his mother is here. I'd never leave him on his own.'

There's another pause.

'Now, I know that no son of Aníbal would do anything too irresponsible, am I right?'

'Absolutely right. I just had a bit too much to drink, that's all. I rarely drink, have no head for it. I'm very sorry for the disturbance and I can assure you it won't happen again.'

'Make sure it doesn't, son. Consider this a verbal warning.'

The policemen take their leave. Olivia slinks back into the kitchen, and Carlos joins her a moment later. He leans against the door jamb and looks at her tiredly.

'I feel like I'm doing nothing but lying,' he says. 'And now I'm lying my head off to the police. I told them I'd been drinking.'

'I heard you.' They exchange a long look.

'You're still bleeding like mad,' says Olivia, looking at his slippers. 'Come and sit down again, let me bandage those feet.'

'First I'm going to check on Leo.'

'Carlos, don't walk blood all over the house!' protests Olivia, but he's gone. Olivia listens to his hesitant steps climbing the stairs, and tears gather behind her eyes as she begins to rehearse in her head how she's going to tell him what she knows she has to tell him very soon – that he can't stay in the house with them any more.

'Were you the one who telephoned the police last night?'

Olivia has collared Senhor António as he walks past the garden gate in his dark business suit, on his way to the private car park he uses. It's already eleven o'clock and what feels like a pre-storm breeze is blowing. Olivia has just let in a windswept Rosa to look

168

after Leo so that she can deliver a painting downtown and meet the dreamworker, Miles, for a talk. Leo is bruised and silent this morning, and since six o'clock Olivia has kept him company as he lies on his floor drawing endless patterns of dolphins. She's keeping him out of school today.

Stopped in his tracks by her voice, Senhor António spins slowly around on his polished shoes and looks straight at her. 'We were woken by shouting again, and I saw your husband tearing out of the house – barefoot, for goodness' sake – with what looked like something bundled up in a coat.' He pushes his silver hair back into place as the wind snatches it. 'He was making the most peculiar noises, as if he were in pain. I thought it best . . .'

'Oh, please don't make out you called the police out of noble reasons!' she exclaims in frustration. 'You just don't want to be disturbed at night, and although that's fair enough –'

'Your husband is turning into a public danger.' Senhor António's mouth is a hard line.

Olivia blinks at him, wondering at the speed at which their polite relationship is deteriorating. She'd felt that these were neighbours who could be relied on in a crisis, and Senhor António's reaction makes her feel isolated. 'Don't you realise my husband is ill? These nocturnal attacks . . .' Her hands float in the air. 'We're seeing a sleep specialist this week.'

He looks at her with no trace of regret. 'What did the police do?'

'Olivia, telephone's ringing!' Rosa appears at the door looking witchy in a black shift dress. 'Shall I answer it?' she adds when she sees Senhor António.

'Um, no, it might be . . . I'm coming.' Olivia turns back to him. 'I'm sorry we've disturbed your sleep three times now. But until we get to the bottom of whatever's causing Carlos' episodes, what we could really do with is a bit of neighbourly understanding.' She curls her fists to stop her fingers shaking, and walks back into the house without giving Senhor António a chance to reply. Rosa pats her on the shoulder as she passes.

It's Professora Celeste, calling to enquire about Leo's absence, as Olivia had known she would. She tries to erase from her voice the emotions her encounter with Senhor António has raised, but she sounds breathless, a little wobbly as she lies. 'He's got a temperature, he's in bed.'

'So there hasn't been a further . . . problem?' insists the teacher.

'No. Not at all. I was just up with him most of the night.' That last part at least is true, but when Olivia hangs up she feels sick.

Rosa is watching her. '*Está tudo tão complicado!* It's all so complicated,' she sympathises.

'And I hate lying.'

'This psychologist you're seeing, she'll have some answers,' soothes Rosa.

'She'd better.'

Chapter Twenty-eight

Miles looks fresh and healthy in a denim shirt. Olivia is surprised to find herself smiling as she walks to his table and sits down opposite him. There's something very reassuring – sane, even – about Miles and, as she slings her bag over the wicker chair arm, she relaxes.

'It was sweet of you to meet me on such short notice.'

'Not a problem, Olivia,' he says warmly. 'Is everything OK? You sounded a little fraught on the phone.'

'I *am* fraught.' Quickly, she fills him in on Carlos' latest episode. They're in Café Amarelo again and the wind is blowing in gusts through the open doors, making the overhead fans wobble on their fittings and paper napkins skitter off the tables.

'This incident happened last night?' Miles' eyes move cautiously over her face and then down her bare arms, as if he's looking for bruising and hopes not to find any.

'At around four-thirty this morning, yes.' Olivia is pleased her spine isn't visible; there's something shameful about being bruised-up and she knows her walk is stiffer than usual, even the set of her shoulders is tenser as her body tries to avoid sudden movements that might aggravate the pain.

'Well, you know, there are stories of sleep disorder sufferers who leave their homes in the night and walk into lakes, drive vehicles, run through the streets to escape hallucinated threats such as a burning house or a bomb attack. Jessica told me of one woman who crawled around trying to find her husband's gun, which he kept under the bed. Luckily, he woke up and stopped her before she found it. Some people bolt into the air as if they're bouncing up from a trampoline. There are some really active dreamers out there.' He smiles a little. 'Your husband's not alone.'

'But he's hardly in what I'd call good company! How do these people's families cope?'

'Well, I have to admit I did a bit of reading up on the internet.' Miles pauses to take a sip of his latte.

'Oh, I tried that, too. I found everything and nothing – the word "nightmare" had something like forty million hits, and when I typed "moving nightmare", all I found were comments by people who'd had a nightmare moving house!' Olivia smiles slightly. 'And when I finally started getting somewhere, it all got a bit dark – you know what it's like on the internet – you look up something innocuous like "headache" and it immediately screams "brain tumour". It's scary, it amplifies everything.' She shrugs. 'I ended up on mental health sites and it freaked me out. I sort of gave up after that.'

'I think "violent moving nightmares" was what worked for me, and I instantly found a lot of pretty crazy stuff,' says Miles. 'Some of it was fascinating though. Some sufferers use water beds and barricades of cushions to help protect themselves and their bed partners from violent movements. Others do as Carlos is doing, and tie themselves down at night with ropes. One man ties himself to his *wife*! Still others sleep alone in a locked room on a mattress on the floor. One guy actually calms his wife down by becoming part of her dream. He'll join in with the action, you know? She'll crouch down on the floor while she's dreaming and scrabble around and he'll say, "What are we doing?" and she'll be like, "We're lifting the roof off the house."' He chuckles.

172

Olivia flicks a strand of hair off her face with a wry smile. 'I bet Carlos' dreams would look like a horror movie clip to anyone on the outside.'

He nods uneasily. 'I believe they would.'

'I think he's dreaming exactly the same dream each time, and it's going a stage further now – you know, with the running.' Olivia frowns. 'I'm trying to work out what happens in the dream. Oh –' she claps a hand to her mouth as she remembers. 'He said there was a dead person behind him.'

'Wow.' For a moment, they look at each other in silence. 'Well, dreams that re-enact real life events are common,' says Miles thoughtfully, 'so this might throw some light on what actually happened in Carlos' past. One mother I read about dreamed she was putting a doll she'd bought for her little daughter under the Christmas tree, but really what she did was take her one-year-old child from her crib and put *her* under the tree.'

'She carried her baby through the house while she was dreaming? Oh, God.'

'Yeah, and there was a young lad who had recurrent moving dreams about saving his sister from drowning after their car went off a cliff. This was a real-life event he subsequently couldn't let go of in his dreams. Weirdly, he later transferred this dream scenario on to his wife, acting out almost identical scenarios with her in the key role. And he never remembers the dreams; his wife has to piece them together from things he shouts out and actions he performs during his episodes.'

Olivia sits very still. 'So maybe this dead person in Carlos' dream scenario is being transferred on to Leo, which would explain why he goes for Leo each time.'

'Each time? You mean he's hurt him before?'

'Yes. I'm sorry I didn't mention it sooner. I didn't know you well enough to trust you. Already we've had the social services round because of his bruises . . .' She tails off. 'I'm so scared of losing him.'

'Oh.' Miles sighs, looking at her with great concern so that Olivia feels compelled to confide in him.

'The police showed up at the door last night,' she says. 'Somehow Carlos blagged his way out of getting any more than a verbal warning.' She sighs, twisting the heavy turquoise ring she wears on her middle finger. 'But still, if the police get involved again, we won't be half as lucky as we were this time. And Carlos . . . well, like I said, he hurt Leo.'

Miles leans across the table. 'You *have* to get either Leo or Carlos out of the house right away.'

'I know, I was geared up to tell Carlos this morning, but before I could say anything, he pointed out that we've only got two nights to get through until we see the specialist and if I tie him up so all the knots are out of his reach, we'll be fine.'

'How do you know that?' He shakes his head.

'He only managed to undo them because he tied them and untied them himself,' insists Olivia, her fingers leaving her ring to turn her water glass around and around on the table. 'Leo has barely spoken all morning and I don't want to traumatise him even more by making *him* leave the house – none of this is his fault, after all.'

Miles' silence is not one of agreement. It's saying quite clearly that Olivia shouldn't give Leo any choice in the matter. He watches her sombrely.

'You don't agree,' she says.

'No, I don't. Olivia, I know it's not my place to say this, but it seems to me you're in denial about the fact that your family is in such jeopardy that you need to get either Leo or Carlos out of the house.' He pauses. 'And logically, it should be Carlos who goes, since then both you and Leo can sleep safely. I know breaking up a living arrangement, even temporarily, can be pretty horrendous – I had to do it myself when my ex-wife became an alcoholic – but in your case I really can't see another choice.'

'Do you have kids?'

He shakes his head. 'We were planning a family but Fran's drinking got out of control and then everything sort of fell apart. She moved out, and back in, and out again . . . Eventually we realised it wasn't going to work.'

'That must've been tough.' Olivia thinks of her and Carlos' second baby whose existence still hangs in the balance.

Miles eyes her kindly. 'People can get used to anything, although I know sometimes it's hard to believe that.'

'I *have* taken your point, Miles,' she assures him. 'I don't know, I'm just blindly pinning all my hopes on this psychologist friend of yours, as if all our problems will dissolve in two day's time when we see her. Silly, I know.'

'Well, she's good, but she's not a miracle worker. She'll do her best for you.' Miles leans back in his chair and runs a hand through his fair hair. 'Your husband sounds as if he's getting more extreme with each episode, though, that's what worries me. Apart from sensing this dead person behind him in last night's dream, has he got no other memory of what he dreams?'

'The only other thing he could recall was a deep, authoritative voice saying, "You must forget."'

'Interesting. It would seem to support the theory that he's trying to suppress some ancient trauma. Perhaps he'd like to do some regressive work? I know a Portuguese woman in Baixa who uses a great combo of hypnosis, body wisdom and Active Imagination.'

'I'll ask him. I'm guessing he'd try anything right now; he's desperate to keep our family under one roof.'

'And you are too,' observes Miles. 'But don't take risks, Olivia. This thing could explode again any time, any night, and I for one feel anxious about just how Carlos' nightmare ends.'

'What do you mean?'

'Well, who is this dead person? Is it a real person, or a symbolic dead person? If it's someone real, then how did he or she die, and who – if anyone – killed him?' Miles lays his hands palms-down on the table and looks at them for a moment before raising his gaze to Olivia's face. 'Olivia, I don't want to frighten you, but if Leo is taking the role of this person in his father's dreams, he could be in line for something unspeakable. You *have* to react.'

Olivia covers her face with both hands and she barely feels Miles' cool fingers touching her arms, pulling them gently from her face. She opens her eyes but instead of seeing Miles, she sees the image his words have conjured: Carlos, glassy-eyed, slamming Leo repeatedly against a wall until it flows red with blood.

Chapter Twenty-nine

12 June 1984

My room is full of sword blades made from the light coming through my shutters. Today is Pedro's birthday, the day of the magic trick. I want to watch the trick, but what if Father finds out I've seen Pedro and sends me away to boarding school? I stumble out of bed with a bang that makes Father grumble somewhere down the corridor. Inês has laid out my clothes for the day, as usual, and I throw off my pyjamas and pull on my white shirt. Father opens the door as I'm struggling with the buttons. He's nearly as tall as the ceiling, which means he's got his outdoor shoes on, not just his slippers, and he's smart in his linen jacket.

'What was all that noise about?' he asks, and I smile at him, on my best behaviour.

'*Bom dia,* Pai.' Good morning, Father.

He steps over and buttons my shirt right up to the collar so it squeezes my neck. 'I'm going to visit your mother.'

I stare at him. Mãe has been in the hospital much longer than Marina said she would be. 'I want to see her.' I press my teeth hard together to stop myself from crying.

Father's voice is kind. 'Next time, if she's still not home, I'll take you with me. Now be good, and tonight at dinner I'll tell you how your mother is.'

Then he goes. I listen to his footsteps all the way down the staircase and out of the house. The front door shuts behind him and I know he'll be away all day, because he always is when he visits her.

After school, Pedro is waiting for me on the wall, juggling. He isn't wearing special birthday clothes, just a long-sleeved shirt so big and loose it comes to his knees, and which maybe very long ago used to be purple but is now more of a funny grey. His bare feet grip the wall and when he sees me he laughs excitedly.

'Trick time,' he says, and jumps down to meet me so the balls fall everywhere. As we chase them, Pedro says, 'My brother showed me a secret place – we can go there to do the trick.'

I mean to tell him that I'm not allowed to see him any more, but instead as I find the last ball, I say, 'Happy birthday – *parabéns*!'

He nods as he puts the balls into his bag. He is pleased about something, his head bobbing as if he's dancing as we start the steep climb with the river blue at our backs. I know he's thinking about his trick. His shoulder bag bulges with secrets. From one corner of it, material flutters as bright as Mãe's headscarves. I think of rabbits coming out of hats, a dove flying from Pedro's big sleeve.

The crow-man is sitting against a wall further up the street. He is all in black and smells of rotten potatoes. His legs are stretched in an open triangle in front of him. When we walk past, he raises his head and hisses like a snake. I look at Pedro and Pedro is looking at the man and whistling at the same time, as if nothing the man does frightens him. But I know Pedro is ready to run. I am, too. I stay close to him, my heart bumping in time with my feet.

'*Maluco*,' says Pedro when we've passed him. 'Mad.' He spits into the dust.

'What'd we do if he came after us?' I whisper.

'I would fly like an eagle, straight up into the sky,' he says and points his arms up, the palms tight together. Then he drops his arms. 'Or I'd throw a stone at his head. What would you do, Carlos?'

I try to think of the worst thing. 'I'd tie him to an ironing board and put him into a white ambulance and he wouldn't be allowed to come back here.'

Pedro laughs and smacks my shoulder to make me laugh too and then he stops walking and I know we've come to the secret place, only it doesn't look secret at all, just a high, narrow bit of the same street.

'I have no birthday gift,' I tell him. 'What can I give you?'

Pedro looks around him at the baskets of red flowers under people's windows, the washing blowing in the breeze, polythene sheets flapping blackly from a covered building site, the caged yellow budgerigars who sit all day on their perches and sing. For a moment I think he's going to dare me to get one of these things and I'm ready to climb the rough stone walls and fetch whatever he wants. But then his eyes stop at my neck. I opened the top buttons as soon as I was sure Father had gone this morning, and Pedro is looking straight at my lucky sapphire amulet. I clutch it in my fist and he laughs.

'Just let me try it on?' he asks. '*Só um minuto* – just for a minute, so I can have good luck, too?'

I take a deep breath. The amulet is cold. I think of the luck of the Casanovas de Albuquerque Moniz: my mother's luck, Marina's, Rosa's. 'It's *our* luck, not just anyone's,' I tell Pedro.

'But luck is like magic, everyone can have a bit, there's always some left over.' Pedro's violet eyes are hopeful and I remember he is my brother who tried to teach me how to juggle and showed me how to get to the centre of the sun and is about to show me his greatest ever trick.

'*Está bem*,' I say. 'All right.'

His eyes flash and he pulls me across the street by the elbow. 'In

179

here, where there's nobody to see.' He pulls back part of a wall that's made not of stone but of black plastic. It scrapes and bends and when Pedro has squeezed through the gap, he holds it open and I squeeze through too, holding my breath.

Inside, it's so quiet. Dust floats on the sunlight and I look up to see the blue, faraway sky. Criss-crossing the blue are slices of stone and I can see this used to be a house but builders have knocked most of it down so the sunshine is everywhere, making every speck of dust stand out. The walls are crumbling pale stone and there are broken off bits of stone all over the ground. For a few moments, we just look around, touching the things we see. Then Pedro whispers, 'Your lucky necklace, Carlos.'

My feet slip on broken stones as I struggle to undo the amulet's gold chain. Pedro has to help me.

When I've fixed it around his neck it sits like a blue star against his tanned throat and he laughs his blackbird laugh and spins in happy circles, shining in the sunlight that drops right on to his head. He looks very lucky to me and I'm about to tell him so when there's a scraping sound and Pedro stops spinning, his eyes go wide and I look behind me, my spine already crawling.

Somebody is coming through the plastic wall, I can hear him breathing as if he ran up the hill, and in all the strange white sunshine I can't see who it is but it's someone *big* . . .

Chapter Thirty

When Olivia arrives back home after meeting Miles, Carlos is lying bare-chested on the grass in the garden, tightening the brakes on Leo's bike, which is turned neatly upside down. 'The brakes were already getting sluggish,' he says when she comes through the gate. 'And yesterday the chain fell off. I'm not happy with the quality, it's not safe for Leo.'

'How's Leo doing?' Olivia drops her bag on the grass and kicks her sandals off. It's a hot, still day and Carlos has beads of sweat across his shoulders.

'He seems a bit brighter. Rosa's taken him off for a walk around the castle ramparts.'

'Oh, good, I've been worrying about how he's been getting on today, he was so silent this morning. How was the shoot?' She tucks her skirt under her and sits beside him, trying to hide her nervousness. The grass is so dry she can feel it spiking through the thin material.

'Not bad. My feet were crying out in pain, though.' He wiggles them and Olivia leans down to look at the stripped-off flesh.

'Ouch. You need more antiseptic cream.'

'Later.' He fiddles with the spanner, squinting against the sun, and checks the brakes, spinning the wheel and then applying them so that the wheel stops with a shudder.

'If you tighten them too much, he'll go over the handlebars.'

'They need to be good and responsive.'

Olivia pulls her hair out of its band and shakes it out over her shoulders. She is uncertain how to begin the conversation she knows they must have, and finds herself side-tracking. 'Before I forget, Carlos, Miles says he knows a woman in Baixa who does regressive therapy work. Would you want to give it a try?'

'Miles?' Carlos lifts his head. 'The dreamworker?'

'Yes. He thinks –'

'Wait – when did you see him?'

'Today,' she admits. 'I wanted to talk to him after you came back covered in blood.'

Carlos absorbs this for a moment. 'What else did he say?'

Olivia repeats Miles' latest stories of sleep-disorder sufferers, which Carlos listens to in silence. When she's finished, he frowns across the garden at the flowering oleander bush and the scattering of Leo's stones beneath it.

'I think Miles is mungering . . . What's the word? Spreading . . . making fear out of nothing.'

'Oh, he's *not* scaremongering, Carlos, and you can hardly call our situation nothing. Anyway . . .' She takes a deep breath. 'I really need to talk to you about something.'

Carlos tosses the spanner onto the grass and wipes his hands on his cut-off jeans. 'What?'

She twists a blade of grass between her fingers, snapping it. 'It's become too risky for us all to sleep in the same house together.'

He tenses. 'What are you saying?'

'I'm really sorry,' she says slowly, 'but I don't want you sleeping here any more.'

'You're kicking me out?' His eyes widen in shock.

'Things have gone way too far.'

He holds up a hand. 'One moment, Olivia. After agreeing this morning that you'd tie me up for the next two nights to make sure you and Leo stay safe, you meet up with the dreamworker, have a nice cosy coffee and share all your troubles with him, and now he's convinced you that rather than doing what we agreed, you should instead throw me, your husband, out of the family home. Is that right?'

Olivia stands up, flustered. 'It's not that simple, Carlos, and you know it.'

'What is it with this man?' He looks hurt and puzzled. 'You *like* him, or something?'

'Carlos!'

'No, don't make this face, Olivia.' He sits up. 'I'm really asking you.'

'Only as a friend! How can you even ask?'

'A friend doesn't encourage you to split up your family.'

'He's seen my bruises, Carlos. It's been a month, and things are only getting worse. I told him you'd hurt Leo . . .'

Carlos baulks visibly. 'What were you thinking? He might contact the police, we don't know this man well. How can you take such a risk?'

Olivia waves his words away. 'Miles won't say a word.' She looks directly at him. 'The biggest risk I'm taking with Leo is letting him sleep under the same roof as you.'

Carlos says nothing for a moment, then drops his gaze. 'It's true. The biggest danger my son has in his life is me, his own father.'

'So you understand why you have to leave?' she asks gently.

'No, I don't understand.' He looks up, cajoling. 'We're seeing the doctor the day after tomorrow. Why not wait until then? Leo can go to Rosa's, and you tie me up and sleep beside me, like we agreed.' He holds his arms out to her. 'What's the worry?'

Olivia makes no move towards him. 'No, Carlos, it's simpler if you just go.'

He drops his arms. 'You *want* me to go?'

'No, of course not.'

'Then I won't go.' He leaps to his feet, grimacing as the grass spikes into his wounds. 'Olivia, I am your husband. We stay together, through everything, *sim*?' He walks to her and stands very close, but doesn't touch her. Olivia can feel the space between them hum as her body responds to his closeness. '*Querida*,' he says softly. 'You are where I want to be. Please don't make me leave.'

Olivia puts her fingers briefly over her eyes, searching her mind for the rest of her carefully prepared arguments. 'Carlos, this isn't fair,' she bursts out, stepping away from him, onto the garden path. 'Don't you dare try to convince me to let you stay when you know how badly you've hurt Leo and I. Why the hell should Leo be expelled from the house? He hasn't done anything wrong. I'm worried about him – he's hardly spoken since you flung him against the wall, he's not himself, he's fearful, unhappy. Why should *he* leave?'

'Only two nights!' Carlos holds up two fingers. 'Two nights with his Aunt Rosa, who he loves, and who can help him better than we can at the moment, then we see the doctor and she cures me.'

'Oh, it's going to be that simple, is it?'

'Why not? Why should it not be simple? None of us deserve to have to live like this.'

Olivia turns away from him, needing a moment to think.

'We're married, Olivia. You're my wife.'

'Yes. But Leo is our son and we have to protect him.'

Carlos comes up behind her and wraps his arms around her. Before she's aware of it, her hand goes up to stroke the dark hairs on his forearm. She watches as an orange butterfly settles, trembling, on a leaf.

'You might kill him,' she says clearly.

Carlos turns her around in a flash, his hands curled around her upper arms. 'Don't say that. Don't tempt fate.'

'But you might!' she cries. 'How does the dream end, Carlos? Does it end with death?'

With a sound of frustration, he releases her. 'I don't know.'

'You have to remember. And until you remember, I can't let you sleep in this house.'

Carlos presses his hands to his temples. 'Don't do this. *Don't* break up our family, Olivia.'

'It would only be for a short time. This isn't the end of anything.'

'It's a first step towards the end, can't you see that? Olivia, our marriage is stronger than these nightmares. Our *family* is stronger than a few violent dreams. Don't you believe that?'

Olivia looks into his eyes and is shocked by the desperation she sees there. 'Carlos, of *course* I believe it.'

'Two more nights,' he pleads. 'Leo stays with Rosa, I stay with you. Then we see the doctor together.'

She sighs. 'And then?'

'Then we talk again.' He reaches out with both hands and cups her face, then slides his fingers through her hair so that her scalp tingles.

Olivia closes her eyes, lets him support the weight of her head.

Chapter Thirty-one

At Rosa's last night, Leo barely slept for worry that he wouldn't be able to help his mum if the sleep monster came. Rosa brought him home straight after breakfast but he knows he'll be staying with her again tonight, and although he loves his aunt, he feels unsettled. It's a Wednesday but he didn't have to go to school today, so he's been playing half-heartedly in the garden all day.

Now he watches as his mother comes out of her studio, drying her hands on a paint-smeared cloth, which she then drapes over the back of a garden chair to dry in the sun. She has the look on her face again, it's almost the same look she has when Leo has a fever; her face is all intense and worried, scared. He knows from this look that she's been working on the painting of his father's nightmare. She won't let anyone else see it but Leo knows it must be horrible to make her so upset each time.

She looks up and sees him. 'Everything OK?'

Leo stands holding two pebbles in his hand which he click-clicks together. 'Why did you work on that painting again?'

Olivia looks surprised. 'You know why – to see if it helps your dad remember his bad dream.'

'But you're afraid of it.'

'Afraid?' Leo can see the movement of his mother's throat as she swallows, and it must be uncomfortable because her fingers go there briefly. 'I don't know that it's fear, Leo,' she says then. 'I just feel . . . the painting is getting a little too powerful, you know?'

Leo nods. He knows. It can happen with anything – teddy bears can grow hideous in the dark, their faces filled with menace. Even fathers can turn into monsters. Just as he thinks this, Carlos emerges from the house and his hand flies out towards Leo's head, so that Leo shies away in sudden fear.

'Leo!' exclaims Carlos, distressed, and Leo understands that this isn't a daylight version of the sleep monster, but only his father wanting to place his big hand on Leo's head the way he always does, as if he's checking he's still there.

'Sorry,' Leo whispers guiltily.

'Sweetheart, don't be scared of your dad,' says Olivia, and he can hear by her voice that she's as shocked as Carlos. He doesn't know how to reply so he spins away from them both and runs to the garden gate. The gate is slatted wood and in the wood there are hundreds of tiny holes.

He hears his father sigh. 'He has every right to be scared of me.'

'Which is why you need to be flexible about our sleeping arrangements.'

'*Por favor*, Olivia, leave it.'

Leo can hear Carlos walking down the path towards him, limping slightly. He knows his father will want to talk, but talking to him is harder now that he looks more and more like the sleep monster, even during the day. There's less to say, the words don't come up the way they used to. But Carlos just crouches next to Leo and says, 'We've got a surprise for you.'

He turns his head and looks at his father warily.

'Olivia phoned Concha's mum today . . .' Carlos begins.

'Yes, and I swear the woman sounded as if she'd been at the gin,' Olivia murmurs behind them. 'At two in the afternoon!'

Jinn, thinks Leo, and flexes his hand, the one the television bit.

'. . . and Rosa has popped down to collect Concha from school. She's coming to visit you, Leo, to cheer you up a bit.'

Leo nods, pleased.

'You know I'd never hurt you on purpose,' Carlos whispers. Leo turns back to the gate and touches one of the tiny holes with his forefinger. His father slips his arms around him and hugs him close, so that Leo's finger is jerked away.

'Leo, Leo!' Concha's voice sings his name as she approaches the house. Carlos releases him and opens the gate and there she is, swinging on Rosa's hand in a battered yellow sundress. 'We've got something amazing!' Her hair is spread over her shoulders in unbrushed glory, and she has a new scab on one of her skinny brown knees.

'What is it?' asks Leo. Just seeing Concha makes him feel lighter.

'Bombs,' says Concha simply, brandishing what looks like a fistful of limp balloons.

Rosa laughs. 'Water bombs. We found them in Dona Maria's general store.'

'We need a bull's-eye, then we can do it from your bedroom window into the garden,' explains Concha on one breath as she ducks through the gate under Carlos' arm. '*You* can be the bull's-eye, Carlos!' she says, throwing him a cheeky look.

'I get to stand in the garden while you two drench me, is that the idea?'

'*Sim!*'

Concha skips over to say hi to Olivia, who bends down to drop a kiss on her forehead. 'I think Carlos might be a bit big to be a bull's-eye. Let's give the two of you a challenge. *Esperem.* Wait a tick.' She darts into her studio.

Leo inspects the water bombs with Concha – there are twenty-five, all of them dark blue – and, in a moment, Olivia is back with a handful of long-handled paintbrushes, a stained wooden palette with generous whorls of red, yellow and blue paint squirted onto it, and a few sheets of foolscap. 'Here,' she says, putting them down on the grass. 'You can paint a few bull's-eyes and we'll pin them up around the garden.'

The children each rapidly draw a circle, Concha holding three paintbrushes dipped in different coloured paint, her swirls generating secondary colours. Leo's circle is thick, red and uneven.

'Hey, we could fill the bombs with paint water,' whispers Concha as they each start on a second sheet.

'I heard that,' chuckles Rosa, gently shaking a clump of Concha's hair. 'No tricks, Senhorita.'

The adults position the targets, slick with paint, around the garden; one on the gate, another pierced by a high branch of the olive tree, two others on the ground.

As they fill their first four bombs with tap water in the kitchen and dash upstairs, leaving a trail of drips, Leo forgets about the pain in his arm and shoulder, the guilt on his father's face, his mother's haunted look when she paints the nightmare. He is only aware of Concha's bare arm pressed against his own as they lean out of the window, her hair tickling his cheek, and the adults' exaggerated shrieks of alarm as the ground near them explodes with flamboyant splashes of water.

Chapter Thirty-two

Doctor Loverock is in her late fifties with yellow-grey hair cut short and curled carefully at the ends. When they're all seated and introductions have been made, she poses a long series of questions in her pleasant Californian drawl to help her build a picture of Carlos' troubled nights. She's meticulous, and her questions go far beyond those they went through on their visit to the bearded GP. Apart from taking a full medical history, she asks Carlos whether he remembers his regular dreams ('sometimes, but I've never paid much attention to them'), how he feels physically after an episode ('exhausted, sweating, as if I've just been through a heart attack'), whether he has a history of physical or sexual abuse ('my father used to hit me now and then but it was nothing out of the ordinary, I think'), whether he can identify the most traumatic events of his life (here, Carlos talks stiltedly about his mother's death), whether he has ever attempted suicide or self-mutilation ('absolutely not!').

When she asks if any of Carlos' relatives have exhibited similar behaviour, Carlos relates what he knows about Marina's conduct and her internment in the psychiatric hospital. Then the doctor turns to Olivia and extracts from her full details of each of Carlos' violent nightmares, listening with calm, professional sympathy to Olivia's fears for Leo and her conviction that Carlos is enacting the same scenario each time.

When the questions are over with, Dr Loverock flips back through her notes in silence. Carlos glances over at Olivia and instinctively their hands bridge the space between their leather armchairs.

'Well, Mr Moniz,' says the doctor, looking up and adjusting her silver-rimmed glasses. 'I can't make a definite diagnosis before I send you for physiological monitoring in the sleep lab, but your symptoms and the testimonials of your wife indicate that you are suffering from a parasomnia which leads to a state of automatism, when the mind is not in control of the body. Parasomnias are abnormal behaviours, perceptions and experiences during sleep, and they tend to unleash primitive aggressions. They're surprisingly common.'

Carlos sits up tensely, his hand slipping from Olivia's. 'You mean a sleep disorder, right? Your colleague Miles and my wife both think it must be RBD.'

'Well, REM Sleep Behaviour Disorder is a sleep pathology characterised by dream-enactment – in fact, it's as much a *dream* disorder as it is a behavioural disorder of sleep – and that is one possibility for the kind of behaviour you've been exhibiting, but it's not the only one.'

Carlos takes a deep breath. 'Do you think I could be mentally ill?'

'When the dream world comes crashing into the real world in the form of sleep violence, reality is bound to feel a little shaky, but at this stage, you have no need to worry that you're losing your sanity, Mr Moniz,' the doctor says firmly. 'Parasomnias are not mental illnesses. However, RBD *can* be a first sign of a neurologic disorder – in men of fifty-plus, over sixty-five per cent of RBD cases are eventually associated with neuro-degenerative brain disorders, such as Parkinson's disease.'

'Oh!' Olivia's heart drops in her chest. 'That's awful.'

The doctor raises a calming hand. 'As I said, we don't yet have an irrefutable diagnosis of RBD, so let's take this one step at a time.' She looks at Carlos. 'First I'm going to refer you to a hospital-based sleep laboratory here in Lisbon for overnight polysomnographic monitoring. It's completely painless,' she adds reassuringly. 'While you sleep, you'll be hooked up to machines which record eye movements, brainwave activity, muscle-twitch activity, heart rate and respiration.'

Carlos and Olivia exchange anxious looks. 'So I'll have to be monitored while an episode takes place?' says Carlos. 'But I never know when I'm going to have one – it could take weeks!'

'No, the emergence of parasomnia behaviours is not absolutely required to make a diagnosis – RBD can be confirmed if there's an excessive increase of muscle tone or phasic muscle twitching during REM sleep. Having said that, we find patients are more likely to experience an episode because the unfamiliar sleeping environment unsettles them, so you may find you have one anyway.'

Carlos is fiddling with the top button of his shirt as if oppressed by its pressure on his neck. 'If it *is* RBD,' he says, 'does that mean I'll have it for life?'

'Spontaneous remissions are rare, but they do occur.'

'Right. And would there be a way to treat it?'

'Clonazepam has proved highly effective in controlling RBD. It's a simple treatment, taken in the form of nightly pills.' Dr Loverock pauses. 'It doesn't work for everyone, and I'm of the opinion that for some sufferers, taking a chemical is not sufficient. But this is all speculation, Mr Moniz, since not all dream-enacting behaviour automatically indicates RBD. We could be looking at something else here.'

'Like what?' asks Carlos. He finally undoes his button and breathes more easily.

The doctor looks briefly down at her notes. 'It could indicate *pavor nocturnus* – night terrors – or nocturnal seizures. These can manifest as dream-enacting behaviours.'

'Seizures?' echoes Carlos. 'Why would I be having seizures?'

'Seizures can occur as a result of anything from an imbalance of chemicals in the brain to fever, illness or trauma.'

Olivia feels frightened; RBD is a dreadful enough prospect but at least she knows a certain amount about it. The word 'seizures' has her imagination working overtime. She fights off a mental image of Carlos convulsing on the floor so violently that his heart stops beating.

'There's a third possibility I'm considering,' continues Dr Loverock. 'From Mrs Moniz's account, your moving nightmares might well be recurrent in terms of content – in other words, you're dreaming the same thing each time.' She pauses to take a sip of sparkling water from a tall glass on her desk. 'With this type of recurring nightmare, I wouldn't rule out the possibility of a repressed trauma resurfacing into consciousness. There's a parasomnia known as Sleep-related Dissociative Disorder which involves the re-enactment of past trauma scenarios during the sleep period. It's said to be the only true psychiatric parasomnia, as it often goes hand in glove with the suppression of memories of sexual, physical or emotional abuse. If this turns out to be your diagnosis, then if you succeed in getting to the root of the traumatic memory, you might be able to halt your violent episodes without recourse to medication.'

'So you're saying that just *remembering* the triggering event – if there is one – could stand in place of taking a course of drugs?' asks Carlos.

'Put it this way. More than twenty-five years' experience of dreamwork have demonstrated to me time and again that nightmares can be indicative of underlying psychological malaise, and that once this malaise has been identified and worked with in a therapeutic way, the nightmares disappear of their own accord. In other words, if your own recurrent nightmares are happening because something has incited your brain to replay a traumatic event from your past, then raising that event to consciousness would be a crucial step in overcoming these violent episodes, which would mean that you'd likely be able to move past this abnormal sleep behaviour without treatment.'

Carlos is nodding. 'I have to remember.' He presses his fingers to his temples. 'The last time it happened, I heard a strong male voice repeating, "You must forget."'

'Whose voice do you think it was?' asks the doctor. Her voice is matter of fact, her expression open and relaxed. Perhaps it's the fact of being asked by a stranger who doesn't have the frightened look Olivia gets on her face when she's questioning him about his dreams, but Carlos answers her unhesitatingly.

'My father's,' he says in surprise.

'And what was it he wanted you to forget?'

Bent slightly forwards in his chair, Carlos seems to be listening out for some memory too far away to hear. Silence stretches around the room and Olivia becomes aware that she's holding her breath. But after a time, he shakes his head. 'All I know is he used to tie me to the bed to stop me running around in my sleep. I think . . . I have a feeling that by ordering me to forget, he was protecting me against something terrible that happened.'

Dr Loverock waits for a while in silence, but Carlos has nothing more to offer. 'I'd urge you to do all you can to recall your nightmare,' she says. 'Would you like to book in with me for a session of regressive dream therapy?'

'I'll do anything you think might help.'

'I know my schedule's a little heavy right now, but I'll ask my secretary to see if she can fit you in as soon as possible, since your case is particularly urgent. I may even be able to see you tomorrow night after my usual consultations, if you don't mind coming in late? Oh, and Mr Moniz, if you have another episode, interrogate yourself on waking from the dream – ask yourself, What was I doing just now?

194

What or who did I see, and what happened?' She looks over at Olivia. 'You can be very helpful to your husband by noting every action he carries out, every word he shouts out while he's dreaming, and then sharing these with him.'

'Yes, that's what I've been doing.'

Carlos is frowning. 'I can't afford to have another episode,' he says, slumping back in his chair. 'The situation is making Olivia threaten to throw me out of our home.'

The doctor nods. 'I see.'

'Not for ever,' protests Olivia. 'Carlos, it's just a temporary measure!'

Carlos keeps his gaze on the doctor. 'How soon can we do this sleep lab observation?'

'I'll check.' While Dr Loverock phones through to the hospital, Carlos and Olivia exchange a long look.

'It wouldn't be for good!' whispers Olivia defensively.

'How do I know that?'

'You have to trust that we're strong enough to cope with living apart for a short time.'

Carlos shakes his head. 'It's much more complicated than that, and you know it.' He shifts restlessly. 'This is all so slow,' he mutters. 'I wanted –'

'They can fit you in for an initial session on Tuesday the twenty-second,' Dr Loverock announces.

'But that's twelve days away. What if –'

'That's unbelievably fast, you know,' she assures him. 'In the meantime, I can prescribe sleeping pills, but there's no guarantee they'll prevent a further episode.'

'I'll take them,' says Carlos quickly.

Soon, they are out in the sunshine under the green canopy of a tree-lined avenue near Marquês de Pombal Square. It feels good to be out of the building, and Olivia strokes Carlos' tight back as they head towards the metro.

'That was very useful,' she says timidly.

He stops walking and turns to face her. 'I'm sorry I'm being so glum,' he says, catching hold of her hands. 'It's just depressing being told I might either have a disorder that could lead to something horrible like Parkinson's, or I'm having brain seizures, or that if I can't remember some deeply buried past trauma, I'll carry on being violent to the people I love most.'

'I know, I know. But listen, Carlos, nothing's sure yet. And at least you're definitely not going mad; you can put *that* fear away, at least.'

'Yeah – for now.'

'I'm going to help you remember your dream,' she tells him.

Looking into her face which is taut with determination, Carlos touches her cheek. 'How?'

'I've nearly finished that painting I'm doing of your nightmare. When it's finished, I'll show you.'

He pulls her into his arms. 'I'm lucky to have you.'

'You're not going to lose me,' says Olivia. 'Or Leo. We're a family.'

On their way up the hill to their home, they see Zebra leaning against the wall of a tumbledown house covered in broken mustard-yellow tiles. He's playing a harmonica and his eyes are slitted against the sunshine.

'*Olá*, my beauties,' he greets them, crossing his legs at the ankle and favouring them with his most irresistible smile. 'Why the long faces?'

The two move into his small patch of shade, so that Olivia has to breathe through her mouth to avoid the smell of stale sweat and wood smoke which hangs about Zebra's body like toxic aftershave. Carlos fills him in on what the doctor said, with Olivia adding the details he misses. Zebra listens, stroking his rope of a beard and barely blinking.

'So everyone is saying to you, "You must remember,"' he

observes. 'But in your nightmare, it's a different story – someone, he wants you to forget. So, *pá*, you must decide what you want. Do you *want* to remember?'

'Of course I do.'

'You sure? Could be something no man wants to remember.'

Carlos shifts his feet impatiently. 'Zebra, I *have* to remember.'

Zebra nods understandingly. 'You have an unhappy woman.'

'Oh, I'm not unhappy exactly,' says Olivia. 'I'm just . . .' She flutters her hands, tries to smile.

Zebra extends a cracked finger and presses it into the space between Carlos' eyebrows. 'Wake up,' he says loudly. 'Wake up!'

Taken aback, Carlos laughs and pulls his head back a little because Zebra's finger is pressing quite hard into his forehead. Zebra shakes his head sorrowfully. 'Recognising what reality you're in is no laughing matter, *pá*.' He withdraws his finger and leans back against the wall, his dark eyes fixed on Carlos. 'I like to call this W.P.R. – Waking Physical Reality. It's *different* from an LSD trip, it's *different* from being mindless drunk, and it's *different* from dream reality, Carlos!' He turns to Olivia with an apologetic shrug. 'I'm trying my hardest with this man of yours.'

Olivia smiles at him. 'I can see that.'

'You must get him to wake up inside his nightmare, then he'll see it for what it really is. No way this big-hearted man would hurt you on purpose.'

'I know, Zebra, I know.'

As they walk on, with Olivia thinking she must take Zebra some of Carlos' old clothes and some oranges for vitamin C, both she and Carlos feel lighter. 'How does he do it?' she asks Carlos, and he knows what she means without having to ask.

'It's the way he stays so calm,' he says as he unlocks their front door. 'Zebra's always the same, he's like a rock and we eddy around him like water with our little problems.'

197

'*Big* problems,' murmurs Olivia, but she feels hopeful.

The house is empty; Rosa is looking after Leo at her place today and has promised to take him to the beach to blow some life into him. He's been off school for three full days, since Carlos' last episode, and Olivia is worried by his listlessness. She wanders into the kitchen and puts the kettle on.

'Olivia!' Carlos' voice is alarmingly urgent, and Olivia hurries into the hall. He's standing by the phone looking agitated.

'What is it?'

'Telephone message. It's that social services woman, Doutora Lurdes. She wants to visit us early next week, "to continue her psychological assessment". She wants Leo to be there, too.'

Olivia thinks of Leo's almost total silence since his father's last episode. She thinks of his left arm, which is mottled with dark-blue bruises. 'No,' she says wildly. 'She can't come. We'll have to pretend we're not in, or take Leo away somewhere and shut up the house . . .'

'She says all three of us are *required* to be here,' says Carlos. 'Olivia, we don't have a choice.'

Chapter Thirty-three

13 June 1984

Blood changes everything.

Father has forbidden me to speak of what happened yesterday and my whole voice is trapped behind a stone. He made me wash off all the blood and when the bathwater went pink and I was white and clean again, that's when the stone came into my throat.

'You must forget.'

Father says this whenever he comes to my room.

'You must forget.'

Inside my head, it's all blinding sunlight and I can't sleep.

Marina says I've had a big shock. She's sitting by my bed looking worried. She strokes my hair, trying to get me to fall asleep. Earlier, she tickled my cheeks with the curling end of her plait, but there was no laughter in me and she sighed very sadly. I wish I could smile for her. There are no happy sounds – Mãe isn't at home to listen to jazz music in her bedroom, and Marina has stopped singing.

Now, I see blue lights whirl on my bedroom ceiling. Car doors slam. Our doorbell chimes and I hear Father answer it.

Marina's eyes jump. 'The police,' she whispers. She opens my door and leans against it in her loose dark dress, listening. The police are talking in the hall, their feet squeak on the tiles.

'What does this have to do with me?' Father's voice is louder than the policemen's voices. 'The neighbours, the neighbours – pah! My son does not consort with beggars. He does not frequent empty building sites. He is a Casanova de Albuquerque Moniz . . .'

The police say something, and Father listens.

Then his voice booms again. 'Carlos is an obedient child.' His voice has great weight, the policemen must be bending away from such power.

Marina turns and her black eyes fix mine. I know what she's asking me: What happened yesterday? Why the blood, who and where and how?

'You may not speak to him, no. The boy is asleep.'

The police sound unhappy, their voices grumble and persuade. Marina is holding her breath, holding her whole body still against the door.

'Are you insinuating that my son, a mere lad of seven, could have been involved in such brutality?' Father's voice is high and uncontrolled. 'Get out of my house. Get out! I'll be speaking to your superintendent about these accusations. I will not have this defamatory talk in my home.'

Now the policemen's voices are low. They rumble and I can feel Father calming himself. When he speaks again, his voice is quieter so I can't hear every word, but I hear him say, 'I understand . . . tragic event . . . doing a good job.'

Soon, the door closes behind the policemen. Marina shuts my bedroom door. Her eyes are wild and frightened as she comes back to my bedside and sits down.

'Carlitos, my little Carlos, what happened? Can you tell your auntie?'

I look into her eyes and in my mind I show her the sunlight, the sparkling amulet, the blood . . . but Marina can't see what I show her. She presses her face close and I know she's about to ask me more questions, more and more, until I can find my voice and speak, but Father opens the door. He stands without coming inside, and he stares at me. Behind his beard, he is pale. He looks and looks, and I look back. Then he looks at Marina and it's like a warning.

Without a word, he goes.

Marina tucks me in, kisses my head, tells me to sleep. Then she leaves too, and I'm alone with the terrible light.

Chapter Thirty-four

'I'd like you to imagine a flight of stairs leading down into darkness. There are ten steps. With each step you descend, you feel more relaxed. One . . . two . . . three . . .'

Dr Loverock's voice has lost its usual briskness, and is warm and reassuring. They are in a small side-room leading off from her office and lit with a mellow orange lamp. Because of the urgency of Carlos' circumstances, the doctor is working later than usual in order to do this initial session with them; when they arrived at 8 pm, the secretary was on her way out of the door for the weekend. Carlos is lying on a comfortably upholstered couch and the doctor sits in a leather armchair beside him, her legs crossed at the ankle, a pad and pen on her lap. Olivia – relegated to a fold-out plastic chair in the corner and asked to remain silent – has only been allowed to stay because Carlos insisted on it. 'If I'm going to be "regressed", I want you there too. I might tumble into a past life and not be able to find my way back,' he joked, and although the doctor explained that this first session is more about establishing a connection with the unconscious, and that this is more easily done when the patient is alone with the therapist, Carlos was adamant.

When she has guided Carlos to the bottom of his flight of stairs, the doctor asks him to shrink his consciousness down to the size of a grain of rice, and imagine it travelling around his body until it comes to rest somewhere. Olivia watches Carlos' face curiously. He looks asleep, his eyelashes trembling now and then, his mouth closed. She can't help thinking how beautiful he is, tanned and handsome and so very familiar.

'Where has the grain of rice come to rest?' asks the doctor.

'My right wrist,' mumbles Carlos. Olivia knows he has intermittent trouble with this wrist, which will suddenly get stiff and painful for no apparent reason. It was the reason he stopped playing tennis and took up running instead.

'So stay there, inside your right wrist. What do you feel?'

There's a pause. 'Terrible guilt.'

'How old are you when you feel this terrible guilt?'

'Seven.'

'Is your mother alive?'

'Yes.'

'Is she well?'

'No, she's very sick.'

'Do you feel this terrible guilt because of your mother?'

'No.'

'Why do you feel this terrible guilt?'

Carlos' lips move, but he says nothing. The doctor waits. Now that the session is underway, she seems like a different person to Olivia: neutral, but infinitely kind and patient. Olivia tries not to move, fearing the plastic chair will squeak and interrupt the reverie. After a long while, the doctor speaks again.

'Staying inside your wrist, look around. What can you see?'

'Nothing . . . darkness.'

The doctor waits, and the moment stretches, but the atmosphere in the room is so relaxing that Olivia finds her own eyelids drooping.

Then Carlos speaks again. 'There's a sort of makeshift door.'

'Good. Can you describe the makeshift door?'

'It's . . . corrugated black plastic. You can bend it back to squeeze through, to go in . . .' He falters.

'Would you like to go in?'

'No!' Carlos rears into a sitting position, clutching his head violently in both hands. 'No!' he yells again, and the terror in his voice has Olivia on her feet in a flash.

'Mr Moniz, relax, I want you to take a deep breath and relax,' says the doctor. She is sitting up very straight and alert. With one hand held in the air, she pre-empts Olivia's impulse to run to Carlos.

'I can't!' he shouts.

'Breathe deeply,' she instructs him, and gradually Carlos begins to breathe again. His head is still buried in his hands, so Olivia can't see whether his eyes are open or closed. She sits back down on her chair, aware of her quickened heartbeat.

'Now that you feel more relaxed, would you like to lie back comfortably again?'

Carlos shakes his head.

'You're happier sitting up?'

He pulls his hands from his face and turns to them, squinting in the dim light. 'I can't do this.'

Olivia wants to leap in and tell him he doesn't have to, but she bites the words back in time.

Dr Loverock leans forwards. 'We can stop the regressive work and just talk, if you want to.' When he nods, she says, 'If you'll just let me guide you back. Close your eyes for a moment, please.'

Carlos closes his eyes and the doctor does a short relaxation with him sitting on the couch, using the stair image in reverse at the end to bring him back up to full waking consciousness. When Carlos opens his eyes again, he is much calmer.

'How do you feel?'

'Better. What the hell happened, why did I get so upset about that door?' When the doctor says nothing, Carlos says, 'It was like the most terrible thing in the world lay beyond it.'

'What lies behind that door might well be the traumatic experience that's causing your nightmares,' says Dr Loverock. Her voice is still gentle, but Olivia can hear that she has switched back into analytical mode. 'You have deep, unresolved feelings of guilt, and there's an incredibly strong lock on them. It seems to me that this lock is what you were fighting against just now, and in your nightmares the lock breaks off so suddenly that you become violent.'

'And the guilt has nothing to do with my mother, her illness, her death,' says Carlos thoughtfully.

'Apparently not, but we can't rule anything out this early on. You know, it's rare for patients to have such violent physical reactions during these sessions,' the doctor adds. 'They might cry, or even shout, but they generally stay lying down on that couch. All of you – your entire conscious mind – is leaping to get away from that memory. That could be why your nightmares are so violent; your whole self is revolting against the raising of this knowledge to consciousness.'

'What can I do about it?'

'What's the worst thing that could happen if you were to remember something terrible that happened in your past?'

'The worst thing?' Carlos runs both hands through his hair, and Olivia notices how much thinner in the face he is, new lines bracketing the edges of his mouth and fanning from the corners of his eyes. 'Not a lot, I guess. I mean, the worst thing would be *never* remembering and continuing to have these dreams and hurt my wife and son and destroy our family. So although I'm apprehensive about what I might discover, I can't imagine the truth could be any worse than what we're going through at the moment.'

'So perhaps open yourself up to the possibility that you *can* remember this – that the knowledge of it won't destroy you. Suggest to yourself that you are ready to remember.'

Carlos shrugs. 'OK.'

'You don't seem convinced.'

'Well, if it was that easy, I'd have remembered by now.'

The doctor nods. 'Sometimes things get easy all of a sudden, when we're least expecting them to,' she says, and for some reason, even though she knows it's probably just some psychological trick, a suggestion designed to melt whatever resistance is within Carlos, hearing the doctor say this makes Olivia feel better. Maybe the power of suggestion is far greater than we know, she thinks. Maybe Carlos can cause a shift in his consciousness by changing the way he thinks. Why not? She remembers Carlos telling her Zebra had made a comment about how both dreams and thoughts can be changed. It's so simple, she thinks – or it could be, if only Carlos could hit on the right way to think. You hear stories about people shrinking cancerous tumours through positive thinking, or pulling themselves back from the brink of terminal illness by meditating.

'And I said I was seven,' muses Carlos. 'My mother's death overshadows everything else I remember from that year. I have no idea what I did each day, what my life was like. There's just a vast blackness over that age.'

Dr Loverock nods again. 'Well, it's up to us to work together to transform that blackness.'

Olivia is relieved the trauma seems to have happened when Carlos was seven: she thinks it must mean that the foreboding Carlos has been feeling, his paranoia about Leo's safety, isn't some terrible premonition of Leo's death after all; it's about Carlos and some ancient memory of his.

'I'm just worried about how long it's going to take to get a proper diagnosis and treatment up and running,' admits Carlos. 'What happens if I have another episode?'

'I'd like to make some suggestions,' says the doctor. 'Each night, before you go to sleep, you could try a progressive muscle relaxation like the one I began the session with, combined with the visualisa-tion of yourself lying calmly in bed all night. It's simple – with each breath, you'll feel yourself becoming more relaxed, and you can sug-gest to yourself that you will sleep well, sleep calmly. This kind of self-hypnosis can be very effective. You could also try fifteen min-utes of meditation before you sleep.' Olivia likes the thought of Carlos meditating, pictures him sitting bare-chested and cross-legged, his eyes serenely closed.

Soon, she and Carlos are stepping into the street, only to be sur-prised at the light summer rain that's falling.

'This is lovely,' exclaims Olivia, tilting her head back and stick-ing her tongue out to taste it. 'It feels like ages since it last rained.'

They stop on the pavement, looking up into the sky, which is still light although it's after nine. Buses and cars dash by, but the smell of summer rises from the warm, wet street and Olivia pulls it into her lungs.

'That was hard,' remarks Carlos, closing his eyes briefly to feel the small splashes of rain.

'Oh, but you're getting there,' says Olivia. 'You got right up to the door that's hiding the memory. That's brilliant, Carlos – it means we're just steps away from finding out the truth!'

He pulls her into his arms. 'My optimist.' He sighs. 'Olivia . . . I want this to be over, have us back to normal, get you pregnant, have another baby, live happily ever after!' He buries his face in her hair. Olivia wraps her arms around him, overcome by a fierce burst of love. They stand like that until her arms ache from hugging him, while the rain polka-dots their clothes.

Chapter Thirty-five

Olivia has been putting the finishing touches to the painting of Carlos' nightmare ever since Leo left for school that morning – the first time he's been back since Carlos threw him against the wall – and her cheeks are flushed, her magenta headscarf unravelling inch by inch so that her hair slips out in limp whorls and sticks to the sweat on the back of her neck. Her smock is heavy on her skin even though she's wearing nothing but a pair of Carlos' boxer shorts underneath it. Scarlet and black paint is splattered across her bare hands. She stands back from the canvas and curls her toes into the floor, hefting a glistening brush in one hand, considering.

The man, dark and muscular, runs from the centre of the image, his screaming mouth contorted, his torso naked, a necklace swinging from one clenched fist. His green eyes are glassy but filled with terror. Behind him, emerging from shadows, is a dead being with helter-skelter arms and a white, desperate face. Olivia has painted white words in wavy lines onto the canvas; the words Carlos has shouted out during his violent episodes. And in red paint across Carlos' torso, she has written 'YOU MUST FORGET'.

Olivia realises she hates this image, hates the way it seems to embody not only Carlos' shadowy side, but her own. Looking at the image is like looking into her own personal hell. She poses her paintbrush and resists the urge to sweep her smock off over her head and allow the breeze from the garden to cool her bare skin; she's going to call Carlos through from the main house to view her work and doesn't want the focus to slip from the painting. Her T-shirt is lying on the floor but it's soaked in water the colour of river mud; she kicked a bowl of water over it earlier while backing away from the painting for the hundredth time to reflect on how it was building. Olivia smiles a little to herself at the thought of Carlos looking appreciatively not at her hours of hard graft but at her bare breasts, then her smile falters as she realises their sex life is suffering as much as every other aspect of their life together; their bedroom has become a place of tension and restriction, especially since the dog leashes made their appearance.

'Don't think about it,' she mutters aloud, and turns her attention to her painting again. This is what his nightmare looks like to me, she thinks. Now let's see what it looks like to him. She picks up her mobile and phones through because she doesn't want to traipse through the house all sticky with paint, and he'll likely be holed up in his darkroom out of earshot.

'Come to the studio,' she tells him when he answers.

'Did you collect Leo from school?'

'No, he's walking back like he always does.'

Carlos sounds displeased. 'If I'd known you weren't going, I'd have gone.'

'You know I almost never collect him,' says Olivia impatiently. 'Just come to the studio, and don't panic – Leo will be back any second.'

Carlos is clean and fresh in a light-blue cotton shirt and white shorts. His hair shines from the shower. Olivia feels hot and dishevelled. She gestures to the easel.

'Oh,' he says. 'Wow.'

'It's your dream,' says Olivia simply. Now that he's here, looking at it, she feels anxious, and when she's anxious she tends to talk, wants to say that if she'd known when she started it that it was probably about something terrible that happened when he was seven, she would have done it differently, painted a child running, not a man . . . but she tries not to speak, just for a moment, so that he can feel the impact of the image.

Carlos steps closer, right up to the canvas, and whistles between his teeth. 'You haven't stinted on the emotion, have you, *querida*? This is pretty horrible, extreme stuff.'

'Your nightmares *are* horrible and extreme.'

He reads the words, looks at the faces. 'So this is me,' he says finally, stepping back.

'You, yes. Running. With a dead person behind you.' She's careful to use the words he himself had used when he'd spoken to her after he'd woken from his nightmare. She wants to trigger something in him, but the composed man beside her in his freshly laundered clothes seems worlds away from the running, dreaming man in the painting. When Carlos says nothing more, Olivia swallows. 'We need to look at your nightmare as if it's a memory being replayed. I'm sure we can piece the whole thing together if we try.'

'OK,' he agrees, and looks at her expectantly.

'So. When you have an episode, you always seem miserable, tortured, your voice full of pain. You howl and sob.'

Carlos shifts his weight from one tanned foot to the other. '*Meu Deus*,' he says, looking back at the painting. 'I howl and I sob . . . how ludicrous.'

Olivia points to the words which zoom across the canvas. 'You become very agitated and you shout: "My luck! You cannot steal my luck!"'

Carlos nods thoughtfully, but she can see he's as blank as she is in terms of being able to guess the meaning of these exclamations. She presses on.

'You go for Leo: seeing him triggers something in you. In your first incident, you shoved him against the wall and wouldn't let go. In the second, you ripped his necklace from his neck, shouting about your luck.' She points to the necklace in the painting. 'And you run, Carlos. After you snatched Leo's necklace that time, you pushed me down the stairs and ran, but only as far as the living room. You sat there and I heard you saying, "So much blood . . ."' She looks at him meaningfully, but his eyes are on the painting, scanning it restlessly. 'So you see, it's the same dream. Only it seems to me it's getting *worse* each time, more specific maybe. In the most recent one, you shoved Leo against the wall and shouted, "No, no, no!" Then you ran away with what must have been your black winter coat, since it seems to have disappeared, bundled in your arms. You said later you were running from something terrible, that there was a dead person behind you. And you heard this powerful male voice – your father's – telling you to forget.'

'You must forget,' murmurs Carlos. Olivia waits for him to say more, but he is quiet, his eyes deep in the painting.

'I think this is definitely a recurrent nightmare, and each time it happens, the action unfolds a little further, like a story. Don't you see? If we use every action and every word you speak in that state as a clue, as Dr Loverock suggested, we might be able to get to the bottom of what happened and work out whether these nightmares really are about some forgotten trauma in your past.' Olivia pulls off the remains of her headscarf and uses it to wipe her perspiring forehead. 'Perhaps the "dead person behind you" is yourself, the part of you that died when this trauma, whatever it was, happened. Your own, traumatised self . . .' She trails off. It's like talking to a wall. Carlos is silent, staring at the painting. His spine is rigid under his cotton shirt.

'Being tied to a bed against your will is traumatic,' Olivia suggests gently. 'Your mother died when you were seven, the whole family went through the crisis of her death . . . Carlos, do you think your father sexually abused you?'

Carlos swings his head towards her sharply. '*What*?'

'He tied you to the bed, after all, and you heard his voice in your head, telling you that you must forget . . . isn't there a possibility that he did something to you that he wanted to hide?' She bites her lip. 'Does that ring any bells at all?'

Carlos sighs, shaking his head. He looks gloomily into the painting. 'Why would I shout about my *luck* being stolen?'

'Luck . . .' Olivia wrinkles her forehead. 'I don't know. Maybe it's symbolic of the loss of something else, something you didn't know the words for as a child.' A thought strikes her and she looks at him with horrified pity. 'Virginity, maybe? Oh, Carlos, I hope your father didn't hurt you.' Carlos shoots her a dark look and she rushes on, trying to make it less dreadful. 'But if he did, we can deal with it, get help, see someone.' She touches his sleeve. 'These days there are so many people who can help.'

He steps away from her angrily. 'I *wasn't* abused by my father. I'm sure of it. Not every nightmare in the world is caused by sexual abuse, you know.' He folds his arms across his chest. 'Could you do me a favour and stop leaping to ridiculously dramatic conclusions, Olivia?'

'I'm sorry.' She holds up a calming hand. 'I'm just trying to jog your memory, for all of our sakes.'

'But there *are* no memories,' groans Carlos. 'It's like sifting my hands through empty sand, looking for a lost jewel. There's nothing there, no cold metal under my fingertips, no sparkle as I lift it to the surface . . .' His gaze is fixed again to the painting. 'The necklace,' he says, and there's something new in his voice: surprise, sadness. Beside him, Olivia becomes absolutely still. Carlos' right hand moves slowly to the dip of his collarbone and he touches the skin there as if he's afraid it might burn him.

'Mãe's amulet,' he says. 'I remember.'

Chapter Thirty-six

The garden gate swings open with a clatter, propelled by Leo's usual after-school shove. Leo comes through, vibrating with nervous tension following his first day back in his normal routine since Carlos' last incident.

'Mum,' he cries. 'My teacher's here!'

Olivia and Carlos are still in her studio, Carlos lit with animation as he begins to talk of his mother's sapphire amulet, the family luck. Leo's cry breaks the mood in a moment. Warily, they emerge to see Professora Celeste standing politely outside the gate, her dark hair held in place with gleaming blue clips. Beside her is Doutora Lurdes. The social worker's expression is grave and when her sharp eyes meet Olivia's, Olivia experiences a thump of foreboding in the centre of her chest.

'Oh, no,' she murmurs under her breath. Carlos gives her hand a warning squeeze and steps forwards, forcing a smile.

'*Boa tarde*,' he greets the two women. '*Façam o favor de entrar*.' Please come in.

They step into the garden and shake hands, Leo hovering beside his mother, amazed at the sight of his teacher standing in his own garden. Olivia caresses his hair, feels beneath it the shape of the bruise on the left side of his skull. They must have found it, or seen the bruising down his left arm. Her breath sticks in her throat.

213

'Professora Celeste telephoned me this morning,' begins Doutora Lurdes smoothly, 'to voice her concern, and under the circumstances I thought it best to move quickly. As you know, I was hoping to visit you in the next few days anyway.' She glances pointedly at Leo, who is leaning against Olivia, listening to every word. 'Perhaps we could talk in private?'

Olivia's hands move to Leo's shoulders as if she's going to insist that he stays near her.

Carlos leans down to his son. 'Leo, there's a bread roll waiting on a plate on the kitchen table for you. Why don't you go and eat that, then play inside the house for a while?'

Leo hesitates, his eyes moving sombrely from face to face. 'Go on,' prompts Carlos. 'I put lots of thick chocolate spread in that roll especially for you.' Reluctantly, Leo goes into the house and Carlos gestures for them all to sit at the garden table.

Doutora Lurdes lays her shiny black handbag on the table and curls the strap neatly on top of it. 'There has clearly been a further . . . incident. Professora Celeste discovered extensive bruising on Leo's upper arm. Your son is exhibiting signs of trauma; Professora Celeste tells me he's been unresponsive today and isolated himself from the other children.'

'Is this true?' Carlos asks the teacher.

She nods. 'He wouldn't speak to the other children, even his little friend Concha couldn't cheer him up, and for most of the morning he was muttering under his breath about sleep monsters and dolphins, telling himself some story or other. That's when I thought I should check for bruises.'

'You undressed my son?' demands Carlos.

'No, of course not. I just asked him if there was any place on his body that hurt and he rubbed his upper arm. I asked him to raise his shirtsleeve, and saw the bruises. That's all.' Professora Celeste sits back in her chair looking offended.

'He was off school last week under false pretexts,' says Doutora Lurdes. 'His mother has dissimulated again, allowing Professora Celeste to believe that no new violence had occurred.' Her eyes move coldly to Olivia's face.

Olivia shakes her head wordlessly. She's in the wrong; what can she say? She holds the woman's gaze, willing her to understand.

'I had another attack,' says Carlos heavily.

'I'm beginning to doubt the veracity of your sleepwalking story, Senhor Carlos. I'd like to remind you that the Segurança Social –' she pulls a sheaf of papers from her bag and hands them to him, 'has the right to take immediate action to protect children from domestic violence.'

Carlos takes the papers and leafs through them, mystified. 'What does this mean?'

'It means that if the Segurança Social judges your son to be in danger, it has the power to move him directly to a foster home while a legal case proceeds.'

'What?' Olivia leans forwards, her hair in disarray. Her fingers grip the mosaic tabletop. 'You could take him away?'

'*Claro*. Of course.' Doutora Lurdes' eyes remain cool, but Professora Celeste has the grace to look uncomfortable. 'It would only be a temporary measure, while we investigated the situation more thoroughly.'

'You have no right!' explodes Olivia.

'Olivia –' begins Carlos.

'Senhora Dona Olivia,' cuts in the social worker. 'Please don't be obstructive. We're only trying to give Leo the protection any child deserves. Clearly under your care –'

'I would do anything to protect my boy,' Olivia cries. Her eyes are bright with tears and fury. 'I'm his mother.'

'Yes, you're his mother. But while in your care, he has been hurt three times that we know of –'

'By someone who has a sleep disorder and had no idea what he was doing!' Olivia gestures towards Carlos, who is flipping frantically through the papers as if he's hoping to find some clause saying this is all a big joke. 'How can someone be blamed for something he did while he was unconscious? Yes, my son has been hurt, and believe me, nobody could be more upset about that than me – it breaks my heart to see his bruises – but we are taking steps to make sure it never happens again. I tie my husband to his bed every night. We've seen a sleep specialist . . .'

'I can get her details for you,' says Carlos, standing in a hurry. He throws the papers down onto the table and goes into the house, touching Olivia meaningfully on the shoulder as he squeezes past her.

Take a deep breath, he's saying to her. Olivia makes a huge effort to calm down.

'We think it would be even more damaging to Leo to split this family up by sleeping in different places, don't you see?' She appeals to the two women. 'I want him to keep getting the love he always gets from us both, as a child in a stable family home. We're trying hard to maintain a sense of normality.'

Doutora Lurdes shakes her head. 'There's nothing normal about a child being repeatedly exposed to a situation where, if your account is to be believed – and let's face it, Senhora Dona Olivia, you have lied before so I hope you can understand my scepticism on this point – his father undergoes a severe personality change at night time and turns into a violent madman.'

Olivia bites her lip. 'I know it sounds crazy. But it's the truth. And Leo needs his father.'

'Well, clearly we can't leave them under the same roof if the result is Leo getting hurt over and over again.'

As she stares at the social worker's thin, intent face, something in Olivia collapses. I have failed to protect my little son, she thinks. What kind of a mother am I? Her eyes swim with tears.

Carlos comes out and presents Doutora Lurdes with a piece of paper. 'Dr Loverock's contact details,' he says. 'Please, call her.'

Doutora Lurdes eyes the paper as if he's just handed her some toilet roll. 'I'd far rather see the official diagnosis you promised you'd get from your doctor the last time we spoke.'

Carlos manoeuvres himself back into his chair, ducking to avoid the low, springy branches of their sapling olive tree. 'I'll only have that once I've been observed in the sleep laboratory,' he explains, his voice husky with tension. 'Then they'll know for sure.'

Sensing that they are losing ground, Olivia speaks up again. 'Would it help if we arranged for Leo to sleep over at his Aunt Rosa's place in Cascais for a few more nights until we have the diagnosis?'

'A few *more* nights?'

'Yes,' says Carlos. 'We sent him there for a couple of nights before we saw the doctor, just to make absolutely sure he'd be safe if it happened again. Since then he's stayed here as the doctor gave me some strong sleeping pills to take.'

'Well, moving Leo back to his aunt's would alleviate the imme-diate danger he's in,' concedes the social worker, 'but even if the diagnosis comes back confirming this sleep disorder, we can't be expected to allow Leo to continue to sleep near someone who hurts children in his sleep.'

'They'd give me medication to control it,' says Carlos. 'We'd all be able to sleep safely in our beds.'

Olivia looks at him, remembering what the doctor had said about the medication not being effective for everyone.

'I'll need the full name and address of Leo's aunt, and the assur-ance that she can take him from tonight,' says Doutora Lurdes briskly. 'And I'll need a copy of the diagnosis and treatment plan as soon as you have it, please, for my files.'

'No problem,' says Carlos, and jots down Rosa's details on the back of the paper he used for Dr Loverock's number. But Olivia frowns, wondering why she hadn't suggested that Carlos go and sleep at Rosa's. Why should poor Leo be the one to leave?

'Olivia?' asks Carlos when he's given the paper to the social worker, but she is staring at the table and won't look at him, her eyes blurred with tears. He turns to the social worker. 'These papers you showed me – are they some kind of legal summons?'

'No. They just set out the Portuguese laws concerning taking children into care. I'm here to officially inform you that we're moving you to a high-alert category.' Doutora Lurdes shifts on her chair. 'I'll need to make a full psychological assessment of Leo, and talk to both of you separately as well over the coming weeks. Leo will need to attend school faithfully every day, providing a valid doctor's note if he's ill, and Professora Celeste will be alert to any fresh signs of distress.'

Olivia looks at Professora Celeste as if she's a spy. The teacher catches her stare and shifts her gaze to the tabletop.

There's nothing left to say. Carlos stands up looking grim, and the two women take his cue and say their goodbyes. Olivia remains sitting at the table, her fingers tracing the ridges of the mosaic. I'm losing him, she thinks. I'm losing my son.

Chapter Thirty-seven

22 June 1984

I can see the building site, the grey rubble on the ground, Pedro spinning in circles . . .

'Carlos, what are you doing out of your bed?' Father's voice is close but it's strange, I can see right through him as if he were a ghost, see the building site through him . . . then the horror hits me and I open my mouth and scream and scream.

'We need to get this child back into his bed. What the hell is going on?'

Father's voice breaks through and I feel myself being lifted in his strong arms, carried back down the lit corridor past Marina, pot-bellied in her white nightgown, and Inês, grim-mouthed. They stand and stare at me as if I am someone they've never seen before. The building site begins to slip away and when Father lies me down on my bed it disappears so that all I can see is his black beard, his worried eyes. His breath smells of mint toothpaste and his face is very close to mine.

'You are not going to suffer from the same madness as your auntie,' he says, very low. 'You will not leave your bed in the night and roam the house doing foolish things, is that clear?'

I nod, but it isn't clear. I think of the way I saw two things at the same time, the corridor with its panelled walls and family portraits, and, behind it or maybe in front of it, the concrete blocks of the building site criss-crossing blue sky.

'*Filho*,' Father says as he arranges the sheet around me. 'Son. You must not think about it again, do you understand? *Tens que esquecer isso*. You must forget.'

But even though I try, I can't forget and it keeps happening – I keep waking in the night to find Father and sometimes Marina or Inês staring at me, their arms out, trying to calm me down, and I realise I've been shouting, or that I've run full pelt into a wall. Once, I woke in the corridor with Father's hand clamped to my mouth so tightly I couldn't breathe.

Tonight, I've just got into bed when my door handle turns and I stop feeling sleepy even though I'm snug under my summer sheet and the street lights are shining soft gold through the gaps in the shutters. The light snaps on and I blink. It's Father.

He has heavy rope coils hanging off his arm like a cowboy lasso.

'Lie flat on your back,' he says with a stern face.

I do as he says, thinking this must be some new punishment. I try to ask him what I've done wrong, but nothing comes out. The stone is going from my throat but I almost never speak. I try to speak sometimes, to make Marina happy. Father won't let her leave the house in case the neighbours see her fat tummy and talk. But there's nothing I really want to say and my voice, when it comes, is very small.

Father stoops and throws one end of the rope under my bed so it slaps against the wall. Then he jerks my bed away from the wall so I rock sideways, and he leans down to pick up the rope. He passes it over my chest. 'You've been thinking too much,' he tells me. 'Shouting out terrible things in the night, things that, for your own

220

sake, *must* be forgotten. This rope will make sure you don't leave your bed again. It's for your own good.'

The rope is heavy on my chest. Father is red in the face as he repeats his actions, passing the rope under the bed two, three more times. When he stands up holding the end, he says, 'How many times have I told you to forget?' I'm not sure how many times, but I know he says it a lot. I'm trying to forget everything. Under the sheet, I close my hands into fists. He starts to pull the rope tight and my chest is stuck down on the bed, then my belly, then the tops of my legs and then my ankles. I try to move and can't. Father ties fat knots in the rope.

'When I close my eyes,' I whisper, 'his face is there.'

Father comes towards me and there's nowhere to escape to because the ropes bite me through the thin sheet as soon as I move. He puts his face right in front of mine and he smells of cigar smoke. He hasn't trimmed his beard today so black spikes prickle out towards me. 'If faces appear, send them away, or you'll end up like your Aunt Marina. This is what comes of my leniency with her night-madness – she's a bad influence on you. I should have acted sooner. There is no madness in the Casanova de Albuquerque Moniz family, do you hear?'

I nod, holding my breath so the stale smell of smoke can't get inside me. Father waits a moment and I feel my eyes start to water. Then, just as I'm about to have to take a big breath of him, he stands up and leaves the room, turning the light off as he goes. He doesn't close the door completely. Light from the landing comes in and makes a long triangle on the ceiling. My arms are stuck to my sides but I can wriggle my fingers. I think about how they must look, wriggling under the sheet. I think of Pedro's brown hands juggling under the stars, of the crow-man's rocklike hands, of Mãe's bony fingers clutching a yellow handkerchief filled with phlegm.

'You can't tie a child to his bed!' Marina's voice is as loud as a bell, it sails up the staircase and comes in through my door and my heart hurts because I want her to come and sit with me and stroke my head the way she has every night since the blood changed everything.

'You've gone too far, Marina.'

'*I've* gone too far? I?'

'*Sim*, you, with your filthy pregnancy, your night lunacy, your interference.'

Marina is walking up and down very quickly, I can hear the clack of her house-shoes on the tiles. 'I know right from wrong, truth from lies, Aníbal. I'm not blind, I *saw* that blood all over him!'

'Hush your mouth. Don't you dare say another word on the subject.' Father's voice is high, as if he might scream if she keeps talking. My whole body is stiff as I listen.

Marina's footsteps stop. 'Why did you lie to the police?'

'Marina, I am *warning* you . . .'

'Get off my arm! Aníbal, you cannot treat a child this way. Untie Carlitos this minute or . . .'

'Or what?' Father's voice is terrifying. 'Or you'll tell the police I lied to protect my son? Will that help Carlos? And who do you think the police will believe? The esteemed head of this household, or the crazy woman who's carrying the bastard child of a sailor? Just remember, Marina, you live here on my charity.'

Father's footsteps stride away and everything goes very quiet. I think of calling for Marina but I'm scared Father will hear. After a long time, I hear Marina's house-shoes walk away very slowly. I hope she isn't crying. I push up and out with my whole body against Father's ropes but they hold me fast, like a fish in a net.

Chapter Thirty-eight

'That bloody teacher, spying on my son!'

Across the living room, Carlos holds up both hands in a calming gesture. 'She's only –'

'*Don't* say she's only doing her job. She's trying to rip our family apart, and she's succeeding.' Olivia knows she's being unreasonable, but she can't stop herself. She paces back and forth, thrusting her fingers through her hair. She's still wearing her blue painting smock and it sits on her uncomfortably, feeling as ungainly as a canvas tent.

Rosa has been and gone, pouring soothing words into the house and leaving rapidly when she saw from Olivia's flared nostrils and tense features that she and Carlos needed to talk. Behind her, she has left the lingering smell of rosemary and thyme from a concoction she was making in her kitchen when Carlos rang her. With her, she has taken a subdued Leo, a compensatory ice lolly in one hand, his little overnight knapsack in the other. She has promised to find out what became of the family amulet. 'We may even still have it,' she said as she left, 'in the safe in the bank with the rest of Mãe's jewellery.'

Olivia turns her face to the wall, recalling the vision she had after their first interview with the teacher, of Leo being carried away from her, kicking and struggling. 'Why didn't I react earlier?' she cries. 'What sort of a mother allows her child to sleep so close to danger?'

'We couldn't know how things would go, *minha querida*,' says Carlos. 'There's no use blaming yourself. How do you think it is for me, knowing I'm the danger you speak of? How could I hurt my son viciously, unknowingly, three times?' His voice falters. 'I can't even look at his bruises.'

Olivia spins around to face him. 'Oh right, yes, it's all very hard for you, isn't it? Don't you realise what happened today? Thanks to you and your awful dreams, we're on high alert in their file now, Carlos.'

'I know. Olivia?' He pauses, waits for her to calm herself enough to listen to him. 'I *know*.'

'Then what do you suggest we do? I don't hear you coming up with solutions.' She jerks her arms into the air and her bracelets slide towards her elbows in a surge of silver. 'I'm fed up with this ostrich behaviour. You can't just sink your head in the sand and pretend you're never going to have another violent dream. You need to remember more about your past, Carlos. You haven't remembered enough!' She juts her chin forwards and stares at him. 'OK, so there was a family amulet, a lucky one that your mother gave to you the summer she died. That's important, but *what happened next*? Think! It frustrates me so much to think that you must *know*, deep inside, what these nightmares are about, and yet all you do is skate the surface. For your family's sake, you must remember!' As she stares across the room at her husband, she is overwhelmed with hopelessness. 'I'm sick, so sick of it all . . .' She begins to sob and once she starts, she doesn't know how to stop. She sinks to her knees, her shoulders shaking.

Carlos is beside her in a moment, his arms around her, trying to pull her back up to a standing position.

'Get off me! I don't want you near me, Carlos. I don't even want to look at you.' She shoves him away in a hot fury, but as soon as he retreats she feels bereft. She stays where she is, down on the floorboards which are smooth with age, and lets the tears come. The minutes pass, and the only sound in the house is Olivia's sobs. She feels as if she's emptying everything inside her into the ground, so that she nearly retches as she weeps. When she finally looks up, she sees Carlos standing in the centre of the room with his arms hanging by his sides. He's not looking at her, and he is eerily still. Olivia wipes her face.

'What? What is it?'

He looks down at her and again it strikes her how much he has aged in the past weeks. His cheeks are thinner, he has frown lines on his forehead where before there were none.

'I think I killed someone.'

Olivia sits up straight with her spine pressed against the wall. She looks at him for a long moment. 'When?' she whispers.

'When I was a boy.' He sits opposite her on the floor, his legs folding so abruptly that Olivia can't be sure whether he chose to sit or whether his legs simply gave way. It feels as if they're sitting in a canoe, deep water rocking all around them. A sensation of dizziness invades Olivia.

'Who do you think you killed?'

'Maybe someone who tried to steal the amulet. You said I shouted, "You cannot steal my luck."'

'But . . .' Olivia struggles to think. The remnants of her sobs are thick in her throat, making her breath judder. 'This is speculation, right? This isn't a real memory, you're just fabricating because I'm pressurising you to remember.'

Carlos shakes his head. He has entirely lost the sparkle he had earlier that day, when he entered her studio to view the painting. Now he droops, reminding her of the way he is after an incident: humbled, devoid of energy. 'I can't remember any actual violence. But just before the social worker arrived this afternoon, when you and I were looking at your painting, I got a flash image of a building site, this peculiar white light hanging over it, and I knew something terrible had happened there . . .' He trails off, looking at her uncertainly.

'But how could a small boy kill anyone?'

'That's the part I don't know. I can't see it, Olivia.' He looks at her pleadingly. 'But something dreadful happened in that place, and it had to do with me. I could feel it in my gut, like a guilty, inconsolable ache. And I knew it meant death, the death of someone . . . I think Father was trying to protect me from whatever it was I did, by telling me to forget.'

'See, Carlos, this is why it's so important to remember,' Olivia says. Her voice is very soft but her eyes burn at him. 'What if during your last episode you'd acted out the killing of whoever it was? You might have killed Leo. Actually killed him.'

'Never say that again.' Carlos' voice is flat, his lips so drawn that his mouth is unrecognisable as his own.

For a long time, they sit on the floor like hurricane victims, staring into each other's faces. Olivia has the sensation of something between them draining away; the hope that everything will turn out to be all right. In the stillness, she can hear the forlorn piping of the knife-sharpener's whistle as he pushes his bicycle through the streets. After a while, Olivia touches her cheeks, which are rough with the dried salt of her tears. She stands up and Carlos follows her face with his gaze. He looks shell-shocked by his own revelation. He is, she imagines, hoping for some gesture of understanding or sympathy. She sways slightly, wondering if she has the strength to smile and tell him they'll get through this. When she does speak, she doesn't say what she intended.

'Carlos, do you think maybe when you were a boy, you killed someone *in your sleep*?'

He stares at her.

'I mean, nobody ties their child to the bed because of a few bouts of sleepwalking – why else would your father have reacted so strongly?'

Carlos sits in silence for a long time, and Olivia stands patiently waiting for him to speak. 'It's like I'm two people,' he says eventually. 'The boy-me, and the man I am now. I can't seem to span the . . . the space between them. I don't have any idea if I did something terrible in my sleep or not. I've told you all I remember. And my father's parenting methods weren't exactly modern. You know he used to hit us.'

Olivia nods. 'Yes. It's something to consider, though.'

'Another terrifying possibility, you mean?' Carlos shakes his head. '*Meu Deus*, Olivia, the theories you come up with are something else.'

'What?' she protests. 'You're the one who said you killed someone!'

'Yeah.' He looks exhausted, and Olivia realises she's losing the will to continue with their situation. Just hours ago, she would have crept into his arms and hugged him until they both felt stronger. Now, as she stands looking down at the faint shadow Carlos' eyelashes cast on his cheeks, and at his fists which are curled loosely in his lap, she understands that this man sitting on the floor isn't just her husband; he's someone dangerously amnesiac, someone who might have killed, and who might kill again.

Chapter Thirty-nine

Leo has been swimming deep under the waves, following a pod of dolphins until the sun is only a faint glimmer on the surface. As his dreams fade, the blue grows stronger, filling out into the hard walls of Rosa's spare room, painted for him when he was a baby. Something is wrong, in a wet, clinging way. Leo shifts his body and a sour smell spreads up from his bedclothes. He tenses in fright, sends one of his hands down to investigate, fearing the worst. The sheets are soaked and smelly with wee, his pyjamas sticking to the tops of his legs. Leo's hand freezes in dismay. What a *baby*, he thinks in Concha's most derisive voice. Tears of shame sting his eyes. He clambers out of the bed and the pong rises like mist, filling the room.

How do I clean this? he thinks in despair, visualising washing machines spinning in efficient rows, as mesmerising as the wall of television screens he has seen in a big electronics shop in Lisbon. He rips the bottom sheet off the bed. It is large, unwieldy, and his urine has left a dark and almost perfectly round stain in the centre, bigger than a Frisbee. The sheet is pale blue and, as Leo fights to control it, he feels he is fighting with the sky. Just as he manages to fold it into a tight rectangle, Rosa knocks at the door.

There's just enough time to kick the sheet under the bed and pull the duvet hastily back into position and then Rosa is there, peering around the door, her eyes full of black sparkle. Leo crosses his hands over his crotch in a gesture which he hopes is casual, but this only makes her look at him closely.

'Everything OK?' she asks. Her voice is deep and safe, hot chocolate on a winter night, but Leo cannot speak. He looks at her from eyes full of misery. He isn't scared Rosa will be angry with him; he just doesn't want her to think any the less of him. Rosa's nostrils flare, and Leo's head sinks. She knows.

'Leo,' she says with her usual brisk kindness. 'Time for your shower.'

He looks up, bewildered. How could she not have noticed? 'But . . .' he begins.

Rosa raises her eyebrows. There's no sign in her eyes that she has noticed anything amiss. 'You don't want to be late for school, do you? *Anda, mexe-te!* Come on – scoot!' she says, opening the door wide for him.

Leo's muscles leap to life and he dashes thankfully past her and into the bathroom, shedding his wet pyjamas outside the door. He knows that Rosa can work magic, and this is one of those times. He knows that when he comes out of the bathroom, the foul pyjamas will have vanished, the guest bed will be dry and sweet-smelling, sea air sweeping through the room. Rosa understands without being told; she knows when words will only cause shame to rise in red waves under the skin. She can turn time back a few clever revolutions so that the bed was never wet, there was never any disgrace. Blissfully, Leo showers, the water hot and sharp on his skin, making him dance. This is like showering in diamonds. The diamonds melt into his skin. When he emerges, he is glittering.

Clean and dressed in a fresh navy T-shirt and his red shorts, Leo heads down the narrow wooden stairs for breakfast, still glittering in places because he didn't dry himself very thoroughly. He sits on the breakfast bench in the kitchen and is startled when Rosa does, in fact, want to talk about it.

'You had a bad dream,' she states as she sets a plateful of toast and Azorean cheeses in front of him.

Leo stiffens, his forgotten shame flooding to his cheeks. '*Peço desculpa –*' he begins, but Rosa brushes his apology away with a flash of her arm in the air.

'I'm not interested in the bed,' she tells him. 'I'm interested in what is happening here –' she reaches across the table and taps him lightly on the head '– and here.' This time her hand touches his heart.

Leo waits, his hands wanting to grab at his food but held back by the force of Rosa's will.

'Will you tell me the bad dream?' she prods.

Leo frowns. He thought his dreams had been good ones, but as he thinks, he recalls a running figure snatching him up, and he knows that last night, before he became a dolphin, he had dreamed about the sleep monster. He drags his eyes from Rosa's and reaches for his toast. She allows him to eat a whole slice before her voice stops him again.

'*Diz-me.*' Tell me.

Leo's eyes remain fixed on his plate. He wonders if he should make something up because Rosa gets upset when he mentions the sleep monster, but he's an honest boy and in any case, when his eyes are irresistibly drawn to hers, it's like looking inside himself, so he simply says, 'The sleep monster stole me away from Mum.'

Beneath her bright flowered top, Rosa's shoulders slump. 'You'll never be separated from your mum, Leo. You're staying with me a few nights just to give your parents some time to get rid of the sleep monster so it's safe for you to sleep at home again.'

Leo's toast is calling to him in a buttery voice, so he eats it, but his gaze never strays from his aunt's face. Her energy has thickened and solidified and her thoughts are too dense to read. He wishes she

230

would grow light again, turn to him with a smile in her eyes and forget about the sleep monster. In his shorts pocket is the hard, reassuring circle of the dolphin eye he found on the beach. When he's licked the crumbs off his fingers, he pulls it out and holds it up so his aunt can see the deep blue shine of it.

Rosa looks at it in silence, then at Leo, who smiles at her. She sweeps to her feet and her face is bright with an idea.

'Come into the larder,' she says.

The larder is a whitewashed space that smells of damp all year round. There's no food in it; the shelves are packed with tubes of glue, jewellery-making tools, and plastic boxes containing semi-precious stones, assortments of beads, silver chains and clasps. In the centre is a high revolving stool that Leo likes to spin around on. He climbs up onto it and watches with a mixture of anxiety and fascination as Rosa fixes the dolphin eye in a clamp and drills a tiny hole through the top of it. 'If it cracks, Leo, I can fix it,' she tells him and, because it's Rosa, he lets her take risks with his treasure. Within minutes, it has become a necklace, the eye swinging off a silver chain. Rosa has to adjust the length of the chain, and this is fiddly, but at last she says, '*Não te mexas, meu amor* – hold still, love,' and fixes it around his neck. 'This is your lucky charm.'

Leo leans back into the plush comfort of Rosa's chest. He touches the eye and smiles.

Chapter Forty

Olivia wakes with a gasp.

She lies still and listens with her whole body. She's used to these moments of nocturnal tension. These days, a slight muscle spasm from Carlos is usually all it takes to wake her: she is immediately alert, ready to field disaster. Tonight, her eyes widen in the darkness as she understands that there is no warm, breathing body beside her, just an empty space. She tests the space by swiping her arm across it, then sits up, wondering. Where are the ropes?

In one fluid movement, Olivia is out of bed. She lifts her knee-length dressing gown off the hook on the back of the door and slips it on as she moves rapidly towards Leo's bedroom. Before she looks for Carlos, she must check that her boy is safely asleep. At the thought of her son's big eyes as he talks of the sleep monster, she feels a pang of sadness which is becoming draggingly familiar. Leo should be a small, contented hump under the bedcovers, his breathing regular, his dreams easy.

When Olivia opens the door to an empty bed, a pang of horror strikes her so forcibly that her hand flies to her chest. She rushes across the room, and only then does she notice that the bed hasn't been slept in, it's as neat as a pin, and she realises – of course – that Leo is safely at Rosa's. She remembers now that instead of using the dog leashes, Carlos had just taken one of the sleeping pills the doctor had prescribed. 'These things completely zonk me,' he'd assured her as he knocked it back.

There's a crashing sound from downstairs, and Olivia runs towards it. Dressed in the red boxers and grey vest he went to sleep in, Carlos is hammering his fists against the thin partition wall in the living room so violently that it trembles. '*Não, não, não!*' he cries in anguish.

Olivia freezes in the doorway. Watching him is like watching a one-man play with ill-assorted props and occasional snippets of dialogue. At moments like this, Carlos actually does seem insane.

Abruptly, he lowers his fists and runs to the front door.

'No, Carlos, you're dreaming,' Olivia yells. 'You must stay in the house.' She follows him and sees him snatch up a coat – her good winter coat – and bundle it against his chest. As he wrenches the door open, his back is a solid wall, warning her off. Only a few weeks ago Olivia would have grabbed his arm, his waist, tried to pull him away, but now she is too afraid of what he might do to her. In this twilight, dreaming state, the powerfulness of his body is such that he could kill her with a flick of his arm. So she hangs back, pleading with him to wake up and remember who and where he is. 'You're at home,' she tells him as he pulls the door open. 'I'm Olivia, your wife. Please wake up, my darling. Stay inside the house so I can take care of you . . . Carlos, *listen* to me!' Her voice is shrill, cutting the night air.

But Carlos has gone, taking her coat with him. She watches him bang out of the garden gate, barefoot, and sprint down the street incredibly fast. Running to the gate, she takes a few steps into the street and watches him disappear down the hill. Olivia shakes her head, staring at the point where Carlos' running figure had vanished. This illness, or condition, is a mystery. How conscious is Carlos right at this second? She pictures him, running through his dream scene. Everyone runs in their dreams, she concedes, only most people's

233

bodies stay put. Most people don't turn into furious beasts and enact every dream action, word and emotion, so why does he?

A lone car speeds past, filling the narrow street. Olivia imagines Carlos half waking from his episode and lying down to sleep further along this same street, then being run over by the car, his body leaping with the violence of it. She remembers hearing about a drunken boy who was walking home after a party in the neighbourhood and who stretched his tired, alcohol-numbed limbs out across an empty road to sleep. He was decapitated by a speeding vehicle. Imagine being the one who found that boy's poor, staring head . . .

Olivia dislikes this part of herself, the part that indulges so heavily in what she thinks of as mother-worry because it has grown much, much worse since she's had Leo. Worst-case scenarios multiply in her head the moment things appear to go wrong. She pushes her mass of hair back from her face and neck, fists it into a ponytail for a moment, then releases it with a sigh, feeling the weight of it roll down her back. Above her head, stars are shining through the orange glow of the city sky, but for once she has no interest in them.

If only she could isolate the cause of these incidents – too much coffee, the stress of an argument, an excess of dairy products, anything. Anything would be better than simply not knowing why they happen. Olivia thinks back to how Carlos had been that day, trying to find clues that amount to him having another episode. There was the obvious stress of the social worker's visit, their discussion once Leo had left with Rosa, their fear of losing him. She realises she's still wearing only her dressing gown. Turning, she goes back into the house, sending out a blessing after her running, dreaming husband, wishing his safe return.

Olivia dozes off sitting in the kitchen with her head propped in her hands, so the sound of Carlos pushing open the front door, which she left on the latch for him, reaches her only faintly. The first thing she notices when she looks up with a gasp to see him standing at the kitchen door in his red boxer shorts and grey vest – the coat gone – is the bloodshot and swollen state of his eyes. He looks as if he has been crying incessantly since he left the house. His shoulders are stooped and his arms dangle heavily by his sides. The altered appearance of his eyes and the blankness of his expression mean that Olivia can't tell whether he's awake or asleep, and she casts her gaze over him anxiously, murmuring his name. That's when she notices the second thing, which alarms her so greatly that she is on her feet in a flash.

Carlos has blood on his hands.

At first, it's hard to tell where the blood is coming from. Olivia's gaze whips down to his feet, thinking that perhaps they are the source and that he has been cradling them in his hands to stem the flow. But his feet seem fine this time – black around the edges with street filth, but no visible blood.

'Carlos, are you awake now, my love?'

'Uh, *sim*,' he says meekly, thick-tongued.

'Good.' She keeps the same clear, deliberate tone. 'Come into the living room and let me look at you.' Obediently, he turns and walks where she indicates. Olivia isn't convinced he's fully awake yet – she knows that this transitional state where he's no longer dominated by his dream imagery but still hasn't retrieved his full waking capacities can take anything from a few seconds to thirty minutes or more. She needs him sitting calmly; smears of blood on the sofa are the least of her worries. As Carlos wanders vaguely into the living room, she ducks into the bathroom and soaks an old hand towel in warm water.

Entering the living room, she finds Carlos sitting as straight-backed as a stranger, his bloodied hands on his knees. She kneels before him and looks closely. He is bleeding not from the knuckles, but from the edges, as if he's been karate-chopping a very hard surface.

'Carlos, did you get in a fight?' she asks faintly.

'I don't remember.' His voice is expressionless. Olivia examines his face for signs of a beating. But there are no bruises here or anywhere else on his body. Only his hands are encrusted with blood, the skin torn away, grit and blood mixed into a black and crimson paste. She begins, very gently, to clean them. Carlos sits in silence and barely seems aware of her touch.

'What *do* you remember?' she asks him. His forehead creases in effort as he thinks back, and it occurs to Olivia that it must be like retrieving memories of very drunken nights where everything is either a blackout or else a strange blur of events and impressions.

'Only that I had to get away.' He sighs, and his torpor is wrapped so thickly around his words that she has to strain to separate them. 'Something was behind me. Something too frightening to face.' She feels his shock reaction through his hands, which jump involuntarily as she holds them through the towel.

'Who or what was behind you? Was it a real person, someone you know?' Olivia is cautious; she keeps her voice calm. She doesn't know if this is the moment for such questions or whether they could trigger a new episode.

Carlos' face shutters, and he shakes his head.

Olivia concentrates on his hands again. She has wiped away much of the blood now; the pale-blue towel is marred all over by patches of reddish-pink. Carlos' palms are unharmed: all the damage, the cuts and bruising, are along the little fingers and the edges of both hands. There are splinters of wood, one of which is quite large, embedded in the flesh. Olivia extracts these with care. Has he been battering a door down? She remembers the way he thumped his fists against the living-room wall before he ran off, and considers his exceptional strength when he's dreaming; it might be a bit like the change of consciousness in the martial arts, she thinks, when practitioners get themselves into a mentally focused, trancelike state and can then

236

karate-chop thick pieces of wood in two. Only instead of Carlos' strength being a question of mind over matter, it's a question of dream over mind. The splinters are too bloody to inspect properly, and Olivia imagines his crazed punches missing their target and swinging instead into furniture. Has he been inside someone's house? Clearly, he has pummelled something or someone so hard that his own skin has split.

When Olivia wonders how much of this blood might be some other man's, the immediate alarm bell of HIV makes her coax Carlos into the bathroom, where she gets him to soak his hands in a strong antiseptic solution. When she's finally satisfied that he is disinfected, she guides him into the shower. While the water rinses the grime off his feet and face, rinses his nightmare away and clears his head, she picks up the bloodied towel and slips back into the kitchen, where she leans against the fridge, thinking. Goosebumps prickle to life on her spine and upper arms and she rubs her arms absently. Just how conscious *is* Carlos when he's dreaming? If he's been violent to someone, she thinks with a rush of panic, how much of him actually knew what he was doing while he slammed his fists into their head?

In the next room, Carlos switches off the shower and the tumble of water ceases, spreading silence through the house. Olivia walks to the sink and rinses the towel she used to clean him up, watching as the blood leaches out and spirals down the plughole.

Chapter Forty-one

16 July 1984

I can't move. The ropes are tight on my legs and across my chest. I can lift my head, though, and when I hear all the shouting in the middle of the night, that's what I do.

'Buttering my cigars and trying to *eat* them. Are you possessed?' I can tell from Father's voice that he's at the bottom of the stairs. 'You've crossed one line too many. Put down that knife and get back in your room this instant!'

'Leave me alone!' Marina sounds angry. 'Leave me, I'll eat what I want.'

Then Father must try to grab Marina and make her go where she doesn't want to go, because she shrieks and I hear the dull slap of her hand across his beard and Father shouts. '*Deixa de comportar-te como uma doida – chega!*' Stop behaving like a madwoman – that's enough!

I don't know what Father does next, but Marina screams so loudly it splits my head.

'I've had it, I've had it with this,' Father exclaims, and I hear his heavy feet come up the stairs, boom-boom-boom. I watch the door with my head still raised, but he stamps past and I hear him talking on the telephone in his bedroom. 'Violent fit . . . found her eating my Cuban *cigars*, for Christ's sake . . . needs psychiatric help . . . can't do this without your help, old friend.'

There's no more shouting for long minutes. I lie my head back on my pillow but I can't sleep. I can hear the thud of Father's slippers going left and right, left and right in the bedroom, no Mãe at home to calm him down, and Marina crashing about in the kitchen, slamming cupboards, rattling pots and pans as she makes herself a midnight feast. I wonder if Father's cigars taste of burned gold if you eat them instead of smoke them. Then the doorbell chimes, making me jump. Father hurries to answer it and another voice – a man's voice, but high and with a different accent from Father's – comes into the house. Father's voice and the new voice talk over Marina's angry protests, and then she is screaming again.

'Get off me, get off me!'

What are they doing to her? The front door is wrenched open – are they leaving?

'Carlitos!' Marina screams.

'Marina!' I fight against the ropes, kick and strain, but Father ties strong knots and they hold me fast.

'*Calma*, Marina, *calma*. I am a doctor,' says the man, and I think he has taken hold of her because his voice comes out in spurts.

The front door bangs shut. My skin is cold and wet with sweat. Marina shouted for me and I couldn't help her – what will she think of me now? I think of the baby the sailor left inside her and I imagine it moving its little arms and legs under her nightgown. The doctor's headlamps send light swinging across the ceiling as he drives Marina and Father down the street towards the river and the main road.

Mãe is at the hospital. Marina is trapped in the doctor's car with Father. Except for Inês – keeping out of the way in her bedroom downstairs – I'm alone in the house. Why can I never help people when they need me? Since the blood, everything is horrible. Hot tears roll from my eyes and I hate them, hate myself. I shiver under my ropes.

What if Marina never comes back?

Chapter Forty-two

Olivia is trying to work on a commission of Sintra's Moorish castle, but she keeps turning involuntarily to the painting of Carlos' night-mare, and every time she does, fear rises in her chest: it's like having a very still but very violent thing crouching in the corner. Looking at it makes her bruises throb, but she can't make herself step right up to it and turn it to face the wall. Even though Carlos has seen it now, and the last thing she wants to do is keep it, Olivia can't imag-ine selling it. It would be like selling an illness, she thinks, or a tumour.

Eventually she stops for a break. As she walks into the garden, Olivia peels off her painting smock – it's far too warm to wear in the heat of the sun, which is beating down, turning their meagre patch of grass browner by the minute. Cooler, she wanders to the gate to col-lect the mail and finds only the daily newspaper, *Diário de Notícias*, which she unfolds absentmindedly and skims as she heads back to the table, her flip-flops clacking softly. By the time she is fully seated, her attention has been caught by a story on the third page. As she reads it, her eyes skittering wildly over the black printed lines, Olivia's heart begins to pound.

It can't be, she thinks. Impossible.

But the more she reads, the worse it becomes and, although she fights it, the facts begin to fall into place: the time at which Carlos left the house, his return with blood and splinters of wood on his fists, his amnesia over what had happened.

MAN SEVERELY BEATEN BY PARTIALLY DRESSED ATTACKER

A man was beaten unconscious on his own doorstep in the Baixa district of Lisbon. On Wednesday 16 June at 3.15 am, furniture salesman Francisco Amorim, 38, opened his door to a barrage of knocking only to be punched to the ground by a man who proceeded to beat him savagely until he lost consciousness, stopping only when Amorim's wife appeared. She described seeing a partially dressed stranger, robustly built and dark-haired, fleeing the scene. Amorim was admitted to São José Hospital suffering a broken jaw and a suspected fractured skull.

Olivia places the newspaper on the table. Staring up at her is a photograph of Francisco Amorim, innocent victim of a savage attack. He is fleshy faced and smiling, unaware of what is to come. He looks nice; the sort of person who would be trusting enough to open his front door in the middle of the night thinking that the person knocking on it was in need of help. It's a coincidence, Olivia tells herself, but she sees again Carlos' disappearance into the darkened streets of the Alfama. Baixa begins just a twenty-minute walk downhill from their part of the Alfama; much less at a sprint, and Carlos had run out of the house just before three in the morning. What do they mean by partially dressed? she agonises, leaning over the text again to check she hasn't missed anything. Why can't they say exactly what the man was wearing? Carlos was in red boxers and a dark-grey Nike vest – she is certain of this, can visualise exactly the way he looked when he startled her in the kitchen. Miles' stories of sleep violence skitter through her mind in a series of dreadful images: a sleeping girl's slim body hurtling down from a window to

242

crash sickeningly into the ground; a man stabbing his parents-in-law in their beds, blood darkening the sheets; Carlos knocking her down the stairs, oblivious to her screams.

If it was him . . .

The thought is unfinishable. Olivia blinks. Tiny yellow butterflies dance overhead and the air is filled with the lightness of summer, but there's a nasty noise in her ears, the kind she's experienced in the past just before fainting. It sweeps through her head like the buzzing of an electric pylon.

This has gone too far, she realises. Just the fact that I'm sitting here entertaining the idea that Carlos might be behind this random attack proves how low we've fallen in the past weeks. How can I trust him when he doesn't know what he's doing? It's impossible, impossible. The smiling face of the unfortunate furniture seller blurs. Carlos is out at a photo shoot in the north of Lisbon, taking pictures of cereal-eating children for a billboard commercial. Olivia thinks for a moment. Then she goes into the house, finds the business card Miles gave her, and calls him, barely registering the leap of pleasure in his voice when he hears her voice. She tells him about the blood on Carlos' hands and the newspaper article.

'Carlos believes he killed someone when he was a boy,' she says, 'although he can't remember a thing about it. And now I'm so frightened he could be behind this new violence – what if he actually did attack that poor man while he was dreaming? How am I supposed to react? What should I do?'

'OK, Olivia,' says Miles. His voice is calm but with an underlying tone of urgency. 'Now listen to me. It's very common for amnesia to surround past traumas, and Carlos may never remember what he did, but it's clear that his episodes are getting much worse, and if he *has* killed before, he's capable of killing again. You and Leo are in extreme danger.'

Olivia bites down hard on her thumbnail. 'What if he didn't kill

243

anyone though? What if he's just trying to find a reason for his violent dreams and only *thinks* he did something terrible?'

Miles makes a faint click of impatience. 'I think the time for "what ifs" has gone, Olivia, don't you? If you suspect he's been violent again while dreaming – and the attack you describe sounds brutal, life-threatening even – then you need to act before something even more dire happens. You know, if you're nervous about telling Carlos to leave, I'd be willing to be present when you talk to him, to give you some support.'

'Oh.' Olivia's head jerks away from the phone for a moment as she imagines Carlos' reaction to that. 'That's very kind,' she says hastily, 'but I think it could be . . . counterproductive.'

'Well, whatever happens, I'm here if you need me.' Miles hesitates. 'I'd like to think we're becoming friends and, as a friend, I'm ready to help you, any time.'

'Miles, I'm touched. That's really very sweet of you.' Olivia is surprised to feel a brief surge of tears.

'Well, you know the stories: people *have* killed other people in their sleep. I keep thinking about that British bloke who strangled his wife while dreaming he was defending them both against an attacker. Now he'll have to live the rest of his life knowing he murdered the person he loved most in the world. And Carlos sounds as if he's only a step away from doing something just as horrific. I can't stand the thought that something similar might happen to you.'

There's a short silence. 'He'll be observed in the sleep lab soon,' says Olivia. 'Then they'll know what it is.'

Miles sighs. 'Olivia.'

'I know, I know.' She bites her lip, looks out of the window at Leo's bike which is lying twisted under the slender twigs of the oleander bush, its front wheel pointed at the sky. 'I'm going to do what needs to be done.'

Chapter Forty-three

The front door bangs as Carlos comes through it. It's late and he looks wired after the long hours of photography and socialising. Olivia reaches across the sofa to the *Diário de Notícias*. As he comes into the room, she flips the article right way up and says, 'Read this, Carlos.'

'What? Hey, is something wrong?' He unhooks his camera bag, sets it carefully on the bookshelf, and pulls off his shoes, sending her a concerned glance as he does so.

'I just want you to read this and tell me what you think.'

'Can I get changed first?' He sees her expression and sighs. 'No?' He comes over and picks up the newspaper. When he reads the headline, he looks sharply at Olivia and sits down, as instantly absorbed as she had been that morning. When he has finished, he sits with his gaze still trained on the print.

'Do you think the attacker could have been you?' Olivia asks him bluntly when she sees that his eyes have stopped scanning the text.

Carlos throws the newspaper onto the table and stares straight ahead. 'What do you mean?'

Olivia twists around on the sofa to face him fully. 'You know what I mean,' she pleads. 'Do you think you did this while you were dreaming? Please look at me, Carlos. Talk to me.'

His jaw tightens and he glances down at his hands.

'The blood,' presses Olivia. 'The blood on your hands, Carlos –'

'*My* blood,' Carlos argues, looking round at her in frustration. 'No one else's – look at the burst skin, the bruises.' He raises loose fists, shows her.

Olivia shakes her head. 'You're so strong when you have an incident, Carlos. You could do that – punch someone so hard you burst the skin on your own fists with the impact.' She leaps to her feet, her agitation too great to contain. 'That *is* what you did; just look at your hands. That *is* what happened.' She wheels away from him, across the room, looking birdlike and dishevelled in her crumpled turquoise clothes, her hair uncombed. 'I'm amazed you didn't break any bones. And although I hope to God it wasn't a person you attacked with those fists, how can we know for certain that it wasn't?'

'For a start, I wouldn't punch a person with the *edges* of my fists, like a girl – I'd punch head-on, with my knuckles. How could you doubt me?' Carlos asks, his voice growing louder with each word. He rarely shouts at her, but, when he does, Olivia's senses sharpen with the awareness that a boundary inside him has been crossed. For the moment, though, she is too emotional to care.

'How can I doubt you?' she repeats, hands on hips. 'Why wouldn't I doubt someone who, when he jumps out of bed at night, doesn't even recognise his own wife and child?'

Carlos, too, is on his feet now, white in the face. 'What exactly are you getting at?' His body radiates tension as he stands facing her across the coffee table, and there's no doubt now that he's shouting.

'Nothing – I'm just saying this thing you've got is completely out of control.' Olivia is nervous now he's standing up. Suddenly he reminds her of the violent man he becomes at night. Instinctively, she starts to move towards the door that leads across the hall to the kitchen, wanting to put a little distance between them.

'No, you're saying more than that,' he insists, turning his body to

246

follow her movement. 'You're saying that I went out on to the street and beat some stranger to within an inch of his life. What the hell do you think I am?'

Olivia opens the door and, as he moves to follow her out of the room, she whips around to face him. 'Carlos, what I'm saying is that you're too dangerous to live with. You could kill Leo, kill me! I'm sorry, but you *have* to move out.'

'Olivia, don't do this!'

The look on his face destroys her but Olivia faces him, breathing hard. 'You're moving out, Carlos.'

'I'll tie myself up again. No more useless bloody sleeping pills –'

'No.' Olivia turns and runs up the stairs.

'Where are you going?' He's behind her, pleading, and she can't stop, can't look back. In the bedroom, she wrestles a battered black suitcase out of the wardrobe and throws it onto the bed.

'Olivia, you always said we'd never sleep apart, never let what happened to your parents happen to us – separate rooms, separate lives . . . Olivia, stop this!' Carlos moves forwards and slams shut the suitcase she has just opened.

'Carlos. You have to sleep alone, behind a locked door.' Olivia is shouting now, her hand on the lid of the case, tugging at it to open it.

Carlos leans down harder on the case and pushes his face close to hers. The hurt in his eyes is unbearable and Olivia has to look away. 'Where will I go?' he demands.

'To a hotel.'

'You want me to sleep in a hotel, like a stranger?'

'I want you to be safe, and I want Leo and me to be safe, and I want the general population to be safe, all right?' Steeling herself, Olivia meets his gaze across the suitcase. 'Either you go, my love, or I will.'

'But sleeping apart . . . Olivia, you always said that's the beginning of the end of a marriage.'

'I know.' Her throat constricts and for a moment they look at each other, their faces inches apart.

'So what are you doing, *querida*? Why do you send me away?'

'You're making me choose!' she cries. 'You're making me.'

'Making you choose what? Olivia, come . . .' He puts his hand on hers but she wrenches it away.

'I never wanted any of this,' she says, stepping back from the bed and fisting the tears from her eyes.

Carlos stands up in concern. 'Talk to me, baby. Choose what?'

Olivia swallows. Her eyes don't leave his. 'Choose between my marriage and my son's well-being.'

'*What?* I never asked you to make this choice.'

'You did, Carlos. By not moving out when you first started to hurt us, you left me to choose. Well, I choose my son, Carlos. I choose Leo.'

Something in Carlos' face collapses. 'You can't choose him or me, don't be crazy. Olivia, we are a *family*. We belong together, all the time.'

'Not any more. Not like this.'

There's an awful silence. Then Carlos opens his palms. 'If you really want me out, I'll go.'

Olivia watches as he goes to the wardrobe, pulls out shirts, trousers, and begins to pile them into the case. She can feel her resolve wearing away, and understands that if she lets him see how tough this is for her, he'll never leave. 'This isn't the end, Carlos,' she says, her voice low. 'It's only until you get yourself well.'

'Is it?' His voice is raw.

'Of course it is, you know that.'

He shrugs again. 'How can I know that? You think I beat the shit out of strangers in my sleep. I've hurt you, hurt our son. Why would you want me back?'

'I'll always want you back,' Olivia whispers, but Carlos has turned away and doesn't hear her.

Chapter Forty-four

Bodies press into Leo on all sides, some unwashed, others perspiring freely in the heat. He's hemmed into an *eléctrico* – one of Lisbon's old yellow trams with brown leather seats and wooden window frames – with Carlos, who had to take him out of school early today for hitting another boy. Although he's pleased to see his father, who looks less like the sleep monster since he moved into a hotel a few nights ago, Leo is subdued, still thinking about the way that José, a sly boy with hamster cheeks, had grown mocking when Leo explained that his dolphin project is a super-spell, one that can disappear any kind of monster. José had snickered and later, when they were clearing up and Professora Celeste wasn't looking, he brought his Tyrannosaurus rex over to Leo's desk and said, 'Let's see if your dolphins can beat my dinosaur.' The sight of José whacking his fragile dolphin collage with a plastic T. Rex made Leo's fist shoot out and punch José's hamster cheek (which was surprisingly solid) before he could stop himself.

He can still feel the ache in his fist, still see José's tears. He wriggles uncomfortably, wondering what his mother will say. Carlos had taken it in his stride, meeting Leo's teacher's gaze calmly as she explained what had happened and, when the two of them were on their own, he hadn't even told him off. 'I need to get some photographic supplies from Baixa, and then we'll go and say hi to Zebra. I haven't seen him for a while and he's good with troubled hearts,' was all he said, and he'd slung his heavy arm across Leo's shoulders so that Leo felt more real again.

The tram rings its bell as it struggles up the narrow hill leading up from Baixa to the Sé Catedral, and Leo peeps through the bodies at the grandmother Carlos whisked him out of his seat for. On her forehead is a hairy mole as big as a mouth. It's eating up her face, thinks Leo. When she smiles at him he jumps guiltily.

'Being in this thing is exhausting me,' announces Carlos. They have only been in it for five minutes, but Leo looks up to see his father's face beaded with sweat. 'Let's get off early and walk up to the *castelo*, what do you say? Get ready to squeeze through behind me,' Carlos warns him as the tram slows, and soon they are jumping down the steps into the heat of the street. When they reach the castle, Zebra's tree is empty. They glance around the café and along some of the low, shady walls where Zebra likes to relax if he's up here during the daytime. Leo sees a woman sitting on one of these walls with walking sticks propped beside her. She is dressed like a raggedy sunset, in gauzy pink scarves, orange socks and a pleated dress that has faded to grey. Beside her is a handwritten sign: *Poesia, 50 cêntimos.* Poetry.

'Pai?' asks Leo, pointing at the sign. 'Ask her to do a poem for you!' Poems are a bit like spells, he thinks.

The woman's body is slender, but her spine appears to be twisted, pushing out her belly in a parody of pregnancy, and one of her legs looks to be considerably shorter than the other. Leo glances at his father and when he sees the way Carlos is looking at the poetry woman, as if he's trying to memorise her, he knows he wants to photograph her.

'*Poesia*,' says the woman in a gravely voice, and scrabbles in her basket where there is a notepad and several chewed-up pens in different colours. Carlos digs in his pocket and the poetry woman accepts his fifty cents.

In red pen, she scribbles a line on a piece of paper, then holds it up.

In a scrambling hand, it reads simply: 'A raindrop is not a teardrop.'

Leo pores over it. 'It's not a very long poem.'

Carlos looks at the woman questioningly. 'More like a Zen koan than a poem, wouldn't you say?'

A small smile appears on her face, and Leo notices a bedraggled pink rose in her hair, its petals furling to brown at the tips. He feels an urge to bring her a new, soft-petalled rose to replace it with. Everything about her is mouldering, wilting.

'What does it mean?' Leo asks.

'Um, I really don't know,' says Carlos. 'Learn to look, maybe. A raindrop is not a teardrop . . . things are not always what they seem?' He is still looking at the poetry woman. 'May I photograph you?'

Her smile freezes. 'What for?'

'For my book. It's called *Street Dwellers: The Beating Red Heart of Lisbon*. It's going to be gritty shots of fire-breathers, jugglers, the mad, the magical, the lost, the destitute.' He grins. 'You'll be one of the magical.'

She grunts, unimpressed. 'One of the destitute, more like. No woman on earth got rich on fifty cents a poem.'

'I already have a steaming dawn shot for the front cover,' Carlos continues persuasively. 'It's of Zebra up his tree, his beard dangling like white rope. You know Zebra?'

'Everyone knows Zebra.' Her face grows wary.

'We came up here looking for him. Have you seen him today?'

She peers at him. 'What d'you want with old Zebra?'

'I'm a friend of his.'

'So am I,' says Leo quickly. He likes this lady.

She studies them both for a moment longer, then says, 'well then, you should know he's been beat up bad.'

Carlos' hand leaps to his heart. 'What?'

She nods grimly. 'Five . . . nah, six nights ago now. He's still in Dona Estefania Hospital, bruised up and battered, poor soul.'

'Six nights ago?' Carlos looks shell-shocked. 'Who did it?'

The poetry woman shrugs. 'Who knows? Some drunk loser who don't like black men, maybe. Got Zebra real good, he did.'

'Dona Estefania Hospital, you say?' Carlos springs up and grabs Leo's hand. 'Let's go.'

It's pure luck that they arrive at the hospital during visiting hours and are allowed to see Zebra straight away. He's in a full ward with grey floors and each bed is separated by a shower curtain but even when they're closed all the way, you can still see through the gaps in the sides, so that Leo sees a man with his foot huge and white-plastered, hanging high as if he's kicking the air, and a bald man who's slumped asleep and snoring.

Zebra's shower curtain is open but his eyes are closed. Leo tiptoes towards the bed and tries to fit together these two very different Zebras: one made from a strong smell of wood smoke and the sound of belly laughter, with sinewy arms and dirt under every fingernail, and this long, skinny man closed in by a white sheet, smelling of antiseptic, his beard fluffier than usual, his skin greyer.

Then Zebra opens his eyes and sees Leo and, despite the bloodshot veins and the bandages on his arms and forehead, he is still Zebra.

'*Boa tarde, menino*,' he grunts, and looks over at Carlos. '*Olá, pá.* Hey, man. Who told you I was in here?'

'The poetry woman,' says Leo.

'Ah. Maria do Mar.'

'What happened to you?' Leo hovers close to Zebra's head, half scared.

'I got got.' Zebra tries to laugh. 'Damn shadow got me when I was looking the other way. Sometimes people get got. It's life's way of getting us to wake up. I shoulda been awake in my sleep, just like I been telling you all this time, huh Carlos? Then I would've seen the guy who did me in. I got myself a fractured arm and a split head from all them punches.'

Carlos sits tensely in the blue plastic chair adjacent to Zebra's bed. 'Have you any idea who it was, why they did it?'

'Nah.' Zebra looks at Carlos lazily. 'Coulda been anyone with too much aggression in his heart, someone who hates himself, maybe. Or someone who hates Zebra!' He grins broadly.

'Or someone who attacks people in his sleep?' Carlos' voice is very low. Leo looks at him, then quickly looks away. On Zebra's bedside table there's a thin bunch of purple flowers, the ones that grow all over Portugal, with petals like three veiny leaves joined at the centre. Leo reaches out and touches a petal so that his father will think he isn't listening.

'What you saying?' Zebra sounds startled.

'Six nights ago, I ran out into the streets, Zebra. While I was dreaming. I came back home with blood on my fists. Blood, broken skin, shards of wood . . . like I'd been beating against something, or someone. Olivia already thinks I hammered some guy whose story she read in the local paper. What if I went on a rampage, stumbled across you, and beat the hell out of you too, Zebra?'

Leo glances sideways and sees Zebra screw his face up. 'Oh, *pá*, do me a fuckin' favour! It wasn't you, or some dreaming version of you. Get real, Carlos.'

'How can you be sure?'

'I'm telling you, I didn't see the guy 'cause of all the blood in my eyes from this split head, but I'm dead certain it weren't the work of no dreamrunner.'

'But how can you be certain?' persists Carlos.

253

Zebra laughs. 'I would've heard that damn camera of yours snapping and clicking away.'

'Very funny.'

'I would've smelt the fresh smell of Carlos, but this guy stank of the sewers,' says Zebra firmly.

'Did he?'

'Oh, hell, what do I know? I was drunk-asleep, gone.' Zebra coughs. 'Some folks get eaten right up by the shadow. When it happens, they either die, or they want to hurt others. It's the dark side of humans, and it can creep up any time.'

'These dreams,' says Carlos in a low voice. 'They're my dark side.'

'Only if you let them be.'

Leo steps back from the flowers and looks across at his father. Carlos is frowning, silent.

'Who gave you the flowers, Zebra?' asks Leo timidly.

'The nurse picked them on her dinner hour!' Zebra's eyes gleam wickedly. 'She's a fine one,' he murmurs. 'It's not bad in here, you know, food every five hours, pretty faces smiling at me, a real bed to lie on.'

'Don't you miss your tree?'

'I miss my tree, *menino*, but that tree ain't going nowhere.' Zebra shifts under his sheet. 'Now cheer that father of yours up, won't you?'

'Sorry, sorry. I should be cheering *you* up,' says Carlos with a grimace. 'But things have gone crazy. Olivia threw me out. I'm in a hotel now.'

'That's bad. That's bad, *pá*, but she's all heart, that woman. She'll forgive and forget.' Zebra smacks his lips. 'Now, have you got any cigarettes?'

Carlos laughs. 'Will you kick me out of the hospital if I haven't?'

'Yep.'

254

'Then it's lucky I bought you two packs.' Carlos digs them out of his pockets.

'Aaah,' croons Zebra. 'Even if I have to smoke in the toilet, being spoiled like this almost makes it worth it.'

'Zebra, if you remember anything about your attacker, tell me,' presses Carlos.

'*Claro, claro.*' Zebra winks at Leo. 'Your dad, he don't let a thing go, does he?' Leo smiles into Zebra's big face, but he sees that his father has gone serious again.

Carlos shrugs, sighs. 'I need to know it wasn't me.'

Chapter Forty-five

'*Bom dia*, Senhora Dona Olivia. This is Doutora Lurdes speaking. Do you have a moment to talk?'

The social worker. Olivia's stomach tightens but she forces herself to sound cheerful. '*Sim, claro.*'

'Good. I'm sure you're aware that Leo has been exhibiting aggressive behaviour at school?'

'Leo is very attached to his dolphin project,' says Olivia apologetically. 'He's been working on it for weeks. The other little boy attacked it with a plastic toy.'

'I see. Still, a punch in the face is quite a strong reaction, wouldn't you agree?'

Olivia pinches the bridge of her nose between thumb and forefinger. She wishes she hadn't answered the telephone. She'd been on her way to her studio to begin the day's painting, and it had started to ring as she passed it in the hallway.

'Would you say this reaction is typical of Leo?' persists the social worker.

'Not at all! He's a sweet, friendly child.'

'So in your opinion, this behaviour is linked to the fact that he's been experiencing violence at home?'

'I didn't say that.' Olivia frowns.

'Did you talk to him about what he did?'

'Yes, of course I did. He was very sorry – he knows hitting is wrong.'

'We're pushing for the paperwork to go through so that we can carry out a full psychological assessment of Leo as soon as possible.'

'There's really no need for all this,' protests Olivia. 'He's a perfectly normal little boy!'

'He's a little boy who has recently been on the receiving end of violence, and who is now being violent himself. But even without the punching incident, we'd be making a full report. As I've said before, when parents start hurting their children, we have to act.'

'Well, Carlos won't hurt Leo in his sleep again, as he isn't sleeping in the house any more.'

There's a pause. 'I see. Is this a permanent arrangement?'

'No! The last thing we want is to split up our family, we're just doing this to make sure Leo stays safe. Carlos is in a hotel until the sleep laboratory research has been done and they find out what the problem is.'

'And which hotel is he in?'

'Hotel Castelo, here in the Alfama.'

'Well, Senhora Dona Olivia, I must say it's a relief to know that you're now taking appropriate steps to protect your son.' Doutora Lurdes' voice is distinctly warmer. 'I'll expect a fax of the official diagnosis as soon as you have it.'

'If the diagnosis shows my husband has a sleep disorder that caused his violence to Leo . . .' Olivia tails off.

'Yes?'

'Would you still be able to take Leo away from us?'

'Taking a child away from his family is an extreme measure, it's not something we *want* to do.' Doutora Lurdes clicks her tongue. 'All I can say is that if the medical evidence demonstrates that the violence was not your husband's fault, and if there's a cure for whatever condition he has, then there will be no reason to take your son into our custody. But at this stage I can't guarantee anything.'

'*Obrigada*,' murmurs Olivia, although she doesn't know what she's thanking the woman for.

'What if the sleep laboratory data is inconclusive? It could take weeks to get a proper diagnosis. We can't sleep apart indefinitely!' Carlos has stopped by to see them after a day shooting in a studio in the west of the city. He has ushered Olivia into the kitchen and is whispering because Leo is in the living room.

Olivia sighs inwardly. 'Look, let's just wait and see what happens, OK?'

'What if I start sleeping here again but take a sleeping pill every night *and* you tie me up?'

She forces a laugh. 'This isn't a negotiation, Carlos. You're still dangerous.'

'I'm still your husband,' he says, aggrieved. 'I should be sleeping with you, not in a hotel where I find dog hairs on the sheets and cigarette burns in the bath.'

'So change hotels!'

'This one is closest.' He spins around and from the table he takes up the folded newspaper he brought in with him. 'And anyway – look.' He finds the right page and points to the paragraph he wants her to read. It's the follow-up to the furniture salesman's attack. Olivia skims the text. The man's attacker has been apprehended. He turned out to be a coke addict on the lowest rung of the dealing ladder, and the salesman owed him money, or some such story – Olivia barely takes in the details.

'It wasn't you,' she says. 'Oh Carlos, that's good news.'

He nods, tosses the paper back onto the table and leans against the fridge, which is covered with Leo's drawings, stuck on with animal magnets. 'Maybe I'm not the huge public danger you think I am.'

'Maybe not.' She hesitates. 'I'm sorry I suggested it was you. It was just the blood on your fists . . . and now Zebra's beating – we still can't be sure what really happened.'

'The blood on my fists – I think I must have just beaten against a tree trunk or something. There were splinters, the skin was ripped . . . Olivia, *tenho saudades tuas*. I miss you. And I want to come home.'

'You sleeping here is dangerous, Carlos! You *know* we can't take any risks.' Olivia moves to put the kettle on. 'That social worker phoned again this morning, asking about Leo's fight. They're all over us.'

He tenses. 'What did you tell her?'

'Well, one of the things I told her was that he's completely safe from harm because you're sleeping in a hotel, and to be honest it felt good to be able to give that reassurance.' She gets out a couple of mugs and hunts for Rosa's sachets of handmade herbal tea. 'Did you want a tea?' she asks belatedly, turning to face him. Carlos shakes his head. 'I know she's going to check you're in that hotel,' she continues, 'so it's doubly important you stay there. She was actually more or less OK to talk to this time – she can see we're taking steps to solve the problem and, as much as I love sleeping in your arms, I'm not risking *anything* any more.'

They exchange a long look.

'The moment the doctors find out what's wrong and give you the treatment you need, you'll be back here again, my love.' Olivia is resolutely upbeat, but every night when she finds herself alone in their bed, she misses him terribly. 'I know you're nervous about tonight at the sleep lab,' she adds. 'But you'll see, it'll be fine.'

Carlos mutters something and turns away.

'What was that dark muttering?' Olivia teases, catching hold of his shirtsleeve. He looks at her unhappily. 'Come on,' she coaxes. 'This isn't like you.'

'What *is* like me? I don't even know any more.'

She shakes her head, still holding on to him. 'Don't be like that. Rationally, we're just dealing with a couple of bad dreams, nothing more.'

'So why do I find myself kicked out of my home?'

'Oh, Carlos.' Olivia releases her hold on his sleeve. 'I don't have the strength to argue in circles like this. Could you *please* stop making this even harder than it already is?' She makes one more attempt to lighten his mood. 'Think of it as a kind of holiday from family life.'

'A holiday? A holiday?'

'OK, look –'

'Olivia, this is no holiday for me. It's one for you, is that it?'

'No!' She brings a finger to her lips, reminding him that Leo is close by. 'I'm just trying to get you to relax a bit – we can't carry on getting more and more stressed around each other with each night that you sleep elsewhere, or things will just . . . disintegrate.'

'Disintegrate?' Carlos stares at her in consternation. 'What will disintegrate?'

'Wrong word – I just mean that things will be even more difficult.' Olivia sighs. 'Please try and take this situation of us *temporarily* sleeping apart a little more lightly.' She watches him as he bites back whatever he'd been about to say. 'For Leo's sake,' she whispers, 'let's not spend the little time we have together arguing.'

Chapter Forty-six

The video image on Dr Loverock's laptop is grey and grainy. It shows the long form of Carlos partially covered by a white bed sheet, the dark slash of his brows just recognisable in the dimness. At the top right of the screen is a digital clock, paused at 3.12 am. Last night, for the first time, Carlos slept in the Cruz Vermelha Hospital sleep laboratory with electrodes positioned on a skullcap and further leads attached to his chest, shins and the corners of his eyes. While he slept, information ranging from brainwaves, airflow, and leg muscle movement was recorded. Olivia can't take her eyes from the screen. Carlos looks so vulnerable asleep under all those wires. As she settles into the chair next to him in the doctor's sunlit room, she aches to be closer still. He has barely smiled at her since she turfed him out of the house, is so serious now whenever she sees him.

'Well, Mr Moniz,' says Dr Loverock. 'As you know, you had a brief moving nightmare last night and the sleep technologist carried out a video polysomnography that recorded the episode. Would you like to see the relevant section of film?'

Carlos shifts in his chair and looks askance at Olivia, who hesitates, then nods. 'It might be good for you to see what you do,' she murmurs. She thinks about reaching out her hand to touch him, but he is frowning intently as the doctor swivels her laptop around to face them and starts the laboratory recording.

'I've only viewed this once myself,' she says. 'I'd like you to watch your actions, Mr Moniz, and see if they bring forth any associations for you. Then we'll talk about the diagnosis.'

'Fine.'

On the screen, the time flashes past in red, digital seconds. At 03.13, the sleeping shape jerks into action; an arm lashes out and then the sheet is thrown off as the sleeper kicks out frantically and leaps from the bed with spectacular speed, trailing electrodes.

Olivia experiences a rush of excitement to see that Carlos has had an episode while under observation and that the doctor has seen this. Surely this is a great step forward? She darts a glance at Carlos and sees him biting down on his lip as he watches. 'It's insane,' he mutters.

The Carlos on the video stands stock-still following his leap, shaking his head violently from side to side. His hands fly out. 'Pedro!' he shouts, his voice thick. Then he twists around, wrenches at the wires taped to his face, and stares uncomprehendingly into space as the seconds tick by.

'At this point, there was no more recording as most of the electrodes had been ripped off,' explains Dr Loverock, and she stops the video. 'The technician then went in and you were in a confused state, so he waited for you to become calm and then reattached the electrodes and you went back to sleep with no further incident.'

Carlos nods, looking disturbed. 'So I didn't run?'

'Not this time.' The doctor looks at him. 'How did it feel, watching yourself?'

Olivia looks at Carlos curiously. He seems numb. 'It felt strange, like watching someone else. I don't remember any of it, not even the technician hooking me up to the machines again. Did I shout "Pedro"?'

'Yes. Do you know who that might be?'

'No idea,' says Carlos.

Olivia feels a surge of impatience. 'Oh, Carlos, you *must* know,' she insists. 'Think back!'

He turns to her indignantly. 'I'm not saying this to irritate you – I really don't know. The only Pedro I know is the guy who rented out your first exhibition space to you, and I barely met him.'

'You may find that other associations return over the next few hours or days,' says Dr Loverock. 'In the meantime, I can tell you that I don't believe you have REM Sleep Behaviour Disorder.'

Carlos leans forwards. 'Really? Even though I do *that* at night?'

The doctor smiles. 'I agree that on the strength of that video clip alone, RBD would be a possible diagnosis, but as I mentioned to you when we first met, RBD isn't the only parasomnia associated with dream-enacting behaviour.' She fiddles with a sheaf of papers in front of her and holds one up for them to see. 'This is a summary of what the electrodes picked up just before and during your episode, before they were ripped off by your movements.'

'OK,' says Carlos, eyeing the figures doubtfully. 'So . . .'

'So when I looked at the physiological data, I discovered that there was no appreciable increase in muscle tone during REM sleep. That rules out REM Sleep Behaviour Disorder.' The doctor places her papers together and looks from Carlos to Olivia. 'The EEG, which records brainwaves, showed no epileptic symptoms, which makes me inclined to think you aren't having nocturnal seizures. Your behavioural incident arose from Stage One sleep. Based on everything you've told me, along with the sleep-laboratory data and our therapy session, I believe what we've got here is a case of SRDD: Sleep-related Dissociative Disorder, a kind of hysterical somnam-bulistic trance, provoked by the emergence of an unresolved or forgotten trauma.'

Olivia and Carlos exchange a look. 'That's the one where if I can

263

recall the trauma, I might not have to take medication, right?' asks Carlos.

'Exactly. In this case, a therapeutic response could be just as effective. I've treated many patients with recurrent nightmares and, as I think I mentioned before, these nightmares were almost always traceable to a traumatic life event. Once that event was brought to consciousness and discussed in a therapeutic way, the nightmares stopped.'

'But with me, it doesn't seem to want to come to consciousness,' says Carlos in frustration.

'We've only had one regressive therapy session so far,' the doctor points out gently. 'You're right at the start of the process, and these things can take time. Another possibility is trying to become aware of the dream while you're in it.'

'You said something about a trance . . . *am* I actually dreaming when it happens?'

Dr Loverock smiles slightly. 'It's a tricky one. A dissociative event can be experienced by the patient as a dream, with moving imagery, but in all probability, this "dream" is a dissociated memory of a past trauma which is being replayed in the mind like a film. To all intents and purposes, you're in an altered state of consciousness – in your case, Stage One sleep – and you're reliving a nightmarish scenario so vividly that reality is lost to you while it's unfolding. In that sense, it's exactly like a recurring nightmare. Studies have shown that dream lucidity can help eliminate recurring nightmares because deep conflicts can be resolved when the sufferer "wakes up" during the traumatic scenario and changes it into something positive.'

'But I'm so unconscious in these nightmares, or whatever they are, I don't remember any imagery, nothing. It's like being in a coma.'

'A dissociative disorder is your mind's way of defending you – the mind tries to protect you from painful memories or emotions by

264

separating and suppressing them. So it's not surprising you don't remember a thing. Before you go to sleep at night, I'd like you to suggest to yourself that you are ready to remember.'

'I'll do that.' Carlos clears his throat. 'We've got the social services on our backs because of the bruises I've inflicted on my son while having these episodes. I've been sleeping in a hotel to make sure he and my wife stay safe, but I'm going to need a written diagnosis, please, preferably with some sort of statement that the violence is not my fault, but part of this, uh, parasomnia I have.'

'Absolutely no problem,' says Dr Loverock understandingly. 'I also think we should continue with the therapy sessions to see whether we can make headway that way. Chronic, relapsing histories are common with this particular disorder, so exploratory psychotherapy is strongly recommended; the faster we make a breakthrough, the sooner your lives can return to normal. And, Mr Moniz, do remember that visualisation is a powerful mental tool. Try to see yourself remembering this trauma, and try to see yourself becoming aware of the state you're in when you next have an episode, so that you can guide events towards a positive conclusion. Are you practising the meditation techniques I suggested last time?'

'Sure – I'm trying everything.'

'And how's that going?'

'I think I'm getting better at it.' Carlos hesitates. 'When I manage to stop listening to all my thoughts, sometimes I sort of float towards a feeling of dread. It's hard to explain . . . it's like a kind of dark cloud.'

'How do you react when you see the dark cloud?'

'Well, at first I would shrink away – I didn't mean to, it just happened – and then my eyes would snap open. But a few nights ago, I managed to stay put and the cloud grew and grew and I started to sweat all over my body, and tremble, and there was this overpowering feeling of dread.' He glances across at Olivia, and she remembers that this happened on Carlos' fourth night alone in the hotel. 'Just when I had the feeling it was about to engulf me, I snapped out of it.'

The doctor nods. 'Well, you're clearly getting somewhere. When it next happens, try to remain calm and receptive. Accept the feeling of dread, and be open to whatever you might see or experience.'

As they are preparing to leave, Dr Loverock says, 'By the way, it's hard to make a diagnosis *in absentia*, but from what you told me in our initial consultation, it sounds as though your aunt may have had SRED – Sleep-related Eating Disorder, where entire meals can be prepared and eaten, often very sloppily, while the person is asleep.'

Carlos looks nonplussed. 'But apparently she got violent and threatened my father with a knife.'

'People with that condition can get aggressive if thwarted in their mission to find and eat food, and someone encountering a sleep-walker might not realise that he or she is in fact asleep. Some dreamers have even been known to drive their cars for fairly long distances in their sleep without causing an accident – so they behave in an outwardly rational manner – and then while in that same state of automatism, where the body is no longer controlled by the rational mind, they perform violent acts on loved ones which they are horrified to learn about afterwards.' She looks at Carlos. 'And of course you know all about that.'

'I do.'

Dr Loverock taps her pen on the desk. 'I'm assuming your aunt must have had other psychiatric symptoms to have been institutionalised the way she was – or should I say, I'm *hoping* she did, but the terrible thing is that many people with sleep disorders have been misdiagnosed in the past, and still are today, and that often results in great suffering.'

There's a brief silence.

'I have to remember,' says Carlos. 'Who the hell is Pedro?' He looks at the doctor. 'There's just nothing there.'

The river is slow and sparkling. Carlos and Olivia are sprawled in giant wicker chairs by the water's edge, sipping freshly squeezed orange juice and going over everything that happened at the doctor's. He has booked himself in for another session of regressive dream-work the following Friday.

'What's she going to do next time, hypnotise me?' he jokes.

'Maybe.' Olivia is serious. She leans her head back and looks up at the sky. 'If it works, we won't complain.'

Carlos passes a hand over his head. 'You know, I had a funny thing as we were driving to this café. It's strange –' He stops.

'No, go on,' says Olivia.

'Well . . . just as we got down to the river, I had this image, of a boy, kind of dirty, standing under a street lamp.'

Olivia sits up with difficulty. 'Do you think "Pedro" is a boy?'

'I don't know – it might have been some random image, something I saw on the TV, or just anything, really.' Carlos stops and thinks. 'But . . . you know, I'm almost sure I had a friend called Pedro when I was small. An imaginary friend.'

'Imaginary?'

His forehead creases. 'I *think* he was imaginary.'

'Maybe Rosa will remember.' Olivia is tapping her fingertips on the table. 'Talk about this boy under the street lamp,' she says. 'Just say anything, really fast, whatever comes into your head.'

Carlos frowns. 'OK. He's small, about seven or eight . . . I *like* him, he's my brother . . . my brother? That's weird.'

'Don't question it, just keep speaking,' urges Olivia, but Carlos seems to have no more to say. She waits in silence for a while, then stands up abruptly.

'What is it?' asks Carlos, shielding his eyes against the sun as he looks at her.

'My luck,' says Olivia. 'You cannot steal my luck . . . did *Pedro* steal your luck?'

'The amulet . . . Pedro . . .' Carlos rubs his brow in frustration.

'We're getting there,' says Olivia. 'You're remembering!'

'But what does it add up to? Nothing.' He squints up at her. 'Do you think he's the person I killed? A little boy?'

Olivia sits down again. 'I don't know.' Her eyes fill with tears. 'I hope not.'

Chapter Forty-seven

5 August 1984

I'm curled up next to Rosa with her warm arm around me. We're on a metal bench in the walled patio at the back of the house, Mãe's favourite place, with its blue *azulejos* of ships and birds, the slim green leaves of hanging plants, and the cool silver fountain that rises from the middle of it all. Since Rosa came home for the summer holidays, we've been playing together every day and she has smiled and tickled my words out of me so that I speak again almost the way I used to before the blood.

I stroke the fine black hairs on Rosa's arm and she laughs. 'I know a secret,' she whispers, and I sit up straight and look into her black eyes.

'Tell me.'

'First you have to cross your heart, Carlitos.'

I cross my heart.

'And second, if I tell you my secret, you must tell me yours.' Rosa's smile has gone.

I shake my head. 'I've forgotten it.'

She pushes me a little bit away from her on the bench and draws her feet under her long red sundress. 'Carlitos, I'm your sister. You can tell me.'

I can't look at her. This is what Marina did after the blood, with smiles so warm I could barely stop my mouth. 'Rosa, I have no secret for you.' I drop my head and try to stop the tears that sting the back of my nose.

'You have a secret, Carlitos. You've changed so much – look at you, so thin! And no words left in you when I came home. Is it Mãe? You're scared she'll leave us like Marina did?'

I shake my head and tears spot my trousers.

Rosa sighs. 'Don't be a crybaby. If Mãe sees you have red eyes, she'll be sad.'

I think of Mãe, who is at home again now but won't even leave her bed to visit her patio any more, and I sniff the tears back where they came from.

'I'll tell you my secret if you cheer up.' Rosa sounds worried and I know she thinks Mãe will tell her off if she finds out Rosa has made me cry.

'It's about Marina,' Rosa says, and I look up at her so she sees the hope on my face.

'When's she coming home?'

'I don't know that. But when I was helping Inês bake bread yesterday morning, she told me where she is.'

'Where?' For the past three weeks, since she left, I've been imagining Marina playing with her tiny baby on the high walls of a castle, the wind blowing through her hair and making her cheeks red and alive.

'She's in a kind of hospital for mad people.' Rosa stares at me, waiting for me to say something.

'Mad people?' Pedro said the crow-man was mad. I shudder when I think of him. Father used to tell Marina she was mad. I picture Marina walking and walking in her white nightdress, almost bumping into other men and women and children who are doing the same thing. But if that's what mad is, I must be mad too, unless Father ties me to the bed and stops me from being it.

'*Sim*, Carlitos, *malucos*. Mad people. That means people who are wrong in their heads, like the whistling man who jiggles his keys when he walks up Rua do Salvador.'

The whistling man is awful; he stinks of dustbins. The crow-man is much worse. I don't want Marina to be with people like them.

'Am I mad?' I ask Rosa quickly.

She laughs. 'You're not mad. Inês said Marina needed to be looked after by doctors, but you don't, do you?'

'Mãe needs doctors too, but she's at home. Why did Marina have to go away?'

We hear a heavy step in the passageway that leads to the patio, and our eyes meet.

'Don't tell,' hisses Rosa, and there's just enough time to cross my heart again before Father strides across the patio towards us. His beard is bushier now. He spends all his time with Mãe, and the more yellow and papery she gets, the greyer he gets.

'What are you two idlers doing out here?'

Rosa sits with her back very straight. 'I'm teaching Carlitos spelling, Pai.'

I look at her in admiration. To lie like that to Father!

'What have you learned, lad?'

My head snaps around to where Father stands, and I can't think of a single word I could spell aloud for him. I see again Marina writing 'P-E-D-R-O' on the dusty tiles of the Santa Luzia viewpoint, and I can't speak even though Father is waiting.

Father's expression softens. 'Still not talking?'

'I'm looking after him,' says Rosa, and again I admire her grown-upness.

'Your *mãe* is very poorly,' he says. 'It's right that you look after your brother.' Then he pats me on the head and smiles kindly, and this surprises Rosa and I so much that it takes us a long moment to make our faces work so that we can smile back. Then Father turns around and leaves us.

'See – he can still smile,' whispers Rosa when he's gone. 'He just saves them all for Mãe.'

'Mãe needs them more than we do,' I whisper back, and vow to give her my best smile when Father next allows me to go up and see her, the smile that makes her say what sparkling teeth I have and what a good boy I am for brushing them so well.

Five days go by where I play hopscotch in the walled patio with Rosa every day and she tells me tales from her school. Things are getting better – even Mãe is coughing less and that must be a good thing.

Then the police come to our house.

This time, Father weeps.

He weeps, and his sobs climb up the stairs to where Rosa and I are lying on my bedroom floor playing marbles. We run to the top of the stairs on our tiptoes and see two policemen below us in the entrance hall, holding their dark-blue caps in their hands. They look very sorry. Inês is staring from a doorway. Mãe begins to call feebly from her bed, wanting to know what is happening.

'Marina!' Father cries. '*A minha irmã*, my sister!' He keeps crying this. *My sister, my sister!*

Rosa sits down suddenly and grips the banisters, peering down at Father. '*Não pode ser*, it cannot be,' she murmurs.

'What?' I ask desperately. Then the impossible happens: the bedroom door opens and Mãe comes out, her face bleak, her mouth twisted. '*Ai não*,' she cries. 'No, no!'

Rosa is crying too. 'Mãe,' she says, and jumps to her feet to help her.

'What, what?' I pull at her sleeve as she tries to pass me.

'Marina has gone.'

'Gone?' She's escaped, I think, gone away from all the mad people, gone to play with the sailor's baby in a high castle.

272

'Dead, *meu querido*,' says Rosa, pushing past me to help Mãe, who is tall and wobbling on thin legs. 'Marina is dead.'

On the day of Marina's funeral, Mãe calls Rosa and me to her room. She's wearing a black dress that Inês had to tuck with her needle so it fits her thin body. Her black hat is trimmed with lace and she's wearing a black wig and there's make-up on her big, tear-filled eyes. Rosa gasps and Mãe smiles a little. She's sitting at her dresser and her jewellery pot is overflowing with diamond and ruby bracelets. I think of the lucky amulet, which I don't have any more. Mãe must have noticed it's gone from my neck, but she never speaks of it. It didn't bring luck to our family after all.

'Fix this to my wrist, will you, *querida*?' Mãe asks Rosa in a small voice. When the bracelet is on, she looks from Rosa to me. 'Death takes people away, and one day I will die. I want the two of you to stick together, help each other through your lives. Do you understand?'

We nod. Rosa is crying again.

'Your father . . .' Mãe hesitates. Her black wig is very shiny. 'Your father is weak,' she whispers. 'He can't look after you as well as he wants to. I fear for him.' She holds out her hands and we take one each. She is queenly, beautiful. 'You must take care of each other, for ever, because I will not always be here.'

When Marina's funeral is over, the whole house feels sad. Inês never tiptoed before but now she does. Father weeps. How can he have so many tears? His beard collects them but they still fall. Rosa says she peeped through a crack in the bedroom door last night and saw him stretched out on Mãe's bed, clutching her and crying, 'You can't leave me, you can't.'

I don't believe I'll never see or touch Marina again. When I walk through the house I think she'll jump out at me from behind a door,

273

and when I'm in bed I think she'll come and sing me a story before I sleep. But where she was there is no noise, no smell of roses, just empty space. I think the doctors who were looking after Marina killed her because she was mad, and if walking in my sleep makes me mad, they might come and get me, too.

Father still comes to tie me to the bed, but his heart isn't in it. He's even stopped telling me to forget, but I tell myself to, every night. I say it in my head before I sleep, so many times that it turns into one jumbly word, and saying it over and over blots out all the blood.

Chapter Forty-eight

Olivia is drugged by sunshine, her limbs reposing blissfully on the sand, protected from the worst of the wind by a barricade of towels and swimming bags. There's a book propped open on her knees but her eyes are closed under an infusion of orange warmth. This is the first time in weeks that she's felt relaxed, she realises. They've made a pact today not to argue about Carlos still sleeping in a hotel, even though it's been nine days now and he is desperate to come home; the goal of this Saturday is to treat Leo to a carefree time on his favourite beach, Guincho. The suncream she has smeared onto her face and arms smells of summer holidays, easier times. Squinting lazily, she can see Leo and Concha mucking around in the sand a way down the beach, Carlos crouched beside them. She wonders why they didn't start their sandcastle nearer to where she and Carlos have set up camp. Are they too cool already, at just seven years old? Smiling to herself, she closes her eyes again and drifts into a state somewhere between sleep and waking.

Carlos, wet from the sea, has been admiring the sand-circus the two children are making.

'Pai, are we allowed ice cream?' asks Leo, and Carlos laughs.

'Your mum might say it's too close to lunchtime.'

'Oh, please!' Both children stare at him.

'All right, why not?' He drops his hand onto Leo's head to ruffle his wet hair, and stands up. 'What do you both want, then?' He takes their orders – a double chocolate cone for Concha and a strawberry Cornetto for Leo – and walks away.

Concha looks expectantly at Leo. 'OK, now I need a bit of washed-up jellyfish, or even a whole baby jellyfish.' She's wearing a pink bikini with worn straps, and there's sand in her tangle of black hair, sand plastered all down her wet arms and legs.

It was Concha's idea to build a circus out of sand, and although Leo had begged his parents for this treat – Concha with him all day, a trip to the beach and later a DVD at Rosa's place – he's finding it tiring to keep up with her demands. He has already sacrificed his stripy beach towel for the roof of the circus tent, and Concha took the rubber strap from his new goggles to make a tightrope which she has expertly stretched from one block of sand to another. 'The jellyfish will be a trampoline, see?' she says excitedly.

Leo nods, but he's not really listening. He watches as his father walks a little way up the beach and pauses next to where his mother is lying. He keeps sneaking looks at his parents today, to see if they're all right. Ever since Carlos stopped sleeping at their house, Leo has felt strange. He needs to look at the two of them together to make sure they don't disappear.

Carlos' voice startles Olivia out of falling into a deeper sleep. The wind is flapping the handles of Concha's plastic beach bag, which is lying beside Olivia, and Carlos' words are partially obscured by the sound.

'Just grabbing a few euros,' he says. 'The kids want ice creams. Do you fancy one?'

'Hmm? No, it's all right, thanks,' Olivia murmurs without opening her eyes.

'OK, we're off to the café, then,' she hears him say, so she knows Leo and Concha will be tagging along with him. She's feeling too sun-struck lazy to crane her head around and watch the three of them walking down the beach, even though watching Leo and Carlos together is something that always makes her happy – Carlos' head bent solicitously towards his son; Leo swinging on his father's hand as he chatters up at him. She pulls her sunhat further down over her face and sighs. Maybe once we've found a cure for Carlos' nightmares, it'll finally be the right time to try for another baby, she thinks, surprising herself with this leap ahead to a happy future. She smiles at the thought of a sister for Leo, a daughter for Carlos. A tiny, green-eyed beauty with curled hands and those funny, flexible toes babies have. Olivia daydreams, dozes off.

'Leo?' Concha waves a blue spade at him. 'The jellyfish?'

Leo's eyes are still on his parents. When his father jogs away along the beach, he hesitates, unconsciously waiting for his mother to search him out with her eyes and wave to let him know she's looking out for him and Concha, but she remains lying down.

'Leo!'

'OK, I'll get you a jellyfish,' he promises, and runs down to the sea, his wet shorts clinging to his thighs, his dolphin-eye necklace bouncing lightly on his clavicle. He stands for a long moment and scans the shoreline. There are no washed-up jellyfish in sight, but the sea is cold and playful. It tugs around Leo's ankles, asking him to join in. He stomps along the edge of the water making splashes, weaving through the smaller kids who stand staring wide-eyed at the sea, holding red buckets or tiny crabs. After a few minutes, he stops looking for jellyfish and starts looking far out into the sea, for dolphins.

Underneath Leo's game is an awareness that his parents aren't watching him. It's just him and this glorious, cheeky sea, and even though part of him recalls the countless repetitions of wave-danger, before he knows it, he is swimming, the waves coating him with salt which has the taste of something just beyond his grasp, something as elusive as dolphins. He revels in the cold roll of the water, its thick glitter rearing just in front of him and descending to crash over his hair which is made up of a hundred damp squiggles plastering his forehead, his eyelashes transformed into long black spikes. Leo's arms, brown and alive, splash forwards, taking him further into this wave-world, only him and the sea now, rolling together, all thoughts of his parents gone. There is only the foam and spray, his toes lifting away from the sand as a wave picks him up like an amusement ride, carrying him onwards and outwards.

The sun is hot on Carlos' shoulders as he walks back from the café with the ice creams. His eyes are on the kite-surfers. Carlos has tried kite-surfing before, enjoyed the feeling of fighting with the wind and making huge leaps into the air. There's a lot of wind today; the waves are white-tipped, crawling with the black bodies of surfers.

He can see Olivia now, sprawled on her back in the strappy white sundress with the bodice that lifts her breasts, the thin material of the skirt flowing over her hips. Her limbs are pleasantly suntanned, her hair blonder than usual after an early start to what is turning into a very hot summer. Although her knees are up and she has rested an open book against them, she doesn't look as if she's reading. He glances to the place where Leo and Concha have set up camp, and sees only Concha. Automatically, he scans the small bodies playing in the shallows.

Leo is nowhere to be seen.

Carlos stops walking, turns, and sends his gaze out over the beach. He feels a twinge of self-righteous annoyance at Olivia, who is sleeping rather than watching their son. But this feeling is immediately erased by a stab of anxiety, and he quickens his pace.

*

Leo licks salt from his lips. What's that, out beyond just a few more lines of white-tipped waves? He kicks frantically, buoying himself up so that he can get a better view. Surely it can't be? But there it is again, the smooth flash of a dark-grey dorsal fin, a shining flank disappearing back under the water.

The dolphins have come to him.

Leo's happiness makes a direct switch into euphoria. He is deliciously aware of the blood singing through his veins, the movement and power of his kicks as he ploughs towards the dolphins. The dorsal fin is like a beckoning, fatherly hand and Leo pictures himself sitting proudly on the dolphin's broad and slippery back, holding on to that same fin. This is his chance to save his father from the sleep monster who, out here in the waves, is no more than the faintest shadow, something that when confronted with a boy riding the finest dolphin in the Atlantic, would have no choice but to disappear.

He swims on manfully, his breath rasping in his throat, water stinging his eyes. His arms are heavy. Where have the dolphins gone? Then, like a manifestation of beauty, he sees three of them – magic three! – leaping in synchrony just ten metres from him, the angle of their arc perfect, the alignment of their sleek bodies millimetre-precise. As they leap, Leo loves every second of their trajectory, admires the curve of their noses, their benignly smiling mouths. He feels himself transported, brought to the brink of the place where magic happens. Instinctively, he knows it's time to make his wish. As the dolphins dive back into the water with barely a splash, Leo gathers his thoughts, treading water with all his strength.

'Save Daddy from the sleep monster,' he prays. 'Please, save my daddy.'

A shimmer runs across the surface of the water, and then it disappears. The ocean seems vast and silent. The dolphins have gone, taking his wish with them.

Leo's breath is laboured, his limbs barely seem his own any more, leaden and unresponsive. And the waves keep coming, not giving him a break. There's a greyness visible in the water now: all signs of that impossible beauty have vanished with the flight of the dolphins. Leo fights to turn around and understands how far he is from the shore; there are waves and waves to battle through. The sea slaps water mean-spiritedly into his face and, as Leo struggles not to choke on it, something Zebra once said to him whispers in his mind: 'The spell is stronger than the spell-maker.'

He spits, coughs, his limbs thrashing now, panicking. Where are the dolphins?

He's alone, more alone than he has ever been in his short life. Not far off, to his left, Leo glimpses the gliding bodies of surfers, but they don't notice his small black head. They are focused on their thrills, jealously watching each other's feats, unaware of any peril. Leo has no spare breath with which to shout; the sea is a tireless, brutal opponent, tossing him further back from safety with each wave.

Leo realises he is too far from the shore, too tired, too cold. He gulps more water, his body hanging in the cold immensity of the ocean, and he feels his muscles give in as the waves suck him downwards.

Chapter Forty-nine

Feeling increasingly worried, Carlos turns back to the sea. He looks at the line where the waves foam onto the sand, forming loops and sideways curves as the strong current sucks them back. The tide is going out. Unwillingly, he lifts his gaze further out. For the moment, there is nothing. Then, in the blink of an eye, just beyond the breaking waves, he sees the white, panicked face of his son turned slightly to one side, his mouth open, his eyes just dots from this distance. The very moment that his father sights him, Leo's head goes under.

Carlos drops his handful of ice creams and loose change and snaps into action, his body no longer his own but a fighting, pumping machine, all muscle and speed and strength as he careers down the sand, no voice in him to shout his son's name, no time to alert Olivia, no thoughts because thoughts would be too dangerous: the distance is too great, there is no way he can reach Leo, who is drowning now, salt water turning to fire in his lungs – no possible way he can reach him before it's too late.

As his legs hammer, something in Carlos understands without thought that all the magnified strength he has in his nightmares is available, ready to be tapped here in waking life. Every pore in his body, every bone, every cell is straining towards the same purpose as he runs, his feet kicking up wet sand, adults snatching their children out of his path, recognising the tragedy they see in his face. Carlos makes a dive into the water, cutting though it, arms knifing, legs pistonlike in their power as he strikes out to his boy though he can't see him any more, has not been able to see him since that first moment of recognition, but Leo's white face is there in his mind's eye like a beacon, every inch of his consciousness is focused on it.

Olivia's eyes spring open as she identifies a feeling of intense unease, which starts somewhere in her chest and mounts towards her neck, making her swallow nervously. It's the same awareness that used to wake her just before Leo cried in the night as a baby. For a second, she tries to throw it off, believing as she does that Leo is safely with Carlos and Concha. Then she pushes off her sunhat and sits up straight, blinking. A little way down the beach, Concha is lying on her belly, decorating a large pile of tightly packed sand, but Leo isn't anywhere near her. Why isn't Concha with Leo and Carlos? Olivia is just about to call to Concha and ask her when there's a commotion on the shoreline.

She looks over to see Carlos diving into the shallow waves and swimming insanely fast in a straight line out towards the breakers. Olivia scrambles to her feet, upturning her novel, scattering sand. Instinctively, she looks out beyond Carlos, following the direction in which he is swimming, but she can see nothing but blue waves. This is a short section of the beach where the waves cut in over rocks and so the surfers avoid it, focusing on the action to the right and left of it.

Olivia's heart begins to pound dizzyingly. She scans the beach. Leo will still be standing in the queue for ice cream; Carlos must have seen someone in trouble, a battered surfer, perhaps. But she finds herself running down to the water's edge, shouting, 'Don't go anywhere!' to a startled Concha as she passes. She slews to a halt in the shallows and stares out at Carlos, his knifing arms. Her eyes jump beyond him to where there is nothing, nobody.

As he swims in a furious front crawl that slices through the waves, Carlos enters a state of absolute awareness. Pictures rise in his mind with startling clarity. He sees himself, asleep and in the throes of destruction. He sees Leo swinging off a tree in Estrela park, sees clearly his little muscles which are developing so well, turning him into a strong boy. Carlos ducks underwater and swims hard and flat beneath the breaking waves, torpedolike, unstoppable.

Sensing that he is approaching the spot where he last saw Leo, his eyes open and he slows. The water is murky, but he can see through it, his eyes stinging terribly. He has breath in his lungs, held tightly. There is nothing here, no kicking legs. The only movement is from the waves above him. Carlos swims forwards, blinking in all directions. His eyes are on fire but he barely notices. Then, away to his right, he sees a limp, star-shaped shadow suspended in the water.

He swims towards it.

Just to the right of Olivia, another man rushes determinedly into the water, with a bodyboard under his arm. Apparently he is going after Carlos. Olivia has the fleeting thought that Carlos is having one of his moving nightmares in broad daylight and has been wreaking havoc. This man must be chasing him to calm him down.

She turns to a woman who is standing near her. 'What is it?' she asks. 'What's happening?'

The woman is middle-aged, wearing a stripy blue one-piece which stretches over her belly. '*Está um menino pequeno na água,*' she says, grim-faced. There's a little boy in the water. A little boy. Olivia's head grows thick with terror. Leo!

Carlos has vanished. Only the man who followed him in can be seen, splashing clumsily through the waves on his board, infinitely slower than Carlos. Of Leo, there is no sign. Nothing. The waves are rolling, lethal.

Olivia runs into the water, her eyes straining as she searches. When the water is thigh deep, she stops.

If they surface, I need to be visible, she thinks through the thud, thud in her head. *When*, she corrects herself. When they surface. But there is nothing to be seen, no bobbing heads, no waving arms. As she stands half-submerged, staring into an empty sea, she sees her life as it will be without them: a grey limbo drained of all beauty. Far out, beyond the brutal smash and roll, there is the flashing leap of something that might be a dolphin, heading out towards the open sea. Olivia finds her voice.

She screams.

Chapter Fifty

Leo's body is a dead weight, his limbs dragging as Carlos lifts him from the water and hefts him over one shoulder as he kicks to stay afloat. There's no movement, no gasping breaths, no coughing.

Spitting out sea water, Carlos whacks Leo on the back, knowing this isn't enough, that it's having no effect. How the hell can I do mouth-to-mouth suspended like this in the ocean? he thinks, twisting his head in a frantic attempt to see Leo's face. Then the water beside him swirls and he looks around to see a man pushing forwards a polystyrene bodyboard. Grey hair is plastered to his skull, and his face is vital and resolute. He holds the board as still as he can and Carlos rolls Leo on top of it. His son's face is so pale it's almost green.

He looks dead, thinks Carlos, but I have to try.

With Leo supported by the board, and the man watching him, Carlos starts pumping Leo's lungs. Sea water gushes out and a wave sloshing over the bodyboard instantly rinses it away. Leo's skin is alabaster white, his face devoid of expression as Carlos squeezes his nostrils closed and begins mouth-to-mouth.

The sea and this small, floating body and the taste of salt is all there is.

Raising his head to snatch another breath of life for his son, Carlos sees that around Leo's fragile neck is a chain, something round and shiny-blue hanging off it, nestling at the base of his throat. As he breathes air into Leo's lungs, feels them puff and rise under his hand, Carlos sees a sapphire amulet, his father's angry face, a vast pool of blood. He dies, he thinks, and now he sees it all again, can remember every detail, and he lifts his head to catch another breath but instead of breathing it into Leo he screams instead, 'Don't die!'

The wind whips his voice away and the man in the water beside him is saying something, his brown eyes narrowed in sympathy or pain.

Sea water gushes from Leo's lungs or his stomach, and this time he splutters, takes his first unassisted breath.

'Leo, stay with me,' cries Carlos. He puts his hand on his son's face but it remains closed and unresponsive, the lips bluish.

'Let's take him in,' shouts the man, and the two of them guide Leo through the waves on his polystyrene bed, stopping twice and treading water so that Carlos can breathe encouraging puffs of air into Leo's lungs.

Standing in the shallows, her arms held out to them, her face blind with horror, is Olivia. She runs towards them, grabs an edge of the bodyboard, leans screaming over Leo.

Guincho is a long, wide beach with dunes which sweep right up to the road and spill over it on windy days. Entire sections of the beach remain unaware of any tragedy, but the bathers within a twenty-metre radius of the small white body laid out on the sand stand as grimly as pall-bearers, incongruent in their bathing suits. The endless beach rituals of repositioning windbreakers, applying suncream, and having a dip in the water cease and there is something uncanny about the craning heads, the solemnly observed progression of the emergency services down the beach to where Leo lies.

As soon as Carlos has laid Leo down, he and Olivia squat on

either side of him, rubbing his chest to prevent the onset of hypothermia. Leo's eyes are closed, his face as still as porcelain. Carlos watches his ragged, uneven breathing. He is terrified that he will stop breathing at any moment. It feels as if the meagre warmth their hands are rubbing into his limbs is the only thing keeping his heart beating.

'I need to keep pumping his lungs empty,' Carlos realises suddenly, and moves to do so.

'No! Leave him now, he's breathing on his own,' Olivia says. Her voice is high and unnatural.

'He could die if I don't.'

'Don't say that, he's fine!'

'He could still die,' says Carlos urgently. He pushes Olivia's hands away and starts to press down on Leo's chest. 'When the lungs are partially clogged with water, the oxygen supply to the rest of the body is blocked. It can result in multiple organ failure, brain damage . . .'

'But I can see him breathing, Carlos. You shouldn't interfere with him!'

'Until we get him to a hospital, there's no way of knowing how much water is still in his lungs,' says Carlos brusquely, continuing to pump.

Olivia pulls at his arm. 'What's wrong with you? You'll damage him!'

'No. If I leave him, he might seem fine for hours, then white foam will come up from his lungs and he'll die. It's called delayed drowning and it happened to a girl at my school.' Carlos pumps grimly. Water trickles from Leo's mouth and he chokes.

'You're all right, Leo, Mummy's here,' Olivia whispers brokenly.

'Leo!' Concha pushes through the slowly gathering crowd and falls to her knees in the sand.

'Concha, you can help Leo by rubbing his feet to warm him up,' Carlos says. Concha sits obediently and takes Leo's feet in her hands.

The ambulance team appear – a dark-haired girl of no more than twenty, and a burly man. Both are wearing brick-red shirts and white slacks. Carlos and Olivia have to move back and let them minister to Leo. After a quick check of his vital signs, they wrap him in a foil blanket. As he's being strapped to a gurney, the ambulance girl tells Carlos to collect his family's belongings and bring them to the ambulance. They start to carry Leo up the beach with Olivia sticking close beside him.

Carlos holds out a hand to Concha, who is shivering in spite of the strong sunshine, her face pinched.

'Leo's done it,' she whimpers as she takes his hand. 'He's turned himself into a dolphin.'

Carlos doesn't reply. He looks away from Concha, looks over her head as he hurries her across to their green and blue parasol. He gathers up Olivia's handbag and their clothes, abandoning the rest. Then, pulling Concha along, he heads quickly up the beach, his eyes on Leo's stretcher. On the way, he sees the man who helped him in the water hovering whey-faced on the edge of the crowd. Carlos nods to him in gratitude, not knowing yet whether Leo's life has actually been saved.

He cranes forwards to keep an eye on his son as he is carried up towards the waiting ambulance. The sight of Leo's bloodless face mixes with the blood and death in Carlos' past so that his chest bursts with it all and, as he walks barefoot up the beach with Concha's small hand in his, he feels as though he can't breathe without seeing the blue shine of the necklace lying against Leo's skin, and the sapphire amulet lying against the skin of a long-dead child. The memories are all there now, slashed through with images of Leo, deathly white. The memories are there and Carlos understands.

It wasn't my fault, he realises. It wasn't my fault Pedro died.

Chapter Fifty-one

12 June 1984

Inside the building site, it's so quiet. Dust floats on the sunlight and I look up to see the blue, faraway sky. Criss-crossing the blue are slices of stone and I can see this used to be a house but builders have knocked most of it down so the sunshine is everywhere, making every speck of dust stand out. The walls are crumbling pale stone and there are broken-off bits of stone all over the ground. The walls have long, black spikes growing out of them.

'What are those?' I ask Pedro, who is watching me look at every-thing.

'Don't know.' He reaches out and grips the thin, grooved middle of one. 'They're just really big nails,' he guesses. On the ground is a hammer, big and old, the wooden handle cracking. We crouch and finger it. Then Pedro whispers, 'Your lucky necklace, Carlos.'

My feet slip on broken stones as I struggle to undo the amulet's gold chain. Pedro has to help me.

When I've fixed it around his neck it sits like a blue star against his tanned throat and he laughs his blackbird laugh and spins in happy circles, shining in the sunlight that drops right onto his head. He looks very lucky to me and I'm about to tell him so when there's a scraping sound and Pedro stops spinning, his eyes go wide and I look behind me, my spine already crawling.

Somebody is coming through the plastic wall, I can hear him breathing as if he ran up the hill, and in all the strange white sunshine I can't see who it is but it's someone *big*, it must be the *maluco*, the crow-man, come to get us with his potato-stinky breath.

But the man climbing through isn't the crow-man.

It's Father.

'Pai!' As he straightens up and I see his face, my knees tremble but I can't move away from where I am. Behind me, I hear the last bit of laughter sigh away from Pedro's mouth.

'Carlos.' Father's voice throbs the way it did the time he hit me for dancing into the table and knocking a crystal glass to the floor. He steps towards me, his shiny shoes crunching on the loose stones. 'I came to get you from school to tell you how your mother is because I thought you cared about her, but what do I see? I see you sneaking off with this street filth.' He clutches my shoulders so hard that I stumble back against the wall and he pins me there, his voice getting louder and angrier. 'How *dare* you disobey your own father?'

'How is my mother?' I whisper, but he ignores me.

'I am no filth.' Pedro's voice is quiet but it stops Father dead.

I turn and look at Pedro in amazement. His chin is high. How brave he is!

'What the hell is that around your neck?' Father stares at the amulet under Pedro's chin. The sapphire glints and flashes in the sunlight. 'Is that . . .?' He turns back to me and his face is terrible. 'My luck!' he roars. 'The family luck, Carlos. Your mother's luck, her *life*, around the neck of a street urchin!'

I open my mouth to tell him about Pedro's birthday wish, about there being enough luck in the amulet for everyone. But everything happens very fast. Father moves towards Pedro, who stands very still, his eyes so big they are more white than violet. Instead of talking, I rush to stop Father, my arms aeroplane-wide.

'Get back, you little fool!' Father's hand catches me across the head and I fall back onto stones and dust, pain shooting through my right wrist. He charges towards Pedro. 'My luck! You cannot steal my luck!'

Pedro leaps, quick as a stag. From the hard ground, I watch his leap. Pedro is a circus boy, made of magic as he springs sideways, his faded shirt swinging loose at the arm so that his phoenix tattoo flashes, his knees bunched high. But Father is quick, too. He throws himself across Pedro's leap, grabbing for the amulet, and knocks into him so hard in mid-air that Pedro goes flying into the wall.

Everything stops. Father freezes. Pedro is still on the wall, like a cartoon character slow to fall.

I run to him, and at first there's so much blood that I don't understand why Pedro doesn't fall. I peer up and through it all I see that his face is stuck on a long, black nail-spike.

'Pedro!'

My hands are under him, trying to hold him up, stop the spike from hurting him, my wrist throbbing in pain, and Father moves and I think, he's strong, he'll help me save Pedro, but when Father looks into Pedro's poor face he swears in a high voice I've never heard him use before, and then he reaches out his hand and rips the amulet off Pedro's neck. The chain snaps and I see Pedro's one eye, which is open but the sparkle has gone; he can't see me. I scream his name and Father has turned and is battering his fists against the wall and strange gasping sounds come from his throat and he shouts, '*Não, não, não!*'

Then he whips around and drags me away and I can't keep Pedro's weight off the spike so he sags, his whole body sags and bleeds. I am fighting but Father is too strong. He hits me so hard across the head that I knock into nowhere for a moment and when

I'm back from nowhere he's wrapped me all bloody in his summer coat and I try to get to Pedro but Father won't let me and there's blood everywhere, so much blood, a thick line running down the wall, a puddle under Pedro.

'Shut up, Carlos. Shut up.' Father's voice is like the sting of a belt.

He grips me to his chest and strides to the corrugated plastic door-way. Up and down the street he looks, I can feel his head turning, his chin moving roughly across the top of my head. Then he's striding, and I'm carried with him, but inside my closed eyes I am with Pedro, hanging like some poor trapped animal, bleeding his life into the wall of the building site, his eyes gone.

Pedro, Pedro, I call to him in my head.

And as Father rushes us up the street, his heart hammering against me as he tells someone his boy is ill, he has to get him home, I see Pedro by golden street light, his wooden hoop in his hand, and he closes his eyes and smiles and he says to me, Carlitos, a boy with no brother:

'I am at the centre of the sun.'

Chapter Fifty-two

Olivia isn't religious, but as the regular sigh of Leo's ventilator counts time in the Condes de Castro Guimarães Hospital in Cascais, she prays.

Leo's face is white and mostly obscured by an oxygen mask, his eyelashes as long as Concha's. Concha is hugging her knees to her chest on a plastic chair at the foot of Leo's bed, and her eyes are drooping closed. A thin hospital blanket is draped around her shoulders because she was shivering in her wet bikini but refused to put on her own clothes. Water is soaking through Carlos' jeans where he pulled them on over his wet swimming shorts as Leo was being loaded into the ambulance. He's sitting opposite Olivia on a chair by Leo's head. Olivia runs things through her mind. The doctors still don't know the extent of the damage; they think Leo was as good as drowned when Carlos got to him – a few seconds later and his life would have been irretrievable. A factor in favour of Leo's survival was the coldness of the water, they say, although Olivia doesn't know why this should be.

For now, Leo is wrapped in blankets and is receiving warmed fluids through an intravenous drip to raise his core temperature. He is receiving oxygen while they await the results of tests done to establish any damage to his liver and other organs. To Olivia's frightened question, 'Will he live?' the doctors replied, 'Let's give it a few hours, then we'll know more.' Olivia tightens her hand on Leo's limp one.

'Come on,' she whispers. 'Come on, my brave boy.'

Carlos shifts closer, bringing his head right up to Leo's face. 'You're the most important thing I've achieved in my life, Leo.' His voice is very soft. 'Living is all about you. Your high laughter . . .' He swallows with difficulty. 'Your games with stones.'

'Don't, Carlos! It sounds as if you're saying goodbye to him.'

Carlos looks up at Olivia. 'Have you heard those stories about parents who do impossible things like lift up cars with their bare hands, to save a trapped child from death?'

Olivia nods.

'That's what happened for me, when I swam to save Leo. I wasn't just Carlos anymore – I had all the strength of my dreaming self. I could have done anything. I knew it was impossible to reach him in time to save him, but I did it anyway. I found him drowned under the waves, Olivia. I found him.' There are tears in Carlos' eyes.

'Without you, he'd be dead,' she says, stunned by the awful fact of this. 'And even though I'm his mother, I didn't know he was in danger. I lay there sunbathing while he swam off unnoticed.' She looks at him desolately. 'I thought he was with you.'

'With me? No, no, I told you I was going down the beach to get the kids ice cream –'

'You said: "OK, we're off to the café, then."'

'I said "*I'm* off to the café." *I*, not we.'

They stare at each other.

'I thought he was with you,' she insists. Her eyes are barely blue any more, stained with red as if she is the one who has been struggling underwater.

'It doesn't matter any more,' he says, shaking his head.

'We nearly lost our son,' she says. She lays a hand on Leo's head. 'It will always matter.'

They are both silent. Then Carlos gets up and walks around the bed, past Concha who has curled up on her chair and is sleeping. He tries to take Olivia in his arms and at first she resists, pushing him away.

'Stupid,' she wails. 'So stupid. The difference between "I'm" and "we're", the sun-fug I was in, too lazy even to open my eyes . . .'

Carlos tightens his grip on her. 'We both should have checked who'd be watching him, the way we normally always do. But Leo is alive, and he's going to stay alive, you'll see. Everything is going to be OK. Olivia? You hear me?'

She nods against the beat of his heart. They both look over at Leo, and listen to the swish, swish of his ventilator.

'Down there in the water, when it happened . . .' says Carlos, still holding on to her, breathing into her hair. 'Leo looked dead when I brought him out. All through my body there was this overpowering feeling of dread, like when I meditated that time and the dark cloud engulfed me. I looked at our child, who I thought was dead, and I saw his blue necklace, like the amulet Mãe gave me, and it was as if a window opened in my mind, all these images suddenly stared me in the face . . . Olivia, I remember now.'

'Remember what?'

'Everything.'

Olivia's eyes widen and she steps back slightly so she can see him. 'You've *remembered*?'

'Yes. I'm not a murderer. I never killed anyone.'

'Oh, Carlos!' She grips his wrists. 'Tell me.'

'Come to the window,' he says, with a glance at the sleeping children.

'It *was* a boy who died,' he says in a low voice. 'A street boy about Leo's age, called Pedro. He was my friend. It wasn't me who killed him – it was my father.'

'Your *father*? But why would he kill a child?'

295

'It was an accident.' Carlos relates all he remembers: Pedro's birthday wish, the building site, his father's face when he saw the amulet around Pedro's neck, their mid-air collision. 'I held Pedro as his heart stopped beating,' he tells Olivia. 'So much blood, running out of him so fast. The nail must have pierced his eye socket.'

Olivia shudders. 'Don't, I can't bear to imagine it.' She leans faintly against the window blind. 'Wow, Carlos. That poor boy. And you, carrying this inside you for so long! No wonder you tried to forget about it.'

'That's just it, though – I didn't "try", Father *made* me forget. That voice I heard, his voice, it was telling me to forget and, when those images came back to me in the sea, I remembered all the rest of it, what he used to do at night. When he tied me to the bed to stop me from sleepwalking, he'd tell me I had to forget what had happened. Worse still, he made me believe it was all my fault!' With a swift look, Carlos checks on Leo and Concha. Leo's eyes are closed and his ventilator is sighing steadily; Concha is still deep asleep on her chair. 'I distinctly remember him saying to me, "No one must know what you have done today."'

'But why would he blame you? To save his own skin?'

He shrugs, looks at the floor. 'He was a deeply unhappy man – Mãe was dying, it was the beginning of the end for him and he didn't . . .'

'Don't make excuses for him, Carlos.' Olivia's mouth twists in revulsion. 'What he did was unforgivable. What sort of a father uses his own child as a scapegoat?'

'Maybe the same sort of father who commits suicide. Someone desperate, depressive, cowardly . . . I don't know.' Carlos shakes his head. 'I feel as if I never really knew Father. The weird thing is, in my nightmares, I *am* the guilty one. All the actions you say I carry out, they're my father's actions. From what you've told me, I enact his role in Pedro's death, ripping that necklace off Leo, running with

296

something bundled in a coat – that's my father running from the building site with *me* wrapped in his coat.'

'Well, to me that makes sense – you're your father in your nightmares because he transferred the blame to you. He brainwashed you into thinking it was *you* who did it.' She shivers, glances across the room to her son. 'I'm glad Leo never met his grandfather.'

'Remembering it all is so crazy, Olivia. I feel as if I've discovered a lost piece of myself, all these memories! And I feel terrible about Pedro, just terrible. If he hadn't become my friend, he wouldn't have died.' Carlos rubs his forehead tiredly. 'I can't change it,' he mutters in frustration. '*Foda-se*! It's all done, he's gone, and even if remembering this whole thing is good for me in some therapeutic sense, and even if it somehow stops my nightmares to have remembered, it won't bring him back. I can't right the wrong that's been done.'

Olivia takes him in her arms and hugs him for a long time, the rhythm of Leo's ventilator sounding reassuringly in her ears. 'Well, that may be true,' she says at last, 'and I understand how upset you must be feeling, but frankly I'm *so* relieved you've remembered at last – I thought you never would. What happened is horrific and dreadful, but, Carlos, at least if the nightmares stop, we can be together again as a family.' She tips her head back to look at him. 'That's got to be worth something!'

'*Claro*,' he murmurs. 'But it doesn't stop me wishing Pedro had survived. He was the brother I never had, a fascinating boy full of ideas and fun. And Marina – when Rosa mentioned her when this whole thing started, I barely remembered any more who she was, but Olivia, I *loved* Marina!' He looks down at her, startled and dismayed. 'How could I have forgotten how sweet she was? It's amazing how much of a life can be swept under the surface.' He steps out of Olivia's embrace, too agitated to stand still. 'She was my Tia Marina, we'd do silly things like see who could stand on one leg the longest, and play marbles on the dining-room floor for hours. Why did Father agree to have her committed? She wasn't mad, she just sleepwalked. Surely he must have known that?' He pauses as something occurs to him. 'Father tying me to the bed like that – he must've been afraid I'd wander around the house shouting out the truth in my dreams. Maybe something similar happened with Marina. Maybe she knew more than he wanted her to know?'

'You mean, maybe he just wanted her out of the way?' Olivia thinks for a moment. 'After what I know about him now, I wouldn't put anything past him. How many lives did that man ruin?' She looks at Leo and at Concha, both of whom seem younger than seven, almost babylike in their sleep. 'That's what triggered this whole thing,' she exclaims with sudden understanding. 'Your first nightmare happened on Leo's seventh birthday. Pedro died on his seventh birthday! Poor little boy.'

She crosses the room and reaches out to touch Leo, her hand trembling on the stiff cotton sheet. 'Leo, you *have* to survive.'

Chapter Fifty-three

Leo knows he's in hospital, on a high white bed, with his parents watching him with exhausting attention. He feels as if he's made from rubber. His hand has a kind of injection in it which is attached to plastic wires that go right up to a bag hanging on a sort of stick. There is a white mask on his face, helping him to breathe. As he is too tired to open his eyes fully, the mask blocks most of his vision with its hard plastic lines. His mouth feels dry. The lights are very bright. His eyes droop closed even though he fights it because he knows what will happen when he shuts out this painfully sharp room: he will go back again to those strange underwater moments. He went back there as the ambulance drove them all to hospital. He manages to open his eyes a crack, and sees his mother's blue eyes very close and filled with love.

'Sleep, my precious,' she murmurs. 'Everything's going to be all right.'

Leo's eyes close, and he is underwater, his thrashing limbs making no difference. His body is cumbersome, so he slips out of it and floats nearby. There in the blue-lit depths, he sees a dolphin. As Leo drifts towards it, he senses the roar of blood to the head as a wave is leaped over, the strike of the sun on a dorsal fin, the cold smack of water. A man jets past him in a stream of pure energy, and Leo sees arms grasp the pale slip of a body floating away to his upper right. The man lifts the body up through the surface, towards the sun. Leo observes the two sets of legs – one pair kicking with great power, the other doll-like and limp. He experiences a deep feeling of disquiet as the smaller set of legs is pulled right above the water. He turns to look for the dolphin, who has receded slightly, as if waiting for something to happen or not happen.

There's a jerk which pulls him through the water and back into the body, which is laid out on a board and, as air makes its painful re-entry, Leo feels again the shape and weight of his limbs, sees in frightened, unfocused glimpses his father's dark eyes which are hot with emotion, his shouting mouth . . .

'Leo, Leo!' His mother is calling his name. 'Calm down, baby, it's OK. Mummy's here.'

Leo's eyes flash open, and it's true – his mother is right there, a strand of her hair falling forwards as she leans into his face, re-adjusting his oxygen mask, stroking his forehead. Leo likes it best when she strokes his cheek but he knows he has no cheeks at the moment because of the mask. He reaches up with his free hand and tries to pull it off his face, but she stops him and he's too weak to resist.

'You had a bad dream,' says his father's voice, and his hand rubs Leo's shoulder with a light, warm touch.

Leo tries to speak, to tell them it wasn't a bad dream at all, that it really happened. But his voice won't work and he experiences a wash of despair. Tears roll from his eyes. In some ways it would have been so much easier to float away with the dolphin.

The next time his eyes open, his parents have turned away from him to talk to a doctor by the door, and it is Concha's face he looks into.

'The doctor said you'll be OK now,' she whispers. Leo blinks to let her know he's listening. 'Leo, you're not a dolphin. You're a boy.'

Concha's whisper is urgent. 'If you want to stay friends with me, you *have* to be a boy, because boys who turn into dolphins drown.'

Leo blinks uncertainly. Concha stares at him. Then she smiles her most gypsy smile, so cheeky and sweet that it usually makes Leo smile back without even thinking about it. He's not sure if he's smiling now or not, but he feels happy for the first time since he ran into the sea.

Then Concha is eased aside as his parents realise he's woken up. They pore over him with eager smiles and his body starts to feel less rubbery. The doctor lifts the mask off his face and he feels lighter.

Rosa has been holding Leo's hand for over an hour, looking at him with tragic eyes, her movements prayerful. '*Tu és o mundo para mim*,' she says repeatedly. 'You are my world.'

When Concha's mother arrives with her smell of nicotine and harsh perfume, she exclaims almost reverently over Leo. In the cold hospital light she looks older, less princess-like. She, Concha, Rosa and Olivia go to the snack bar on the ground floor of the hospital together, and Leo finds himself looking into his father's broad face.

'Everything OK, *filho*?'

Leo hesitates. '*Sim.*' His throat is still sore from all the vomiting so his voice sounds croaky. 'In my imagination,' he says, 'I can be anything.'

Carlos nods gravely.

'A flying squirrel,' continues Leo, raising his head a little. 'An eagle, or . . .' He falters. 'Or a dolphin,' he says with effort.

His father's green eyes are steady, listening.

'But when I'm in the world with you and Mum and Concha and Rosa, I'm just a boy.' The utter misery of it sinks him; he collapses back into his pillows and bites his lip.

For a long moment, Carlos is silent. Leo can't look at him; all his energy has gone into trying to make himself understood. Has it worked? He waits with the quiet patience of the physically shattered.

Carlos strokes Leo's pale forehead, then leaves his palm there, as if to recharge him. 'Leo,' he says, his voice low. 'Imagining things is lovely, and I don't want you to stop doing it, but you always need to know where imagination stops and real life begins. And while it's true that you don't have wings or fins, and your bones are breakable and your lungs need constant air, being a boy is a beautiful thing. You're a human child, a miracle of muscles and tendons with a strong, beating heart and the ability to dream. Do you see?'

Leo's nod is faint under the weight of Carlos' hand, but his eyes are locked to his father's.

'And on top of all that, you, Leo, have a mum and dad and auntie who love you absolutely and for ever,' whispers Carlos. His voice is so kind that Leo's throat constricts with love.

When Olivia and Rosa come back, they bring a *bolo de arroz*, a sweet rice cake, for Carlos. Rosa's eyes are red-rimmed, but Olivia is composed.

'You'll have home-made chocolate cake tomorrow or the day after,' she promises Leo. 'Once you're out of here.' She strokes the soft hairs at the edge of his hairline. 'My strong boy. You're coming through this like a super-hero!'

The air in Leo's lungs is a relief, a balm. His parents and aunt lean over him, as full of wonder as if he were a newborn, and under their triple gaze – magic three, he thinks sleepily – he falls into a peaceful sleep.

Chapter Fifty-four

They have fire, and a hosepipe.

Rosa checks the hose, spraying a thin film of water over Leo's and Concha's bare legs so that they jump away squealing. Leo has been out of hospital just five days but his energy levels have already returned to normal. Carlos is fiddling with firelighters and matches. A small can of petroleum stands on the garden table, just in case.

Since Carlos told her about the dream he had this morning in his hotel room, Olivia feels as if she can breathe again. She tests the feeling, filling her lungs with morning air.

'*Querida*?' asks Carlos, resting his arm briefly across her shoulders. 'You're happy to do this?'

'I *need* to do this.'

'So do I!' Leo grins and rubs his hands together. It's already hot and having stripped off his T-shirt and thrown it onto the garden table, he's dressed only in a pair of yellow shorts. He and Concha are fizzy with excitement.

'We seem to be adopting Concha,' murmurs Olivia to Carlos. 'Her mother just asked if we could have her for three weeks over the summer holidays.'

'Fine by me,' says Carlos immediately. 'What's Concha's mum going to be doing?'

'Well, she *says* she wants to get her act together.' Olivia shrugs. 'We'll see.' She disappears into her studio and returns with the painting. When she's in the centre of the garden, she stops dramatically with it held out in front of her so that they can all see it.

'*Meu Deus*,' murmurs Rosa. 'That's dark.'

'He's even uglier than the real one,' Leo tells a wide-eyed Concha, and this makes Carlos chuckle.

Olivia lowers the painting face up onto the rough circle of barbecue stones that Carlos has arranged on the garden path. 'Ready,' she says, and Carlos sets a match to four firelighters and positions them under the four corners of the canvas. Within seconds, flames are rising, burning dripping holes in the material.

'*É pá!* It's pretty flammable,' says Rosa.

Olivia stands very straight in her cut-off jeans and halter top. She stares at the canvas, which is caving in already, the paint bubbling as black smoke begins to stretch upwards. 'I've never destroyed a painting before.'

'It's not a painting, it's the sleep monster.' Leo touches her with his hand as he dances around the fire with Concha close on his heels.

'Don't trip!' Olivia watches him anxiously. 'You be careful too, Concha. The garden's too small for this, really.'

Carlos strokes his hand down the length of Olivia's hair. 'Who was it that said painting isn't an aesthetic operation, but a form of magic?'

'Pablo Picasso.' Olivia hooks her thumbs into her belt hooks. 'He said painting is a way of seizing power by giving form to our terrors as well as our desires. But if we're burning a painting, what does that mean?'

'Double magic,' calls Leo from the other side of the fire.

'We'll have to hope the social services lady doesn't drop by for a surprise visit,' Carlos mutters, and Olivia makes a face. When she faxed Dr Loverock's sleep disorder diagnosis to Doutora Lurdes, she got a cautiously positive call from her the next morning to say that she and her colleagues were willing to accept that Carlos had acted violently through no fault of his own, but that they expected him to continue to stay in a hotel until his nightmares were under control, and that they would be keeping tabs on the family to make sure things settled down. Carlos' latest dream makes Olivia feel hopeful that soon enough, the social services will back off for good.

'Oh, she'd have a field day, wouldn't she?' Rosa agrees. 'Pyromaniac philistines, destroying artwork on a Sunday morning . . .'

'And a child who nearly drowned last week, playing with fire this week,' says Carlos. His eyes never leave Leo. 'I think that's enough dancing, you two.'

'She wouldn't come on a Sunday,' reasons Rosa, who is clearly enjoying watching the cavorting children.

'No, come here now, both of you.' The unusual strictness of Carlos' voice brings both children reluctantly to his side.

'Do you know what we're doing here?' he asks them, and together they look at the melting nightmare figure in the centre of the flames.

'We're killing the sleep monster,' says Leo.

'And making a bad smell.' Concha pinches her nostrils closed.

It's true that the paint fumes stink, another reason to keep the kids out of harm's reach, thinks Olivia. She moves towards them, as does Rosa, so the five of them are bunched together on the sun-bleached grass, watching the fire. The smoke is thick and rises vertically, moving into black spirals once it clears the hedge.

'Yes, we're killing the sleep monster, and I hope he'll never be back,' says Carlos. 'But we're also saying goodbye to a little boy I once knew, a boy your age with a red and green phoenix tattoo on his arm.'

'*Que fixe*! How cool!' Concha holds up her hands and twists them in the air. 'My *mãe* did henna on me once, it looked soooo beautiful.'

'Can I get a phoenix tattoo, Pai?'

'Not yet. But you can come with me when I get mine done.'

'You're getting a tattoo like Pedro's?' Olivia touches Carlos' arm. 'That's so like you.'

'Is Pedro coming today?' asks Concha.

'Pedro's been dead for a very long time.'

Leo looks from the burning painting to his father's face. 'Did the sleep monster kill him?'

'Uh . . . I guess you could say a version of the sleep monster killed him, yes.'

'*How*?' Leo's eyes are bright with curiosity and fear.

Olivia glances at Rosa and sees the suffering in her eyes. I never want Leo to know what his grandfather did, she thinks. For a second, she's worried that Carlos is about to tell the children the whole story. 'Don't give them nightmares,' she says quickly.

'It doesn't matter any more how Pedro died. He had a wooden hoop, juggling balls, he knew magic tricks . . .' Carlos pulls the children down onto the grass and as the three of them sit cross-legged and watch the flames, he starts telling them everything he has remembered about himself and Pedro, two seven-year-olds just like Leo and Concha. Leo's eyes are on the burning heap in front of him, but he leans into his father's words, imagining.

Olivia and Rosa stand shoulder to shoulder, watching the fire and half listening to Carlos.

'I encouraged Leo, you know,' says Rosa after a while, softly, so the others can't hear. 'His dolphin obsession . . . I'm afraid I stoked it, strengthened his belief that anything was possible. I should have noticed he was in too deep.'

Olivia squeezes her arm. 'I think we all blame ourselves for what happened on that beach. I still feel sick when I think of myself lying in the sun while he swam off into danger. Carlos blames himself even though he saved him – he says the fact of him not remembering what happened to Pedro nearly ended up being the death of Leo. But Leo's safe, that's all that matters now.' She nods towards the fire. 'I know it's awful, but watching the flames is making me think of poor Marina.'

'*Eu também*. Me, too. Even if it was only indirectly, my father was responsible for her terrible death.' In her thin grey-green dress, her arms folded tightly across her chest, Rosa appears shrunken. 'I never found out what he did with the amulet,' she adds. 'I asked the bank to resend me details of the family jewellery we have in the vault, and it wasn't listed.'

'Maybe he sold it.'

'Or threw it into the Tejo when Mãe died.' Rosa shrugs. 'You know, even though Father survived another five years, on the day Mãe died, Carlos and I became orphans.' She flings her arms out, startling Olivia. 'I don't care any more that I found Father dead. He took an overdose in the attic, you know. A jar of sleeping tablets and two bottles of *Porto*. I found him stretched out on the floor, surrounded by photographs. None of Carlos and me! All of them were of Mãe.'

Rosa's face is sad as she watches the fire, and Olivia slips an arm protectively around her shoulders. The painting gives a large crack as the frame snaps, and Olivia looks up to see Zebra standing at the gate, his beard dangling over it, a big smile on his face.

'Zebra!' Carlos jumps up. As Olivia watches him greet Zebra, she wonders about this friendship, and the way Carlos immortalises street people with his camera. Even the forgotten past has the power to shape us, she thinks.

'*É pá*, I thought all this black smoke looked to be coming from your place!' laughs Zebra as he comes into the garden, one arm in a sling. 'So you're burning your shadows?' His face still shows signs of his beating; the pink line of a new scar divides the deep wrinkles on his forehead. There's a clean glow about him, though, thinks

Olivia. Maybe all the washing his beard got in hospital hasn't worn off yet.

'Is it that obvious?' she asks with a smile.

'This nose can smell burning shadows from a long way off,' he chuckles, sniffing dramatically for the children's benefit. 'I hear *your* shadow nearly got you,' he says to Leo, who answers with a baffled look so that Zebra has to clarify. 'You nearly died, *menino*. In the sea.'

'Pai saved me,' Leo says with pride.

'He *had* to save him because Leo's not a dolphin,' says Concha.

'Yeah, I'm a boy.'

Zebra looks him up and down. 'Well, that's true.'

'Can I touch your beard?'

Zebra half laughs, half groans. '*Sim, sim, vamos.*' He leans forwards and allows both children to curl their hands around the swinging white rope of hair.

'It's so rough!' Leo exclaims.

'It feels alive, like a weasel's tail,' marvels Concha.

'You've never felt a weasel's tail.' Leo gives her a reproachful nudge with his elbow.

'Have.' But Concha winks so that Leo knows she hasn't.

'How are you healing, Zebra?' asks Olivia when he straightens up, the children's fingers slipping reluctantly from his hair.

'Well. And friends of mine found out who got me that night. Bastard came snooping around, asking if I'd died of my injuries.' Zebra smacks his lips scornfully. 'Pah! Who'd die from such a pathetic beating, I'd like to know?'

'So who was it?' Carlos' voice is light with relief.

'The Time Man. Has forty-three digital watches hanging off his clothes and sets the alarms so they go off at different times during the day. He beeps his way through life. Street dweller for eighteen years, and thought he could steal my tree. It was three, four weeks ago. I

308

turfed him out and apparently his feelings were offended.' Zebra guffaws. 'My tree, *pá*! Who in their right mind tries to steal another man's tree? I threw his blankets and all his tat into the fountain while he hopped and beeped.'

Leo is still, listening. 'What if he comes back to get you again?'

Zebra looks satisfied. 'My friends scared him right away. He'll be on the other side of the city now, or even further, maybe.' He looks at Carlos. 'I read about you in the local paper that nice nurse brought me in the hospital. "Father's superhuman sea rescue", that sorta shit. I'm impressed, *pá*.'

'Well.' Carlos smiles a little. 'Maybe you'll be even more impressed when I tell you what happened this morning. I had the nightmare, the one that makes me get violent and crazy. It started and this time I remember the way it went. I was a big, angry man, trying to rip an amulet off a little boy's neck because the amulet was my luck and my dying wife's luck, and I needed it back. And just as I was about to plunge towards the boy, I realised I was dreaming.'

Zebra raises his eyebrows. '*Boa, boa*.'

'And I stopped. Everything in the dream stopped, and I looked at the boy, who had violet eyes and a great sapphire hanging around his neck. Although I was dreaming, I knew everything that I know now, all the memories were there, as clear and fresh as day. And I thought, what do you say to a murdered child? After a long moment of the two of us staring at each other, I said, "From my heart, I am sorry."' Carlos shakes his head. 'Then I watched as he ran out on to the street, and he had a hoop with him and he was bowling it along. It bounced on the cobblestones and, as he ran out of sight, I could hear him laughing. It was so real. Then I woke up.'

'And from what he's told me, he didn't jump up in his sleep and go mad,' adds Olivia.

''Course not,' says Zebra. 'No need to any more. You've come through all the layers, *pá*. It doesn't control you now.' He winks at

Olivia. 'You'll have to let him come back home now, no more excuses, eh?'

'You might be right.' Her gaze shifts back to the smouldering painting. Carlos' reference to murder makes her remember how, right after his first episode, she had feared Leo and herself could become the victims of accidental murder, when all the time it had already happened to Pedro, twenty-six years earlier.

Rosa hands Zebra a cold glass of mint tea and he toasts them with it, holding it briefly against the sky before he drinks. He moves to sit on one of the garden chairs, and Rosa indicates the burning mess on the garden path. All the paint has run away or been evaporated by the flames, and the canvas is black and broken. 'It looks as if the sleep monster's dead and gone. Who wants to help me douse the flames?'

'Me!' Concha runs to her side, and Leo's about to go too when Carlos intercepts him, swinging him high in the air so that Leo dangles there, laughing in his yellow shorts, his dolphin-eye necklace put aside since that day on the beach so that his torso is undecorated, all silky little-boy skin. Olivia moves close to Carlos, out of the way of Leo's kicking legs. She can see her son's face against a halo of sky. Just looking at him is enough, seeing him breathe in and out. Having seen him so close to death, she understands that the fear of losing him will never go away. Will having another child dilute the fear, she wonders, or double it? She thinks of Leo saying, 'Double magic' as he danced around the fire.

Leo kicks his legs back and up and extends his arms like wings, his fingers splayed wide. 'I'm a Pegasus, a dragon, a phoenix!'

Living, thinks Olivia, is a moment-by-moment thing. Reaching up a hand, she cups Leo's laughing face.

Acknowledgements

My husband, Markus, helped me work out my ideas and gave me endless love and support. As always, love and thanks to my family and friends, for being there.

Warmest thanks go to my agent, Jane Conway-Gordon, for her encouragement and her belief in my writing, and to my editor, Emma Beswetherick, for her stellar suggestions, energy and enthusiasm. Huge thanks to all the team at Piatkus.

I am grateful to Carlos H. Schenck, MD, for his swift diagnosis of the fictional Carlos and for generously sharing his parasomnia expertise with me. The conferences of the International Association for the Study of Dreams enabled me to meet sleep disorder researchers whose stories fired my interest. My thanks to the old school friend who spoke to me frankly about his enactment of violent dreams and the effect this was having on his relationship.

Luisa Leite Santos Roldão kindly checked through the Portuguese language in the book for me, and Lina Afonso helped me with character names and forms of address.

My love and gratitude go to Yasmin, for saying yes to life.

Author Note

While I was finishing *Dreamrunner*, a tragic case of homicidal somnambulism came to light in the UK. Devoted husband Brian Thomas was acquitted of strangling his wife of forty years because he was asleep at the time, dreaming that he was fighting off intruders. Thomas suffered from night terrors and sleepwalking episodes, and the court accepted that this was a case of automatism, where the mind no longer controls the body. People have driven cars while asleep, swum in lakes, and sustained injuries by throwing themselves from buildings during vivid dreams of fleeing from fire or armed pursuers. It is estimated that four per cent of adults sleepwalk, two per cent have night terrors, and two per cent engage in sleep violence.

Parasomnias, the behavioural disorders of sleep, are therefore quite common, affecting millions of people. Most of them are treatable, but even today they often remain misdiagnosed or unrecognised. All of the sleep disorders that appear in this novel – Sleep Related Dissociative Disorder (SRDD); REM Sleep Behaviour Disorder (RBD); and Sleep Related Eating Disorder (SRED) – are bona fide parasomnias as defined by the *International Classification of Sleep Disorders*, 2nd ed. (2005). Night terrors, sleep paralysis, narcolepsy, sleep-sex and sleepwalking are just some of the other parasomnias out there, and all can have upsetting effects on the lives of sufferers and their families.

I've never suffered from a sleep disorder, but, like many people, as a child I sleepwalked on several occasions. When I began to research parasomnias for the novel, I had a semi-lucid dream in which I was asleep next to a man who went straight into a violent dream-enactment scenario, smashing into wardrobes, yelling and screaming. Part of me knew I was dreaming this and that I was witnessing the effects of a sleep disorder on a bed partner. As I continued to combine conventional research with dreaming into the subject, I also had a series of *literal* examples of how it feels to wake up moving due to an action I'd been performing in a dream: once I woke in a half-sitting position, with my hand outstretched, and experienced all the disorientation of someone struggling from a dream into waking reality.

Such incidents were very helpful to the writing process, enabling me to internalise the experience of dream enactment, but I was relieved when they stopped, as their occurrence made me sense how easily sleep disorders might happen to anyone. So in some ways, writing *Dreamrunner* was an uncomfortable experience, because sleep disorders can have a dark side, as with the examples of sleep violence. But witnessing someone physically enacting a dream must be like having a partially opened window into their dream life, and that in itself fascinated me.

In *Dreamrunner*, apart from exploring the psychological impact that the onset of a violent sleep disorder can have on a family, I was also interested in examining therapeutic responses to such disorders. If the origin of a recurrent nightmare is discovered, then the core conflict can often be resolved, and the nightmares then cease. I found myself wondering whether the resolution of the central conflict could potentially eliminate the need for medication in some cases of violent sleep behaviours which involve nightmares. Techniques such as meditation, self-hypnosis, dream replay or psychotherapy could be beneficial to this process, while lucid dreaming provides a way of penetrating the heart of a nightmare in such a way that the conflict can be resolved in situ. Lucid dreaming has been shown to be effective in eliminating nightmares (Saint-Denys 1867, Arnold-Forster 1921, LaBerge & Rheingold 1990, Spoormaker 2005). *Wrestling with Ghosts: A Personal and Scientific Account of Sleep Paralysis*, by Jorge Conesa Sevilla, PhD, explores ways of transitioning from the terrifying apparitions which often accompany sleep paralysis, to the potentially healing and positive state of lucid dreaming.

For those interested in learning more about parasomnias, I highly recommend *Paradox Lost: Midnight in the Battleground of Sleep and Dreams*, by Carlos H. Schenck, MD, available from www.parasomnias-rbd.com. This book provides clinical interviews with patients suffering from a wide variety of sleep disorders and, in doing so, it adeptly reveals the human aspect of parasomnias. This was my primary source material for *Dreamrunner*, and it provides fascinating insights into the strangeness of sleep disorders: my fictional character Marina buttering and eating Cuban cigars might stretch the reader's belief, but this was inspired by a case study of a person with SRED who actually buttered pop cans and tried to eat them! Dr Schenck was generous enough to answer my questions when I was tying up the medical chapters. Any clinically incorrect details or misrepresentations of parasomnia behaviours are purely my mistake. Dr Schenck's *SLEEP: A Groundbreaking Guide to the Mysteries, the Problems, and the Solutions*, examines a range of parasomnias, from those linked with sleep apnoea and restless legs syndrome, all the way to sexsomnia and exploding head syndrome. His award-winning DVD documentary, *Sleep Runners: The Stories Behind Everyday Parasomnias* is available at www.amazon.com, with the Deluxe Academic Edition at www.sleeprunners.com.